Praise for

RED SQUARE

"As good as popular fiction should be."
                    —*The Washington Post Book World*

"Devilishly alarming . . . It lives up to the Red-noir standards of Renko and reminds us of the working human condition of love and death, lunacy and fun, that always seemed to be there beyond the cold war scrim."
                    —*The New York Times Book Review*

"With its twists and turns and romantic subtext, played against a backdrop of decadence and despair, *Red Square* functions much like an off-shore *Maltese Falcon*. Yet Smith's approach, while street-smart and wry is ultimately rich and affirmative. . . . What ultimately sets the Renko books apart is the careful writing, and, more importantly, the knowledge of the human heart that is carried through it, through them, first to last."   —*Chicago Tribune*

"Welcome home, Arkady Renko. The hero of *Gorky Park* and *Polar Star* returns to Moscow in a thriller so dense with observation and atmosphere, it rivals John le Carré. . . . Renko [is] the most touching character to grace the pages of a novel since *The Spy Who Came in from the Cold*."
                    —*Cosmopolitan*

"Arkady Renko is one of the more memorable creations of cold-war fiction, as clever, guilt-ridden, and self-effacing as any George Smiley."   —*Newsweek*

"A solid and entertaining winner." —New York *Daily News*

"Gripping . . . Vividly capture[s] the essence of the new Russia . . . The climax of *Red Square* takes place in Moscow during the hard-line coup attempt of August 1991. The texture of that remarkable time is captured quite adeptly: The moment is simultaneously tense and festive, bizarre and ordinary, grave and absurd. It's Mr. Smith at his best."
                                                 —*The Wall Street Journal*

"*Red Square* is a pleasure to read. It moves well, its dialogue is superb and its depiction of underground Moscow is chilling. Just as we read, say, Tony Hillerman to learn about the Navajo, we read Martin Cruz Smith for a ringside seat at the messy brawls that passed for life in the last days of the Soviet Union."   —*Newsday*

"Martin Cruz Smith is a fine writer, and not just by the standards of the thriller. *Red Square,* a serious novel of contemporary history, enlightens even as it entertains."   —*USA Today*

"Ingenious . . It's Renko's dispirited character that makes *Red Square* compelling. . . . Communism, capitalism—whatever the *ism,* there'll always be a need for a good homicide cop."
                                                 —*Entertainment Weekly*

RED SQUARE

MARTIN CRUZ SMITH

RED SQUARE

A NOVEL

Ballantine Books New York

2007 Ballantine Books Trade Paperback Edition

Published in the United States by Ballantine Books, an imprint of The Random House Publishing Group, a division of Random House, Inc., New York.

BALLANTINE and colophon are registered trademarks of Random House, Inc.
MORTALIS and colophon are trademarks of Random House, Inc.

Originally published in hardcover in the United States by Random House, an imprint of The Random House Publishing Group, a division of Random House, Inc., in 1992.

Grateful acknowledgment is made to Little, Brown and Company for permission to reprint six lines from "The Last Toast" from *Poems of Akhmatova*, selected, translated, and introduced by Stanley Kunitz with Max Hayward. Copyright © 1973 by Stanley Kunitz and Max Hayward. First appeared in *American Poetry Review*. Reprinted by permission of Little, Brown and Company.

The Don Swaim interview of Martin Cruz Smith is courtesy of the WOUB Center for Public Media and the Donald L. Swaim Collection in the Mahn Center for Archives and Special Collections at Ohio University. The interview can be heard in its entirety at Wired for Books, Wiredforbooks.org/martincruzsmith/.

ISBN 978-0-345-49772-7

Printed in the United States of America

www.mortalis-books.com

2 4 6 8 9 7 5 3 1

FOR EM

ACKNOWLEDGMENTS

I must acknowledge the guidance I received in Moscow from Vladimir Kalinichenko, Alexander Stashkov and Yegor and Chandrika Tolstyakov; in Munich from Rachel Fedoseyev, Jörg Sandl and Nougzar Sharia; and in Berlin from Andrew Nurenberg and Natan Federowskij. Generous assistance was also given by George Albov, Nan Black and Ellen Irish Smith, courage by Knox Burger and Katherine Sprague.

Once again, the compass of this book was Alex Levin.

The errors are all mine.

CONTENTS

I

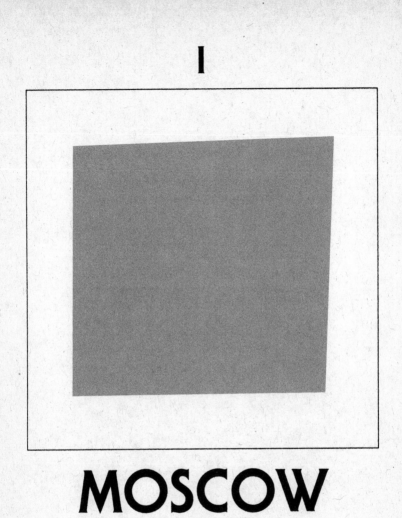

MOSCOW

■

August 6–August 12, 1991

1

In Moscow, the summer night looks like fire and smoke. Stars and moon fade. Couples rise and dress and walk the street. Cars wander with their headlights off.

"There." Jaak saw an Audi passing in the opposite direction.

Arkady slipped on headphones, tapped the receiver. "His radio's out."

Jaak U-turned to the other side of the boulevard and picked up speed. The detective had askew eyes set in a muscular face and he hunched over the wheel as if he were bending it.

Arkady tapped out a cigarette. First of the day. Well, it was one A.M., so it wasn't much to brag about.

"Closer," he said, and pulled the phones off. "Let's be sure it's Rudy."

Ahead were the lights of the peripheral highway that circled the city. The Audi swung onto the ramp to merge with highway traffic. Jaak edged between two flatbed trucks carrying steel plates that clapped with every undulation of the road. He passed the lead truck, the Audi and a tanker. On the way, Arkady had caught the driver's profile, but there were two people in the car, not one. "He picked someone up. We need another look," he said.

Jaak slowed. The tanker didn't pass, but a second later, the Audi slid by. Rudy Rosen, the driver—a round man with soft hands fixed to the wheel—was a private banker to the mafias, a would-be Rothschild who catered to Moscow's most primitive capitalists. His passenger was female, with the wild look achieved by Russian features on a diet, somewhere between sensual and ravenous, with short, stylishly cut blond hair brushed back to the collar of her black leather jacket. As the Audi passed, she turned and sized up the investigators' car, a two-door Zhiguli 8, as a piece of trash. In her thirties, Arkady thought. She had dark eyes, and a wide mouth and puffy lips, parted slightly as if starving. As the Audi swung in front, it was followed by the sound of an outboard engine and the appearance of a Suzuki that inserted itself between the two cars. The motorcycle rider wore a black dome helmet, black leather jacket and black high-tops that sparkled with reflectors. Jaak eased off. The biker was Kim, Rudy's protection.

Arkady ducked and listened to the headset again. "Still dead."

"He's leading us to the market. There are some people there, if they recognize you, you're dead." Jaak laughed. "Of course then we'll know we're in the right place."

"Good point." God forbid anyone should exercise sanity, Arkady thought. Anyway, if anyone recognizes me it means I'm still alive.

All the traffic squeezed off the same exit ramp. Jaak tried to follow the Audi, but a line of "rockers"—bikers—swarmed in between. Swastikas and czarist eagles decorated their backs, all wreathed in the rising smoke of exhaust pipes stripped of mufflers.

At the end of the ramp, construction barriers had been pushed to one side. The car bounced as if they were crossing a potato field, and yet Arkady saw silhouettes that loomed high against the faint northern sky. A Moskvitch went by, its windows crammed with swaying rugs. The roof of an ancient Renault wore a living-room suite. Ahead, brake lights spread into a pool of red.

The rockers drew their bikes into a circle, announcing their stop with a chorus of roars. Cars and trucks spaced themselves roughly on a knoll here, in a trough there. Jaak killed the Zhiguli in first; the car had no neutral or parking gear. He emerged from the car with the smile of a crocodile who has found monkeys at play. Arkady got out wearing a padded jacket and cloth cap. He had black eyes and an expression of bemusement, as if he had recently returned from a long stay in a deep hole to observe changes on the surface, which wasn't far from the truth.

This was the new Moscow.

The silhouettes were towers, red lights at the top to warn off planes. At their bases were the chalky forms of earthmovers, cement mixers, stacks of good bricks and mounds of bad, rebars sinking into mud. Figures moved around the cars and more were still arriving, an apparent convention of insomniacs. No sleepwalking here, though; instead, the swarming, purposeful hum of a black market.

In a way it was like walking through a dream, Arkady thought. Here were cartons of Marlboros, Winstons, Rothmans, even despised Cuban cigarettes stacked as high as walls. Videotapes of American action or Swedish porn sold by the gross for distribution. Polish glassware glittered in factory crates. Two men in running suits arranged not windshield wipers, but whole windshields, and not merely carved out of some poor sod's car, but new, straight from the assembly line. And food! Not blue chickens dead of malnutrition, but whole sides of marbled beef hanging in a butcher's truck. Gypsies lit kerosene lamps beside attaché cases to display counterfeit gold czarist rubles in mint condition, sealed and sold in plastic strips. Jaak pointed out a moon-white Mercedes. Further lamps appeared, spreading the aura of a bazaar; there might be camels browsing among the cars, Arkady thought, or Chinese merchants unrolling bolts of silk. An encampment to themselves was the Chechen mafia, men with pasty, pocked complexions and black hair who sprawled in their cars like pashas at their ease. Even in this setting, the Chechens enforced a space of fear.

Rudy Rosen's Audi was in a choice central location near a truck unloading radios and VCRs. A well-behaved line had formed outside the car under the gaze of Kim, who stood, one foot on his helmet, about ten meters away. He had long hair that he pushed away from small, Korean features. His jacket was padded like armor and open to a compact model of the Kalashnikov called Malysh, Little Boy.

"I'm getting in line," Arkady told Jaak. "Get some license-plate numbers, then watch Kim."

Arkady joined the queue while Jaak loitered by the truck. From a distance, the VCRs seemed solid Soviet goods. Miniaturization was a virtue for consumers of other societies; generally, Russians wanted to show what they bought, not to hide it. But were they new? Jaak ran his hand along the edges, searching for the telltale cigarette burns of a used machine.

There was no sign of the golden-haired woman who had come with Rudy. Arkady felt himself being scrutinized, and turned toward a face whose nose had been broken so many times it had developed an elbow. "What's the rate tonight?" the man asked.

"I don't know," Arkady admitted.

"They twist your prick here if you have anything but dollars. Or tourist coupons. Do I look like a fucking tourist?" He dug into his

pockets and came out with crumpled bills. He held up one fist: "Zlotys." He held up the other: "Forints. Can you believe it? I followed
these two from the Savoy. I thought they were Italian and they turned
out to be a Hungarian and a Pole."

"It must have been pretty dark," Arkady said.

"When I found out I almost killed them. I *should* have killed them
to spare them the pain of trying to live on fucking forints and zlotys."

Rudy rolled down the window on the passenger side and called to
Arkady, "Next!" To the man waiting with zlotys, he added, "This will
take a while."

Arkady got in. Rudy was well wrapped in a double-breasted suit, an
open cashbox on his lap. He had thinning hair combed diagonally
across his scalp, moist eyes with long lashes, a blue cast to his jowls. A
garnet ring was on the hand that held a calculator. The backseat was
an office of neatly arrayed file boxes, laptop computer, computer battery, and cases of software, manuals and computer disks.

"This is a thoroughly mobile bank," Rudy said.

"An illegal bank."

"On my disks I can hold the complete savings records of the Russian Republic. I could do a spreadsheet for you some other time."

"Thanks. Rudy, a rolling computer center does not make for a satis-
fying life."

Rudy held up a Game Boy. "Speak for yourself."

Arkady sniffed. Hanging from the rearview mirror was something
that looked like a green wick.

"It's an air freshener," Rudy said. "Pine scent."

"It smells like armpit of mint. How can you breathe?"

"It smells cleaner. I know it's me—cleanliness, germs—it's my problem. What are you doing here?"

"Your radio's not working. Let me see it."

Rudy blinked. "You're going to work on it here?"

"Here is where we want to use it. Behave as if we're conducting a
normal transaction."

"You said this would be safe."

"But not foolproof. Everybody's looking."

"Dollars? Deutsche marks? Francs?" Rudy asked.

The cashbox tray was stuffed with currencies of different nationalities and colors. There were francs that looked like delicately hand-
tinted portraits, lire with fantastic numbers and Dante's face, oversized Deutsche marks brimming with confidence and, most of all,

compartments of crisp-as-grass green American dollars. At Rudy's feet was a bulging briefcase with, Arkady assumed, much more. Tucked by the clutch there was also a package wrapped in brown paper. Rudy lifted the hundred-dollar bills from the tray to reveal a transmitter and microrecorder.

"Pretend I want to buy rubles," Arkady said.

"Rubles?" Rudy's finger froze over the calculator. "Why would anyone want to buy rubles?"

Arkady played the transmitter's power switch back and forth, then fine-tuned the frequency. "You're doing it, buying rubles for dollars or Deutsche marks."

"Let me explain. I'm exchanging. This is a service for buyers. I control the rate, I'm the bank, so I always make money and you always lose. Arkady, nobody buys rubles." Rudy's small eyes swelled with sympathy. "The only real Soviet money is vodka. Vodka is the only state monopoly that really works."

"You have some of that, too." Arkady glanced at the rear floor, which was littered with silvery bottles of Starka, Russkaya and Kuban vodka.

"It's Stone Age barter. I take what people have. I help them. I'm surprised I don't have stone beads and pieces of eight. Anyway, the rate is forty rubles to the dollar."

Arkady tried the On button of the recorder. The miniature spools didn't move. "The official rate is thirty rubles to the dollar."

"Yes, and the universe revolves around Lenin's asshole. No disrespect. It's funny, I deal with men who would slit their mother's throat and are embarrassed by the concept of profit." Rudy became serious. "Arkady, if you can just imagine profit apart from crime, then you have business. What we're doing right now is normal and legal in the rest of the world."

"He's normal?" Arkady looked in the direction of Kim. His eyes fixed on the car, the bodyguard had the flat face of a mask.

Rudy said, "Kim's there for effect. I'm like Switzerland, neutral, everybody's banker. Everybody needs me. Arkady, we're the only part of the economy that works. Look around. Long Pond mafia, Baumanskaya mafia, local boys who know how to deliver goods. Lyubertsy mafia, a little tougher, a little dumber, just want to improve themselves."

"Like your partner, Borya?" Arkady tried tightening the spools with a key.

"Borya's a great success story. Any other country would be proud of him."

"And the Chechens?"

"Granted, Chechens are different. If we were all rotting bones, they wouldn't mind. But remember one thing, the biggest mafia is still the Party. Never forget that."

Arkady opened the transmitter and slapped out the batteries. Through the window he noticed customers growing restless, though Rudy seemed in no hurry. If anything, after his initial nervousness, he was in a serene, valedictory mood.

The problem was that the transmitter was militia goods, never strong cause for confidence. Arkady twisted the connecting jacks. "You're not scared?"

"I'm in your hands."

"You're only in my hands because we have enough to put you in a camp."

"Circumstantial evidence of nonviolent crimes. Incidentally, another way to say 'nonviolent crimes' is 'business.' The difference between a criminal and a businessman is that the businessman has imagination." Rudy glanced at the rear seat. "I have enough technology here for a space station. You know, that transmitter of yours is the only thing in this car that doesn't work."

"I know, I know." Arkady lifted the contact prongs and gently slipped the batteries back in. "There was a woman in your car. Who is she?"

"I don't know. I *really* don't know. She had something for me."

"What?"

"A dream. Big plans."

"Is greed involved?"

Rudy let a modest smile shine. "I hope so. Who wants a poor dream? Anyway, she's a friend."

"You don't seem to have any enemies."

"Chechens aside, no, I don't think I do."

"Bankers can't afford enemies?"

"Arkady, we're different. You want justice. No wonder you have enemies. I have smaller aims like profit and pleasure, the way sane people live around the world. Which of us helps other people more?"

Arkady hit the transmitter with the recorder.

"I love to watch Russians fix things," Rudy said.

"You're a student of Russians?"

"I have to be, I'm a Jew."

The spools started to roll. "It's working," Arkady announced.

"What can I say? Once again I'm amazed."

Arkady laid transmitter and recorder under the bills. "Be careful," he said. "If there's trouble, shout."

"Kim keeps me out of trouble." When Arkady opened the door to leave, Rudy added, "In a place like this, you're the one who has to be careful."

As the line outside pressed forward, Kim pushed it back with rapid shoves. He gave Arkady a black stare as he brushed by.

Jaak had bought a shortwave radio that hung like a space-age valise from his hand. The detective wanted to stow his purchase in the Zhiguli.

On the way to the car, Arkady said, "Tell me about this radio. Shortwave, long-wave, medium-wave? German?"

"All waves." Jaak squirmed under Arkady's gaze. "Japanese."

"Did they have any transmitters?"

They passed an ambulance that offered vials of morphine in solution and disposable syringes still in sterile American cellophane. A biker from Leningrad sold acid from his sidecar; Leningrad University had a reputation for the best chemists. Someone Arkady had known ten years before as a pickpocket was now taking orders for computers; Russian computers, at least. Tires rolled out of a bus straight to the customer. Women's shoes and sandals were arrayed on tiptoe on a dainty shawl. Shoes and tires were on the march, if not into the daylight, at least into the twilight.

There was a white flash and a gust of glass from behind them, in the middle of the market. Perhaps a camera bulb and a broken bottle, Arkady thought, though he and Jaak started to return in the direction of the disturbance. A second flash erupted like a firework that caught each face in recoil. The flash subsided to an everyday orange, the sort of fire men start in an oil can to warm their hands on a winter's eve. Little stars rose and danced in the sky. The acrid smell of plastic was tinged by the heady bouquet of gasoline.

Some men staggered back with sleeves on fire and, as the crowd spread and Arkady pushed through, he saw Rudy Rosen riding a blazing phaeton, upright, face black, hair aflame, hands clasped to the wheel, brilliant in his own glow but motionless within the thick, noxious storm clouds that whipped from the interior and out the gutted windows of his car. Arkady got near enough to look through the windshield at Rudy's eyes sinking into the smoke. He was dead. There was that silence, that gutted gaze in the middle of the flames.

Around the burning car other cars were moving. Spilling rugs, gold coins, VCRs, a mass evacuation flowed to the gate. The ambulance lumbered off, plowing over a figure in its headlights, followed by a Chechen motorcade. Cycles split into several streams, searching for gaps in the site fence.

Yet some men stayed and, as the stars drifted overhead, fought to catch them. Arkady himself leaped and plucked from the air a burning Deutsche mark, then a dollar, then a franc, all lined with worms of burning gold.

2

Although the ground was still in shadow, Arkady could see that the site was a layout of four twenty-story towers around a central plaza; three of the towers were faced in precast concrete while the last was still in a skeletal girders-and-crane phase that in the hopeful light of dawn appeared both gargantuan and frail. On the ground floors, he supposed there would be restaurants, cabarets, perhaps a cinema, and in the middle of the plaza, when the earthmovers and cement mixers were gone, a view of tour buses and taxis. Now, however, there were a forensic van, the Zhiguli and the black shell of Rudy Rosen's Audi sitting on a black carpet of singed glass. The Audi's windows were hollow and the heat of the fire had exploded and then burned the tires, so at least it was the stench of burnt rubber that was strongest. As if listening, Rudy Rosen sat stiffly upright.

"Glass seems to be evenly distributed," Arkady said. Polina followed with her prewar Leica and took a picture every other step. "Glass is melted closer to the car, which is a four-door Audi. Left doors shut. Hood shut, headlights burned out. Right doors shut. Trunk shut, taillights burned out." There was nothing to do but get on his hands and knees. "Fuel tank is blown. Muffler separated from exhaust pipe." He got up. "License plate black now but a Moscow number is legible and identified as property of Rudik Rosen. By the wide spread of glass, origin of fire seems to have been inside the passenger compartment, not out."

"Pending expert reports, of course," Polina said to maintain her reputation for disrespect. Young and tiny, the pathologist wore one coat and one smirk summer and winter, her hair piled high and stabbed ferociously with pins. "You should get the thing up on a lift."

Arkady's comments were written down by Minin, a detective with the deep-set eyes of a maniac. Behind Minin a cordon of militia marched across the site. Arson dogs dragged their handlers around the towers, racing from pillar to post, raising their legs.

"Exterior paint is peeled," Arkady went on. "Chrome on the door latch is peeled." There go prints, he thought; nevertheless, he wrapped a handkerchief around his hand to open the front passenger door.

"Thank you," Polina said.

At Arkady's touch the door swung open, spilling ash on his shoes. "Interior of the car is gutted," he continued. "Seats are burned down to frames and coils. Steering wheel seems to have melted and disappeared."

"Flesh is tougher than plastic," Polina said.

"Rear rubber floor mats melted around what appears to be puddled glass. Rear seat burned to springs. Charred computer battery and residue of nonferrous metal. Flecks of gold probably from conductors." Which was all that was left of the computer Rudy was so proud of. "Metal shuttles from computer disks." The megabytes of information. "Covered with ash." The file boxes.

Reluctantly, Arkady moved to the front. "Flash signs by the clutch. Fragments of charred leather. Plastic residue, batteries in dash compartment."

"Naturally. The heat was intense," Polina leaned in to snap a shot with her Leica. "Two thousand degrees, at least."

"On the front seat," Arkady said, "a cashbox. The tray is empty and charred. Under the tray are small metal contacts, four batteries, perhaps the remains of a transmitter and tape recorder. So much for surveillance. Also on the seat is a metal rectangle, perhaps the back of a calculator. Key in the ignition is turned to Off. Two other keys on the ring."

Which brought him to the driver. This was not where Arkady excelled. In fact, this is where he could have used a long walk and a cigarette.

"With the burned ones you have to open the camera aperture all the way just to get any detail," Polina said.

Detail? "The body is shrunken," Arkady said, "too badly charred to be immediately identified as male or female, child or adult. Head is resting on the left shoulder. Clothes and hair are burned off, some skull shows through. Teeth do not appear salvageable for molds. No visible shoes or socks."

Which didn't really describe the new, smaller, blacker Rudy Rosen riding on the airy springs of his chariot. It didn't capture his transformation into tar and bone, the particular nakedness of a belt buckle hanging in the pelvic saddle, the wondering sockets of the eyes and the molten gold of his fillings, the pants stripped for speed, the way his right hand gripped an invisible steering wheel as if he were cruising through hell and the fact that the pearlized wheel had melted like pink taffy on his fingers. It didn't convey the mysterious way bottles of Starka and Kuban vodka had liquefied and pooled, how hard currency and cigarettes had vanished in a puff. "Everybody needs me." Not anymore.

Arkady turned away and saw that as black as Rudy Rosen was, Minin's face registered nothing but satisfaction, as if this sinner had suffered barely enough. Arkady took him aside and aimed him at some of the searchers among the militia who were stuffing their pockets. The ground was strewn with goods abandoned in the panic of the evacuation. "I told them to identify and chart what they found."

"You didn't mean for them to keep it."

Arkady took a deep breath. "Right."

"Look at this." Polina probed a corner of the backseat with her hairpin. "Dried blood."

Arkady went over to the Zhiguli. Jaak was in the backseat questioning their only witness, the same unlucky man Arkady had met when he was waiting to talk to Rudy. The mugger with too many zlotys. Jaak had tackled him just inside the fence.

According to his ID and work papers, Gary Orbelyan was a Moscow resident and hospital orderly, and, by the looks of his coupons, due for a new pair of shoes.

"You want to see ID?" Jaak said. He pulled back Gary's sleeves. On the inside of the left forearm was the picture of a nude sitting in a wineglass and holding the ace of hearts. "He likes wine, women and cards," Jaak said. On the right forearm was a bracelet of spades, hearts, diamonds and clubs. "He loves cards." On the left little finger, a ring of upside-down spades. "This means conviction for hooliganism." On the right ring finger, a knife through a heart. "This means he's ready to kill. So let's say Gary did not wash up in a basket of reeds. Let's say Gary is a multiple offender who was apprehended at a gathering of speculators and who should cooperate."

"Fuck you," Gary said. In the daylight his broken nose looked welded on.

"Still have your forints and zlotys?" Arkady asked.

"Fuck you."

Jaak read from his notes. "The witness states that he spoke to the fucking deceased because he thought the deceased was someone who owed him money. He then left the fucking deceased's car and was standing at a distance of approximately ten meters about five minutes later when the fucking car exploded. A man the witness knows as Kim threw a second fucking bomb into the car and then ran."

"Kim?" Arkady asked.

"That's what he says. He also says he burned his fucking hands trying to save the deceased." Jaak reached into Gary's pockets to pull out handfuls of half-burned Deutsche marks and dollars.

It was going to be a warm day. Already the dewiness of dawn was turning to beads of sweat. Arkady squinted at a sunlit banner that hung limply across the top of the western tower. NEW WORLD HOTEL! He imagined the banner filling with a breeze and the tower sailing away like a brigantine. He needed sleep. He needed Kim.

Polina knelt on the ground on the passenger side of the Audi. "More blood," she called.

AS ARKADY UNLOCKED Rudy Rosen's apartment door, Minin pressed forward with a huge Stechkin machine pistol. Definitely not standard issue.

Arkady admired the weapon but he worried about Minin. "You could saw a room in half with that thing," he told him. "But if someone's here, they would have opened the door or blown it off with a shotgun. A pistol won't help now. It just scares the ladies." He dispensed a reassuring nod to the two street sweepers he had gathered as legal witnesses to the search. They answered with shy glimpses of steel teeth. Behind them, a pair of forensic technicians pulled on rubber gloves.

Search the home of someone you don't know and you're an investigator, Arkady thought. Search the home of someone you do know and you're a voyeur. Odd. He had watched Rudy Rosen for a month but never been inside his apartment before.

Upholstered front door with peephole. Living/dining room, kitchen, bedroom with TV and VCR, another bedroom turned into an office, bathroom with whirlpool. Bookcases with hardbound collections of culture (Gogol, Dostoyevsky), bios of Brezhnev and Moshe Dayan, stamp albums and back issues of *Israel Trade, Soviet Trade, Business Week* and *Playboy*. At once the forensic technicians began a survey, Minin one step behind them to make sure nothing disappeared.

"Don't touch a thing, please," Arkady told the street sweepers, who stood reverentially in the middle of the room as if they had stepped into the Winter Palace.

A kitchen cabinet held American scotch and Japanese brandy, Danish coffee in aluminum-foil sacks; no vodka. In the refrigerator, smoked fish, ham, pâté, butter with a Finnish label, a cool jar of sour cream and, in the freezer, a chocolate bar and an ice cream cake with pink and green frosting in the shape of flowers and leaves. It was the sort of cake that used to be sold in common milk shops, and was now a fantasy found only in the most special buffets—a little less rare, say, than a Fabergé egg.

Kilims on the living-room floor. On the wall, matched portrait photographs of a violinist in formal clothes and his wife at a piano. Their faces had the same roundness and seriousness as Rudy's. The front window looked down on Donskaya Street and, over rooftops, north toward the giant Ferris wheel slowly rolling nowhere in Gorky Park.

Arkady moved on to an office with a Finnish maple desk, StairMaster, telephone and fax. A power-surge protector at the outlet, so Rudy had used his laptop computer in the apartment. The drawers held paper clips, pencils, stationery from Rudy's hotel shop, savings book and receipts.

Minin opened a closet and slapped aside American warm-up outfits and Italian suits. "Check the pockets," Arkady said. "Check the shoes."

In the bedroom bureau even the underwear had foreign labels. Bristle brush on the television set. On the night table, travelogue videotapes, satin sleep mask and alarm clock.

A sleep mask was what Rudy needed now, Arkady thought. Safe but not foolproof, was that what he had told Rudy? Why did anyone ever believe him?

One of the street sweepers had followed him as silently as if she moved in felt slippers. She said, "Olga Semyonovna and I share a flat. We have Armenians and Turkmen in the other rooms. They don't speak to each other."

"Armenians and Turks? You're lucky they don't kill each other," Arkady said. He unlocked the bedroom window for a view of a courtyard garage. Nothing hanging outside the sill. "The communal apartment is death to democracy." He thought about it. "Of course democracy is death to the communal apartment."

Minin entered. "I agree with the chief investigator. What we need is a firm hand."

The sweeper said, "Say what you want, in the old days there was order."

"It was rough order but it was effective," Minin said and they both turned to Arkady with such expectation that he felt like a mad dog on a pedestal.

"Agreed, there was no shortage of order," he said.

At the desk, Arkady filled in the Protocol of Search: date, his name, in the presence of—here he entered the names and addresses of the two women—according to search warrant number, entered Citizen Rudik Davidovich Rosen's residence, apartment 4A at 25 Donskaya Street.

Arkady's eye was caught by the fax again. The machine had buttons in English—for example, Redial. Gingerly he lifted the phone and pushed the button. The receiver produced tones, a ring, a voice.

"Feldman."

"I'm calling for Rudy Rosen," Arkady said.

"Why can't he call himself?"

"I'll explain when we talk."

"You didn't call to talk?"

"We should meet."

"I don't have time."

"It's important."

"I'll tell you what's important. They're going to shut the Lenin Library. It's collapsing. They're turning off the lights, locking the rooms. It's going to be a tomb, like the pyramids at Giza."

Arkady was surprised that anyone associated with Rudy cared about the state of the Lenin Library. "We still have to talk."

"I work late."

"Anytime."

"Outside the library, tomorrow at midnight."

"Midnight?"

"Unless the library comes down on top of me."

"Let me just check the phone number."

"Feldman. F-e-l-d-m-a-n. Professor Feldman." He recited the number and hung up.

Arkady set the receiver down. "Terrific machine."

Minin had a bitter laugh for one so young. "The forensic bastards will strip this place and we could use a fax."

"No, we leave everything, especially the fax."

"Food and liquor, too?"

"Everything."

The second sweeper's eyes grew larger. The magnetic force of guilt made her stare at pearls of vanilla ice cream that traced a trail in the Oriental carpet to the refrigerator and back.

Minin whipped open the freezer door. "She ate the ice cream while our backs were turned. And the chocolate's gone."

"Olga Semyonovna!" The first sweeper was also shocked.

The accused lifted her hand from a pocket and seemed to sink at the knees as if the weight of the incriminating chocolate bar were too much. Tears coursed down the folds of her cheeks and dropped from her trembling chin as if she had stolen a silver cup off an altar. Terrific, Arkady thought, we've made an old woman cry over candy. How could she not succumb? Chocolate was an exotic myth, a whiff of history, like the Aztecs.

"Well, what do you think?" Arkady asked Minin. "Should we arrest her, not arrest her but beat her, or just let her go? It would be more serious if she had taken the sour cream, too. But I want to know your opinion." Arkady really was curious to learn how zealous his assistant was.

"I suppose," Minin said finally, "we can let her go this time."

"If you think so." Arkady turned to the women and said, "Citizens, that means you both will have to help the organs of the law a little more."

Soviet garages were mysteries because steel siding was not legally for sale to private citizens, yet garages constructed of such siding continued to appear magically in courtyards and multiply in rows down back streets. Rudy Rosen's second key opened the mystery in the courtyard. The hanging bulb Arkady left untouched. In the sunlight he could see a tool kit, cases of motor oil, windshield wipers, rearview mirrors and blankets kept to cover the car in winter. Under the blankets there was nothing more unusual than tires. Later Minin and the technicians could dust the bulb and tap the floor. The sweepers had stood timidly in the open door the entire time; the old dears hadn't tried to make off with even a lug wrench.

WHY WASN'T HE tired or hungry? He was like a man with a fever but no diagnosed disease. When he caught up with Jaak at the Intourist Hotel lobby, the detective was swallowing caffeine tablets to stay awake.

"Gary's full of shit," Jaak said. "I don't see Kim killing Rudy. He was his bodyguard. You know, I'm so sleepy that if I find Kim, he's going to shoot me and I won't even notice. He's not here."

Arkady looked around the lobby. To the far left was a revolving door to the street and the outdoor Pepsi stand that had become a landmark for Moscow prostitutes. Inside stood a line of security men who scrupulously let in only prostitutes who paid. Camped within the grotto darkness of the lobby, tourists waited for a bus; they'd been waiting for some time and had the stillness of abandoned luggage. The information stands were not only empty, but seemed to express the eternal mystery of Stonehenge: why were they built? The only action was to the right, where a semi-Spanish courtyard under a skylight invited attention to the tables of a bar and the stainless-steel glitter of slot machines.

Rudy's lobby shop was the size of a large armoire. A case displayed postcards with views of Moscow, monasteries, the fur-trimmed crowns of dead princes. On the back wall hung ropes of amber nuggets and the bunting of peasant shawls. On the side shelves, wooden hand-painted dolls of ascending sizes crowded around plaques for Visa, MasterCard, American Express.

Jaak unlocked and opened the glass door. "One price for credit cards," he said, "half-price for hard currency, which, when you consider that Rudy bought the dolls from idiots for rubles, still gave him a profit of a thousand percent."

"Nobody killed Rudy over dolls," Arkady said. Handkerchief on his hand, he opened the counter drawer and flipped through a ledger. All figures, no notes. Minin and forensics would have to come here, too.

Jaak cleared his throat and said, "I have a date. See you in the bar."

Arkady locked the shop and wandered across the courtyard to the slots. The machines displayed draw poker or revealed plums, bells and lemons on wheels of chance under instructions in English, Spanish, German, Russian and Finnish. All the players were Arabs who circulated joylessly, setting down cans of orange Si Si soda to stack tokens. In the middle of the machines an attendant poured a silvery stream of tokens into a mechanical counter, a metal box with a crank that he kept in furious motion. He jumped when Arkady asked him for a light. Arkady caught his own reflection on the side of a machine: a pale man with lank, dark hair in desperate need of sunshine and a shave, but not frightening enough to account for the way the attendant wrestled with his lighter.

"Did you lose count?" he asked.

"It's automatic," the clerk said.

Arkady read the numbers off the counter's tiny dials. Already 7,590. Fifteen canvas sacks were full and tied shut, five empty sacks to go.

"How much are they?" he asked.

"Four tokens for a dollar."

"Four into . . . well, I'm not good at mathematics, but it seems enough to share." When the clerk started around looking for help, Arkady said, "Just joking. Relax."

Jaak was sitting at the far end of the bar, sucking sugar cubes and talking to Julya, an elegant blonde dressed in cashmere and silk. A pack of Rothmans and a copy of *Elle* were open beside her espresso.

Jaak pushed a cube across the table as Arkady joined them. "Hard-currency bar, they don't take rubles."

"Let me buy you lunch," Julya offered.

"We're staying pure," Jaak said.

She gave him a rich smoker's laugh. "I remember saying that myself."

Jaak and Julya had once been man and wife. They had met on the job, so to speak, and fallen in love, not a unique situation in their callings. She had gone on to bigger and better things. Or he had. Hard to say.

The buffet had pastries and open-faced sandwiches under banners for Spanish brandy. Was the sugar the product of imported Cuban sugarcane or the plain but honest Soviet sugar beet? Arkady wondered. He could become a connoisseur. Australians and Americans traded monotones along the bar. At nearby tables, Germans wooed prostitutes with sweet champagne.

"What are they like, the tourists?" Arkady asked Julya.

"You mean, special kinks?"

"Types."

She allowed him to light her cigarette and took a thoughtful drag. She crossed her long legs in slow motion, drawing eyes from around the bar. "Well, I specialize in Swedes. They're cold but they're clean and they're regular visitors. Other girls specialize in Africans. There's been a murder or two, but generally Africans are sweet and grateful."

"Americans?"

"Americans are scared, Arabs are hairy, Germans are loud."

"What about Russians?" Arkady asked.

"Russians? I feel sorry for Russian men. They're lazy, useless, drunk."

"But in bed?" Jaak asked.

"That's what I was talking about," Julya said. She looked around. "This place is so low-class. Did you know that there are fifteen-year-old girls working the sidewalk?" she asked Arkady. "At night girls work the rooms, knocking on doors. I can't believe Jaak asked me here."

"Julya works at the Savoy," Jaak explained. The Savoy was a Finnish venture around the corner from the KGB. It was the most expensive hotel in Moscow.

"The Savoy says they don't have any prostitutes," Arkady said.

"Exactly. It's very high-class. Anyway, I don't like the word *prostitute.*"

Putana was the word most often used for high-class hard-currency prostitutes. Arkady had the feeling that Julya wouldn't like that word either.

"Julya's a multilingual secretary," Jaak said. "A good one, too."

A man in a warm-up suit set his athletic bag on a chair, sat down and ordered a cognac. A few sprints, a little cognac; it sounded like a good regimen. He had the knotty hair of a Chechen, but worn long in back, short on the sides, with curly bangs dyed an off-orange. The bag looked heavy.

Arkady watched the attendant. "He doesn't seem happy. Rudy was always here when he counted. If Kim killed Rudy, who's going to protect him?"

Jaak read from a notebook. "According to the hotel, 'Ten entertainment machines leased by TransKom Services Cooperative from Recreativos Franco, S.A., show total average reported receipts of about a thousand dollars a day.' Not bad. 'The tokens are counted daily and checked daily against the meters in the backs of the machines. The meters in the slots are locked in; only the Spanish can get into them and reset them.' You saw . . ."

"Twenty sacks," Arkady said.

Jaak calculated. "Each sack holds five hundred tokens and twenty sacks is twenty-five hundred dollars, so that's one thousand dollars for the state and fifteen hundred dollars a day for Rudy. I don't know how he did it, but by the sacks he beat the meters."

Arkady wondered who TransKom was. It couldn't be just Rudy. That kind of import-and-lease needed Party sponsorship, some official institution willing to be a partner.

Jaak turned his eyes to Julya. "Marry me again."

"I'm going to marry a Swede, an executive. I have girlfriends in Stockholm who've already done it. It's not Paris, but the Swedes appreciate someone who's good with money and knows how to entertain. I've had proposals."

"And they talk about the Brain Drain," Jaak said to Arkady.

"One gave me a car," Julya said.

"A car?" Jaak was more respectful.

"A Volvo."

"Naturally. Your bottom should touch nothing but foreign leather." Jaak implored her, "Help me. Not for cars or ruby rings, but because I didn't send you home the first time we took you off the street." He explained to Arkady, "The first time I saw her she was wearing gumboots and a mattress. She's complaining about Stockholm and she came from somewhere in Siberia where they take antifreeze to shit."

"That reminds me," Julya said, unfazed, "for my exit visa I may need a statement from you saying you don't have any claims on me."

"We're divorced. We have a relationship of mutual respect. Can I borrow your car?"

"Visit me in Sweden." Julya found a page in her magazine that she was willing to deface. She wrote three addresses in curly script, folded the margin and tore it along the crease. "I'm not doing you a favor. Personally, Kim is the last person I'd want to find. You're sure I can't buy you lunch?"

Arkady said, "I'll just treat myself to one more cube before we go."

"Be careful," Julya told Jaak.

On the way out, Arkady caught another glance of himself in the bar mirror. Grimmer than he thought, not the kind of face that woke up expecting sunshine. What was that old poem by Mayakovsky? "Regard me, world, and envy: I have a Soviet passport!" Now everyone just wanted a passport to get out, and the government, ignored by all, had collapsed into the sort of spiteful arguments that erupted in a whore-house where no customers had come to call in twenty years.

WHAT COULD EXPLAIN this store, this country, this life? A fork with three out of four tines, two kopecks. A fishhook, twenty kopecks, used, but fish weren't choosy. A comb as small as a seedy mustache, reduced from four kopecks to two.

True, this was a discount shop, but in another, more civilized world, wasn't this trash? Wouldn't it all be thrown away?

Some items had no discernible function. A wooden scooter with rough wooden wheels and no pole, no bars to hang on to. A plastic tag embossed with the number 97. What were the odds someone had ninety-seven rooms, ninety-seven lockers or ninety-seven anything and was only missing the number 97?

Perhaps it was the *idea* of buying. The idea of a market. Because this was a cooperative shop and people wanted to buy . . . something.

On the third table was a bar of soap, shaved and shaped out of a larger, used bar of soap, twenty kopecks. A rusty butter knife, five kopecks. A blackened light bulb with a broken filament, three rubles. Why, when a new bulb was forty kopecks? Since there were no new light bulbs for sale in the stores, you took this used bulb to your office, replaced the bulb in the lamp on your desk and took the good bulb home so that you wouldn't live in the dark.

Arkady slipped out the back door and walked across the dirt toward the second address, a milk shop, cigarette in his left hand, which meant that Kim had not been inside the cooperative. Up the street, Jaak seemed to be reading a newspaper in a car.

There was no milk, cream or butter in the milk shop, though the coolers were stacked with boxes of sugar. The empty counters were staffed by women in white coats and caps who wore the boredom of a rear guard. Arkady lifted a sugar box. Empty.

"Whipped cream?" Arkady asked a clerk.

"No." She seemed startled.

"Sweet cheese?"

"Of course not. Are you crazy?"

"Yes, but what a memory," Arkady said. He flashed his red ID and walked around the counter and through the swinging door into the rear. A truck was in the bay and a delivery of milk was being unloaded directly into another, unmarked truck. The store director came out of a cooler; before the door snapped shut, Arkady saw wheels of cheese and tubs of butter.

"Everything you see is reserved. We have nothing, nothing!" she announced.

Arkady opened the cooler door. An elderly man huddled like a mouse in a corner. In one hand he clutched a certificate naming him a volunteer civilian inspector to combat hoarding and speculation. In his other hand was a bottle of vodka.

"Staying warm, uncle?" Arkady asked.

"I'm a veteran." The old man touched the bottle to the medal on his sweater.

"I can see that."

Arkady walked around the storeroom. Why did a milk shop need bins?

"Everything here is special order for invalids and children," the director said.

Arkady opened a bin to see sacks of flour stacked like sandbags. When he opened another, pomegranates rolled around his feet and over the storeroom floor. A third bin, and lemons poured over pomegranates.

"Invalids and children!" the director shouted.

The last bin was stacked with cigarettes.

Arkady stepped carefully around the fruit and exited through the bay. The men loading the milk tucked their faces away.

From the back of the shop, his cigarette still in his left hand, Arkady walked across a yard seeded with broken glass to the main street. On it, apartment houses rusted in seams along drainpipes and window casings. Cars had the creased and rusted look of wrecks. Kids hung on to a rust-orange carousel without seats. The school seemed to be built of bricks of rust. At the end of the street, the local Party headquarters was sheathed like a sepulcher in white marble.

At Julya's last address for Kim, Arkady dropped the cigarette as he approached a pet shop whose plaster had fallen from its façade in large, geographic sections. He heard Jaak and the car rolling close behind.

The only animals for sale seemed to be chicks and cats peeping and mewing in wire cages. The clerk was a Chinese girl carving what looked like liver for a customer. When the liver stirred, Arkady saw that it was actually a spreading mound of bloodworms. He stepped behind the counter and into a back room as the girl followed with her cleaver and warned, "This is no entry."

In the back were sacks of wood shavings and chicken pellets, a refrigerator with a calendar for the Year of the Sheep, shelves with tall glass jars of teas, mushrooms and fungi, man-shaped ginseng and items labeled only in Chinese characters, but which he recognized from the herbal shops he had seen in Siberia. What looked like tar in a jar was black-bear bile; a larger bottle held a lumpish mass of coagulated pig's blood, good for soup. There were dried seahorses and deer penises that resembled peppers. Bear paws, another illegal delicacy, were stacked on a rope. An armadillo stirred, half-alive, on a string.

"No entry," the girl insisted. She couldn't have been more than twelve and the cleaver looked as long as her arm.

Arkady apologized and left. A second door led up stairs littered with birdseed to a metal door. He knocked and pressed himself against the wall. "Kim, we want to help you. Come out so we can talk. We're friends."

Someone was inside. Arkady heard the careful easing of a floorboard and a sound like rustling sheets. When he pounded the door, it popped open. He walked into a storeroom that was dark except for a shoebox that was burning from the top down in the middle of the floor; he smelled the lighter fluid that had been poured onto it. Around the walls were television cartons, on the floor a bare mattress, tool kit, hot plate. He pulled the curtains aside and looked out the open window at a fire escape leading down to a yard knee-deep in pet-shop trash: birdseed bags, steel netting, dead chicks. Whoever had been here was gone. He tried the switch. The light bulb was gone, too. Well, that showed forethought.

Arkady made a complete circuit of the room, looking behind the cartons, before he returned to the burning box. The sound of the flames was soft and furious at the same time, a miniature firestorm. It wasn't a shoebox. The side of it said "Sindy" and showed a doll with a blond ponytail sitting at a table, pouring tea. He recognized it because Sindy dolls were the most popular import in Moscow, displayed in every toy-store window, nonexistent on the shelves. The box's illustration also showed a dog, perhaps a Pekingese, that sat at the doll's feet and wagged its tail.

Jaak rushed in to stamp out the fire. "Don't." Arkady pulled him back.

The fire line edged down into the picture. As Sindy's hair burst into flame, her face darkened in alarm. She seemed to raise the teapot, then stand, as her upper half was consumed. The dog waited faithfully as paper burned down around him. Then the entire box was black, twisted, spider-webbed with red, turning gray and gauzy, with a layer of ashes that Arkady blew away. Inside was a landmine, lightly charred, its two pressure pins up, triggered, still waiting for Jaak's foot to push them down.

3

Arkady drew a cartoon car on a piece of paper. Crayons, he thought, were about all he lacked. Amenities for rehabilitated Special Investigator Renko included desk and conference table, four chairs, files and a closet that held a combination safe. Also, two "Deluxe" portable typewriters, two red outside phones with dials and two yellow intercoms without. He had two windows dressed with curtains, a wall map of Moscow, a rollaway brownboard, an electric samovar and an ashtray.

On the table Polina spread a black-and-white 360-degree panorama of the construction site and approaching shots of the Audi, then detailed color shots of the gutted car and driver. Minin hovered zealously. Jaak, forty hours without sleep, stirred like a boxer trying to rise before the count of ten.

"It was vodka that made the fire so bad," Jaak said.

"Everyone thinks of vodka," Polina sneered. "What really burns are seats because they're polyurethane. That's why cars burn so quickly, because they're mostly plastic. The seat adheres to the skin like napalm. A car is just an incendiary device on wheels."

Arkady suspected that not so long ago Polina had been the girl in pathology class with the best reports, illustrated and footnoted in punctilious detail.

"In these photographs, I first show Rudy still in the car, then after we've peeled him off and removed him, then a shot through the springs to show what fell through from his pockets: intact steel keys, kopecks melted with floor trash, hardware from the seat, including what was left of our transmitter. The tapes burned, of course, if there ever was anything on them. In the first photographs you'll notice that I have circled in red a flash mark on the sidewall by the clutch." She had indeed, right by the charred shinbones and shoes of Rudy Rosen's legs. "Around the flash mark were traces of red sodium and copper sulfate, consistent with an explosive incendiary device. Since there are no remains of a timer or fuse, I assume it was a bomb designed to ignite on contact. There was also gasoline."

"From when the tank blew," Jaak said.

Arkady drew a stick figure in the car and, with a red pen, a circle around the stick feet. "What about Rudy?"

"Flesh in that condition is as hard as wood, and at the same time bones break as soon as you cut. It's hard enough to pick the clothes off. I brought you this." From a plastic bag Polina produced a newly buffed garnet and a hard puddle of gold, what was left of Rudy's ring. The cool pride on her face reminded Arkady of the sort of cat that brings mice to its owner.

"You checked his teeth?"

"Here's a chart. The gold ran and I haven't found it, but there are signs of a filling in the second lower molar. This is all preliminary to a complete autopsy, of course."

"Thank you."

"Just one thing," she added. "There's too much blood."

"Rudy was probably pretty cut up," Jaak said.

Polina said, "People who are burning to death don't explode. They're not sausages. I found blood everywhere."

Arkady squirmed. "Maybe the assailant was cut."

"I sent samples to the lab to check the blood type."

"Good idea."

"You're welcome." Chin up, contemptuous from then on of the proceedings, she even sat just like a cat.

Jaak diagrammed the market on the brownboard, showing the relative positions of Rudy's car, Kim, the line of customers, then, at a distance of twenty meters, the truck with VCRs. A second grouping was arranged in a loose orbit of ambulance, computer salesman, caviar van; then more space and half an orbit that included Gypsy jewelers, rockers, rug merchants, the Zhiguli.

"It was a big night. With Chechens there we're lucky the whole place didn't erupt." Jaak stared at the board. "Our only witness states that Kim killed Rudy. At first I found it hard to believe, but looking at who was actually close enough to throw a bomb, it makes sense."

"This is from a memory of what you saw in the confusion in the dark?" Polina asked.

"Like much of life." Arkady searched his desk for cigarettes. No sleep? A little nicotine would take care of that. "What we have here is a black market, not the usual daytime variety for ordinary citizens, but a black market at night for criminals. Neutral territory and a very neutral victim in Rudy Rosen." He remembered Rudy's description of himself as Switzerland.

"You know, this was like spontaneous combustion," Jaak said. "You get together enough thugs, drugs, vodka, throw in some hand grenades and something's going to happen."

"A type like that probably cheated someone," Minin suggested.

"I liked Rudy," Arkady said. "I forced him into this operation and I got him killed." The truth was always good for embarrassment. Jaak looked pained by Arkady's lapse, like a good dog that sees his master trip. Minin, on the other hand, seemed grimly satisfied. "The question is, why two firebombs? There were so many guns around, why not shoot Rudy? Our witness —"

"Our witness is Gary Orbelyan," Jaak reminded him.

Arkady continued, "Who identifies Kim as an assailant. We saw Kim with a Malysh. He could have emptied a hundred bullets into Rudy more easily than throwing a bomb. All he had to do was pull the trigger."

Polina asked, "Why two bombs instead of one? The first was enough to kill Rudy."

"Maybe the point wasn't just to kill Rudy," Arkady said. "Maybe it was to burn the car. All his files, every piece of information—loans, deals, paper files, disks—were on the backseat."

Jaak said, "When you kill someone, you want to leave the area. You don't want to have to start moving files."

"They're all smoke now," Arkady said.

Polina changed to a happier subject. "If Kim was close to the car when the device ignited, maybe he was injured. Maybe it was his blood."

"I alerted hospitals and clinics to report anyone coming in with burns," Jaak said. "I'll add lacerations to that. I just find it hard to believe that Kim would have turned on Rudy. If nothing else, Kim was loyal."

"How are we on Rudy's place?" Arkady asked while he followed the at-once tantalizing and repellent smell of stale tobacco to a bottom drawer.

Polina said, "The technicians lifted prints. So far they've only found Rudy's."

In the back of a drawer, Arkady found a forgotten pack of Belomors, a true gauge of desperation. He asked, "You haven't finished the autopsy?"

She said, "There's a wait for morgue time, I told you."

"A wait for morgue time? That's the ultimate insult." The Belomor lit with a puff of black fumes like diesel exhaust. Hard to smoke it and hold it away at the same time, but Arkady tried.

"Watching you smoke is like watching a man commit suicide," Polina said. "No one has to attack this country, just drop cigarettes."

Arkady changed the subject. "What about Kim's place?"

Jaak reported that a more complete search of the storeroom had turned up more empty cartons for German car radios and Italian running shoes, the mattress, empty cognac bottles, birdseed and Tiger Balm.

"All the fingerprints from the storeroom matched the militia file on Kim," Polina said. "The prints on the fire escape were smudged."

"The witness identified Kim throwing a bomb into Rudy's car. You find a landmine in his room. How much doubt can there be?" Minin asked.

"We didn't actually *see* Kim," Arkady said. "We don't know who was there."

"The door opened and there was a fire inside," Jaak said. "Remember when you were a kid? Didn't you put dog shit in a bag and set the bag on fire to see people stamp it out?"

No, Minin shook his head; he'd never done anything like that.

Jaak said, "We used to do it all the time. Anyway, instead of dog shit there was a landmine. I can't believe I fell for it. Almost." A photo in front of Jaak showed the mine's oblong case, the raised pins. It was a small army antipersonnel mine with a trinitrotoluol charge, the kind nicknamed "Souvenir for . . ." The detective lifted his eyes and regained his poise. "Maybe it's a gang war. If Kim went over to the Chechens, Borya will be looking for him. I bet the mine was left for Borya."

Polina had never removed her coat. She stood and buttoned the top with quick fingers that expressed both decisiveness and disgust. "The mine in the bag was left for you. The bomb in the car was probably meant for you, too," she told Arkady.

"No," he said and was about to explain to Polina how backward her reasoning was when she left, shutting the door as her last word. Arkady killed the Belomor and regarded his two detectives. "It's late, children. That's enough for one day."

Minin rose reluctantly. "I still don't see why we have to keep a militiaman at Rosen's apartment."

Arkady said, "We want to keep it the way it is for a while. We left valuable items there."

"The clothes, television, savings book?"

"I was thinking of the food, Comrade Minin." Minin was the only Party member on the team; Arkady fed him "comrade" as occasional slops to a pig.

SOMETIMES ARKADY HAD the feeling that while he had been away, God had lifted Moscow and turned it upside down. It was a nether-Moscow he had returned to, no longer under the gray hand of the Party. The wall map showed a different, far more colorful city painted with grease pencils.

Red, for example, was for the mafia from Lyubertsy, a workers' suburb east of Moscow. Kim was unusual for being Korean, but otherwise he was typical of the boys who grew up there. The Lyubers were the dispossessed, the lads without elite schools, academic diplomas and Party connections, who had in the last five years emerged from the city's metro stations first to attack punkers and then to offer protection to prostitutes, black markets, government offices. Red circles showed Lyubertsy spheres of influence: the tourist complex at Izmailovo Park, Domodedovo Airport, video hawkers on Shabalovka Street. The racetrack was run by a Jewish clan, but they bought muscle from Lyubertsy.

Blue was for the mafia from Long Pond, a northern dead-end suburb of barrack housing. Blue circles marked their interest in stolen cargo at Sheremetyevo Airport and prostitutes at the Minsk Hotel, but their main business was car parts. The Moskvitch auto factory, for example, sat in a blue circle. Rudy's friend Borya Gubenko had not only risen to the top of Long Pond but had also brought Lyubertsy under his influence.

Islamic green was for the Chechens, Moslems from the Caucasus Mountains. A thousand lived in Moscow, with reinforcements that arrived in motorcades, all answering to the orders of a tribal leader called Makhmud. The Chechens were the Sicilians of the Soviet mafias.

Royal purple was reserved for Moscow's own Baumanskaya mafia, from the neighborhood between Lefortovo Prison and the Church of the Epiphany. Their business base was the Rizhsky Market.

Finally, there was brown for the boys from Kazan, more a swarm of ambitious hit-and-run artists than an organized mafia. They raided restaurants on the Arbat, moved drugs and ran teenage prostitutes on the streets.

Rudy Rosen had been banker for them all. Just following Rudy in his Audi had helped Arkady to draw this brighter, darker Moscow. Six mornings a week—Monday through Saturday—Rudy had followed a set routine. A morning drive to a bathhouse run by Borya on the north side of town, then a swing with Borya to pick up pastries at Izmailovo Park and meet the Lyubers. Late-morning coffee at the National Hotel with Rudy's Baumanskaya contact. Even lunch at the Uzbekistan with his enemy, Makhmud. The circuit of a modern Moscow businessman, always trailed by Kim on the motorcycle like a cat's tail.

The night outside was still white. Arkady wasn't sleepy or hungry. He felt like the perfect new Soviet man, designed for a land with no food or rest. He got up and left the office. Enough.

THERE WAS GRILLWORK at each landing of the stairwell to catch "divers," prisoners trying to escape. Maybe not only prisoners, Arkady thought on the way down.

In the courtyard, the Zhiguli was parked next to a dog van. Two dogs with bristling backs were chained to the van's rear bumper. Ostensibly Arkady had two official cars, but gas coupons enough for only one because the oil wells of Siberia were being drained by Germany, Japan, even fraternal Cuba, leaving a thin trickle for domestic consumption. From his second car he'd also had to cannibalize the distributor and battery to keep the first one running, because to send the Zhiguli to the shop was equivalent to sending it on a trip around the world, where it would be stripped on the docks of Calcutta and Port Said. Gas was bad enough. Gas was the reason that defenders of the state slipped from car to car with a siphon tube and can. Also the reason dogs were leashed to bumpers.

Arkady got in through the passenger side and slid over to the wheel. The dogs shot the length of their chains and tried to claw through his door. He prayed and turned the key. Ah, at least a tenth of a tank of gas. There was a God.

Two right turns put him in Gorky Street's gamut of shop windows, still lit. What was for sale? A scene of sand and palm trees surrounded a pedestal surmounted by a jar of guava jam. At the next store, mannequins fought over a bolt of chintz. Food stores displayed smoked fish as iridescent as oil slicks.

At Pushkin Square, a crowd spilled into the street. A year before there had been exhilaration and tolerance between competing bullhorns. A dozen different flags had waved: Lithuanian, Armenian, the czarist red, white and blue of the Democratic Front. Now all were driven from the field except for two flags, the Front's and, on the opposite side of the steps, the red banner of the Committee for Russian Salvation. Each standard had its thousand adherents trying to outshout the other group. In between were skirmishes, the occasional body down and being kicked or dragged away. The militia had discreetly withdrawn to the edges of the square and to the metro stairs. Tourists watched from the safety of McDonald's.

Cars were stopped, but Arkady maneuvered up an alley into a courtyard of plane trees, a quiet backwater to the lights and horns on the avenue outside. A playground's chairs and a table were set into the ground, waiting for a bears' tea party. At the far end, he drove up a street narrowed by trucks straddling the sidewalk. They were heavy, with massive military wheels, the backs covered by canvas. Curious, Arkady honked. A hand drew aside a flap, revealing Special Troops in gray gear and black helmets, with shields and clubs. Armed insomniacs—the worst kind, Arkady thought.

THE PROSECUTOR'S OFFICE had offered him a modern flat in a suburban high-rise of apparatchiks and young professionals, but he had wanted to feel he was in Moscow. That he was, in the angle formed by the Moscow and Yauza rivers, in a three-story building behind a former church that produced liniment and vodka. The church spire had been gilded for the '80 Olympics, but the interior had been gutted to make way for galvanized tanks and bottling machinery. How did the distillers decide which part of their production was vodka and which was rubbing alcohol? Or did it matter?

While he was removing windshield wipers and rearview mirror for the night, Arkady remembered Jaak's shortwave radio, still in the car trunk. Radio, wipers and mirror in hand, he considered the food shop on the corner. Closed, naturally. He could either do his job or eat; that seemed to be the option. If it was any consolation, the last time he had made it to the market he'd had a choice of cow head or hooves. Nothing in between, as if the bulk of the animal had disappeared into a black hole.

Since access to the building could be gained only by punching numbers into a security box, someone had helpfully written the code by the door. Inside, the mailboxes were blackened where vandals had shoved newspapers in the slots and torched them. On the second floor, he stopped by a neighbor's for his mail. Veronica Ivanovna, with the bright eyes of a child and the loose gray hair of a witch, was the closest thing to a guard the building had.

"Two personal letters and a phone bill." She handed them over. "I couldn't get you any food because you didn't remember to give me your ration card."

Her apartment was illuminated by the airless glow of a television set. All the old people in the building seemed to have gathered on chairs and stools around the screen to watch, or rather to listen with their eyes closed to, the image of a gray, professorial face with a deep, reassuring voice that carried like a wave to the open door.

"You may be tired. Everyone is tired. You may be confused. Everyone is confused. These are difficult times, times of stress. But this is the hour of healing, of reconnecting with the natural, positive forces all around you. Visualize. Let your fatigue flow out your fingertips, let the positive force flow in."

"A hypnotist?" Arkady asked.

"Come in. It's the most popular program on television."

"Well, I *am* tired and confused," Arkady admitted.

Arkady's neighbors leaned back in their seats as if from the radiant heat of a fireplace. It was the fringe of beard under the chin that gave the hypnotist a serious, academic caste. That and the thick glasses that enlarged his eyes, as intense and unblinking as an icon's. "Open yourself up and relax. Cleanse your mind of old dogmas and anxieties because they only exist in your mind. Remember, the universe wants to work through you."

"I bought a crystal on the street," Veronica said. "His people are selling them everywhere. You place a crystal on the television set and it focuses his emanations directly on you, like a beacon. It amplifies him."

In fact, Arkady saw a row of crystals on her set. "Do you think it's a bad sign when it's easier to buy stones than food?" he asked.

"You will only find bad signs if you're looking for them."

"That's the problem. In my work I look for them all the time."

FROM HIS REFRIGERATOR Arkady took a cucumber, yogurt and stale bread that he ate standing at an open window, looking south over the church toward the river. The neighborhood had ancient lanes on real hills and an actual wood burner's alley hidden behind the church. Behind the houses were back lots that used to hold dairy cows and goats, which sounded good now. It was the newer parts of the city that looked abandoned. The neon signs above the factories were half-dark, half-lit, delivering illegible messages. The river itself was as black and still as asphalt.

Arkady's living room had an enamel-topped table with a coffee can of daisies, armchair, good brass lamp and so many bookshelves that the room seemed to have been built against a dam of books, a paper-back bulwark from the poet Akhmatova to the humorist Zoshchenko, and including a Makarov, a 9-mm pistol he kept behind the Pasternak translation of *Macbeth*.

The hall had a shower and WC and led to a bedroom with more books. His bed was made, he gave himself credit for that. On the floor were a cassette player, headphones and ashtray. Under the bed he found cigarettes. He knew he should lie down and close his eyes, yet he discovered himself wandering back through the hall. He still wasn't sleepy or hungry. Merely as an occupation he looked into the refrigerator again. The last items were a carton of something called "Berry of the Forest" and a bottle of vodka. The carton demanded a mauling to permit a stream of brown, gritty juice to plop into a glass. By taste, it was either apple, prune or pear. Vodka barely cut it.

"To Rudy." He drank and filled the glass again.

Since he had Jaak's radio, he placed it on the table and turned on a garble of shortwave transmissions. From distant points of the earth came spasms of excitable Arabic and the round vowels of the BBC. Between signals the planet itself seemed to be mindlessly humming, perhaps sending those positive forces the hypnotist had talked about. On a medium band he heard a discussion in Russian about the Asian cheetah. "The most magnificent of desert cats, the cheetah claims a range that extends across southern Turkmenia to the tableland of Us- tyurt. Distribution of these splendid animals is uncertain since none have been seen in the wild for thirty years." Which made the cheetahs' claims about as valid as czarist banknotes, Arkady thought. But he liked the concept of cheetahs still lurking in the Soviet desert, loping after the wild ass or the goitered gazelle, gathering speed, darting around tamarisk trees, leaping skyward.

He found he had gravitated to the bedroom window again. Veron- ica, who lived below, said he walked a kilometer from room to room every night. Just claiming his open range, that's all.

A different voice on the radio, a woman's, read the news about the latest Baltic crisis. He half-listened while he considered the landmine at Kim's address. Arms were stolen from military depots every day. Were army trucks going to set up shop at every street corner? Was Moscow the next Beirut? Filmy smoke hung over the city. Below, the same smoke swirled around empty vodka cases.

He drifted back to the living room. There was a strange slant to the broadcast, yet the voice itself sounded vaguely familiar. "The right- wing organization 'Red Banner' stated that it planned a rally tonight in Moscow's Pushkin Square. Although Special Forces are on the alert, observers believe the government will once again sit on its hands until chaos escalates and it has the excuse of public order to sweep away political opponents on both the right and the left."

The indicator needle was between 14 and 16 on the medium wave and Arkady realized he was listening to Radio Liberty. The Americans ran two propaganda stations, the Voice of America and Radio Liberty. VOA, staffed by Americans, was a buttery voice of reason. Liberty was staffed by Russian émigrés and defectors, hence offered vitriol more in character with its audience. An arc of jamming arrays had been built south of Moscow simply to block Radio Liberty, sometimes chas- ing the signal up and down the dial. Although full-time jamming had stopped, this was the first time since then that Arkady had heard the station.

The broadcaster talked calmly about riots in Tashkent and Baku.

She reported new findings on the poison gas used in Georgia, more thyroid cancer from Chernobyl, battles along the border with Iran, ambushes in Nagorno-Karabakh, Islamic rallies in Turkestan, miners' strikes in the Donbas, railroad strikes in Siberia, drought in the Ukraine. In the rest of the world, Eastern Europe still seemed to be rowing its lifeboats away from the sinking Soviet Union. If it was any consolation, the Indians, Pakistanis, Irish, English, Zulus and Boers were making hells of their parts of the globe. She finished by saying that the next news would be in twenty minutes.

Any reasonable man would have been depressed, yet Arkady checked his watch. He got up, assembled cigarettes and took the next vodka straight. The program between newscasts was about the disappearance of the Aral Sea. Irrigation for Uzbek cotton fields had drained the Aral's rivers, leaving thousands of fishing boats and millions of fish foundered in slime. How many nations could say they had wiped out an entire sea? He got up to change the water for the daisies.

The news came on at the half hour for only one minute. He listened to the blissful chirping of Belorussian folk songs until the news returned again at the hour for ten minutes. The stories didn't change; it was her voice he sat forward to attend to. He laid his watch on the table. He noticed he had lace curtains. Of course he knew his windows had curtains, but a man can forget these niceties until he sits still. Machine-made, of course, but quite nice, with a floral tracery fading into the pale light outside.

"This is Irina Asanova with the news," she said.

So she hadn't married, or else she hadn't changed her name. And her voice was both fuller and sharper, not a girl's anymore. The last time he had seen her she was stepping across a snowy field, wanting to go and wanting to stay at the same time. The bargain was that if she went, he stayed behind. He had listened for her voice so many times since, first in interrogation when he was afraid she had been caught, later in psycho wards where his memory of her was grounds for treatment. Working in Siberia, he sometimes wondered whether she still existed, had ever existed, was a delusion. Rationally he knew he would never see or hear her again. Irrationally he always expected to see her face turning the next corner or hear her voice across a room. Like a man with a condition, he had waited every second for his heart to stop. She sounded good, she sounded well.

At midnight, when programming started to repeat, he finally turned the radio off. He had a last cigarette by the window. The church spire blazed like a golden flame against the gray, under the arch of the night.

4

The museum had a catacomb's low ceiling and compressed atmosphere. Unlit dioramas were spaced down the walls like abandoned chapels. At the far end, instead of an altar, open crates held unpolished plaques and dusty flags.

Arkady remembered the first time he had been granted admittance twenty years before, and the ghoulish eyes and sepulchral tone of his elderly guide, a captain whose only duty was to instill in visitors the glorious heritage and sacred mission of the militia. He tried the light switch on a display. Nothing.

The next switch did work and illuminated a foreshortened Moscow street circa 1930 with the hearselike cars of that period, model figures of men striding importantly, women shuffling with bags, boys hiding behind lampposts, all apparently normal except for, lurking on the corner, a doll with his coat collar turned up to his hat brim, a miniature paranoid. "Can you find the undercover officer?" the captain had proudly asked.

The younger Arkady had arrived with other high school boys, a group picture of sniggering hypocrisy. "No," they chorused with a straight face while they traded smirks.

Two more dead switches, then a scene of a man skulking into a house to reach for an overcoat hanging in the foyer. In an adjoining parlor a plaster family listened contentedly to the radio. A caption revealed that when this "master criminal" was captured he had a thousand coats in his possession. Wealth beyond compare!

"Can you tell me," the captain had asked, "how this criminal, without drawing suspicion, carried these coats home? Think before you answer." Ten blank faces stared back. "He wore them." The captain looked each boy in the eye so that everyone understood the sheer brilliance and inventive deceit of the criminal mind. "He *wore* them."

Other models continued the historical survey of Soviet crime. Not a tradition of subtlety, Arkady thought. See photos of slaughtered children, see the ax, see the hair on the ax. Another display of disinterred bodies, another murderer with a face half-erased by a lifetime of vodka consumption, another carefully preserved ax.

Two scenes in particular were designed to draw gasps of horror. One was of a bank robber who made his getaway in Lenin's car, equal to stealing an ass from Christ. The other featured a terrorist with a homemade rocket that had narrowly missed Stalin. Find the crime, Arkady thought: trying to kill Stalin or missing him.

"Don't dwell in the past," Rodionov said from the door. The city prosecutor delivered his warning with a smile. "We're the men of the future, Renko, all of us, from now on."

The city prosecutor was Arkady's superior, the all-seeing eye of Moscow courts, the guiding hand of Moscow investigators. More than that, Rodionov was also an elected deputy to the People's Congress, a barrel-chested totem of the democratization of Soviet society at all levels. He had the frame of a foreman, the silvery locks of an actor and the soft palm of an apparatchik. Perhaps a few years ago he had been just one more clumsy bureaucrat; now he had the particular grace that comes from performing for cameras, a voice modulated for civil debate. As if he were bringing together two dear friends, he introduced Arkady to General Penyagin, a larger, older man with deep-set, phlegmatic eyes whose blue summer uniform was marked by a black armband. The chief of Criminal Investigation had died only days before. Penyagin was now head of CID, and though he had two stars on his shoulder boards, he was distinctly the new bear in the circus, taking his cue from Rodionov. The city prosecutor's other companion was a different type altogether, a jaunty visitor named Albov who looked less Russian than American.

Rodionov dismissed the displays and cartons with a wave and told Arkady, "Penyagin and I are in charge of cleaning out the Ministry archives. These will all be junked, replaced by computers. We joined Interpol because as crime becomes more international, we have to react imaginatively, cooperatively, without outdated ideological blinders. Imagine when our computers here are hooked up to New York,

Bonn, Tokyo. Already Soviet representatives are actively assisting in investigations abroad."

"No one could escape anywhere," Arkady said.

"You don't look forward to that prospect?" Penyagin asked.

Arkady wanted to please. He had once shot a prosecutor, a fact that lent relations a certain delicacy. But was he thrilled by that prospect? The world as a single box?

"You've worked with Americans in the past," Rodionov reminded Arkady. "For which you suffered. We all suffered. That's the tragic nature of mistakes. The office suffered the loss of your services during crucial years. Your return to us is part of a vital healing process that we all take pride in. Since this is Penyagin's first day at CID, I wanted to introduce him to one of our more special investigators."

"I understand you demanded certain conditions when you returned to Moscow," Penyagin said. "You were given two cars, I hear."

Arkady nodded. "With ten liters of gas. That makes for short car chases."

"Your own detectives, your own pathologist," Rodionov reminded him.

"I thought a pathologist who wouldn't rob the dead was a good idea." Arkady glanced at his watch. He had assumed they would leave the museum for the usual conference room with baize table and double sets of aides taking notes.

"The important point," Rodionov said, "is that Renko wanted to run independent investigations with a direct channel of information to me. I think of him as a scout in advance of our regular forces, and the more independently he operates, the more important the line of communication between him and us becomes." He turned to Arkady and his tone became more serious. "That's why we have to discuss the Rosen investigation."

"I haven't had time to review the file," Penyagin said.

When Arkady hesitated, Rodionov said, "You can talk in front of Albov. This is an open, democratic conversation."

"Rudik Davidovich Rosen." Arkady recited from memory. "Born 1952, Moscow, parents now dead. Diploma with distinction in mathematics from Moscow State University. Uncle in the Jewish mafia that runs the racetrack. During school vacations, young Rudy helped set the odds. Military duty in Germany. Accused of changing money for Americans in Berlin, not convicted. Came back to Moscow. Motorpool dispatcher at the Commission on Cultural Work for the Masses, where he sold designer clothes retail out of cars. Switchyard director at the Moscow Trust of the Flour and Groats Industry, where he stole wholesale by the boxcar. Up to yesterday, managed a hotel souvenir shop from which he ran the lobby slot machines and bar, which were sources of hard currency for his money-changing operation. With the slots and the exchange, Rudy made money at both ends."

"He lent money to the mafias, that's it?" Penyagin asked.

"They have too many rubles," Arkady said. "Rudy showed them how to invest their money and turn it into dollars. He was the bank."

"What I don't understand," Penyagin said, "is what you and your special team are going to do now that Rosen is dead. What was it, a Molotov cocktail? Why don't we leave Rosen's killer to a more ordinary investigator?"

Penyagin's predecessor at CID had been that rare beast who actually had risen from the detective ranks, so he would have understood without having everything explained. The only thing Arkady knew about Penyagin was that he had been a political officer, not operational. He tried to educate him gently. "As soon as Rudy agreed to put my transmitter and recorder in his cashbox, he became my responsibility. That's the way it is. I told him I could protect him, that he was part of my team. Instead I got him killed."

"Why would he agree to carry a radio for you?" Albov spoke for the first time. His Russian was perfect.

"Rudy had a phobia. He was hazed in the army. He was Jewish, he was overweight and the sergeants got together and put him in a coffin filled with human waste and nailed him in for a night. Since then he had a fear of close physical contact or dirt or germs. I only had enough to put him in camp for a few years, but he didn't think he could survive. I used the threat to make him carry the radio."

"What happened?" Albov asked.

"The militia equipment failed, as usual. I entered Rudy's car and tinkered with the transmitter until it worked. Five minutes later he was on fire."

"Did anyone see you with Rudy?" Rodionov asked.

"Everyone saw me with Rudy. I assumed no one would recognize me."

"Kim didn't know that Rosen was cooperating with you?" Albov asked.

Arkady revised his opinion. Though Albov had the physical ease and blow-dried assurance of an American, he was Russian. About thirty-five, dark brown hair, soulful black eyes, charcoal suit, red tie and the patience of a traveler camping with barbarians.

"No," Arkady said. "At least I didn't think he did."

"What about Kim?" Rodionov asked.

Arkady said, "Mikhail Senovich Kim. Korean, twenty-two. Reform school, minors colony, army construction battalion. Lyubertsy mafia, car theft and assault. Rides a Suzuki, but we expect him to take any bike off the street, and of course he wears a helmet, so who knows who he is? We can't stop every biker in Moscow. A witness identifies him as the assailant. We're looking for him, but we're also looking for other witnesses."

"But they're all criminals," Penyagin said. "The best witnesses were probably the killers."

"That's generally the case," Arkady said.

Rodionov shuddered. "The whole thing is a typical Chechen attack."

"Actually," Arkady said, "Chechens are more partial to knives. Anyway, I don't think the point was to only kill Rudy. The bombs burned the car, which was a computerized mobile bank stuffed with disks and files. I think that's why they used two bombs, in order to make sure. They did a good job. It's all gone now, along with Rudy."

"His enemies must be happy," Rodionov said.

"There was probably more incriminating evidence about his friends on those disks than about his enemies," Arkady said.

Albov said, "It sounds as if you liked Rosen."

"He burned to death. You could say I sympathized."

"Would you describe yourself as an unusually sympathetic investigator?"

"Everyone works in a different way."

"How is your father?"

Arkady thought for a moment, more to adjust to this shift of ground than to search for an answer.

"Not well. Why do you ask?"

Albov said, "He's a great man, a hero. More famous than you, if you don't mind my saying so. I was curious."

"He's old."

"Seen him lately?"

"If I do, I'll tell him you asked."

Albov's conversation had the slow but purposeful motion of a python. Arkady tried to catch the rhythm.

"If he's old and sick, you should see him, don't you think?" Albov asked. "You select your own detectives?"

"Yes." Arkady was trying to answer the second question.

"Kuusnets is an odd name—for a detective, I mean."

"Jaak Kuusnets is the best man I have."

"But there aren't that many Estonians who are Moscow detectives. He must be especially grateful and loyal to you. Estonians, Koreans, Jews—it's hard to find any Russians in your case. Of course some people think that's the problem with the whole country." Albov had the calm gaze of a Buddha. Now he let it incline toward the prosecutor and the general. "Gentlemen, your investigator seems to have both a team and a goal. The times demand that you let initiative have its head, not bring it to a halt. I hope we don't make the same mistake with Renko that we made before."

Rodionov could tell the difference between a red light and a green. "My office is totally committed to our investigator, of course."

"I can only repeat that the militia wholeheartedly supports the investigator," Penyagin said.

"You're from the prosecutor's office?" Arkady asked Albov.

"No."

"I didn't think so." Arkady added up the suit and ease. "State Security or Ministry of the Interior?"

"I'm a journalist."

"You brought a *journalist* to this meeting?" Arkady asked Rodionov. "My direct channel to you includes a journalist?"

"An international journalist," Rodionov said. "I wanted a more sophisticated point of view."

Albov said, "Remember, the prosecutor is also a people's deputy. There's an election to consider now."

"Well, that *is* sophisticated," Arkady said.

Albov said, "The main thing is, I've always been an admirer. This is a turning point in history. This is Paris in the Revolution, Petrograd in the Revolution. If intelligent men can't work together, what hope is there for the future?"

Arkady was still stunned after they left. Maybe Rodionov would show up next time with the editorial board of *Izvestia* or cartoonists from *Krokodil.*

And what would become of the crates and dioramas of the militia museum? Were they really going to be replaced by a computer center? And what would become of all the bloody axes, knives and threadbare

overcoats of Soviet crime? Would they be stored? Of course, he answered himself, because the bureaucratic mind saved everything.
Why? Because we might need it, you know. In case there was no
future, there was always the past.

JAAK DROVE, SKIPPING lanes in the manner of a virtuoso pianist going up
and down a keyboard.

"Don't trust Rodionov or his friends," he told Arkady as he shouldered another car to the side.

"You don't like anyone from the prosecutor's office."

"Prosecutors are political shits, always have been. No offense." Jaak
glanced over. "But they're Party members. Even if they quit the Party,
even if they become a people's deputy, in their hearts they're Party
members. You didn't quit the Party, you were thrown out, that's why I
trust you. Most prosecutors' investigators never leave their office.
They're part of the desk. You get out. Of course you wouldn't get far
without me."

"Thanks."

One hand on the wheel, Jaak handed Arkady a list of numbers and
names. "Plates from the black market. The truck nearest Rudy when
he blew up is registered to the Lenin's Path Collective Farm. I think it
was supposed to be carrying sugar beets, not VCRs. There are four
Chechen cars. The Mercedes was registered in the name of Apollonia
Gubenko."

"Apollonia Gubenko," Arkady tried it on the tongue. "There's a
round name."

"Borya's wife," Jaak said. "Of course Borya has a Mercedes of his
own."

They looped ahead of a Lada whose windshield was patched with
pins, paper and glue. Windshields were hard to come by. The driver
steered with his head out the side.

"Jaak, what is an Estonian doing in Moscow?" Arkady asked. "Why
aren't you defending your beloved Tallinn from the Red Army?"

"Don't give me any more of that shit," Jaak warned. "I was in the
Red Army. I haven't been to Tallinn in fifteen years. What I know
about Estonians is that they live better and complain more than anyone else in the Soviet Union. I'm going to change my name."

"Change it to Apollo. You'd still have an accent, though—that nice Baltic click."

"Fuck accents. I hate this subject." Jaak made an effort to cool down. "Speaking of dumb, we're getting calls from a coach at Red Star Komsomol who says Rudy was such a club supporter that the boxers there gave him one of their trophies. The coach thinks it should be among Rudy's personal effects. An idiot but a persistent guy."

As they approached Kalinin Prospect, a tour bus tried to cut in front of Jaak. It was an Italian bus with tall windows, baroque chrome and two tiers of stupefied faces—almost a Mediterranean trireme, Arkady thought. The Zhiguli accelerated with a burst of blue smoke. Jaak tapped the brakes just enough to threaten the finish on the bus's front bumper and raced ahead, laughing triumphantly. "Homo Sovieticus wins again!"

AT THE GAS station Arkady and Jaak got into separate lines for meat pies and soda. Dressed like a lab technician in white coat and toque, the pie vendor whisked flies from her wares. Arkady remembered the advice of a friend who picked mushrooms to stay away from those surrounded by dead flies. He reminded himself to check the ground when he reached the pushcart.

A far longer line, all male, stretched from a vodka store at the corner. Drunks sagged and leaned like broken pickets on a fence. Their clothes had the grayness of old rags, their faces were raw red and blue, but they clutched empty bottles in the solemn knowledge that no new bottle would cross the counter except in exchange for an empty. Also, it had to be the right size empty bottle: not too big, not too small. Then they had to pass militiamen stationed at the door to check coupons for out-of-towners trying to buy vodka marked for Moscow. As Arkady watched, a satisfied patron left the store, cradling his bottle like an egg, and the line inched forward.

There was a selection, which was what was holding up Arkady's line: meat or cabbage pies. Since the filling was sure to be no more than a suggestion—a delicate soupçon of ground pork or steamed cabbage, a fine line within dough first steeped in boiling fat and then allowed to cool and congeal—it was a choice that demanded a fine palate, not to mention hunger.

The vodka line also stalled, held up by a customer who had swooned on his way into the store and dropped his empty. The bottle rang as it rolled to the gutter.

Arkady wondered what Irina was doing. All morning he had denied to himself that he was thinking about her. Now, with the chiming of the bottle, the very strangeness of the sound, he saw her having her midday meal not on the street but in a Western cafeteria of gleaming chrome, brightly lit mirrors, smoothly rolling carts bearing white porcelain cups.

"Meat or cabbage?"

It took him a moment to return.

"Meat? Cabbage?" the vendor repeated and held up identical pies. Her own face was as round and coarse, her eyes sunk in a crease. "Come on, everyone else knows what they want."

"Meat," Arkady said. "And cabbage."

She grunted, sensing indecision rather than appetite. Maybe this was his problem, Arkady thought, lack of appetite. She made his change and handed over two pies embellished by paper napkins dripping grease. He checked the ground. No dead flies, though the ones buzzing around looked depressed.

"You don't want it?" the vendor asked.

Arkady was still seeing Irina, feeling the warm pressure of her and smelling not the rancid fumes of grease but the clean crispness of sheets. He seemed to be moving quickly through progressive stages of insanity, or else Irina was moving from oblivion to the unconscious, then to the conscious areas of his mind.

As the vendor leaned over her cart, a transformation took place. In the middle of her face appeared what was left of a girl's embarrassment, of sad eyes lost between jowls, and she shrugged apologetically with round shoulders. "Eat it, don't think about it."

When Jaak brought the sodas Arkady awarded him both pies.

"No, thanks." Jaak recoiled. "I used to like them before I started working with you. You ruined them for me."

5

On Butyrski Street, past a long storefront of lingerie and lace, was a building of barred windows with a driveway that dipped by a guardhouse down to entrance stairs. Inside, an officer issued numbered aluminum tags to Arkady and Jaak. A grille with a heart-shaped pattern slid open and they followed a guard across a parquet floor, down a stairwell with rubber treads and into a corridor of calcified stucco lit by bulbs in wire cages.

Only one person had ever escaped from Butyrski Prison and that was Dzerzhinsky, the founder of the KGB. He had bribed the guard. In those days a ruble meant something.

"Name?" the guard asked.

A voice behind the cell door said, "Orbelyan."

"Article?"

"Speculation, resisting arrest, refusal to cooperate with proper organs—what the fuck, I don't know."

The door opened. Gary stood stripped to the waist, his shirt tied turban-style around his head. With his rakishly broken nose and torso of tattoos, he looked more like a pirate marooned on a desert island than a man who had spent one night in jail.

"Speculation, resisting and refusal. Great witness," Jaak said.

The interrogation room had a monastic simplicity: wooden chairs, metal desk, icon of Lenin. Arkady filled out the protocol form: date, city, his own name under the grand title "Investigator of Very Important Cases under the General Prosecutor of the USSR," interrogated Orbelyan, Gary Semyonovich, born 3/11/60, Moscow, passport number, Armenian nationality . . .

"Naturally," Jaak said.

Arkady went on. "Education and specialization?"

"Vocational. Medical industry," Gary said.

"Brain surgeon," Jaak said.

Unmarried, hospital orderly, not a Party member, criminal record of assault and possession of drugs for sale.

"Government honors?" Arkady asked.

Both Jaak and Gary laughed.

"It's the next question on the protocol," Arkady said. "Probably just looking to the future."

After he wrote out the exact time, the questioning began, going over the same ground Jaak had covered at the crime site. Gary had been walking away from Rudy's car when he saw it blow up, and then Kim throw in a second bomb.

"You were walking backwards from Rudy's car?" Jaak asked. "How did you see all this?"

"I stopped to think."

"You stopped to *think*?" Jaak asked. "What about?"

When Gary fell silent, Arkady asked, "Did Rudy change your forints and zlotys?"

"No." Gary's face went dark as a cloud.

"You were pretty mad."

"I would have twisted his fat neck."

"Except for Kim?"

"Yeah, but then Kim did it for me." Gary brightened.

Arkady drew an *X* in the middle of a page and handed Gary the pen. "This is Rudy's car. Mark where you were, then mark what else you saw."

With concentration, Gary drew a stick figure with trembly limbs. He added a box with wheels: "Truck with electronic goods." Between him and Rudy, a blacked-in figure: "Kim." A box with a cross: "Ambulance." A second box: "Maybe a van." Lines with heads: "Gypsies." Smaller squares with wheels: "Chechen cars."

"I remember a Mercedes," Jaak said.

"They were already gone."

"*They?*" Arkady asked. "Who was they?"

"A driver. I know the other one was a woman."

"Can you draw her?"

Gary drew a stick figure with a big bust, high heels and curly hair. "Maybe blond. I know she was built."

"A real careful observer," Jaak said.

"So you saw her out of the car, too," Arkady said.

"Yeah, coming from Rudy's."

Arkady held the paper a couple of ways. "Good drawing."

Gary nodded.

Arkady thought so, too. With his blue body and busted face, Gary looked just like the stick figure on the page, rendered more human by his picture.

THE SOUTH PORT car market was bounded by Proletariat Prospect and a loop of the Moscow River. New cars were ordered in a hall of white marble. No one went inside; there were no new cars. Outside, gamblers laid cardboard on the ground to play three-card monte. Construction fences were papered with offers ("Have tires in medium condition for 1985 Zhigulis") and pleas ("Looking for fan belt for '64 Peugeot"). Jaak wrote down the number for the tires, just in case.

At the end of the fence was a dirt lane of used Zhigulis and Zaporozhets, two-cylinder German Trabants and Italian Fiats as rusty as ancient swords. Buyers moved with eyes that scrutinized tire tread, odometer, upholstery, dropping to one knee with a flashlight to see whether the engine was actively leaking oil on the spot. Everyone was an expert. Even Arkady knew that a Moskvitch built in far-off Izhevsk was superior to a Moskvitch built in Moscow, and that the only clue was the insignia on the grille. Around the cars were Chechens in warm-up outfits. They were dark, bulky men with low brows and long stares.

Everyone cheated. Car sellers went to the market clerk's wooden shack to learn—depending on model, year and condition—what price they could demand (and on which they would pay tax), which bore no resemblance to the money that actually passed between seller and buyer. Everyone—seller, buyer and clerk—understood that the real price would be three times higher.

Chechens cheated in the most devious way. Once a Chechen had title in hand, he paid only the official price, and there was as much chance of a seller getting the rest of his money as taking a bone from the jaws of a wolf. Of course the Chechen turned around and sold the car for full price. The tribe amassed fortunes at the South Port market. Not off every sale—that would destroy the incentive that brought fresh cars—but off an intelligent percentage. Chechens culled the market as if it were a flock of sheep that was all their own.

Jaak and Arkady stopped halfway down the line and the detective nodded toward a car parked by itself at the end of the lane. It was an old, black, once-official Chaika sedan with a scalloped chrome grille rubbed to a mirror finish. Curtains were drawn across the side windows of the backseat.

"Fucking Arabs," Jaak said.

"They're no more Arab than you are," Arkady said. "I thought you were free of prejudice. Makhmud is an old man."

"I hope he's got the strength to show you his collection of skulls."

Arkady went on alone. The last car for sale was a Lada so dented that it looked as if it had been rolled to the market end over end. Two young Chechens with tennis bags stopped him to ask where he was headed. When Arkady mentioned Makhmud's name, they escorted him to the Lada, pushed him into the back, felt his arms, legs and torso for a gun or a wire and told him to wait. One went to the Chaika; the other got in front, opened his bag and turned to slide a gun between the two front seats so that the muzzle nestled in Arkady's lap.

The gun was a new single-barrel "Bear" carbine cut to half-length and retooled for shot. The visors of the car were fringed with beads, the dash decorated with snapshots of grapevines, mosques and decals of AC/DC and Pink Floyd. An older Chechen got in behind the wheel, ignored Arkady and opened the Koran, droning aloud as he read. He had a heavy gold ring on the pinky finger of each hand. Another got in beside Arkady with a skewer of shashlik wrapped in paper and handed pieces of meat around, including Arkady, not in a friendly fashion, more as if he were a despised guest. All they needed were mustachios and bandoliers, Arkady thought. The Lada pointed away from the market, but in the rearview mirror he occasionally caught sight of Jaak examining different cars.

Chechens had nothing to do with Arabs. Chechens were Tartars, a western tide of the Golden Horde that had settled in the fastness of the Caucasus Mountains. Arkady studied the postcards on the dash. The city with the mosque was their mountain capital of Grozny, as in "Ivan Grozny"—Ivan the Terrible. Did that twist the Chechen psyche a little bit, growing up with a name like that?

Finally the first Chechen returned, accompanied by a boy not much bigger than a jockey. He had a heart-shaped face with raddled skin and eyes full of ambition. He reached into Arkady's jacket for his ID, studied it and slipped it back. To the man with the shotgun he said, "He killed a prosecutor." So by the time Arkady got out of the car, he was accorded some respect.

Arkady followed the boy up to the Chaika, where the rear door opened for him. A hand reached out and pulled him in by the collar.

Vintage Chaikas had a stately Soviet style: upholstered ceiling, elaborate ashtrays, banquette seats with corded piping, air-conditioning, plenty of room for the boy and driver up front and Makhmud and Arkady in back. Also bulletproof windows, he was sure.

Arkady had seen pictures of mummified figures dug from the ashes of Pompeii. They looked like Makhmud, bent and gaunt, no lashes or brows, skin a parchment gray. Even his voice sounded burned. He turned stiffly, as if hinged, to hold his visitor at arm's length and stare with eyes as black as little coals.

"Excuse me," Makhmud said. "I had this operation. The wonder of Soviet science. They fix your eyes so you don't have to wear glasses anymore. They don't do this operation anywhere else in the world. What they don't tell you is from then on you only see at one distance. The rest of the world is a blur."

"What did you do?" Arkady asked.

"I could have killed the doctor. I mean, I really could have killed the doctor. Then I thought about it. Why did I have this operation? Vanity. I'm eighty years old. It was a lesson. Thank God I'm not impotent." He held Arkady steady. "I can see you right now. You don't look very good."

"I need some advice."

"I think you need more than advice. I had them keep you down there while I asked some questions about you. I like to have information. Life is so various. I've been in the Red Army, White Army, German Army. Nothing is predictable. I hear that you've been an investigator, a convict, an investigator again. You're more confused than I am."

"Easily."

"It's an unusual name. You're related to Renko, that madman from the war?"

"Yes."

"You have mixed eyes. I see a dreamer in one eye and a fool in the other. You see, I'm so old now that I'm going around a second time and I appreciate things. Otherwise you go crazy. I gave up cigarettes two years ago for the lungs. You have to be positive to do that. You smoke?"

"Yes."

"Russians are a gloomy race. Chechens are different."

"People say that."

Makhmud smiled. His teeth looked oversized, like a dog's. "Russians smoke, Chechens burn."

"Rudy Rosen burned."

For an old man, Makhmud changed expression quickly. "Him and his money, I heard."

"You were there," Arkady said.

The driver turned. Though he was big, he was almost as young as the boy beside him, with acne clustered at the corners of a pouty mouth, hair long in back, short on the side, bangs a spray-painted orange. It was the athlete from the Intourist bar.

Makhmud said, "This is my grandson Ali. The other is his brother Beno."

"Nice family."

"Ali is very fond of me, so he doesn't like to hear this sort of accusation."

"That's not an accusation," Arkady said. "I was there, too. Maybe we're both innocent."

"I was at home asleep. Doctor's orders."

"What do you think might have happened to Rudy?"

"With this medication I have and oxygen tubes, I look like a cosmonaut and I sleep like a baby."

"What happened to Rudy?"

"My opinion? Rudy was a Jew, and a Jew thinks he can eat with the devil and keep his nose from being bitten off. Maybe Rudy knew too many devils."

Six days a week, Rudy and Makhmud had taken Turkish coffee together while they bargained over exchange rates. Arkady remembered seeing the fleshy Rudy across the table from the bone-thin Makhmud, and wondering who would eat whom.

"You were the only one he was afraid of."

Makhmud rejected the compliment. "We had no problem with Rudy. Other people in Moscow think the Chechens should go back to Grozny, back to Kazan, back to Baku."

"Rudy said you were out to get him."

"He was lying." Makhmud dismissed the idea like a man used to demanding belief.

"It's hard to argue with the dead," Arkady noted as tactfully as he could.

"Do you have Kim?"

"Rudy's bodyguard? No. He's probably looking for you."

Makhmud said to the front of the car, "Beno, could we have some coffee?"

Beno passed back a thermos, small cups and saucers, spoons and a paper bag of sugar cubes. The coffee came out of the thermos like black sludge. Makhmud's hands were large, fingers and nails curved; the rest of him might have shrunk with age, but not the hands.

"Delicious," Arkady said. He felt his heart fibrillate with joy.

"The mafias used to have real leaders. Antibiotic was a theatrical promoter, and if he liked a show he'd hire the whole hall for himself. He was like family to the Brezhnevs. A character, a racketeer, but his word was good. Remember Otarik?"

"I remember he was a member of the Writer's Union even though his application had twenty-two grammatical errors," Arkady said.

"Well, writing was not his main occupation. Anyway, now they're replaced by these new businessmen like Borya Gubenko. It used to be that a gang war was a gang war. Now I have to watch my back two ways, from hit men *and* militia."

"What happened to Rudy? Was he part of a gang war?"

"You mean a war between Moscow businessmen and bloodthirsty Chechens? We're always the mad dogs; Russians are always the victims. I'm not addressing you personally, but as a nation you see everything backwards. Could I give you a small example from my life?"

"Please."

"Did you know that there was a Chechen Republic? Our own. If I bore you, stop me. The worst crime of old people is to bore young people." Even as he said this, Makhmud clutched Arkady's collar again.

"Go on."

"Some Chechens had collaborated with the Germans, so in February 1944, mass meetings were called in every village. There were soldiers and brass bands; people thought it was a military celebration and everyone came. You know what those village squares are like—a loudspeaker in each corner playing music and announcements. Well, this announcement was that they had one hour to gather their families and possessions. No reason given. One hour. Imagine the scene. First the pleading, which was useless. The panic of looking for small children, for grandparents, forcing them to dress and dragging them out the door to save their lives. Deciding what you should take, what you can carry. A bed, a bureau, a goat? The soldiers loaded everyone into trucks. Studebakers. People thought the Americans were behind it and Stalin would save them!"

In Makhmud's stare, Arkady saw black irises locked like the lens of a camera. "In twenty-four hours there wasn't a Chechen left in the Chechen Republic. Half a million people gone. The trucks put them on trains, in unheated freight cars which traveled for week after week after week in the middle of winter. Thousands died. My first wife, my first three boys. Who knows at what siding the guards threw their bodies out? When the survivors were finally allowed to climb down from the cars they found themselves in Kazakhstan, in Central Asia. Back home, the Chechen Republic was liquidated. Russian names were given to our towns. We were removed from maps, histories, encyclopedias. We disappeared. Twenty, thirty years went by before we managed to return to Grozny, even to Moscow. Like ghosts, we make our way back home to see Russians in our houses, Russian children in our yards. And they look at us and they say, 'Animals!' Now you tell me, who's been the animal? They point fingers at us and shout, 'Thief!' Tell me, who's the thief? When anyone dies, they find a Chechen and say, 'Murderer!' Believe me, I would like to meet the murderer. Do you think I should feel sorry for them now? They deserve everything that's happening to them. They deserve us."

Makhmud's eyes became their most intense, dead coals come alive, and then dimmed. His fingers unclenched and released Arkady's lapel. Fatigue folded into a smile across his face. "I apologize, I wrinkled your jacket."

"It came wrinkled."

"Nevertheless, I got carried away." Makhmud smoothed the jacket. He said, "I'd like nothing more than to find Kim. Grapes?"

Beno handed back a wooden bowl overflowing with green grapes. By now, Arkady could see not so much a family resemblance among him, Ali and Makhmud as a likeness of species, like the bill of a hawk. Arkady took a handful. Makhmud opened a short knife with a hooked blade to carefully slice off a bunch. When he ate, he rolled down the window to spit on the ground.

"Diverticulitis. I'm not supposed to swallow the seeds. It's a terrible thing to grow old."

6

Polina was dusting Rudy's bedroom for prints when Arkady arrived from the car market. He had never seen her out of her raincoat before. Because of the heat, she wore shorts, had knotted her shirt into a halter and tied her hair up in a kerchief, and with her rubber gloves and little camel's-hair brush she looked like a child playing house.

"We dusted before." Arkady dropped his jacket on the bed. "Aside from Rudy's prints, the technicians got nothing."

"Then you have nothing to lose," Polina said cheerfully. "The human mole is in the garage tapping for trapdoors."

Arkady opened the window over the courtyard and saw Minin in his hat and coat in the open door of the garage. "You shouldn't call him that."

"He hates you."

"Why?"

Polina rolled her eyes, then climbed a chair to dust the bureau mirror. "Where's Jaak?"

"We've been promised another car. If he gets it, he'll go to the Lenin's Path Collective Farm."

"Well, it's potato time. They can use Jaak."

At a variety of odd locations—on hairbrush and headboard, inside the medicine-cabinet door and under the raised toilet lid—were the shadowy ovals of brushed prints. Others had already been lifted with tape and transferred to slides lying on the night table.

Arkady pulled on rubber gloves. "This isn't your job," he said.

"It isn't your job, either. Investigators are supposed to let detectives do the real work. I have the training for this and I'm better than the others, so why shouldn't I? Do you know why no one wants to deliver babies?"

"Why?" Immediately, he was sorry he asked.

"Doctors don't want to deliver babies because they're afraid of AIDS and because they don't trust Soviet rubber gloves. They wear three or four at a time. Imagine trying to deliver a baby wearing four pairs of gloves. They don't do abortions either, for the same reason. Soviet doctors would rather set women out about a hundred meters away and watch them explode. Of course there wouldn't be so many babies if Soviet condoms didn't fit like rubber gloves."

"True." Arkady sat on the bed and looked around. Though he had followed Rudy for weeks, he still knew too little about the man.

"He didn't bring women here," Polina said. "There are no crackers, no wine, not even a condom. Women leave things—hairpins, pads, face powder on a pillow. It's too neat."

How long was she going to be up on the chair? Her legs were whiter and more muscular than he would have expected. Perhaps she'd wanted to be a ballerina at one time. Black curls escaped from the discipline of her kerchief and coiled at the nape of her neck.

"You're working room by room?" Arkady asked.

"Yes."

"Shouldn't you be out with your friends playing volleyball or something?"

"It's a little late for volleyball."

"Did you lift prints from the videotapes?"

"Yes." She bounced a glare off the mirror.

"I got you more morgue time," Arkady said to mollify her. Isn't that the way to soothe a woman, he thought, by offering her more time in a morgue? "Why do you want to go back inside Rudy?"

"There was too much blood. I did get laboratory results on the blood from the car. It was his type, at least."

"Good." If she was happy, he was happy. He turned on the television and VCR, inserted one of Rudy's tapes, pushed Play and Fast Forward. Accompanied by high-speed gibberish, images rushed across the screen: the golden city of Jerusalem, Wailing Wall, Mediterranean beach, synagogue, orange grove, high-rise hotels, casinos, El Al. He slowed the tape to catch the narration, which was more glottal than Russian. "Do you speak Hebrew?" he asked Polina.

"Why in the world would I speak Hebrew?"

The second tape showed in rapid succession the white city of Cairo, pyramids and camels, Mediterranean beach, sailboats on the Nile, muezzin on a minaret, date grove, high-rise hotels, Egyptair. "Arabic?" Arkady asked.

"No."

The third travelogue opened in a beer garden and raced through etchings of medieval Munich, aerial views of rebuilt Munich, shoppers on the Marienplatz, beer cellar, polka bands in lederhosen, Olympic stadium, Oktoberfest, rococo theater, gilded angel of peace, autobahn, another beer garden, nearby Alps, vapor trail of Lufthansa. He rewound to the Alps to listen to a narration that was both ponderous and exuberant.

"You speak German?" Polina asked. The dusted mirror was starting to look like a collection of moth wings, each one an oval of whorls.

"A little." Arkady had spent his army years in Berlin listening to Americans and had picked up some German in the truculent fashion that Russians approach the language of Bismarck, Marx and Hitler. It wasn't only that Germans were a traditional foe; it was because for centuries the czars had imported Germans as taskmasters, not to mention that the Nazis had regarded all Slavs as subhuman. There was a certain accretion of national ill will.

"Auf Wiedersehen," said the television.

"Auf Wiedersehen." Arkady turned the set off. "Polina, *auf Wiedersehen.* Go home, see your boyfriend, go to a movie."

"I'm almost done."

So far Polina seemed to have sensed more about the apartment than Arkady had. He knew he was missing not so much clues as essence. Rudy's phobia about physical contact had created an apartment that was solitary and sterile. No ashtrays, not even butts. He craved a cigarette, but didn't dare upset the apartment's hygienic balance.

Rudy's single weakness of the flesh appeared to be food. Arkady opened the refrigerator. Ham, fish and Dutch cheese were still cool, in place and overwhelming even to a man who had just eaten an appetizer of Makhmud's grapes. The food was probably from Stockmann's, the Helsinki department store that delivered complete smorgasbords, office furniture and Japanese cars for hard currency to Moscow's foreign community; God forbid they should live like Russians. In its rind of wax, the cheese shone like a mushroom cap.

Polina stepped into the bedroom doorway, one arm already thrust into her raincoat. "Are you examining the evidence or consuming it?"

"Admiring it, actually. Here is cheese from cows who graze on grass that grows on dikes a thousand miles away, and it's not as rare as Russian cheese. Wax is a good medium of prints, isn't it?"

"Humidity is not the best atmosphere."

"It's too humid for you?"

"I didn't say I couldn't do it, I just didn't want to get your hopes up."

"Do I look like a man with high hopes?"

"I don't know; you're different today." It was not characteristic of Polina to be uncertain about anything. "You—"

Arkady put a finger to his lips. He heard a barely audible noise, like the fan of a refrigerator, except that he was standing by the refrigerator.

"A toilet," Polina said. "Someone's relieving themselves on the hour."

Arkady went to the water closet and touched the pipes. Usually pipes banged and rang like chains. This sound was fainter, more mechanical than liquid, and inside Rosen's apartment, not out. It stopped.

"On the hour?" Arkady asked.

"On the dot. I looked, but I didn't find anything."

Arkady went into Rudy's office. The desk was undisturbed, the phone and fax silent. He tapped the fax and a red "alert" light blinked. Tapped harder and the button winked as regularly as a beacon. The volume had been turned all the way down. He pulled the desk forward and found facsimile paper that had scrolled between the desk and the wall. "First rule of investigation: pick things up," he said.

"I hadn't dusted here yet."

The paper was still warm. On top was the transmission date and time, one minute ago. The message, typed in Russian, read: "Where is Red Square?"

Anyone with a map could answer that. He read the previous message. The transmission time on it had been sixty-one minutes ago: "Where is Red Square?"

You didn't need a map. Ask anyone in the world—up the Nile, in the Andes or even in Gorky Park.

There were five messages in all, each sent on the hour, with the same insistent demand: "Where is Red Square?" The first also said, "If you know where Red Square is, I can offer contacts with international society for ten percent finder's fee."

A finder's fee for Red Square sounded like easy money. The machine had automatically printed a long transmitting phone number across the top. Arkady called the international operator, who identified the country code as Germany and the city as Munich. "Do you have one of these?" he asked Polina.

"I know a boy who does."

Close enough. Arkady wrote on Rudy's stationery: "Need more information." Polina inserted the page, picked up the receiver and dialed the number, which answered with a ping. A light flashed over a button that said Transmit, and when she pushed the button the paper started to roll.

Polina said, "If they're trying to reach Rudy, they don't know he's dead."

"That's the idea."

"So you'll get pointless information or find yourself in an embarrassing social situation. I can't wait."

THEY WAITED AN hour without an answer. Finally Arkady went downstairs and visited the garage, where Minin was tapping the floor with the butt end of a shovel. The hanging light bulb had been replaced by one with greater wattage. Tires were moved to the side and stacked according to size; rubber belts and oil cans were enumerated and tagged. Minin's only concession to the heat had been to remove his coat and jacket; his hat stayed on his head, casting an umbra across the middle of his face. The man in the moon, Arkady thought. When he saw his superior, Minin came to sullen attention.

Arkady thought the problem was that Minin was the classic dwarf child. Not that he was small, but Minin was the unloved creature, the sort who always felt despised. Arkady could have removed him from the team—an investigator didn't have to accept everyone assigned to him—but he didn't want to justify Minin's attitude. Also, he hated to see an ugly man pout.

"Investigator Renko, when Chechens are on the loose, I think I would be of better use on the street than in this garage."

"We don't know if we're after the Chechens, and I need a good man doing this. Some people would slip the tires under their coat."

Humor seemed to give Minin a wide berth. He said, "Do you want me to go upstairs and watch Polina?"

"No." Arkady tried human interest. "There's something new about you, Minin. What is it?"

"I don't know."

"That's it." On Minin's sweat-darkened shirt was the enamel pin of a red flag. Arkady never would have noticed it if he hadn't taken off his jacket. "A membership pin?"

"Of a patriotic organization," Minin said.

"Very stylish."

"We stand for the defense of Russia, for the repeal of so-called laws that steal the people's wealth and give it to a narrow group of vultures and money changers, for a cleansing of society and an end to chaos and anarchy. You don't mind?" It was a challenge as much as a question.

"Oh, no. On you it looks right."

DRIVING TO BORYA GUBENKO's, it seemed to Arkady that the summer evening had fallen like a silence. Streets vacant, taxis camped outside hotels, refusing to carry anyone but tourists. One store was besieged with shoppers, while stores on either side were so empty they looked deserted. Moscow looked like a cannibalized city, without food, gas or basic goods. Arkady felt like a cannibalized man, as if he might be missing a rib, a lung, some part of his heart.

It was oddly reassuring that someone in Germany had asked a Soviet speculator about Red Square. It was confirmation that Red Square still existed.

BORYA GUBENKO PICKED up a ball from a pail, set it on his tee, cautioned Arkady about the backswing, concentrated, drew the club back so that it seemed to encircle his body, uncoiled and lashed the ball on a line. "Want to try it?" he asked.

"No, thanks. I'll just watch," Arkady said.

A dozen Japanese teed up on squares of plastic grass, drew back their clubs and drove golf balls that sailed as diminishing dots the interior length of the factory. The irregular pop of balls sounded like small-arms fire—appropriately since the factory used to turn out bullet casings. During the White Terror, Patriotic War and Warsaw Pact, workers had manufactured millions of brass and steel-core cartridges. To convert to a golf range, assembly lines had been scrapped and the floor painted a pastoral green. A couple of immovable metal presses were screened by cutout trees, a touch appreciated by the Japanese, who wore golf caps even indoors. Besides Borya, the only Russian players Arkady could see were a mother and daughter in matching short skirts taking a lesson.

On the far wall, balls thudded against a green canvas marked in ascending distances: 200, 250, 300 meters.

Borya said, "I confess, I overestimate a little bit. A happy customer is the secret of business." He posed for Arkady. "What do you think? The first Russian amateur champion?"

"At least."

Borya's big frame was tamed by a plush pastel sweater, his unruly hair wetted into sleek golden wings around a watchful, angular face with eyes of crystal blue.

"Look at it this way." Borya plucked another ball from the pail. "I spent ten years playing football for Central Army. You know the life: terrific money, apartment, car, as long as you can perform. You get injured, you start to slip, and suddenly you're on the street. You go right from the top straight to the bottom. Everyone wants to buy you a beer, but that's it. That's the payoff for ten years and your busted knees. Old boxers, wrestlers, hockey players, same story. No wonder they go into the mafia. Or worse, start playing American-style football. Anyway, I was lucky."

More than lucky. Borya seemed to have crystallized into a new, successful persona. In the new Moscow, no one was as transcendentally popular and prosperous as Borya Gubenko.

Behind the driving range, slot machines sang beside a bar decorated with Marlboro posters, Marlboro ashtrays and Marlboro lamps. Borya lined up his shot. If possible, he looked more robust than in his playing days. Also sleek, like a well-groomed lion. He swung and froze, studying a drive that faded as it rose.

"Tell me about this club," Arkady said.

"It's hard-currency, members only. The more exclusive you make it, the more foreigners want in. I'll tell you the secret," Borya said.

"Another secret?"

"Location. The Swedes have poured millions into an eighteen-hole resort outside town. It's going to have conference facilities, communications center, super security so that businessmen and tourists can come without ever really staying in Moscow. In comparison, we're downtown, right on the river, practically across from the Kremlin. Look what it took—a little paint, AstroTurf, clubs and balls. We're in guidebooks and foreign magazines, and all of it was Rudy's idea." He looked Arkady up and down. "What sport did you play?"

"Football in school."

"Position?"

"Mainly goal." Arkady wasn't going to claim any athletic distinction in Borya's company.

"Like me. The best position. You study, see the attack, learn anticipation. The game comes down to a couple of kicks. And when you commit, you commit, right? If you try to save yourself, that's how you get hurt. For me, of course, playing was a way to see the world. I didn't understand what food was until we went to Italy. I still referee some international games just to eat well."

"To see the world" had to be a mild description of Borya's ambition, Arkady thought. Gubenko had grown up in the concrete "Khrushchev Barracks" of Long Pond. In Russian, *Khrushchev* rhymed with *slum,* giving bite to the title. Borya would have been raised on cabbage soup and cabbage hopes, and here he was talking about Italian restaurants.

Arkady asked, "What do you think happened to Rudy?"

"I think that what happened to Rudy was a national disaster. He was the only real economist in the country."

"Who killed him?"

Without hesitating, Borya said, "Chechens. Makhmud is a bandit with no concept of Western style or business. The fact is, he holds everyone else back. The more fear, the better—never mind that it closes a market down. The more unsettled everyone else is, the stronger the Chechens become."

On the tees a tier overhead, the Japanese hit a unified salvo, followed by excited shouts of *"Banzai!"*

Borya smiled and pointed his club up. "They fly from Tokyo to Hawaii for a weekend of golf. I have to throw them out at night."

"If Chechens killed Rudy," Arkady said, "they had to get past Kim. For all his reputation—muscleman, martial arts—he doesn't seem to have been much protection. When your best friend, Rudy, was looking for a bodyguard, didn't he come to you for advice?"

"Rudy carried a lot of money and he was concerned about his safety."

"And Kim?"

"The factories in Lyubertsy are closing down. The problem with interacting with the free market, Rudy always said, is that we manufacture shit. When I suggested Kim to Rudy, I thought I was doing them both a favor."

"If you find Kim before we do, what will you do?"

Borya aimed the club at Arkady and dropped his voice. "I'd call you. I would. Rudy was my best friend and I think Kim helped the Chechens, but do you think I'd endanger all this, everything I've achieved, to take some sort of primitive revenge? That's the old mentality. We have to catch up with the rest of the world or we're going to be left behind. We'll all be in empty buildings and starving to death. We have to change. Do you have a card?" he asked suddenly.

"Party card?"

"We collect business cards and have a drawing once a month for a bottle of Chivas Regal." Borya controlled a smile, barely.

Arkady felt like an idiot. Not an ordinary idiot, but an outdated, socially uninformed idiot.

Borya put down his driver and proudly led Arkady to the buffet. In chairs upholstered in red, white and black Marlboro colors were more Japanese in baseball caps and Americans in golfing shoes. Arkady suspected that Borya had hit upon the exact decor of an airport lounge, the natural setting of the international business traveler. They could have been in Frankfurt, Singapore, Saudi Arabia—anywhere—and for this very reason felt at home. Above the bar a television showed CNN. The crowded buffet offered an array of smoked sturgeon and trout, red and black caviar, eggplant caviar, German chocolates and Georgian pastries around bottles of sweet champagne, Pepsi, pepper vodka, lemon vodka and five-star Armenian cognac. Arkady was dizzy from the smell of food.

"We also have *karaoke* nights, putting tournaments and corporate parties," Borya said. "No prostitutes, no hustlers. It couldn't be more innocent."

Like Borya? The man had not only gone from football to the mafia, but had made the second, steeper evolutionary leap to entrepreneur. The way his Western sweater draped his shoulders, the directness of his eyes, the freer gestures of clean hands, all said: businessman.

Borya gave a discreet, proprietary wave and a uniformed waitress immediately arrived from the buffet and set a plate of silver herring on the table in front of Arkady. The fish seemed to swim before his eyes.

Borya asked, "Remember unpolluted fish?"

"Not well enough, thanks." Arkady dug a last cigarette from the pack. "Where do you get the fish?"

"Like anyone else. I trade this, barter that."

"On the black market?"

Borya shook his head. "Direct. Rudy said there wasn't a farm or fishing collective that wasn't willing to do business if you could offer more than rubles."

"Rudy told you what to offer?"

Borya held Arkady's eyes with his. "Rudy started out as a football fan. He ended up as an older brother. He simply wanted to see me happy. He gave me advice. That doesn't sound like a crime to me."

"It depends on the advice." Arkady wanted to provoke a reaction.

Borya's eyes were clear as water, without a ripple. "Rudy always said there was no need to break the law, just to rewrite it. He looked ahead."

"Do you know an Apollonia Gubenko?" Arkady asked.

"My wife. I know her well."

"Where was she the night Rudy died?"

"What does it matter?"

"There was a Mercedes registered in her name at the black market about thirty meters from where Rudy died."

Borya took a little longer to answer. He glanced at the television, where an American tank was rolling through a desert. "She was with me. We were here."

"At two in the morning?"

"I often close after midnight. I remember we went home in my car because Polly's was in the garage being repaired."

"You have two cars?"

"Between Polly and me, two Mercedeses, two BMWs, two Volgas and a Lada. In the West people can invest in stocks and bonds. We have cars. The trouble is, as soon as a nice car goes to the garage, someone borrows it. I can try to find out who."

"You're sure she was with you, because a woman was seen in it."

"I treat women with respect. Polly is her own person, she doesn't have to answer to me for every second of her time, but that night she was with me."

"Did anyone else see you here?"

"No. The secret of business is, you stay close to the cash register and lock up yourself."

"There are a lot of secrets in business," Arkady said.

Borya leaned forward and spread his hands. Although Arkady knew he was a big man, he was surprised at the wingspan. He remembered how Borya the player used to roar out of the Central Army goal to stop penalty kicks. Gubenko let his hands fall. His voice was soft. "Renko?"

"Yes?"

"I'm not going to kill Kim. That's your job."

Arkady looked at his watch. It was eight P.M. He had already missed the first broadcast and his mind was starting to wander. "I have to go."

Borya steered Arkady through the bar. Another discreet signal had been sent because the waitress caught up to them with two packs of cigarettes which Borya stuffed into Arkady's jacket.

The mother and daughter made their way around the tables. They shared the same fine features and gray eyes. When the woman spoke, she had a faint lisp; Arkady was relieved to hear an imperfection.

"Borya, the teacher's waiting for you."

"The pro, Polly. The pro."

"ARMENIAN NATIONALISTS ATTACKED Soviet Internal troops again yesterday, inflicting ten deaths and as many wounded," Irina said. "The object of the Armenian attack was a Soviet Army depot, which they ransacked, removing small arms, assault rifles, mines, a tank, a personnel carrier, mortars and antitank guns. The Moldavian Supreme Soviet yesterday declared its sovereignty, three days after the Georgian Supreme Soviet did the same."

Arkady set a table of brown bread, cheese, tea and cigarettes and sat facing the radio as if it had come to dinner. He should have returned to Rudy's apartment; yet here he was, a man with no will, in time for her broadcast. What apocalyptic news she had, but it didn't matter.

"Rioting continued in Kirghizia between Kirghiz and Uzbeks for the third straight day. Armored personnel carriers patrolled the streets of Osh after Uzbeks took control of the downtown tourist hotels and directed automatic fire at the local offices of the KGB. Deaths in the unrest now total two hundred and the question of draining the Uzgen Canal to find more bodies has been raised."

The bread was fresh and the cheese was sweet. A breeze drifted in the open window and the curtain stirred like a skirt.

"A Red Army spokesman admitted today that Afghan insurgents have penetrated the Soviet border. Since Soviet troops withdrew from Afghanistan, the border has become accessible to drug runners and to religious extremists who are urging Central Asian republics to begin a holy war against Moscow."

The sun hung on the northern horizon, onion domes and chimney pots. Her voice was a shade huskier and her Siberian accent sounded more schooled and sophisticated. Arkady remembered her gestures, sometimes flamboyant, and the color of her eyes, like amber. Listening, he found himself leaning toward the radio. He felt ridiculous, as if he should be holding up his side of the conversation.

"Miners in Donetsk yesterday demanded the resignation of the government and the removal of the Party, and announced the start of a new strike. Work stoppages have also begun in all twenty-six mines in the Karaganda Basin and in twenty-nine mines in Rostov-on-Don. Mass rallies in support of the strikers were held by miners in Sverdlovsk, Chelyabinsk and Vladivostok."

The news was not important; he hardly heard it. It was her voice and breath transmitted across a thousand miles.

"Last night in Moscow, the Democratic Front rallied outside Gorky Park to call for the 'de-legalization' of the Communist party. At the same time, members of the right-wing 'Red Banner' met to defend the Party. Both groups demanded the right to march in Red Square."

She was Scheherazade, Arkady thought. Night after night she could tell tales of oppression, insurrection, strikes, and natural disaster, and he would listen as if she were spinning stories of exotic lands, magical spices, flashing scimitars and pearl-eyed dragons with scales of gold. As long as she would talk to him.

7

At midnight, Arkady waited across from the Lenin Library, admiring the statues of Russian writers and scholars that hovered along the roof line. He remembered what he had heard about the building being ready to collapse. True enough, the statues looked ready to jump. When a shadow emerged and locked the door, Arkady crossed the street and introduced himself.

"An investigator? I'm not surprised." Feldman wore a fur hat, carried a briefcase and looked like Trotsky, down to a goat's beard of snow white. He started a vigorous shuffle toward the river and Arkady fell in step beside him. "I have my own key. I didn't steal anything. You want to search?"

Arkady ignored the invitation. "How do *you* know Rudy?"

"It's the only time to work. I thank God I'm an insomniac. Are you?"

"No."

"You look like one. See a doctor. Unless you don't mind."

"Rudy?" Arkady tried again.

"Rosen? I didn't. We met once, a week ago. He wanted to talk about art."

"Why art?"

"I'm a professor of art history. I told you I was a professor on the phone. You're a hell of an investigator, I can tell already."

"What did Rudy ask?"

"He wanted to know everything about Soviet art. Soviet avant-garde art was the most creative, most revolutionary period in history, but

Soviet man is an ignoramus. I couldn't educate Rosen in half an hour."

"Did he ask about any paintings in particular?"

"No. But I catch your point and it is amusing. For years, the Party demanded Socialist Realism and people hung paintings of tractors on their walls and hid avant-garde masterpieces behind the toilet or under the bed. Now they're dragging them out. Suddenly Moscow is full of art curators. You like Socialist Realism?"

"Socialist Realism is one of my weakest areas."

"Are you talking about art?"

"No."

Feldman regarded Arkady with a more wary, interested eye. They were in the park behind the library, where steps ran between trees down to the river near the southwest corner of the Kremlin. Spotlights made the lower branches into lattices of gold that turned to black.

"I told Rosen that what people forget is that there actually was idealism at the beginning of the Revolution. Starvation and civil war aside, Moscow was the most exciting place in the world to be. When Mayakovsky said, 'Let us make the squares our palettes, the streets our brushes,' he meant it. Every wall was a painting. There were painted trains, boats, airplanes, balloons. Wallpaper and dinner plates and gum wrappers were all created by artists who genuinely thought they were making a new world. At the same time women were marching for free love. They all believed anything was possible. Rosen asked how much one of those gum wrappers would be worth now."

"The same question occurred to me," Arkady admitted.

Feldman stomped down the stairs in disgust.

"Since avant-garde art was not approved, you chose a fairly suicidal specialty. Is that how you got used to working late at night?" Arkady asked.

"Not a totally stupid observation." Feldman stopped short. "Why is red the color of revolution?"

"It's traditional?"

"Prehistoric, not traditional. The two earliest habits of the ape-man were cannibalism and painting himself red. Soviets are the only ones who still do it. Look what we did to the genius of the Revolution. Describe Lenin's tomb."

"It's a square of red granite."

"It's a Constructivist design inspired by Malevich. It's a red square on Red Square. There's more to it than just Lenin laid out like a smoked herring. Art was everywhere in those days. Tatlin designed a revolving skyscraper taller than the Empire State Building. Popova drew high fashions for peasants. The artists of Moscow were going to paint the trees of the Kremlin red. Lenin did object to that, but people thought that anything was possible. Those were days of hope, days of fantasy."

"You lecture on this?"

"No one wants to hear. They're like Rosen, they only want to sell. I spend all day authenticating art for idiots."

"Rosen had something to sell?"

"Don't ask me. We were supposed to meet two days ago. He didn't come."

"Then why do you think he had something to sell?"

"Today everyone is selling everything they have. And Rosen said he found something. He didn't say what."

At the embankment Feldman looked around with such fervor that Arkady could nearly imagine painted trees in the Kremlin gardens, amazons marching on Gorky Street, dirigibles towing propaganda posters under the moon.

"We live in the archeological ruins of that new world that never was. If we knew where to dig, who knows what we would find?" Feldman asked and trudged on alone across the bridge.

ARKADY WANDERED ALONG the embankment wall toward his flat. He didn't feel sleepy, but he didn't feel like an insomniac. Just the word made him restless.

He found no amazons along the river. There were fishermen baiting hooks. A couple of years of his exile had been spent on a Pacific trawler. He had always appreciated how at dusk the rustiest, most nondescript ship became a dazzling and intricate constellation of stars, with fishing lights on masts, booms, gunwales, bridge, ramp and deck. It occurred to him now that the same could be done for Moscow's nocturnal fishermen, with batteries and lamps on their hats, belts and the tips of their poles.

Maybe the problem wasn't insomnia. Maybe he was crazy. Why was he trying to find out who killed Rudy? When an entire society was collapsing like so many rotten beams, what difference did it make who murdered one black-market speculator? Anyway, this wasn't the real world. The real world was out there where Irina lived. Here he was one more shadow in a cave, where he couldn't sleep anyway.

Straight ahead the silhouette of St. Basil's stood like a crowd of turbaned Moors backlit by the all-night floodlights of the square. In shadow at the stone base of the cathedral were about a hundred soldiers from the Kremlin barracks in full field gear with radio packs and submachine guns.

Red Square itself rose as a vast hill of cobblestones. To the left, the Kremlin was illuminated, bricks nearly white, with swallowtail battlements that were grace notes on a fortress that seemed to stretch as far as the Chinese Wall. The spires above the gates looked like churches that had been captured, roped, dragged from Europe and erected as trophies to a czar, topped now by ruby stars. Shimmering in upturned lights, the Kremlin was midway between reality and dream, an immense, oppressive vision. From the gate at Spassky Tower a black sedan issued like a bat and flitted across the stones. Far off, at the head of the square, a four-story banner for Pepsi covered the façade of the Army Museum. To his right the classical stone face of GUM, the world's largest and emptiest department store, shrank into the dark. From the roof of GUM and from the Kremlin wall, cameras constantly monitored the square, but no floodlights were bright enough to penetrate the valley of shadow in its center, where he stood. No individual here would be more than a blip on a gray screen. The sheer size of scale and awesome vacuum of the square didn't so much uplift the soul as both hide it and suggest how inconsequential it was.

Except for one soul. When Lenin lay dying, he begged for no memorials. The mausoleum Stalin built for him was a vengeful pile of crypts, a squat ziggurat of red and black under the battlements of the Kremlin wall. Empty tiers of white marble flanked it, the area where dignitaries would sit for the May Day parade. Lenin's name was inscribed in red letters above the door of the tomb. At the door, two honor guards, boy sergeants with white gloves and faces as pale as waxworks, swayed with fatigue.

Ordinary traffic was barred from the square, but as Arkady turned away from the tomb a black Zil rolled out of Cherny Street and, racing at official speed, crossed in front of GUM toward the river and sank into the dark around St. Basil's. Tires squealed, a sharp sound of protest that reverberated the length of the square.

The Zil came back. Because the car's headlights were dark, it was too late when Arkady realized it was coming straight at him. When he started to run for the museum, the Zil followed, its bumper almost on his heels. He darted left toward the tomb and the big car roared by and cut in front. He dodged the rear bumper and headed for Cherny Street. The Zil tipped, settled and lumbered toward him in a wider circle, the car's centrifugal force accelerating.

When his escape intersected the path of the car, Arkady dove. He rose and started dizzily back toward St. Basil's but slipped on the stones. Headlights rose up. He fell to one knee and raised his arm across his eyes.

The Zil stopped directly in front of him. Four uniforms emerged from the halos exploding in his eyes. Dark dress-green general's uniforms with brass stars, fringed shoulder boards and mosaics of medals behind ropes of golden braid. But as his vision returned, Arkady saw that the men inside the uniforms were strangely shrunken, holding each other up. As the driver got out he almost fell. He wore a civilian sweater and jacket, topped by a sergeant major's cap. He was drunk and his eyes were leaking tears that rolled from his eyes to his jowls.

"Belov?" Arkady asked as he stood.

"Arkasha." Belov's voice was as deep and hollow as a barrel. "We were at your address and you were not at home. We went to your office and you weren't there. We were just driving around when we saw you, and then you ran."

Arkady dimly recognized the generals, though they were gray and stunted versions of the tall, impressive officers who used to trail behind his father. Here were the staunch heroes of the Siege of Moscow, the tank commanders of the Bessarabian offensive, the vanguard of the push to Berlin, each of the four properly wearing an Order of Lenin awarded for "a decisive action that significantly altered the course of the war." Except that Shuksin, who had always slapped his boots with a crop, was now so shriveled and bent that he was hardly much higher than the top of those boots, and Ivanov, who had always claimed the privilege of carrying his father's field case of plans, was as stooped as an ape. Kuznetsov had turned as round as a child, whereas Gul was a skeleton, his vigor and ferocity reduced to hair bristling from his brows and ears. Though Arkady had hated them all his life—despised them, really, because they had abused him out of sycophancy rather than evil—he was astonished at their feebleness.

Boris Sergeyevich was different. He had been Sergeant Belov, his father's driver, the very same bodyguard who had escorted the boy Arkady to Gorky Park. Later Boris became Investigator Belov, though his gift was less for legal scholarship than for devotion to orders and ironclad loyalty. His attitude toward Arkady had never been less than adoration. Arkady's arrest and exile was something Belov had never grasped—like, say, French or quantum mechanics.

Belov removed his cap and placed it under his left arm as if reporting for duty. "Arkady Kirilovich, it is my painful task to inform you that your father, General Kiril Ilyich Renko, has died."

The generals advanced and shook Arkady's hand.

"He should have been marshal of the army," Ivanov said.

Shuksin said, "We were comrades in arms. I marched into Berlin with your father."

Gul waved a rusty arm. "I marched here in this same square with your father and laid a thousand fascist flags at Stalin's feet."

"Our most sincere condolences for this immeasurable loss." Kuznetsov sobbed like an aunt.

Belov said, "The funeral is already arranged for Saturday. That's soon, but your father left instructions for everything, as usual. He wanted me to give you this letter."

"I don't want it."

"I have no idea of the contents." Belov tried to push an envelope inside Arkady's jacket. "Father to son."

Arkady knocked Belov's hand away. He was surprised by his own brusqueness to a good friend and by the depth of his revulsion for the others. "No, thanks."

Shuksin took a wobbly step toward the Kremlin. "*Then* the army was appreciated. Soviet power meant something. *Then* the Fascists shit their pants whenever we blew our nose."

Gul picked up the theme. "Now we crawl to Germany to kiss their ass. That's what we get for letting them get off their knees."

"And what do we get for saving Hungarians and Czechs and Poles except the spit on our face?" The passion of his question was too much for Ivanov; the ancient bearer of the field case slumped against the fender of the car. They were all so thoroughly soaked with vodka, Arkady realized, that a match would set them off like rags.

"We saved the world, remember?" Shuksin demanded. "We saved the world!"

Belov pleaded, "Why?"

"He was a killer," Arkady said.

"That was war."

Gul asked, "Do you think *we* would have lost Afghanistan? Or Europe? Or a single republic?"

"I'm not talking about the war," Arkady said.

"Read the letter," Belov begged.

"I'm talking about murder," Arkady said.

"Arkasha, please!" Belov's eyes were as pleading as a dog's. "For me. He's going to read the letter!"

The generals rallied, regrouped and crowded round. One push and they would probably collapse and turn to piles of dust, Arkady thought. Who did they see, he wondered? Him, his father, who? This could be his moment of vindictive triumph, a child's long-awaited fantasy. But it was too pathetic, and the generals, grotesque as they were, also were at their most human in this last stage of fangless dotage. He took the letter. It had a luminous quality and his name printed in spidery letters. It felt light, as if empty, to the hand.

"I'll read it later," Arkady said and walked away.

"The Vagankovskoye Cemetery," Belov called after him. "Ten A.M."

Or I'll throw it away, Arkady thought. Or burn it.

8

The following day was the final one of so-called "hot investigation," the last day of official alerts at travel points, a peak time for frustration and argument. Arkady and Jaak chased false sightings of Kim north, west and south at all three Moscow airports. On the fourth tip, they headed east toward the dead end known as Lyubertsy.

"A new informant?" Arkady asked. He was driving, which was always a sign of bad humor.

"Totally new," Jaak insisted.

"Not Julya," Arkady said.

"Not Julya," Jaak maintained.

"Borrow her Volvo yet?"

"I will. Anyway, it isn't Julya, it's a Gypsy."

"A Gypsy!" With an effort Arkady stayed on the road.

"You always say *I'm* prejudiced," Jaak said.

"When I think of Gypsies, I think of poets and musicians. I don't think of reliable informants."

Jaak said, "Well, this guy would sell out his brother and that's what I call a reliable informant!"

KIM'S MOTORCYCLE WAS there, an exotic midnight-blue Suzuki, propped on a chrome kickstand in back of a five-story apartment house. Arkady and Jaak walked around the machine and admired it from every angle, taking an occasional glance at the building. The upper floors had balconies that were illegally enclosed. The ground was littered with refuse that seemed to have rained down from the windows: paper cartons, mattress springs, broken bottles. The next house was a hundred meters away. It was an incomplete landscape of houses set far apart, sewer pipes lying in open trenches, concrete walkways that intersected among weeds. No one was walking. The sky was soiled with that particular kind of smog which expressed both industrial poison and despair.

Lyubertsy was what all Russians feared, which was to be outside the center, to not be in Moscow or Leningrad, to be forgotten and invisible, as if the steppes started here, only twenty kilometers from the Moscow city limits. This was the vast population that moved on a straight track from day care to vocational school to assembly line to the long vodka line to the grave.

Lyubertsy was also what Muscovites feared because its young factory workers took the train into Moscow to beat up privileged urban kids. It was only natural that Lyubers developed into a mafia with a special talent for tearing up rock shows and restaurants.

Jaak cleared his throat. "In the cellar," he said.

"The cellar?" It was the last thing Arkady wanted to hear. "If we're going into the cellar, we should have bulletproof vests and lamps. You didn't order those?"

"I didn't know Kim was going to be here."

"You didn't really believe your reliable informant, did you?"

"I didn't want to cause a lot of fuss," Jaak said.

The trouble was that Lyubertsy cellars were not ordinary cellars, because until recently the private practice of unarmed Oriental self-defense had been against the law. In response, Lyuber musclemen had gone underground, refitting coal bins and boiler rooms as secret gymnasiums. Wandering alone around a Lyubertsy basement was not a prospect Arkady looked forward to, but he knew it would take a day to get special gear out of Moscow.

Three babushkas sat on the steps of the apartment house and watched over a playground where toddlers climbed into a sandbox that was made from rotting boards. The women had the gray heads and black coats of crows.

Jaak asked, "Remember the Komsomol Club that called about a trophy for Rudy?"

"Vaguely."

"Did I mention they keep calling?"

"Is this a good time to mention it?" Arkady asked.

"What about my radio?" Jaak asked.

"Your radio?"

"I bought it, I'd like to listen to it. You keep forgetting to bring it in."

"Come by my place tonight and pick it up."

They couldn't stand around the bike all day, Arkady thought. They had already been seen.

Jaak said, "I have the gun, so I'll go in."

"As soon as someone goes in, he's going to run. Since you have the gun, you wait here and stop him."

Arkady walked up to the steps. The women regarded him as if he had arrived from a different solar system. He tried a smile. No, they didn't accept smiles here. He looked at the playground. It was empty; the kids were chasing cottonwood fluffs across the lot. He glanced back at Jaak, who was sitting on the bike and watching the building.

He moved along the base of the house until he found stairs leading down to a steel door. The door was unlocked and the other side of it was as black as an abyss. He called, "Kim! Mikhail Kim! I want to talk to you!"

The answer was a profound hush. This was the sound of mushrooms growing, Arkady thought. He didn't want to enter the cellar. "Kim?"

He felt around until he found a chain. When he pulled it a dozen dim light bulbs appeared, hanging from an electrical line tacked directly to bare support beams, not so much illumination as markers in the dark. As he stooped down it was like slipping into shallow water.

Clearance from floor to ceiling was a meter and a half, sometimes less. It was crawl space excavated into a tunnel that worked its way over and around exposed pipes and valves. The underside of the house creaked overhead like a ship. He peeled cobwebs from his face and held his breath.

Claustrophobia was an old friend come along for the trip. The main thing was to keep moving from one tiny, shivering light bulb to the next. To breathe more evenly. To not think about the weight of the building pressing down on his back. To not consider the low quality of Soviet construction. To not imagine for a moment that the tunnel resembled a moldering grave.

At the last light bulb, Arkady squeezed through a second hatch and found himself on his hands and knees inside a low, windowless room that was smoothly plastered and painted and lit by a fluorescent tube. On the floor were mattresses, barbells and pulleys. The barbells were

homemade from steel wheels crudely slotted to fit over bars. The
pulleys were boiler plates cut up and strung with wire. On the walls
were a full-length mirror and a picture of Schwarzenegger in total flex.
A heavy bag hung by a chain from the ceiling. The air was pungent
with sweat and talc.

Arkady got to his feet. Beyond was a second room with benches and
weights on blocks. Books on bodybuilding and nutrition lay on a mattress. One bench was slick and showed the imprint of a sneaker. Set in
the ceiling above the bench was a metal plate. There was a switch on
the wall. Arkady turned the light off so that he wouldn't be a silhouette. He stood on the bench, lifted the plate and slid it back. He was
beginning to hoist himself up when a gun pressed against his head.

It was dark. Arkady's head was halfway through the floor behind the
stairs of the building foyer. The bench was a million miles below his
swaying feet. The odor of stale urine wafted from the foyer floor. He
could see a tricycle with no wheels, the corner detritus of cigarette
packs and condoms and, on the other end of the automatic, Jaak.

"You scared me," Jaak said. He pointed the gun up.

"Really?" Arkady felt as if more than his feet were dangling.

Jaak pulled him up. The foyer faced the opposite street from the
way they had approached the building. Arkady leaned against the
mailboxes, which were torched, as usual. The foyer light was broken,
of course. No wonder people got killed.

Jaak was embarrassed. "You were taking forever, so I came around
to see if there was another way in just as you popped up."

"I won't do it again."

Jaak said, "You should have a gun."

"If I had a gun, we'd be a suicide pact."

Arkady still felt dizzy when they went outside.

"Let's just watch the motorcycle," Jaak suggested.

When they came around the building, Kim's beautiful bike was
gone.

THE MILITIA TOWED vehicular wrecks to a dock near the South Port,
handy to the metal stamps and auto factories of the Proletariat Borough. Whatever was remotely reusable had been stripped from them.
These were the bones of cars, and they had a kind of dignity, like
dried flowers. The dock had a vista of the entire southern end of

Moscow; it was not Paris, granted, but it possessed a certain sweep, the occasional gold cap of a church flashing in the shadow of industrial chimneys.

The evening sky was still lit. Arkady found Polina at the end of the dock working with a brush, cans of paint and squares of pressed wood. She had unbuttoned her raincoat, a concession to the balmy weather.

"Your message sounded urgent," Arkady said.

"I thought you should see this."

"What?" He looked around.

"You'll see."

He was losing patience. "There's no emergency? You're just working?"

"You're working, too."

"Well, I lead an obsessed but empty life. Don't you want to go dancing or see a movie with a friend?" Irina's newscasts had begun and he knew there was something he would rather be doing.

Polina daubed green paint on a square of wood balanced on the fender of a Zil from which doors and seats had been removed. She herself made rather a pretty picture, Arkady thought. If she had an easel and a little more technique . . . But she just slapped the paint on.

She seemed to sense his mind wandering. "How did you do with Jaak?"

"It was not a day covered in glory." He looked over her shoulder. "Very green."

"You're a critic?"

"Artists are so temperamental. I meant, as in 'expansively, generously green.'" He stood back to study the cityscape of black river, gray cranes and chimneys melting into a milky sky. "What exactly are you painting?"

"The wood."

"Ah."

Polina had four different pots of green paint labeled CS1, CS2, CS3, CS4, separated from four pots of red labeled RS1, RS2, etc. Each pot had its own brush. The green paint had an infernal reek. He searched his pocket, but he had left Borya's Marlboros in his other jacket. When he did find Belomors, Polina blew the match out. "Explosives," she said.

"Where?"

"Remember, in Rudy's car we found traces of red sodium and copper sulfate? As you know, that's consistent with an incendiary device."

"Chemistry wasn't my strong point."

"What we couldn't understand," Polina went on, "was why we didn't find a timer or remote receiver. I did some research. You don't need a separate source of ignition if you combine red sodium and copper sulfate."

Arkady looked at the pots at his feet again. RS: red sodium, marine-paint red, a deep carmine with an ocher tinge. CS: copper sulfate, a vile stewpot green with a sniff of the devil. He put his matches away. "You don't need a fuse?"

Polina set the wet board down on the Zil's front seat and brought out another on which the green paint was dry. Over the board she taped brown paper. "Red sodium and copper sulfate are relatively harmless individually. Together, however, they react chemically and generate enough heat to spontaneously ignite."

"Spontaneously?"

"But not immediately and not necessarily. That's the interesting part. It's a classic binary weapon: two halves of an explosive charge separated by a membrane. I'm testing different barriers such as cheesecloth, muslin and paper for time and effectiveness. I've already put painted boards in six cars."

Polina took the brush from a can marked RS4 and started painting the paper in broad strokes of red sodium. Arkady noticed that she started with a *W,* like a house painter. "If they did ignite immediately, you'd know by now," he said.

"Yes."

"Polina, don't we have militia technicians with bunkers and body armor and very long brushes to do this sort of thing?"

"I'm faster and better."

Polina was quick. She kept red drips from falling into green cans and in less than a minute covered the papered board so that it had a completely scarlet surface.

Arkady said, "So when the wet red sodium soaks through the paper and makes contact with the copper sulfate, they heat up and ignite?"

"That's the idea, put very simply." Polina took a notepad and pen from her raincoat and jotted the paint numbers and the time down to the second. With finished board and brush in hand, she started to stroll down the line of wrecks.

Arkady walked with her. "I can't help thinking you'd be better off skipping through a park or sharing an ice cream sundae with some-one."

The cars on the dock were crushed, rusted and stripped. A Volga was so twisted that its axle aimed at the sky. A blunt-nosed Niva wore its steering wheel through the front seat. They passed a Lada with its engine block resting ominously in the rear. Around the dock were darkened factories and military depots. Out on the river, the last hy-drofoil of the evening slid by like a snake of lights.

Polina laid the red board by the brake pedal of a four-door Moskvitch and painted a 7 on the left front door. When she saw Arkady begin to approach the other six cars on the end of the dock, she said, "You'd better wait."

They sat in a Zil from which windshield and wheels had been re-moved, affording a low, clear view of the dock and the far bank.

Arkady said, "A bomb inside the car, Kim outside. It seems a little redundant."

Polina said, "At the assassination of Duke Ferdinand, which started World War I, there were twenty-seven terrorists with bombs and guns at different points along the procession route."

"You've made a study of assassinations? Rudy was only a banker, not an heir to the throne."

"In contemporary attacks by terrorists, especially against Western bankers, the car bomb is the weapon of choice."

"You *have* made a study of this." It made his heart sink.

"I'm still confused about the blood in Rudy's car," Polina admitted.

"I'm sure you'll figure it out. You know, there's more to life than . . . death."

Polina had the dark curls of a girl painted by Manet, Arkady thought. She ought to be in a lace collar and long skirt, sitting at a wrought-iron table on sun-dappled grass, not in a wreck on a dock talking about the dead. He noticed her eyes observing him. "You really do lead an empty life, don't you?" she said.

"Wait a second," Arkady said. Somehow the conversation seemed to have been, without any warning or logic, reversed.

"You said so yourself," she pointed out.

"Well, you don't have to agree."

"Exactly," Polina said. "You can lead your empty life, but you criti-cize how I lead mine, even though I'm working day and night for you."

The first car blew with a muffled sound like a damp drum. A white flash mixed with the explosion of windshield and windows. After a blink, and while crystallized glass was still raining down, the car interior filled with flames. Polina entered the time in her notepad.

Arkady asked, "That didn't have a blasting cap or a fuse? Just chemicals?"

"Just what you saw, although with solutions at different concentrations. I have others with phosphorus and aluminum powder. Those need a blasting cap or some sort of blow to detonate."

"That one seemed pretty effective," Arkady said.

He had expected some sort of spontaneous combustion, but not an explosion of such strength. Already the fire had taken root, the front seat and dash covered with lapping flames that produced dark, noxious smoke. How did anyone ever escape car fires? "Thanks for not letting me take a closer look," Arkady said.

"Entirely my pleasure."

"And I apologize for criticizing even by suggestion your professional dedication, since you're the only member of the team who has shown any competence. I'm in awe, really."

While Polina scrutinized him for sarcasm, he lit a cigarette. "I'd roll down the window if there were a window," he said.

The second car burst into flame without the explosive force of the first, and the bomb in the third car was even weaker—hardly a blast at all, though it was followed by a steady, hardworking flame. The fourth met the initial standard. By now Arkady was a veteran observer and could appreciate the sequence: the initial eruption of crystallized safety glass, the blinding flare of ignition, the *whump* of compacted air, and then the two-step flowering of roseate flames and brown, toxic smoke. Polina jotted down notes. She had delicate hands made even smaller by the rolled cuffs of her coat. Her rapid writing was as neat as type.

Belov had said there would be a funeral for his father. Were they going to bury the body or a pot of ashes? They could skip the crematorium and bring the old man out here for a glorious postmortem ride in one of Polina's flaming chariots. Irina could report it on the news as one more Russian atrocity.

It occurred to Arkady that cars were not meant for Russians. First of all, Russia didn't have enough roads free of frost heaves and mud wallows. More important, vehicles capable of any speed should not be placed in the hands of people given to vodka and melancholy.

"Did you have something else planned tonight?" Polina asked.

"No."

The fifth and sixth cars exploded almost simultaneously, then burned very differently, one developing into a bowl of fire and the other, already a burned-out shell, subsiding into guttering flames. No fire engines had arrived yet. The era of night shifts was long over, and at this hour the factories around the dock were empty except for watchmen. Arkady wondered how much of the city he and Polina could torch before anyone noticed.

As she leafed through her notes, Polina said, "I wanted to put dummies in the cars."

"Dummies?"

"Mannequins. I wanted thermometers, too. I couldn't even find oven thermometers."

"Everything's so hard to find."

"Because chemical combustion is inexact, especially in the lead time to ignition."

"It's my impression that it would have been more exact for Kim to spray Rudy with a submachine gun. Not that I'm not having a wonderful time watching cars blow up. It's sort of like suttee. You know, how Indian women immolate themselves on their husbands' funeral pyres? This is like a grand suttee on the Ganges, except that we're on the Moscow and it's not the middle of the day, it's the middle of the night, and we neglected to bring any widows. Even dummies. Otherwise it's practically romantic."

Polina said, "That's hardly an analytical approach."

"Analytical? I wouldn't need an oven thermometer. I smelled Rudy. He was done."

Polina was stung. Arkady was shocked at himself. What could he say now? That he was tired, upset, wanted to be home cupping his ear to his radio? "I'm sorry," he said. "That was mean."

"I think you'd better get a different pathologist," Polina said.

"I think I'd better go."

As he got out, the seventh car exploded, shooting fountains of glass high into the air. After the clap of detonation, the glass rang like chimes as it fell and scattered in crystals around his feet. The Moskvitch burned like a furnace at full blast, white flames leaping excitedly from window to window, broadcasting a circle of heat that made Arkady flinch and step back. As the seat burned, the nature of the flames changed into roiling purplish smoke rich with toxin. Paint bubbled and the whole dock glowed with shining glass, like coals.

He noticed that Polina was making notes again. She would have made a good assassin, he thought. She was a good pathologist. He was an idiot.

9

It's sad about Rudy. He was very human, warm, concerned about Soviet youth." Antonov winced as one boy backed another into a corner and knocked out his mouthpiece. "Many's the time he was here, encouraging the kids, telling them to mind the straight and narrow." Antonov bobbed sympathetically as the beleaguered fighter slipped free. "Stick him, stick him, *move!* Well, that's a good imitation of a propeller! Anyway, Rudy was like an uncle. This is not the center of Moscow. These kids are not going to special schools for ballerinas. Hit him! But youth is our most precious possession. Every boy and girl in Komsomol gets a fair chance. Model planes, chess, basketball. I bet Rudy sponsored every club here. Backpedal! Not you! *Him!*"

Jaak hadn't checked in yet. Polina had called, but the last place Arkady had wanted to start the day was the morgue. Didn't she ever get her fill of gore? On the other hand, watching boys pummel each other was proving no cure for a headache. Master of Sport Antonov gave the impression of a man whose brains had long since been pounded into more solid stuff. He had a gray crew cut and flat, utilitarian features, and in his fists, so knotted that he seemed to have extra knuckles, he held a bell mallet and a watch. The boys in the ring wore leather helmets, tank tops, shorts. Their skin was as pale as potato flesh except where they had been hit. Sometimes they looked like they were boxing, the next moment as if they were dancing badly. Besides the ring, the Leningrad Borough Komsomol gymnasium also gave room to wrestling mats and weights, so the walls resounded with the puffing of wrestlers and lifters. There were two different psychological types, Arkady thought; weight lifters were soloists of grunts, while wrestlers couldn't wait to get tangled. A dim light penetrated whitewashed windows, and an ancient reek clung to the air. Wrestling and boxing ladders framed the door and a sign that said CIGARETTES AND SUCCESS DON'T MIX!, which reminded Arkady that he had unconsciously put on the jacket with Borya's two packs of Marlboros, so there was a bright side to things.

"Rudy was a sports enthusiast—that's why you asked me to come? You had a trophy for him?"

Antonov asked, "He's really dead?"

"Absolutely dead."

"Follow up, follow up!" Antonov shouted up at the ring. To Arkady he said, "Forget the trophy."

"Forget the trophy?" Antonov had called the office twice a day about the trophy.

"What's Rudy going to do with a trophy now?"

"That's what I wondered," Arkady said.

"I don't want to be disrespectful, but I had a question. Say, in a cooperative, the person who signs the checks dies. Does that mean the other partner in the cooperative gets whatever money is left in the account?"

"You were partners with Rudy?"

Antonov sneered as if the question were ridiculous. "Not me personally, no. The club. Excuse me. Don't switch leads! If you're right-handed, stay right-handed!"

Arkady started to wake up. "The club and Rudy?"

"Local Komsomols are allowed to be in cooperatives. It's only fair, and sometimes it helps to have an official partner involved when you want to bring in certain stuff."

"Slot machines?" Arkady took the happiest guess.

Antonov remembered his watch and whacked the mallet on a pail. The fighters reeled away from each other, neither able to raise a glove.

"It's perfectly legal," Antonov said and lowered his voice. "Trans-Kom Services, with a capital *K.*"

TransKom. The Young Communist League plus Rudy equaled the Intourist slots. Seen in the light of Rudy's talent, this dingy little Komsomol club was dross turned to gold. For Arkady it was a minor victory, admittedly inconsequential compared to finding Kim.

Antonov said, "You'll see, the club's on the cooperative papers.

There were the names of the partners, statement of services, bank accounts, everything."

"You have the papers?"

"Rudy had all the papers," Antonov said.

"Well, I think Rudy took them with him."

The dead were perverse.

IN THE MORGUE they were patient. Gurneys lined the hall, the bodies under soiled sheets waiting their turn on the table with a final, supine lack of urgency. No matter to them if they rotted for lack of formaldehyde. There was no offense taken if an investigator lit an expensive American cigarette to mask the stench. Rudy was in a drawer, internal organs in a plastic bag between his legs. Polina, however, was gone.

Arkady found her midway in a line of a thousand people queuing for beets in the small park next to Petrovka. Rain fell in a steady, insinuating drizzle that sparkled around lamplights. Some umbrellas were up, though not many, because people needed both hands free for bags. At the head of the line soldiers piled sacks in the mud. With her raincoat buttoned to her chin, drops beaded on her dark hair, Polina looked as if she were being borne forward by a centipede of pinched eyes and mouths. There were other lines for eggs and bread, and a line that wound around a kiosk for cigarettes. Food vigilantes patrolled the lines to make sure no one switched. Arkady didn't have his coupons, so all this plenty was wasted on him.

Polina said, "I came here after the dock to finish up Rudy. I told you there was too much blood. He's all yours now."

Arkady doubted there could ever be too much blood for Polina, but he maintained an attitude of appreciation. Obviously she had worked all night.

"Polina, I'm sorry about the dock. I'm terrible about forensic medicine and pathology. You have more nerve than I do."

Behind Polina, a woman with a gray shawl, gray brows and mustache leaned toward him to demand, "Are you trying to cut in?"

"No."

The woman said, "They should shoot people who cut in."

"Watch him," advised the man behind her. He was a short, bureaucratic type with an impressive briefcase, the kind that could hold a lot of beets. All the way down the queue, Arkady saw faces regarding him with suppressed fury. They moved one lockstep forward, crowding to make a wall he couldn't breach.

"How long have you been in line?" Arkady asked Polina.

"Just an hour. I'll get some beets for you," she said and glared at the pair behind her. "Fuck them."

"What do you mean, 'too much blood'?"

Polina shrugged; she had offered. "Describe the explosions when Rudy died," she said. "What you saw, exactly."

"Two bursts of flame," Arkady said. "The first was a surprise. It was brilliant, white."

"That was the red sodium–copper sulfate device. The second burst?"

"The second was bright, too."

"As bright?"

"Less." He had run them together in his mind before. "We didn't have a clear view, but maybe more orange than white. Then we saw burning money rising in the smoke."

"So two bursts of flame, but only one hot enough to leave a flash point in the car. Did you smell anything after the second burst?"

"Gasoline."

"The gas tank?"

"That blew later." Arkady watched a brawl at the kiosk, where a customer claimed he had been given only four packs for the month, not five. A pair of soldiers carried him like a suitcase, one arm around his neck and one around his crotch, and threw him into a van. "Gary told us that Kim threw a bomb into the car. It could have been a Molotov cocktail, a bottle of gasoline."

"It was better than that," Polina said.

"What's better?"

"Gelled gasoline. Gelled gasoline sticks and burns and burns. That's why there was so much blood."

Arkady still didn't understand. "Before, you said burning didn't cause bleeding."

"I went over Rosen again. He simply didn't have the number or kind of cuts to produce all that blood inside the car and out. I know that the lab said it was his blood type, but this time I checked it myself. It wasn't his type. It wasn't even human blood. It was cattle blood."

"Cattle blood?"

"Drain the blood through a cloth and use the serum. Mix it with gasoline and a little coffee or baking soda. Stir until it gels."

"A bomb of blood and gasoline?"

"It's a guerrilla technique. I would have caught on faster if the lab result had been correct," Polina said. "You can thicken gasoline with soap, eggs or blood."

"That must be why they're in short supply," Arkady said.

The couple behind Polina were listening intently. "Don't get eggs," the woman warned. "The eggs have salmonella."

The bureaucrat countered, "That is a baseless rumor started by persons who intend to keep all the eggs to themselves."

The line shuffled forward another step. Arkady wanted to stamp his feet to keep warm. Polina was in open sandals, but she could have been a plaster bust for her reaction to rain, blood and the insanity of the wait. Her entire attention was focused on the nearing scales. The rain fell harder. Drops ran along the contour of her temple and webbed the pagoda curve of her hair.

"Are they selling by weight or by count?" she asked her neighbors.

"Dear," the old woman said, "it all depends whether they have rigged scales or little beets."

"Do we get beet greens, too?" Polina asked.

"There's another line for greens," the woman said.

Arkady said, "You did a good job. I'm sorry it had to be so gruesome."

Polina said, "If it bothered me, I'd be in the wrong profession."

"Maybe *I'm* in the wrong profession," Arkady said.

Most of the transactions at the scales were mute and sullen exchanges of rubles and ration chits for beets, though every fourth or fifth erupted into an accusation of cheating and a demand for more, denunciations that sang with frustration, hysteria and rage, which drew the line anxiously closer until soldiers pushed it back and the customer on, so that there was a constant eddy and pulse within the line. At least the rain washed the beets, showing their scarlet under a lamppost. In its light Arkady could see that the sacks heaped behind the scales exhibited the effects of their rough passage from the country, dirt and bruises staining the wet burlap. The wetter sacks were smeared bright red, the ground around them was steeped red, and the scales were dyed a winy vermilion speckled with the skins of beets. In the reflection off the water running from the sacks, the entire park glowed in a spreading lens of red. Polina stared down at her toes and open sandals, which were already stained pink. Arkady watched her face turn to wax, and he caught her as she dropped.

"Not the morgue, not the morgue," she said.

Arkady put her arm over his shoulder and half-carried, half-walked her out of the park and down Petrovka Street in search of someplace she could sit. Across the street an ambulance was leaving the gate of a buff-colored mansion, the sort of pre-Revolutionary building the Party loved to use for offices. It seemed to be some kind of clinic.

As soon as he got her into the courtyard, though, Polina insisted, "Not a doctor."

On one side of the courtyard was a rustic wooden entrance whimsically painted with crowing roosters and dancing pigs. They went through into an empty café. Small tables were surrounded by leather banquettes, and a row of stools stood along a padded bar. In back of the counter was an arsenal of orange-juice presses.

Polina sat at a banquette, put her head between her knees and said, "Shit, shit, shit, shit, shit."

A waitress appeared from the kitchen to chase them away, but Arkady held up his ID and asked for brandy.

"This is a medical clinic. We don't serve brandy."

"Then medicinal brandy."

"For dollars."

Arkady put a pack of Marlboros on the table. The waitress stared, unmoved. He added the other pack. "Two packs."

"And thirty rubles."

She disappeared, returned a moment later and in one circular motion set down a flask of Armenian cognac with two glasses and scooped up the cigarettes and money.

Polina sat up and let her head loll back. Her hair hung in sad ringlets. "That's half your weekly salary," she said.

"What was I going to save it for? Beets?" He poured her a glass that she downed in one swallow. "I don't think you really wanted borscht, anyway," he said.

"That lousy body. Once you know what happened, it's worse, not better." She tried long, deliberate breaths. "That's why I went outside. Then I saw the food lines and joined the nearest one. No one makes you go back to work if you're shopping."

At the bar, the waitress dug under her apron for a lighter, lit a cigarette and exhaled with a sensuality that hooded her eyes. Arkady envied her. "Excuse me," he called. "What kind of clinic is this? A café with leather seats and soft lighting, it's rather fancy."

"It's for foreigners," the waitress said. "It's a diet clinic."

Arkady and Polina shared a glance. There must be hysteria in the air, he thought, because she seemed ready to laugh and cry at the same time, and he felt the same way himself. "Well, Moscow is certainly the right place," he said.

"They couldn't come to a better place," Polina said.

Arkady saw color return to her cheeks. It was interesting how quick recovery was in someone young, like roses. He poured her another glass and one for himself. "It's insane, Polina. It's Dante's Inferno with breadlines. Maybe there's a diet center in hell."

"Americans would go," she said. "They'd do aerobics." There was a real smile on her face, perhaps because there was a real smile on his. It merely took appreciating insanity together. "Moscow *could* be hell. This *could* be it," she said.

"Good cognac." Arkady poured two more glasses. It had a terrific impact on an empty stomach. "To hell," he added. He could feel the damp in his clothes rising like steam. He called to the waitress, "What kind of food is on this diet?"

"Depends." She screwed her lips around the cigarette. "Whether you're on a fruit diet or a vegetable diet."

"Fruit diet? Do you hear that, Polina? Like what?" he asked.

"Pineapples, papayas, mangoes, bananas." The waitress rattled them off casually as if she were intimately acquainted with them.

"Papayas," Arkady repeated. "Polina, you and I would be willing to stand in line for seven or eight years for a papaya. I'm not sure I even know what a papaya looks like. They could give me a potato and I'd probably be happy. Then I wouldn't lose weight. Luxury is wasted on people like you and me." He asked the waitress, "Could you show us a papaya?"

She studied them. "No."

"She probably doesn't even have a papaya," Arkady said. "She just says it to impress her friends. Feel better?"

"I'm laughing, so I must feel a little better."

"I've never heard you laugh before. It's a nice sound."

"Yes." Polina slowly rocked back and forth. Her smile sank. "At medical school we used to ask each other, 'What is the worst way to die?' After Rudy, I think I know. Do you believe in hell?"

"There's a question out of the blue."

"Well, you're like the devil. You take a secret glee in your work, like you've come to grab the damned. That's why Jaak likes to work with you."

"Why do you work with me?" He didn't think she was going to quit now.

Polina took a moment. "You let me do things right. You let me get involved."

Arkady knew this was the problem. The morgue was a simple theater of black and white, dead or alive. Polina had been full of analytical detachment, a blind determinism perfect for labeling the dead as so many cold and inert specimens. But a pathologist who became involved in the investigation outside the morgue started seeing bodies as living people, and then the cadaver on the table became the picture of someone's worst and ultimate breath on earth. He had robbed her of professional distance. In a way he had corrupted her.

"Because you're smart." Arkady left it at that.

She said, "I've been thinking about what you said last night. Kim had a gun. Why use two different kinds of bombs on Rudy? It's such a complicated way to kill him."

"The point wasn't just to kill him; the point was to burn him. Or burn all the records and computer disks and every piece of information that would connect him to someone else. I'm more sure of that all the time."

"So I am a help."

"A Hero of Red Labor." He toasted her.

Polina drank her cognac and leveled her gaze. "I heard that you left once," she said. "There was a woman, I heard."

"Where do you hear all these things?"

"You're avoiding the question."

"I don't know what people say. I was out of the country for a short time and then I came back."

"The woman?"

"Did not come back."

"Who was right?" Polina asked.

Now that, Arkady thought, was a question asked only by the very young.

10

Irina said, "The Soviet Defense Minister conceded that Soviet troops attacked civilians in Baku to prevent the overthrow of the Azerbaijan Communist regime. The army had stood aside when Azeri activists rioted against Armenians in the capital, but went into action when an Azeri crowd threatened to burn down Party headquarters. Tanks and troops broke through blockades set up by anti-Communist militants and stormed into the city, firing dumdum bullets and spraying apartment buildings without provocation. Hundreds, perhaps thousands, of civilians are estimated to have died in the assault. Although the KGB had spread rumors that Azeri militants would be armed with heavy machine guns, only hunting rifles, knives and pistols were found among the dead."

Arkady had left Polina and hurried home in time to catch Irina's first broadcast. Drinks with one woman, then rushing to the voice of another. What a sophisticated life, he thought.

"Official justification for the military operation was the mob violence against Armenians by militants who showed documents identifying themselves as leaders of the Azeri Popular Front. Since the Front does not issue such documents, a KGB provocation is once again suspected."

While Arkady listened, he changed to a dry shirt and jacket.

Who was right? She was. He was. There was no choice, no right or wrong, no black or white. He wished for one blinding ray of certainty; even to be wrong would be a relief. He had stepped back in his memory so many times his tracks would have worn through stone, and he still didn't know what else he could have done. He had told Polina, "We'll never know."

Irina said, "Increasingly, Moscow has cited nationalist tensions to justify the continued presence of Soviet Army troops in different republics, including the Baltic states, Georgia, Armenia, Azerbaijan, Uzbekistan and the Ukraine. Tanks and missile launchers that were supposed to be scrapped in the arms-control agreement with NATO have instead been moved to bases in the dissident republics. At the same time, nuclear missiles have been removed from those republics to the Russian Republic."

He hardly heard her words. Every rumor he heard was worse than her reports; reality was worse than her reports. So, like a beekeeper separating honey from a comb, he was able to hear only her voice and not the words. She had a darker sound tonight. Had it rained in Munich? Were there traffic jams on the autobahn? Was she with anyone?

She could have said anything and he would have gone on listening. Sometimes he felt as if he were going to fly out the window and wheel in the sky above Moscow. He would home in on that voice like a beacon, which would lead him, lead him, lead him away.

WHEN THE NEWS went to a tape, Arkady left his apartment not with wings but with wipers, attached them to his car and plunged into the midnight traffic. Night and rain combined to make disoriented streets and paint smears of light across the windshield. At the embankment road he had to stop for a convoy of army trucks and personnel carriers as long and slow as a freight train. While he waited he felt his jacket for cigarettes, found an envelope and winced when he recognized the letter Belov had given him in Red Square. His name was written across the face of the envelope with a fine nib in letters that started as slashes and ended in sprawls, as if the hand had been too weak to wield a pen or a knife.

Polina had asked what the worst way to die was. Holding the letter, letting it rest lightly across his palm with the shadow of water running over his name, Arkady knew the answer. It was to realize that when you died no one would care. It was to realize that you were already dead. He didn't feel that way now; he would never feel that way. Just hearing Irina made him come so alive his heart shook with every beat. What had his father written? The wise course, he thought, would be to leave the letter on the street. The rain would wash it down a storm drain, the river would carry it to the sea, where the paper would unfold and fall apart and the ink would run and fade like poison. Instead, he slipped it back into his pocket.

MININ LET HIM into Rudy's apartment.

The detective was agitated because of the rumor that speculation would become legal. "This undermines the basis of our investigation," he said. "If we can't go after money changers, who can we arrest?"

"There are still murderers, rapists and violent thieves. You'll always be busy," Arkady reassured him and gave him his hat and coat. Getting Minin out of the place was like unearthing a mole. "Catch some sleep. I'll take over here."

"The mafia's going to open banks."

"Very likely. I understand that's how they start."

"I searched everything," Minin said and stepped reluctantly onto the threshold. "Nothing hidden in books, bureaus, under the bed. I left a list on the desk."

"It's suspiciously clean, isn't it?"

"Well . . ."

"That's what I thought, too," Arkady said as he started to shut the door. "And don't worry about a lack of crime. In the future we'll have a better class of criminal—bankers, brokers, businessmen. You'll need lots of sleep for that."

Alone, the first place Arkady went was to the office desk to see whether anything new had come in on the fax. The paper was clean and bore the same faint pencil dot on the reverse side that he had left after tearing off the messages about Red Square. He picked up Minin's list. The detective had cut open Rudy's mattress and springs, inspected bureau and drawers, unscrewed switches, tapped baseboards, disassembled and reassembled the apartment, and found nothing.

Arkady ignored Minin's list. What could be found, he thought, would be more obvious. Sooner or later an apartment fit a man like a shell. He might be gone, but his outline stayed in a worn chair, a photo, a crust of food, a forgotten letter, in the smell of hope or despair. In part he took this approach because technological support for investigations was so weak. The militia had invested in German and Swedish gear, spectrographs and hemotypers, which lay unused for lack of parts for dearth of funds. There was no computer matching of blood or license plates, let alone of something so laughably out of reach as "genetic fingerprints." What Soviet forensic labs possessed were archaic chemistry sets of blackened test tubes, gas burners and curlicues of glass piping that the West hadn't seen in fifty years. Polina had extracted answers from the body of Rudy Rosen in spite of her equipment, not because of it.

Since the chain of hard evidence tended to be thin, a Soviet investigator was more dependent on softer clues, on social nuance and logic. Arkady knew investigators who believed that with a sufficiently clear understanding of the scene of a homicide, they could deduce a murderer's sex, age, occupation and hobbies. The only place in the Soviet Union where psychological analysis was allowed to thrive was criminal investigation.

Of course Soviet investigators had always relied on confession, too. Confession solved everything. But confession really worked only with amateurs and innocents. Makhmud or Kim would no more confess to a crime than suddenly burst into Latin.

What had this apartment said so far? One thing: "Where is Red Square?"

Was Rosen religious? There were no menorahs, Torahs, prayer shawls or Sabbath candles. The portraits of his parents were the bare minimum of family history; generally Russian homes were photo galleries of sepia ancestors in oval frames. Where were Rudy's pictures of himself or of friends? He was hygienic. The walls were smooth, scrubbed clean, not a nail hole to mar the blank space, as if he had effaced himself.

Arkady pulled books and magazines from the shelves. *Business Week* and *Israel Trade* were in English and indicated an international breadth of ambition. Did the stamp album speak of a solitary youth? Inside was a regular aquarium of outsized stamps of tropical fish issued by miniature nations and islands around the world. In a paper sleeve were loose stamps of nondescript variety: Czarist two-kopecks, French "Libertés," American "Franklins." No valuable red squares.

He stacked the books and moved to the bedroom, where he balanced the pile on the night table. The sleep mask had a poignant quality, suggesting that a combination of rich food and diet pills made for uneasy nights.

There was no chair in the bedroom. Arkady removed his shoes, sat on the bed and at once had the shock of hearing the complaint of springs that anticipated Rudy's weight. He packed the pillows behind his back, the way Rudy would have, and flipped through the books.

Every home had a few classics just to prove literacy. Rudy read his. Arkady found underlined the humorous passage in the immortal Pushkin's *The Captain's Daughter* in which a hussar offers to teach a young man the game of billiards: " 'It's quite essential to us soldiers,' he said. 'One can't always be beating Jews, you know. So there is nothing to it but to go to the inn and play billiards; and to do that one must be able to play.' "

"Or beat Jews with cues," was scribbled below the line. Arkady recognized Rudy's handwriting from the bankbook.

Deep in Gogol's *Dead Souls,* Rudy had marked "For some time, Chichikov made it impossible for smugglers to earn a living. In particular, he reduced Polish Jewry almost to despair, so invincible, so almost unnatural, was the rectitude, the incorruptibility which led him to refrain from converting himself into a small capitalist." In the margin, Rudy had added, "Nothing changes."

There had to be more, Arkady thought. Thanks to Jewish emigration, the Moscow mafia had good connections with Israeli criminals. He put on the television set and replayed the Jerusalem videotape, skipping from place to place, from Wailing Wall to casino.

His mind wandered to what Polina had said: "Too much blood."

He agreed. If gasoline could be thickened with blood, it could also be thickened with a dozen other agents easier to get ahold of. He'd seen blood in some other strange form recently, but couldn't remember where.

He looked at the Egyptian tape again. It was warming to see the tawny hues of the Sinai desert while rain tapped on the windows, and he crowded closer, like a man to a fireplace. He reached into his jacket for cigarettes, and before he remembered that he had given them away he had pulled the letter from his pocket. He could count the number of letters he had received from his father. One a month while Arkady was in Pioneer camp. One a month when the general was in China, at a time when relations with Mao were fraternal and deep. All those missives were brisk, militarylike reports that ended with instructions for Arkady to be hardworking, responsible and worthy. About twelve letters altogether. He received one more after choosing the university over officers' school. He was impressed because his father had cited the Bible, namely the episode in which God demanded from Abraham the sacrifice of his only son. This was where Stalin improved on God, the general said, because he not only would have allowed the execution but would have been glorified by Abraham all the more. Besides, there were some sons, like weak calves, who were fit only for sacrifice. Too much blood? For his father there was never enough.

The father renounced his son, the son renounced his father, one cutting off the future, the other the past, and neither daring to mention, it occurred to Arkady now, the one point in time where they would always dwell together. At the dacha, boy and man had stared from the dock at feet caught in the drowsy, warm river that ran by the edge of the dacha's lawn. The feet were bare, and they neither floated up nor plunged down to deeper water; instead, they lazed beneath the surface like underwater flowers. Farther down, Arkady could make out his mother's white dress billowing and swaying in the current, to his child's mind waving good-bye.

Dhows tipped and cruised the waters of the Nile. Arkady realized that he had stopped consciously watching the television. He replaced the letter in his jacket as delicately as if it were a razor, then punched the Egyptian tape out of the VCR and pushed in the one from Munich. He paid more attention now because in a rudimentary way he understood German, and because he needed to focus on something besides the letter. Of course he watched with Russian eyes.

"*Willkommen* to München . . ." the tape began. On the screen was an etching of medieval monks watering sunflowers, turning a spitted boar, pouring beer. It didn't look like such a bad life. The next image was of modern, rebuilt Munich. The narration managed to be boastful of this phoenixlike accomplishment without directly mentioning any world wars, suggesting that a "sad and tragic" plague had reduced the city to rubble. Munich had been liberated by Americans, and there was the plastic feel of an American mall to the images on the screen. From the figure of the belled jester turning in the Marienplatz clock tower to the checkerboard walls of the Old Court, every historical site was sterilized to quaintness. Virtually every other image was of a beer garden or a beer hall, as if the brew were an anointing oil of innocence —Hitler's beer-hall putsch aside, of course. Yet Munich was undeniably attractive. People looked so wealthy and well dressed that they seemed to be shopping on a different planet. Cars looked inexplicably clean and sounded like the brass horns of a hunt. Swans and ducks flocked to the city's lakes and river; when was a swan last seen on the Moscow?

"Munich is a city with the stamp of royal builders," the narrator intoned. "Max-Joseph-Platz and the National Theater were built by King Max-Joseph, Ludwigstrasse by his son, King Ludwig I, the "Golden Mile" of Maximilianstrasse by Ludwig's son, King Max II, and Prinzregentenstrasse by his brother, Prince Regent Luitpold."

Ah, but do we get to see the the beer hall where Hitler and his Brownshirts started their first premature march to power? Will we see the square where Göring took the bullet meant for Hitler and in so doing captured *der Führer*'s heart forever? Will we tour Dachau? Well, Munich's history is so packed with people and events that we can't see everything on one tape. Arkady admitted his attitude was unfair, jaundiced and corroded with envy.

"At last year's Oktoberfest, celebrants drank over five million liters of beer and consumed seven hundred thousand chickens, seventy thousand pork knuckles and seventy roasted oxen . . ."

Well, they could come to Moscow to diet. The nearly pornographic display of food glazed Arkady's eyes. After opera in the National Theater—"built by a tax on beer"—refreshment in a romantic beer cellar. After a spin on the autobahn, a pit stop in the beer garden. After an Alpine hike up the Zugspitze, well-earned beer at a rustic inn.

Arkady stopped the tape and rewound to the hike. Vista of Alps leading to the stone-and-snow escarpment of the Zugspitze. Hikers in lederhosen. Tight shot of edelweiss. Silhouettes of mountaineers high above. Drifting clouds.

Beer garden of the inn. Honeysuckle climbing yellow plaster. The enervated stillness of Bavarians after lunch, except for one woman in short sleeves and sunglasses. Cut to a vapor trail leading from clouds to a Lufthansa jet.

Arkady rewound and ran the scene in the garden again. The tape quality seemed the same, but both the narrator's voice and the music were absent. In their place was the scraping of chairs and the off-screen sounds of traffic. The sunglasses were a mistake; in a professional tape they would have been off. He went back and forth from Alps to airliner. The clouds were the same. The beer garden scene had been inserted.

The woman raised her glass. Blond hair was brushed back like a mane from her broad brow and broader cheeks, short chin, medium height, mid-thirties. Dark sunglasses, gold necklace, black short-sleeved sweater—contrasts that were more sensual than pretty in any ordinary sense. Red nails. Fair skin. Red lips half-open in the same slack, reckless study she had once given Arkady through a car window lifting a corner of a half-smile. She mouthed, "I love you."

Her lips were easy to read because her promise was in Russian.

11

I don't know," Jaak said. "You saw her better than I did. I was driving."

Arkady drew the curtains so that his office was lit only by the glow of the beer garden. On the monitor a glass was lifted and held by the Pause button of the VCR.

"The woman who was in Rosen's car looked at us."

"She looked at you," Jaak said. "My eyes were on the road. If you think she's the same woman, that's good enough for me."

"We need stills. What's the matter?"

"We need Kim or the Chechens; *they* killed Rudy. Rudy as good as told you they would. If she's German, if we drag foreigners in, we have to spread the circle and share with the KGB. You know how that goes: we feed them and they shit on us. You told them?"

"Not yet. When we have more." Arkady turned off the monitor.

"Like what?"

"A name. Maybe an address in Germany."

"You're going to run this one around them?"

Arkady handed Jaak the tape. "We just don't want to bother them until we have something definite. Maybe the woman is still here."

Jaak said, "You've got brass balls. You must ring when you walk."

"Like a belled cat," Arkady said.

"The bastards would just take all the credit anyway." Jaak reluctantly accepted the tape, then brightened and waved a pair of car keys. "I borrowed Julya's. The Volvo. After I run your errand, I'm headed for the Lenin's Path Collective. Remember the truck that sold me the radio? It's possible they saw something when Rudy was killed."

"I'll bring the radio," Arkady promised.

"Bring it to Kazan Station. I'm meeting Julya's mother at the Dream Bar at four."

"Julya won't be there?"

"She wouldn't be caught dead at Kazan Station, but her mother's coming in on the train. That's how I got the car. Unless you want to keep the radio."

"No."

When he was alone, Arkady opened the curtains. The rain had stopped, leaving weepy stains around the windows of the courtyard. The skyline was a ring of damp chimney pots upraised like spades. Perfect weather for a funeral.

THE MAN AT the Ministry of Foreign Trade said, "A joint business venture requires a partnership between a Soviet entity—a cooperative or a factory—and a foreign company. It helps if there is sponsorship from a Soviet political organization—"

"Meaning from the Party?"

"Yes, to be plain, but it's not necessary."

"This is capitalism?"

"No, this is not pure capitalism; this is an intermediate stage of capitalism."

"Can the joint venture take rubles out?"

"No."

"Can it take dollars out?"

"No."

"This is a very intermediate stage."

"It can take oil. Or vodka."

"We have that much vodka?"

"For sale abroad."

Arkady asked, "All joint ventures must be approved by you?"

"They should be, but sometimes they aren't. In Georgia or Armenia they tend to make their own arrangements, which is why Georgia and Armenia don't ship anything to Moscow anymore." He giggled. "Fuck them."

His office was on the tenth floor with a view of squalls moving east to west. No factory smoke, though, because parts hadn't arrived from Sverdlovsk, Riga, Minsk.

"What did TransKom register as its purpose?"

"Importation of recreational equipment. It is sponsored by the Leningrad Borough Komsomol. Boxing gloves, things of that nature, I suppose."

"Like slot machines?"

"Apparently."

"In trade for what?"

"Personnel."

"People?"

"I guess so."

"What kind of people? Olympic boxers, nuclear physicists?"

"Tour guides."

"Touring where?"

"Germany."

"Germany needs Soviet guides?"

"Apparently."

Arkady wondered what else the man would believe. That the baby Lenin left coins under pillows in exchange for teeth?

"TransKom has officers?"

"Two." The man read from the file in front of him. "Many positions, but all filled by two people, Rudik Davidovich Rosen, Soviet citizen, and Boris Benz, a resident of Munich, Germany. TransKom's address is Rosen's. There may be any number of investors, but they're not listed. Excuse me." He covered the file with *Pravda*.

"The Ministry has no names for the tour guides?"

The man folded the newspaper in halves and quarters. "No. You know, people come here to register a venture to import medicine, and the next thing you know they're bringing in basketball shoes or building hotels. Once conditions exist here for a free market, it will be like watering the ground."

"What will you do when capitalism is in full swing?"

"I'll find something."

"You're inventive?"

"I have to be." From a drawer he took a ball of string, bit off an arm's length and put it and *Pravda* in his jacket. "I'll walk you out. I was on my way to lunch." Bureaucrats survived on the butter, bread and sausage they took home from cafeterias. The jacket was loose and its pockets were jowls dappled with grease.

■ ■ ■

VAGANKOVSKOYE CEMETERY WAS lovingly but casually tended. A coverlet of wet leaves lay unswept around limes, birches, oaks; dandelions were allowed to line the walk, and overall spread the soft embrace of natural decay. Many of the gravestones were busts of Party stalwarts hewn from granite and black marble: composers, scientists, writers of Socialist Realism with broad brows and commanding gazes. More timid souls were represented by photographs set like cameos on their stones. Since the graves were surrounded by iron fences, the faces on the tombstones seemed to peer from black bird cages. Not all, though. The first grave inside the gate belonged to the roughneck singer-actor Vysotsky, and was heaped so high with daisies and roses freshly watered by the rain that it stirred with the hum of bumblebees.

Arkady found his father's funeral procession halfway down the central path. Cadets bearing a star of red roses and a cushion covered with medals were followed by a porter pushing a handcart and coffin, then a dozen shuffling generals in dress dark-green uniforms and white gloves, two musicians with trumpets and two with dented tubas playing a funeral march from a sonata by Chopin.

Belov was in the rear guard, wearing civilian clothes. His eyes lit when he saw Arkady. "I knew you would come." Solemnly he pumped Arkady's hand with both of his. "Of course you couldn't stay away, it would have been disgraceful. You saw *Pravda* this morning."

"Being used as food wrap."

"I knew you'd want this." He gave Arkady an article that seemed to have been meticulously torn from the newspaper with a ruler.

Arkady stopped to read the obituary. "General of the Army Kiril Ilyich Renko, a prominent Soviet military commander . . ." It was a long piece and he read it in small handfuls. ". . . after completing the M. V. Frunze Military Academy. K. I. Renko's active involvement in the Great Patriotic War was a brilliant page in his biography. Commander of a tank brigade, he was cut off by the first rush of the fascist invasion but joined partisan forces and mounted raids behind enemy lines . . . fought successfully in battles for Moscow, in the Battle of Stalingrad, the campaign in the steppes and operations around Berlin. . . . After the war, he was responsible for stabilizing the situation in the Ukraine and then for command of the Urals Military District." Or to put it another way, Arkady thought, the general, now numbed to slaughter, was responsible for a mass execution of Ukrainian national-ists so bloody that he had to be exiled to the Urals. ". . . twice awarded the title Hero of the Soviet Union and awarded four Orders of Lenin, the Order of the October Revolution, three Orders of the Red Banner, two Orders of Suvorov (First Class), two Orders of Kutuzov (First Class) . . ."

Belov had pinned a plaque of fading ribbons onto his jacket. His white crewcut was a sparse stubble, and badly shaved wattles covered his collar.

"Thanks." Arkady put the obituary in his pocket.

"You read the letter?" Belov asked.

"Not yet."

"Your father said it would explain everything."

"That would be quite a letter." It would take more than a letter, Arkady thought; it would take a heavy tome bound in black leather.

The generals marched ahead in creaky lockstep. Arkady had no desire to catch up. "Boris Sergeyevich, do you remember a Chechen named Makhmud Khasbulatov?"

"Khasbulatov?" Belov adjusted slowly to the change of subject.

"What's interesting is that Makhmud claims he's been in three ar-mies: White, Red and German. According to the records, he's eighty. In 1920, during the Civil War, he would have been ten years old."

"It's possible. There were plenty of children on each side, White and Red. Those were terrible times."

"Let's say that at the time of Hitler, Makhmud was in the Red Army."

"Everyone served, one way or another."

"I was wondering, in February 1944, was my father in the Chechen military district?"

"No, no, we were pushing toward Warsaw. The Chechen operation was completely rear echelon."

"Hardly worth the time of a Hero of the Soviet Union?"

"Not worth a second of his time," Belov said.

Wasn't it wonderful, Arkady thought, how completely some people retired? Belov had only recently left the prosecutor's office; now Arkady had asked him about the head of the Chechen mafia and the old sergeant had not made the connection at all, as if his mind had already retreated forty years.

They started walking again in silence. Arkady felt watched. In mar-ble and bronze, the dead stood over their graves. A dancer whirled dreamily in white stone. An explorer paused, compass in hand. Against a bas-relief of clouds, a pilot pulled aviator goggles from his eyes. They shared a somber, communal gaze, restless and restful at the same time.

"It was a closed coffin, of course," Belov muttered.

Arkady was distracted because moving in the opposite direction on a parallel path was another, longer procession with an empty cart, a larger battery of horns and tubas and, among the mourners, some familiar faces. Bolstering a widow on either side were General Penyagin and Rodionov, the city prosecutor, both of them with black bands on their sleeves. Arkady remembered that Penyagin's predecessor at CID had died only days ago; presumably the woman was the dead man's wife. The three were trailed by a slow-moving entourage of militia officers, Party officials and relatives parading fixed expressions of boredom and grief. None of them noticed Arkady.

His own cortege had turned down an alley of shaggy pines and stopped at a gate open to a fresh hole in the ground. Arkady looked around. Since Soviet tombstones were not anonymous slabs, he felt introduced to his father's new neighbors. Here was a statue of a singer listing to music inscribed in granite. There, a sportsman with bronze muscles shouldered an iron javelin. Behind the trees grave diggers hunkered over cigarettes, hands on their shovels. Beside the open grave was a small marker of white marble almost flush with the ground. Space was tight at Vagankovskoye, and sometimes husbands and wives were stacked on top of each other, but not this time, thank God.

As the generals formed ranks by the grave, Arkady recognized the four he had seen in Red Square. Shuksin, Ivanov, Kuznetsov and Gul looked even smaller in the daylight, as if the men he had feared and detested as a child had magically bent into beetles with carapaces of green serge and gold brocade, their sunken chests stiffened by tiers of campaign medals, honors and orders, a dazzling clatter of ribbons, brass stars and coins. They were all weeping bitter vodka tears.

"Comrades!" Feebly Ivanov unfolded a piece of paper and began to read. "Today we say good-bye to a great Russian, a lover of peace, yet a man forged . . ."

Arkady was constantly amazed at peoples' faith in lies. As if words had the remotest relationship to the truth. This band of veterans were nothing but little butchers bidding a mawkish farewell to a great butcher. Take the arthritis from their joints and they would drive the knife home as vigorously as in their glorious youth, and they believed every lie they uttered.

By the time Shuksin took Ivanov's place, Arkady wanted his own cigarette and a shovel.

" 'Not one step back!' Stalin ordered. Yes, Stalin. His name is still sacred to my lips. . . ."

"Stalin's favorite general" was what his father had been called. When they were surrounded and without food and ammunition, other generals would dare surrender their men alive. General Renko never surrendered; he wouldn't have surrendered if he'd had nothing but dead to command. Anyway, the Germans never caught him. He broke back through the lines to join the defense of Moscow, and a famous photograph showed him and Stalin himself, like two devils defending hell, studying a subway map to plot the shifting of troops from station to station.

The round Kuznetsov took his turn and balanced on the lip of the grave. "Today, when every effort is made to libel our army's glorious duty . . ."

Their voices had the hollow tremor of busted cellos. Arkady would have felt sorry for them if he didn't remember how they would troop into the dacha, like so many lesser shadows of his father, for the midnight dinners and drunken songs that ended in the army roar "Arrrrrrrraaaaaaaaaagh!!!"

Arkady wasn't sure why he had come. Perhaps for the sake of Belov, who had faithfully maintained the hope of a reunion between father and son. Perhaps for his mother. She would have to lie side by side with her own murderer. He stepped forward to brush dirt off the white marker.

"Soviet power, built on the holy altar of twenty million dead . . ." Kuznetsov droned on.

No, not metamorphosed into beetles, Arkady thought. That was too kind, too Kafkaesque. More like hoary, three-legged dogs, senile but rabid, baying at a pit.

Gul wavered, his green tunic weighted with medals and hanging from his bones. He removed his hat, revealing hair the color of ashes. "I recall my last encounter with K. I. Renko a very short time ago." Gul laid his hand on the coffin of dark wood with brass handles, slim as a skiff. "We remembered comrades in arms whose sacrifices burn like an eternal flame in our hearts. We talked of the present period of doubt and self-mortification so different from our own iron resolve. I give you now the words the general gave me then. 'Those who would shovel dirt on the Party. Those who forget the Jewish historical sins. Those who would distort our revolutionary history, debase and vulgarize our people. To them I say, my banner was and is and always will be red!' "

"Well, that's about as much as I can take," Arkady told Belov and started back down the path.

"There's more." Belov caught up.

"That's why I'm going." Gul was still ranting on.

"We were hoping you would say a few words now that he's dead."

"Boris Sergeyevich, if I had been the investigator of my mother's death, I would have arrested my father. I gladly would have killed him."

"Arkasha—"

"Just the idea that this monster died quietly in his bed will haunt me for the rest of my life."

Belov's voice dropped. "He didn't."

Arkady stopped. He forced himself to be calm. "You said it was a closed coffin. Why?"

Belov had trouble drawing breath. "At the end the pain was so great. He said the only thing holding him together was cancer. He didn't want to die that way. He said he preferred the officer's way out."

"He shot himself?"

"Forgive me. I was in the next room. I . . ."

As Belov's knees gave way, Arkady eased him onto a bench. He felt incredibly stupid; he should have seen what was in the old man's face before this. Belov dug into his jacket, twisted around and gave Arkady a gun. It was a black Nagant revolver and four squat bullets as polished as old silver. "He wanted you to have this."

"The general always had a good sense of humor," Arkady said.

THERE WAS BRISK business at a kiosk beside Vysotsky's grave when Arkady got back to the gate. Now that the sun was out, fans were buying pins, posters, postcards and cassettes of the singer, dead ten years and more popular than ever. The number 23 tram stopped right across the street; it was the handiest souvenir run in Moscow. Around the gate were beggars, peasant women with white kerchiefs and sun-browned faces, legless men with crutches and carts. They congregated around worshipers leaving the cemetery's little yellow church. Coffin lids dressed in crepe and wreaths of sharp-smelling evergreens and carnations rested against the church front. Seminarians sold Bibles from a card table, asking forty rubles for the New Testament.

Carrying his father's gun in his pocket, Arkady felt a little dizzy and had some difficulty in discriminating. As much as he saw the ceremonies of human grief—a widow polishing the photo on a headstone—he saw just as clearly a robin wrestling a worm from a grave. He had no sense of focus. A funeral bus pulled inside the gate and the family clambered down its front steps. A coffin was slid out the rear, slipped and hit the ground with a bang. A girl in the family made a comic grimace. That was the way Arkady felt. Outside the gate, the Rodionov-Penyagin party was still milling around the sidewalk. Arkady didn't feel in decent enough shape to talk to either the prosecutor or the general, so he slipped into the church.

There was a crowd inside. All standing, no pews. The atmosphere was like a crowded, colorful train station, with incense for cigarette smoke, and instead of a loudspeaker, an unseen choir whose voices hovered in the vaulted ceiling singing about the lamb of God. Icons— Byzantine, age-darkened faces in cutouts of bright silver—tipped down from the walls. Icon candles were wicks suspended in glass cups of oil. Strategically placed on the floor were cans of oil to keep the flames alight. Votive candles came in thirty-kopeck, fifty-kopeck and one-ruble sizes. Candles burned and sputtered in pools of pearly wax; candle stands glowed like softly burning trees. Lenin had described religion as a hypnotic flame for a reason. Women in black gathered contributions on brass plates covered with red felt. To the left, a store sold postcards of miraculous relics. To the right, three women, also in black dresses and scarves, hands crossed on their breasts, lay in open coffins surrounded by candles on arms of wrought iron and wax.

In a chapel next to the coffins, a priest taught a boy how to bow by pushing down his head. Arkady found himself forced by the sheer press of bodies into the "devil's corner," where confessions were heard. A priest in a wheelchair looked up expectantly, his long beard as white as rays of the moon. Arkady felt an interloper because his disbelief was not an institutional attitude, but the fury of a son who had deliberately and in a rage left his father's camp. Yet his father had not been a believer; for all the good it had done her, it was his mother who had secretly slipped like a bird into the few churches open in

Stalin's Moscow. Kopecks dropped. Wax dripped. Collection plates circulated around the faithful as the glorious music unfolded, descant climbing over descant, appealing to the Almighty: *Hear us and watch over us.* No, Arkady thought, better to beg that He was deaf and blind. The voices pleaded, *And be merciful, be merciful, be merciful.* At least mercy was the last thing the general ever wanted.

ARKADY LOOPED AROUND the horse track to Gorky Street, stuck the blue light on the car roof, leaned on his horn and raced down the middle lane while traffic officers, like so many semaphores in slickers and batons, cleared the way ahead. The rain had started again, marching in gusts up the street, raising umbrellas on the sidewalk. He wasn't going anywhere in particular. It was the sound of water tearing under the wheels, the blur of a windshield without wipers, the gondola flow of running lights and the melting of store windows that he pursued. At the Intourist Hotel, prostitutes fluttered for cover like pigeons.

Without braking, Arkady swung into Marx Prospect. Rain turned the wide square into a lake that taxis surged through like motorboats. Move fast enough and you could move through time, he thought. Gorky Street, for example, had been given back its old title of Tverskaya, Marx Prospect was being renamed Mokhovaya and Kalinin, just ahead, was once again New Arbat. He imagined Stalin's ghost wandering the city in confusion, lost, looking into windows, frightening babes. Or worse, seeing the old names and not being confused at all.

Through the rain Arkady saw that a traffic officer had stopped a taxi in the middle of the square. Trucks blocked him on the right; to his left were oncoming cars. He hit his brake pedal and fought the squirming wheels as the faces of the officer and the taxi driver gaped in the lights. The Zhiguli skidded up to their trouser legs.

Arkady jumped out. The officer wore a plastic cover on his cap. A license was in one hand and a blue five-ruble note in the other. The taxi driver had a narrow face with eyebrows frightened to his hairline. Both looked as if they had been struck by lightning and were waiting for the thunder's clap.

The militiaman stared at the car bumper, miraculously stopped. "You almost killed us." He waved the ruble note, which was damp and limp. "Excellent, it's a bribe. A lousy five rubles. You can take me off and shoot me, you don't need to run me down. Fifteen years and I make two hundred and fifty rubles a month. You think my family can live on that? I have two bullets in me and they gave me a traffic light, as if that made up for it. Now you want to kill me over a bribe? I don't care. I no longer care."

"You're not hurt?" Arkady asked the taxi driver.

"No problem." The man snatched his license back and dove into his car.

"You, too?" Arkady asked the officer; he wanted to be sure.

"Yes, fuck, who cares? Still on duty, comrade." The officer saluted. He became braver when Arkady turned his back. "As if you never saw a little extra. The higher you go, the more you get. At the top it's a golden trough."

Arkady sat in the Zhiguli and lit a Belomor. He was soaked— soaked and likely crazy. As he put the car in gear he noticed that the officer had stopped all traffic for him.

He drove more carefully along the river. The major question was whether he should pull over to put the windshield wipers on. Was it worth getting even more wet just so he could see? Was he a good enough driver for it to make a difference?

Clouds drifted in his way as the road dipped south by the swimming pool where the Church of the Saviour used to stand, and he found himself forced to drive onto the sidewalk and stop. It was stupid. Stalin had torn down the church. How many Muscovites actually remembered the Church of the Saviour? Yet that was how they identified the pool. Once Arkady got out to put the wipers on, he lost interest in the task. The car looked like a jar draped with wet leaves on the outside and airless as a grave within. He needed a walk.

Was he in an emotional state? He supposed so. Wasn't everybody, all the time? Had anybody ever, awake or asleep, experienced a totally *non*emotional state? To his right, a swale of trees sank into steam flowing from the pool. He climbed down and then up through them using branches as handrails until he came to a real handrail of metal, cold and sweaty to the touch, and pulled himself onto an apron of concrete.

He walked around a locked and shuttered changing house until he came to the edge of the water. Vapor rose not in wisps but as white and dense as smoke off the surface of the water. This was the largest swimming pool in Moscow, a perfect factory for the fog that wrapped around him and made his eyes smart from chlorine. He knelt. The water was heated, warmer than he had expected. Although he had assumed the pool was closed, the lamps were on, sodium halos hanging in the mist. He heard the slap of water against the sides, and then not words but perhaps someone humming. He wasn't sure of the direction, but he thought he heard feet strolling around the pool's perimeter. Whoever it was hummed not so much tunelessly as idly and in snatches, in the manner of someone who believes himself or herself totally alone. Arkady guessed from the lightness of the step and voice that it was a woman, probably an attendant or a lifeguard who felt herself at home.

Fog was a great confuser. On a trawler, Arkady remembered a veteran seaman who had listened to a distant foghorn for an hour before discovering that the sound came from an open bottle ten meters away. "Chattanooga Choo Choo"—that's what she was humming. A classic. Unless no one was there, because suddenly she was silent. Waiting for her to start again, he tried to light a cigarette, but the match was dowsed instantly and the cigarette crumpled into wet paper and tobacco. How hard was it raining? He heard her from a new direction, straight ahead and higher, nearly level with the lamps. Her voice faded, paused, and he heard the flexing of a diving board. There was a flash of white dropping through the steam and the swallowed splash of a clean entry.

Arkady resisted the temptation to clap for what was, he thought, an unusual dive at every stage: finding the ladder, climbing the rungs by feel, walking out onto the high board and keeping her balance while locating the board's end with her toes, finally pushing down against the strength of the board and flying off into . . . nothing. He expected to hear her surface; he imagined she would be an expert swimmer, the sort who did laps with languid, tireless strokes. But there was no sound besides the steady drumming of rain on the pool and the irregular, barely audible rush of traffic from the embankment road.

"Hello?" Arkady called. He stood and walked along the side. "Hello?"

12

The other customers in the Dream Bar of the Kazan Railway Station carried suitcases, duffels, cardboard boxes and plastic bags, so Arkady didn't feel out of place with Jaak's radio. Julya's mother was a stocky peasant dressed in discards sent her over the years by a chic, long-legged daughter: rabbit-fur coat, denim skirt and lacy hose. She consumed sausages and beer while Arkady ordered tea. Jaak was half an hour late.

"Julya won't meet her own mother's train. She won't even send Jaak, oh, no. She sends a stranger." She studied Arkady. His jacket smelled like wet wash and sagged around the gun in his pocket. "You don't look Swedish to me."

"You've got a good eye."

"She needs my permission to go, you know. That's the only reason I'm here. But the princess is too good to come to the train herself. And now we have to wait?"

"Let me get you another sausage."

"Big spender."

They waited another thirty minutes before he took her outside to the taxi line. Clouds smothered the spire lights of the two other railway stations across Komsomol Square. Taxis slowed as they approached the line, perused the prospects and drove on.

"A trolley might be faster," Arkady said.

"Julya told me in an emergency to use this." As she waved a pack of Rothmans, a private car skidded to a stop. She hopped in the front and rolled down the window to say, "I'm warning you, I'm not going back home in any rabbit-fur coat. I may not go home at all."

Arkady returned to the Dream Bar. Still no Jaak. He was never this late.

Kazan Station was "The Gateway to the East." The information hall had walls of flipping destination cards under a brick, mosquelike dome. A bronze Lenin, striding, right hand raised, looked strangely like Gandhi. A Tadzhik girl wore a brilliant scarf over braided hair and a dull raincoat over loose, multicolored pants. Gold earrings played at her neck. All the porters were Tatars. Arkady recognized Kazan mafia in black-leather jackets making the rounds of their prostitutes, pasty-faced Russian girls in jeans. A shop in the corner dubbed music on cassettes. As an inducement it played the lambada. Arkady felt like a fool carting the radio around. He had gone to his apartment and stared at it for an hour before forcing himself to return it to its rightful owner, as if it were the only one in Moscow that could receive Radio Liberty. He would get one of his own.

On the outdoor platforms, army patrols searched for deserters. In the cab of a locomotive Arkady saw two engineers, a man and a woman. He was seated at the controls, a muscular man stripped to the waist; she wore a pullover and coveralls. Arkady couldn't see their faces but he could imagine a life on the tracks, the whole country passing by the window, eating and sleeping behind the momentum of a diesel engine.

He returned to the Dream Bar, crossing a waiting room that was so crowded and still that it could have been a madhouse or a prison. Row after row of faces were raised toward a silent, rolling image of folk dancers on a television screen. Militia prodded sleeping drunks. Whole Uzbek families bedded on huge pillowlike sacks that contained all their earthly possessions. By the bar, two Uzbek boys in knit caps played a Treasure Box. For five kopecks they manipulated a grip that controlled a robot hand within a glass case. The bottom of the case was covered with sand, and strewn on this miniature beach were prizes that could be, with luck, picked up and deposited to the winner in a sliding tray. A tube of toothpaste the size of a cigarette, a toothbrush with a single row of bristles, a razor blade, a stick of gum, a piece of soap. Each in turn slid out of the grasp of the hand. When he looked more closely, he could see that the prizes had been in the case for years. The yellow bristles, the curling wrappers, the veins in the soap were not so much treasure as trash occasionally sorted, never removed. But the boys played enthusiastically, undeterred, since the idea wasn't the getting as much as the grasping.

After an hour and a half, Arkady gave up. Jaak wasn't coming.

LENIN'S PATH COLLECTIVE FARM was north of the city on the Leningrad Highway. Women bundled in scarves against the rain held up bouquets and buckets of potatoes to cars and trucks passing by.

Where Arkady left the highway, the road turned immediately to a dirt lane that rose and fell through a village of dark cabins with painted eaves, newer houses of cinder blocks and gardens of tomato poles and sunflowers. Black-and-white cows wandered on the road and through the yards. At the end of the village the road split into two tracks. He chose the one more deeply rutted.

The country around Moscow was flat potato fields. Picking was still done bent over, by hand. Students and soldiers were ordered out for the harvest, straggling behind peasants who tirelessly filled sacks; at any time, scavengers could always glean a few potatoes from a field. But he saw no one at all, only mist, turned earth and a glow in the distance. He followed the road to a burning pile of cardboard boxes, burlap and corn husks. It was a dirty country habit to mix trash with brown coal for incineration. Not usually in the evening, though, and not in the rain. Around the fire were livestock pens, trucks and tractors, water and gas tanks, barn, garage, shed. Collectives were smaller farms where workers shared according to the time they put in. Someone should be on watch, but no one answered his horn.

Arkady got out and, before he was aware of it, stepped into water that overflowed the yard from an open pit. The sharp odor of lime overlaid ambient barnyard smells. In the pit, garbage, slops and animal bones stripped of skin floated in a stew that was pocked by rain. The fire was half again as tall as he was. It blazed in some sections and smoldered in others, individual flames blossoming around newspapers, gnawing on spoiled potatoes. A can rolled from the top of the pyre to the bottom, next to two neatly placed man's shoes. Arkady picked one up and as quickly dropped it. The shoe was hot, literally steaming.

The whole yard glowed. The tractors were ancient models with rusty harrow disks, but both trucks were new, one the truck from which Jaak had bought his radio. Tractor attachments—reapers, balers, plows—were laid out along the shed; morning glories had grown around them, twined around tines, their petals folded for the night. Nothing stirred in the pens, no piggish grunts, no nervous clacking of a goat bell.

The garage was open. There were no working switches, but the light of the fire was sufficient for Arkady to see a white four-door Moskvitch with Moscow plates squeezed between oil cans and a tire vise. The car doors were locked.

The barn was cement, with empty stalls on one side. The other side was a butchering house. A white coat hung on a wall. It took a while for Arkady to see that it was a pig on a hook. The pig was headless, upside down and speckled with flies. Below it was a pail with cheese-cloth black with crusted blood. Beside it was a long tallow paddle for stirring fat. The floor was cement, with blood grooves leading to a central drain. Against one end were butcher blocks, meat grinders and tallow pots as big as kettle drums on hooks standing before a hearth. On the blocks were perfume vials with labels that claimed both Suma-tran origin and the rejuvenating powers of rhino horn. Why an endangered species would be famous for reproductive prowess, Arkady didn't understand.

The shed's double doors stood ajar, bent where a crowbar had forced the lock. Arkady swung them wide to the light of the fire. Unpacked VCRs, CD players, personal computers, hard disks and video games were stacked to the ceiling. Running suits and safari wear hung on racks, and a Japanese copier stood on slabs of Italian marble —all in all, a scene like a customs depot, except that it was in the middle of a potato field. The Lenin's Path Collective hadn't worked as a real farm for years, he realized. On the floor was a prayer rug; on a card table were dominoes and a newspaper. The paper's headline was in Arabic script, but the masthead was half in Russian and said *Grozny Pravda.*

Arkady went outside to the fire. It was uneven, blazing through excelsior here, creeping through damp hay there. Paint rags burned in their own aura of colors. He pulled out a burning hoe shaft, poked in the flames and found nothing but charred brand names, Nike falling over Sony crashing onto Luvs, threatening to collapse over him.

As he stepped back, he noticed that the reflections of the fire betrayed a narrow track of footsteps leading between the butchering house and the shed to a meadow of tall wild grass that obscured two berms, low earthen walls serving no apparent purpose. At the end of one, cement steps went down to a steel hatch with a wheel lock that wore a bar and heavy padlock.

The second berm had a similar hatch without a bar. Arkady crouched as he entered because he felt how tight the space was. His lighter produced a weak glow, enough for him to see that he had stumbled into an army bunker. Command bunkers—capsules of buried reinforced concrete like this—had been built all around Moscow, then mothballed when the nuclear holocaust didn't arrive. Elaborate venting and radiation monitors surrounded the hatch. On a long communications desk were a dozen phones; two of them he recognized from his own service as radio-frequency phones, artifacts of the past. There was even a high-speed Iskra system, phone and code modem intact. He lifted a receiver and got an earful of static, but was astonished that the line was alive at all.

He returned to the yard. There was too much water to make out individual tire treads. He walked the periphery without finding any other tracks except to the road, and he had come that way. It struck him that since the truck and tractor tires weren't smeared with lime, the overflow was recent. There was no flooding anywhere else.

In the reflection of the fire the overflow was molten gold, though Arkady knew that in daylight it would look like watered milk. He guessed the pit was about five meters square. He sank the hoe; it was at least two meters deep. An object bobbed to the surface that resembled a cross-section of sausage; it rolled to show the circular jowls, cone ears and snout of a pig, a face made smooth and hairless by corrosive lime, then rolled and sank again. Feathers and hair lay pasted on the scum. A stench deeper and more profound than simple rot pervaded the mist.

Arkady reached into the middle of the pit with the hoe and hit metal. He hit metal and glass. As he walked back and forth along the pit he traced the outline of a car beneath the surface. By now he was breathing in shallow gasps not only because of the smell. He thought he heard Jaak inside the car; he was beating on the roof of Julya's Volvo and screaming. Not that the sound escaped the pit, but Arkady could feel it.

He pulled off his jacket and shoes and dove in. He kept his eyes closed against the lime and felt his way down the side window to the door, found a latch and pulled without success because of the pressure of the water. He broke the surface, breathed and dove again. The motion of his dive disturbed the pit and unseen things rose, poking, prodding, as if trying to nudge him from the door. The second time he came up for air, the surface was crowded with the sweetmeats of the bottom, overwhelming with the smell of death.

On the third dive, he got both legs against the car and opened the door a crack. That was enough. As water leaked in, pressure equalized, faster by the second. He held on because he wasn't going up and down again. As the door opened, water flowed in with a rush, Arkady with it. He swam blindly onto the front seat, then climbed into the back, where Jaak was starting to float.

The door shut with the suction of the water. Eyes still closed, Arkady located the inside latch, but the door wouldn't budge and he couldn't get decent purchase for his feet with Jaak bobbing every which way around him. What a tight, well-made car, Arkady thought. He rolled down the window, and as the car filled up, the door eased open and he kicked himself out, towing Jaak behind him.

He crawled over the lip of the pit and pulled the detective by the arms up onto the yard. Jaak didn't look too bad—wet, eyes wide, curly hair matted like a lamb's—but he was too cold and uncooperative, without a pulse at the wrist or neck, and his irises could have been glass. Arkady tried the breath of life, lifting Jaak's arms and then beating life into his chest until a raindrop exploded in the center of Jaak's eye and he didn't blink. Without trying, Arkady's hand found a small entry wound at the back of Jaak's skull. No exit wound. Small caliber; the slug probably just bounced around the brain.

The pig bobbed to the crowded surface of the pit. No, this head was smaller, ears shorter, followed by the surfacing X-form of outstretched limbs. Arkady realized that his problem getting out of the car had been because there were two bodies, not one, in the backseat. What a regular fishing hole, this pit! With the hoe he pulled the body close and dragged it up beside Jaak. It was an older man, not Korean or Chechen, the features slack and dirty but familiar. Killed the same way, a hole in the back of the skull that the tip of his little finger fit into. A black mourning band on the left sleeve was how Arkady recognized him. It was Penyagin.

What was the chief of Criminal Investigation doing with Jaak? Why was Penyagin at the Lenin's Path Collective Farm? If it was a payoff, since when did generals collect in person? Arkady resisted the temptation to kick him back into the pit. Instead, he peeled open Penyagin's jacket to remove the dead man's internal passport, Ministry pass and

Party card. Inside the vinyl book that held the card a list of phone numbers was pressed against the image of Lenin's damp cheek.

The car keys in Penyagin's pocket unlocked the Moskvitch in the garage. Under the dashboard shelf was a briefcase stuffed with the pasteboard-and-ribbon folders of Soviet officialdom: Ministry directives and memoranda, raw reports and "correct analyses," two oranges and a ham wrapped in a copy of the Tass news digest *For Official Use Only*.

Arkady locked the briefcase and car, wiped his prints from the car door, replaced the keys in Penyagin's pants and radioed from his own car for help. He returned to Jaak and emptied the detective's pockets of keys. Two were house keys, a third was large and looked as if it had been fashioned to open a castle door. The Volvo keys were probably still in the car. Whoever put it in the pit had probably just set the car in Drive.

He walked around Jaak. Was this worth it? His entire body stung. He found himself in front of the fire, which blazed away, cartons roaring, ignoring the rain. He remembered Rudy's words: "legal anywhere else in the world." Kim had led them on. Jaak had come close. For what? Things were no better; they were worse. A flaming carton tumbled from the top of the pyramid, a rolling cube lit inside and out. It crashed, split and sputtered on a tide of Russian shit. "Some things never change"; Rudy had said that, too.

ARKADY UPENDED A bucket and let the water flow over his head, chest and back. Waiting for his radio call to be answered, he had built a fire in the hearth of the butchering house using cardboard and coal. Now the yard was lit like a circus with a generator truck, lamps, tow truck, fire engine and two forensic wagons, and animated by the silhouettes of Ministry troops racing back and forth in combat gear. But the only person in the butchering house with Arkady was Rodionov, the city prosecutor, who kept to the shadow beside the door. As the fire in the hearth shifted, the pig on the hook took on a restless aspect. Water spread in rays from Arkady's feet, the runoff following the blood grooves of the floor.

"Kim and the Chechens are obviously working together," Rodionov said. "It seems clear to me that poor Penyagin was abducted and brought here, shot either before or after he arrived, and then the detective was murdered afterwards. You agree?"

"Oh, I understand Kim killing Jaak," Arkady said. "But why would anyone go to the bother of shooting the chief of Criminal Investigation?"

"You've answered your own question. Naturally they'd want to remove someone as dangerous as Penyagin."

"Penyagin? Dangerous?"

"Some respect, please." Rodionov glanced at the doorway.

Arkady walked to the butcher block, where a towel lay over the cast-off plain clothes that had been brought from the prosecutor's office. His shoes and jacket were beside them. As far as he was concerned, his own clothes could be burned. He started to towel off.

"Why are there Ministry troops out here? Where's the regular militia?"

Rodionov said, "Remember, we're outside Moscow. We got the men who were available."

"They certainly got here quickly, and they look like they're available to go to war. Is there something I'm not aware of?"

"No," Rodionov said.

"I'd like to add this to the Rosen investigation."

"Definitely not. The killing of Penyagin is an assault on the entire structure of justice. I'm not going to tell the Central Committee that we added General Penyagin to the investigation of a common speculator. I can't believe that this morning Penyagin and I were together at a funeral. You can't imagine the shock."

"I saw you."

"What were you doing at the cemetery?"

"Burying my father."

"Oh." Rodionov grunted as if he had expected a more imaginative excuse. "Condolences."

Through the door, the yard was so full of incandescent lamps that it looked ablaze. As the Volvo was winched from the pit, water poured in bright fountains from the doors.

"I'll fold the Rosen investigation into the Penyagin investigation." Arkady pulled on dry pants.

Rodionov sighed as if a difficult decision had been forced on him. "We want someone working full-time on Penyagin and nothing else. Someone fresh, more objective."

"Who are you placing in charge? Whoever it is will have to spend time getting briefed on Rudy."

"Not necessarily."

"You're going to bring in someone cold?"

"For your sake." Rodionov glanced around to demonstrate solidarity with Arkady. "People will say that if Renko had found Kim, Penyagin would still be alive. They'll blame you for the tragic deaths of both your detective and the general."

"We have no evidence that Penyagin was abducted. All we know is that he's here."

Rodionov was pained. "This sort of innuendo and speculation is uncalled for. See, you're too close to this case."

The shirt was a sail with sleeves. Arkady tucked it in and slipped his bare feet into the shoes. "So who are you putting in charge of the investigation?"

"A younger man, someone who can bring more vigor to this case. In fact, this person is very well versed on Rosen. There should be no problems of coordination at all."

"Who?"

"Minin."

"*My* Minin? Little Minin?"

Rodionov became firmer. "I've already talked to him. We're raising him a grade so that he'll have equal authority to you. I think we may have made a mistake by bringing you back to Moscow, by glorifying you and letting you loose on the city. You should be careful or you're going to fall further than you did before. I must tell you that not only will Minin bring more vigor to this case, he will also bring a clearer sense of direction."

"He'd kill that bucket if you told him to. Is he here now?"

"I told him not to come until you were gone. Send him a report."

"There'll be overlap between investigations."

"No."

Arkady had started to take his jacket from the butcher block. He put it down. "What are you trying to say?"

As he answered, Rodionov carefully made his way across the floor. "This is a crisis that demands forceful action. The murder of Penyagin is not just the loss of a single man, it's a blow against the body of the state. Everything we do, our office and militia, must have one overriding goal, finding and arresting the elements responsible. We will all have to make sacrifices."

"What's my sacrifice?"

The prosecutor lifted a face lined with sympathy. The Party still turned out great actors, Arkady thought.

Rodionov said, "Minin will take over the Rosen investigation, too. It will be part of this case, as you suggested. Tomorrow I want all your files and evidence on the case delivered to him—as well as a report on tonight's events, of course."

"This is my case."

"The debate is over. Your detective is dead. Minin is reassigned. You don't have a team and you don't have an investigation. You know, I think we've been demanding too much of you. You must have been in an emotional state after your father's funeral."

"Still am."

"Take a rest," Rodionov said. As he handed Arkady his jacket from the block, a pocket rang against a tile.

"My god, an antique," Rodionov said when Arkady took out the Nagant.

"An heirloom."

"Don't point that at me." The prosecutor backed away from the revolver.

"No one's pointing it at you."

"Don't threaten me."

"I'm not threatening you. I was just wondering. Penyagin and you were at the cemetery out of respect for . . ." He tapped the gun on his head to remember.

"Asoyan. Penyagin succeeded Asoyan." The prosecutor edged to- ward the door.

"Right. I never met Asoyan. Good man. I forget, just what did Asoyan die of?"

But the city prosecutor had escaped to the blinding lights of the yard.

13

On his way into town, Arkady parked behind the apartment complex by Dynamo Stadium, where a blue militia-precinct lamp on the corner announced what looked like an all-night bar. In the street, a drunk and his wife had a domestic conversation. He said something and she slapped him. He said something else and she slapped him again. He leaned into the blows as if he agreed with her point of view. Another drunk, in good clothes lightly dusted, walked in circles, as if one foot were nailed to the sidewalk.

Inside the station, the desk officer was helping to subdue a drunk who, stripped to the waist and blinded by methanol, was trying to fly, beating his tattooed arms against the wall and leading a chorus of drunks who shouted from separate tanks. Passing through, Arkady showed his ID, not bothering to open it. He might be dressed in odd sizes, but in this crowd he looked pretty good. Upstairs, where all the doors were padded in gray upholstery, a bulletin board displayed photos of Afghan vets on the force. In the Lenin room—the meeting place for political reinforcement and morale—militiamen were sacked out on long tables, towels across their faces.

Jaak's key opened a door to a room with a linoleum floor and yellow walls. Since a precinct "undercover" room was home to different detectives working different hours, the furniture was sparse and the decoration was anonymous: two desks facing each other at the window, four chairs, four hulking prewar safes made of iron plate. A car poster, a soccer poster and a scene of a world's fair were taped to the wall. A corner door was open to a pissoir, a foul nosegay to the room.

The desks shared three phones: an outside line, an intercom and a dispatch connection to Petrovka. The drawers held old sheaves of wanted faces, car descriptions and calendars that went back ten years. Around the legs of each desk chair the linoleum was scarred by cigarettes.

Arkady sat down and lit a cigarette. He realized he had always believed that one day Jaak would decamp for Estonia, be reborn as an ardent nationalist and heroically defend the fledgling republic. He had believed Jaak had the capacity to have a different life. Instead of this. The difference between him and Jaak was not so great, dead or alive.

The first phone call he made was to his own office.

He was answered on the second ring. "Minin here."

Arkady hung up.

A naïf might ask why Minin hadn't gone to the Lenin's Path Collective. Arkady knew from experience that there were two types of investigations: one that uncovered information, and the more traditional type that covered it up. The second was actually more difficult since it demanded someone to cover the crime scene and someone to control information in the office. As Arkady's superior, Rodionov had to be the man at the collective. Minin, hardworking Minin, upgraded Minin, would be entrusted with gathering all the evidence and dossiers that showed any connection between the martyred General Penyagin and Rudy Rosen.

Arkady pulled out the short list of phone numbers he had taken from Penyagin's Party book. The first he recognized as Rodionov's; the other two were Moscow numbers but were new to him. He glanced at his watch: two A.M., an hour when all good citizens ought to be home. He picked up the outside line and dialed one of the unfamiliar numbers.

"Yes?" a man's voice answered, calmly coming awake.

"I'm calling about Penyagin," Arkady said.

"What about him?"

"He's dead."

"That's terrible news." The voice stayed well spoken, soft, calmer than before. "Did they catch anyone?"

"No."

There was a pause; then the voice corrected itself. "I mean, how did he die?"

"Shot. At the farm."

"Who am I talking to?" The very polish of the voice was unusual, Russian birch painted with foreign lacquer.

"There was a complication," Arkady said.

"What complication?"

"A detective."

"Who is this?"

"Don't you want to know how he died?"

There was a pause at the other end. Arkady could almost hear an intelligence becoming fully alert. "I know who this is."

The line went dead, but not before Arkady had recognized Max Albov's voice, too. Even if they had met only for an hour, because it was recently and in Penyagin's company.

He dialed the other number, feeling like a night fisherman dropping a hook in black water to see what would bite.

"Hello!" This time it was a woman, wide awake, yelling over a background of television babble. She had a lisp. "Who is it?"

"I'm calling about Penyagin."

"Wait a second!"

While he waited, Arkady listened to what sounded like an American relating a tedious story interspersed by explosions and the popping of small arms.

"Who is this?" A man came on the line.

"Albov," Arkady said. Not that he was nearly as smooth as the journalist, but he modulated his voice a bit and there was that racket on the other end. "Penyagin's dead."

There was a pause, not a silence. With a musical segue, the American in the background moved on to a different story. The small-arms fire continued, though, with echoes that suggested a luxury of space.

"Why are you calling?"

Arkady said, "There were problems."

"The worst thing you can do is call. I'm surprised at a sophisticated man like you." The voice was strong, with the radiant humor and confidence of a successful leader. "You don't start panicking in the middle of the game."

"I'm worried."

There was the click of a well-hit ball, a burst of applause and enthusiastic shouts of *"Banzai!"* By now Arkady could picture a bar of Marlboro colors and contented golfers. He could hear the ringing of the cash register and, in softer tones, the distant chimes of slot machines. He could also see Borya Gubenko cupping the receiver, starting to be concerned.

"What's done is done," Borya said.

"What about the detective?"

"You of all people know this is not a conversation to have on the phone," Borya said.

"What next?" Arkady asked.

It was the middle of the night now. The television's American voice had a reassuring mutter. Arkady could almost feel the campfire glow of the screen, an international sameness of news that must accompany businessmen everywhere. Once Americans were going to save Russia. Then the Germans were going to save Russia. Whoever was going to save Russia now would bring their golf clubs to Borya's, Arkady thought; he had said that the Japanese were always the last to leave. "What do we do?" he asked again.

He heard the launch of another ball. Was it bouncing off one of the cutout trees standing on the factory floor? Or sailing long and true to the grass-green canvas on the far wall?

"Who is this?" Borya asked, then hung up.

Leaving Arkady with . . . nothing. First, he had not taped the conversations. Second, what if he had? He had captured no confession, nothing that couldn't be explained by sleepiness, noise, misunderstanding, a bad connection. So what if Penyagin had their phone numbers? Albov had been introduced as a friend of the militia, and the militia protected Borya Gubenko's driving range. So what if Albov and Gubenko knew each other? They were sociable members of the New Moscow, not hermits. Arkady had proof of nothing at all except that the Rosen case had taken Jaak to a collective farm, where he was killed and was found in the same car with Penyagin. And Arkady had bungled the Rosen case. He didn't have Kim, and what evidence he did have was being seized at this moment by Minin.

On the other hand, Jaak might be dead, but he was not a bad detective. Arkady looked through all the drawers and under them, and then brought out Jaak's oversized key. Each undercover detective had his own safe, a locked repository of his work. He tried the key on all four ancient safes in turn, fishing for a tumbler, until the last lock yielded and the iron door swung open to the three private shelves of Jaak's life. On the lower shelf were dead files tied in red ribbon, a basement of Jaak's professional memory. On the top shelf were personal items: loose photos of a boy and a man fishing, of the same boy and man holding a model plane, of that boy now grown into an army uniform and recognizable as Jaak posing with a happy but self-conscious woman smoothing her apron. They stood on the steps of a dacha. Light covered Jaak's eyes, shade covered his mother's. A picture of soldiers in their tent, singing, the one with the guitar Jaak. Divorce papers, eight years old, torn apart and taped back together. A snapshot of Jaak with Julya in an earlier phase of dark hair, blurred because they were plummeting on an amusement ride, also torn and taped together.

On the middle shelf was a gray criminal code book stuffed with the sloppy addenda of daily changing laws: protocol forms for investigation, search, interrogation; red directory of detectives in the Moscow region; loose Makarov slugs in copper casings. There were a surveillance photo of Rudy, a mug shot of a younger Kim, Polina's pictures of the black market and of the burned shell of Rudy's car. Also an interoffice envelope. Arkady opened it and found the German videotape he had given Jaak, along with two developed stills. So Jaak had got the pictures done.

They were individual photographs of the woman in the beer garden. On the reverse side of one, Jaak had written: "Identified by reliable source as 'Rita,' emigrated to Israel 1985."

A romantic name, Rita, short for the flower, marguerite. He guessed Julya was the source. If Rita had married a Jew and got out, Julya would remember her.

Israeli? The combination of blond hair, black sweater and gold chain struck Arkady as a classic German style, added to a full red mouth and line of the cheek that were pure Slav. Why wasn't she in the Jerusalem tape instead of the Munich one? Why had Arkady seen her in Rudy's car and intercepted a glance from her that had read him and his Zhiguli as a man and machine all too familiar? Why had he seen her mouth on the tape, "I love you"?

The second picture was identical. On its back, Jaak had written: "Identified by Soyuz clerk as Mrs. Boris Benz. German. Arrived 5-8, departed 8-8." Two days ago.

The Soyuz Hotel was not one of Moscow's best, but it was the closest to where he and Jaak had sighted her with Rudy.

The outside line rang. He picked it up.

"Who's there?" Minin demanded.

Arkady laid the receiver on the desk and softly left.

■ ■ ■

BY NOW THEY would be watching his apartment. Arkady drove to the south bank of the river, parked and walked to stay awake.

Moscow was beautiful at night. The other day when he was in the café with Polina, he had recited a poem by Akhmatova. " 'I drink to our ruined house, to the dolor of my life, to our loneliness together; and to you I raise my glass, to lying lips that have betrayed us, to dead-cold, pitiless eyes, and to the hard realities: that the world is brutal and coarse, that God in fact has not saved us.' " Polina, the romantic, had insisted that he recite it again.

Moscow was the ruined house, a cityscape that looked half-burned at night. Yet a street lamp showed an iron gate open to a court of graceful linden trees around a marble lion on a pedestal. Another light, askew, shone on a church cupola, azure, studded with gold stars. As if in Moscow anything that wasn't ugly dared display itself only at night.

His own bitterness surprised Arkady. He had been willing to tolerate a background of meanness and corruption if he could carry out his own work at a certain level of efficiency, the way a surgeon might be content with setting bones in the middle of an endless catastrophe. His own honesty had become a shell for him, a way to both deny and accept the general misrule. See the contradiction, Arkady told himself —a lie, to be precise. Still, if he had lost Rudy and Jaak, never even caught sight of Kim and probably been an evil influence on Polina, just how good was he?

What did he want? What he wanted was far away. For years he had been patient, yet for the last week he had felt that every second was like another grain of sand rolling through his fingers, ever since he had heard Irina's voice on the radio.

If he felt this way, maybe he was in the wrong city. Was it possible to escape from the ruins of his own life?

THE CENTRAL TELEGRAPH on Gorky Street was open twenty-four hours a day. At four A.M. its grand hall was populated by Indians, Vietnamese and Arabs wiring home, and by equally desperate Soviets trying to reach relatives in Paris, Tel Aviv or Brighton Beach.

The air tasted of ashes, and the odor lingered on the teeth. Writers sat with telegram blanks to compose messages at five kopecks a word, men wadding up rejected attempts, women sitting more thoughtfully over theirs. Family groups collaborated in a circle of heads, usually brown heads with bright scarves. Occasionally a guard wandered in to make sure that no one stretched out on a bench, so the drunks in the hall made every effort to keep their bones assembled in a sitting position. There was an expression: "A Russian is not drunk while there's a single blade of grass to hold on to." Maybe it was a law, Arkady wasn't sure. On the other side of a high counter, clerks maintained a quiet hostility. They held their own prolonged and whispered phone calls, turned their backs to read novels in privacy, disappeared for discreet naps. Their understandable grudge was that their shift gave them no chance to shop during working hours. Clocks above the counter showed the time: 0400 in Moscow, 1100 in Vladivostok, 2200 in New York.

Arkady stood at the counter and studied the two identical photographs, one of a Russian prostitute in Israel, the other of a well-dressed German tourist. Was either identification correct? Neither? Both? Jaak probably had the answer.

On the back of a telegram blank, he drew Rudy's car, the approximate positions of Kim, Borya Gubenko, the Chechens, Jaak and himself. On the side, to give her a name, he added Rita Benz.

On a second blank, he wrote "TransKom" and listed Leningrad Komsomol, Rudy and Boris Benz.

On a third, under "Lenin's Path Collective": Penyagin, Rudy's killer, maybe Chechens. From the blood, maybe Kim. Rodionov absolutely.

On a fourth, under "Munich": Boris Benz, Rita Benz and an "X" for whoever had asked Rudy, "Where is Red Square?"

On a fifth, under "Slot Machines": Rudy, Kim, TransKom, Benz, Borya Gubenko.

Frau Benz was the connection between the black market and Munich, and the contact between Rudy and Boris Benz. If Borya Gubenko had slots, too, was he part of TransKom? Who better to introduce Rudy to his unlikely associates at a Komsomol gym than a former football idol? And if Borya was in TransKom, then he knew Boris Benz.

Finally Arkady drew a diagram of the farm, indicating road, yard, pens, barn, shed, garage, fire, Volvo, pit. He marked it with an estimate of distances and an arrow north, then added a diagram of the barn, with a sketch of the pail and cheesecloth of gore.

He thought of the pet shop under Kim's apartment and the shelf of dragon's blood and the blood in Rudy's car. This reminded him of Polina. Public phones took only tiny two-kopeck pieces, but he found one in his pocket and dialed her home.

Her voice had the lower register of half-sleep, then was instantly awake. "Arkady?"

"Jaak is dead," he said. "Minin is taking over."

"Are you in trouble?"

"I am not your friend. You have always been suspicious of my leadership. You felt the investigation had strayed onto nonproductive paths."

"In other words?"

"Stay clear."

"You can't order me to do that."

"I'm asking you." He whispered into the phone, "Please."

"Call me," Polina said after a silence.

"When everything is straightened out."

"I'll take Rudy's fax and put it on my number. You can leave a message."

"Be careful." He hung up.

Suddenly exhaustion overwhelmed him. He stuffed the blanks into the pocket with the gun and assumed a semi-upright position at the end of a bench. As soon as his eyes closed he was half asleep. He didn't dream as much as feel that he was falling down a soft, loamy hill in the dark, rolling lazily and without a sound, following the course of gravity. At the bottom of the hill was a pond. Someone ahead dove in and ripples spread in white rings. He hit the water without a struggle, sank and then really was asleep.

TWO EYES STARED up from a face of loose, badly shaven cheeks. A hand raised a black pistol. The fingers were filthy and callused and shaky. Another dirty hand held Arkady's ID. As he came fully awake he saw a plaque of war ribbons sewn onto a stained jacket. He also saw that the man, legless, stood on a wooden truck. By its casters lay two blocks surfaced with strips of rubber tread for him to propel himself with.

The face unveiled steel teeth and a breath like gasoline fumes. A human car, Arkady thought.

The man said, "I was only looking for a bottle. I didn't know I was going to run into a fucking general. I apologize."

The pistol was the Nagant. Carefully he handed it to Arkady butt first. Arkady took the ID, too.

The man hesitated. "Spare some coins? No?" He picked up the blocks to push himself away.

Arkady checked the clock; it was five A.M. He said, "Wait."

Something had occurred to him. While the idea was fresh, he laid his gun and ID down and pulled out the sketch of the farm. On a fresh blank he drew the interior of the shed as best he could remember: door, table, stacks of VCRs and computers, racks of clothes, copier, dominoes, telltale Grozny newspaper on the table, prayer rug on the floor. Referring to the farm sketch, he added an arrow north. Now that he thought about it, the rug had been new, with no wear from knees or forehead, and it had been aligned east-west. But from Moscow, Mecca was directly south.

"Do you have a two-kopeck piece?" Arkady asked. "For a ruble?"

The beggar dug a change purse from his shirt and produced a coin. "You're going to make a businessman out of me."

"A banker."

He used the same phone he had called Polina on. For once he felt he had the advantage. Rodionov wasn't used to being confused and in the dark, but Arkady was.

14

At Veshki, on the verge of the city, the Moscow River seemed to hesitate among sedges and reeds, reluctant to leave a village where the drumming was the sound of frogs, the water reflected the morning hunt of swallows and the steam of dawn wreathed beds of lilies.

Arkady had sailed here as a boy. He and Belov would tack back and forth, disturbing the ducks, reverently trailing the swans that summered in Veshki. The sergeant would draw the boat up on the beach and he and Arkady would walk up to the village through a maze of lanes and cherry orchards to buy fresh cream and sour candies. The sun always seemed to be uphill, beyond the crows that roosted in silhouette on the belfry of the church.

Better, the village was surrounded by the lush tangle and wonderful disrepair of old forest. Tier upon tier of birches, ash, broad-leafed beeches, larches, spruces and oaks that the sun penetrated only in providential single rays that searched for mushrooms. Everything was still and moving at once: ground litter alive with the tunneling of shrews and moles, an explosion of needles and leaves when a hare left its cover, warblers and tits cleaning branches of caterpillars, woodpeckers ministering to the trunks, the cello drone of insects. Veshki was the fantasy of all Russians, the village of perfect dachas.

Nothing had changed. When he slipped into the woods he followed paths that were familiar even in the mist. The same solitary oaks, not quite so dark and grandiose. A stand of birches with pale, trembling leaves. Someone had once tried to set out a lane of pines, but vines and smaller trees had sprung up around them and hauled them down.

Everywhere ferns, ivy, the boughs of secondary growth tried to hide the way.

Fifteen meters to the left, a squirrel with tufted ears swayed on a lower branch, hanging upside down to scold an overcoat lying in the leaves. Minin lifted his face, which only annoyed the squirrel more. Arkady counted a windbreaker huddled in the bushes and a pants leg farther to Minin's left. He moved right, behind a screen of pines.

He stopped when he caught sight of the road. It was smaller and the macadam more frayed than he remembered. A jogger went by in a warm-up suit, a Gypsy with caved-in cheeks and black eyes on the woods. A woman rode by on a bicycle, chased by a terrier. When she was well past, he took the last few steps into the clear.

In one direction, the road continued for fifty meters, then veered right, approaching and then pulling away from a high gate, a black square framed by green trees. In the other direction, only ten meters away, were Rodionov and Albov. The city prosecutor looked surprised to see his investigator, though this was the appointed hour and place. Some people resented missing even a single night's sleep, Arkady thought. Rodionov walked stiffly, angrily, as if it were cold, instead of the pleasant summer day that was unfolding. Albov, however, appeared well rested, in tweed jacket and slacks, with an aura of aftershave. "I told Rodionov we wouldn't spot you," he said as a greeting. "You must have visited here quite a lot."

Rodionov said, "You were supposed to return to your office and write your account of what happened at the farm. Instead, first you disappear, and then you call and demand that we meet you in the middle of nowhere."

"Hardly nowhere," Arkady said. "Let's walk." He started to amble in the direction of the gate.

Rodionov stayed by his side. "Where is that report? Where did you go?"

The road was still deep in shadow. Albov lifted his eyes appreciatively to sunlight spilling halfway down a wall of trees. "Stalin had a number of dachas around Moscow, didn't he?" he asked.

"This was his favorite," Arkady said.

"Your father visited frequently, I'm sure."

"Stalin liked to drink and talk all night. In the morning, they would walk here. Notice that the larger trees are firs. Behind every fir was a soldier who had to stay absolutely silent and out of sight. Of course, times have changed."

From either side of the road came the sound of crashing, as if heavy-footed mice were trying to keep pace.

Rodionov was exasperated. "You didn't write a report."

He jumped back when Arkady reached into his jacket. Instead of the Nagant, however, he produced a folded sheaf of yellow pages neatly filled with handwriting.

Rodionov said, "It will have to be typed on the proper forms. That's just as well. We'll go over it together at the office."

"And then?" Arkady asked.

Rodionov was encouraged. A report, even handwritten, was a token of surrender. "We're all shaken by the death of our friend General Penyagin," he said, "and I understand how upset you must be over the murder of your detective. Nevertheless, nothing excuses your disappearance and wild accusations."

"What accusations?" Arkady kept walking. So far he had made no mention of his phone calls to Albov and Borya Gubenko. Neither had Albov.

"Your erratic behavior," Rodionov said.

"Erratic in what way?" Arkady asked.

"Your disappearance," Rodionov said. "Your unprofessional reluctance to cooperate in the Penyagin investigation simply because you will not be in charge. Your fixation on the Rosen case. The pressure of being back in Moscow was too much. For your own sake a change is in order."

"Out of Moscow?" Arkady asked.

"It's not a demotion," Rodionov said. "The fact is that there are crimes in other cities besides Moscow, real hot spots. I'm always lending investigators where they're needed. Without the Rosen case you are available."

"Where?"

"Baku."

Arkady had to laugh. "Baku is not just out of Moscow, it's out of Russia."

"They asked for my very best man. This is a chance for you to recoup some honor."

Between the three-way civil war going on between Azeris, Armenians and the army, in addition to mafia battles over the drug trade, Baku was a combination of Miami and Beirut. There was no easier place on earth for an investigator to vanish.

Twenty meters back, Minin stepped into the road to brush leaves from his overcoat, which was a signal for other men to emerge from the trees. The Gypsy jogged back to Minin's side.

To Arkady it looked as if the stroll had become a parade. "A fresh opportunity," he said.

"That's the way to look at it," Rodionov agreed.

"I think you're right; it is time for me to leave Moscow," Arkady said. "But I wasn't thinking of Baku."

"Where you go is not up to you," Rodionov said. "Or when."

They had reached the gate. Up close, it wasn't black but dark green, with a guard walk over double doors of wood backed with steel plates and guard towers on the sides. In front was a striped barrier to keep the curious away, but how could anyone resist? Arkady stepped over and ran his hands over the lacquer finish, still lovingly maintained. Through it the long sedans used to roll another fifty meters to the dacha, to the midnight dinners and the after-midnight writing of the lists of names, when men and women passed, even while they slept, from the living to the dead. Sometimes children were brought to the dacha to decorate a lawn party or present a bouquet, but always during the day, as if they were safe only in the sun.

This was the door of the dragon, Arkady thought. Even if the dragon was now dead, the gate should be charred black and the road should be scarred by claws. Bones should be hanging from the branches. The soldiers in greatcoats should at least have stayed on as statues. Instead, watching from the guard walk, was the solitary wide-angle eye of a security camera.

Rodionov hadn't noticed. "Minin will—"

"Shut up," Albov said and looked up at the lens. "Smile." He asked Arkady, "There are other cameras on the road?"

"The entire way. The monitors are in the dacha. They're actively watched and taped. It's a historical area, after all."

"Naturally. Do something about Minin," Albov said softly to Rodionov. "We don't want strong-arm tactics. Get the fool out of here."

Confused but beaming with goodwill, Rodionov waved to Minin while Albov turned to Arkady with the expression of a man who keeps honest score. "We're friends who are concerned about your well-being. We have every reason to meet you out in the open. So someone is watching a television monitor and wondering whether we're bird-watchers or amateur historians."

"I'm afraid Minin won't pass as either," Arkady said.

"Not Minin," Albov agreed.

Rodionov stepped down the road to shoo Minin off.

"Slept?" Albov asked Arkady.

"No."

"Eaten?"

"No."

"It's miserable being on the run." He sounded sincere. He also sounded in control, as if Rodionov had been allowed to chair the meeting as long as items on the agenda were followed in order. The camera at Stalin's gate had changed that. Albov held his cigarette to his mouth as he spoke. "The call was clever."

"Penyagin had your phone number."

"Then it was obvious."

"My best ideas are obvious."

Arkady had also called Borya, as Albov must know by now. The question was implicit: what other phone numbers had Penyagin written down?

When Rodionov returned, Albov lifted the report from the prosecutor's pocket. "Telegram blanks," Albov said. "He was at Central Telegraph all night."

Rodionov glanced at the camera and muttered, "We were covering train stations, known addresses, the streets."

"Moscow is a big city," Arkady said in the prosecutor's defense.

"Did you send any telegrams?" Albov asked Arkady.

"We can find out," Rodionov pointed out.

"In a day or two," Arkady agreed.

"He's threatening us," the prosecutor said.

Albov said, "With what? That's the question. If he knows anything about Penyagin, the detective or Rosen, he's legally bound to inform his superior, who is you, or the investigator of record, who is Minin. Otherwise, he'll be regarded as a raving maniac. The streets are full of raving maniacs these days, so no one's going to listen to him. He's also obligated to follow orders. If you send him to Baku, that's where he goes. He can stand under this camera all day long. It's a dead end; there aren't any floodlights, so you can pick him up tonight and tomorrow he'll wake up in Baku. Renko, let me tell you something from experience. You don't stop running until you've got something to trade. You have nothing, do you?"

"No," Arkady admitted. "But I have other plans."

"What other plans?"

"I was thinking of pursuing the Rosen investigation."

Rodionov looked down the road. "Minin is in charge of that now."

"I wouldn't be in Minin's way," Arkady said.

Albov asked, "How could you not be in Minin's way?"

"I'd be in Munich."

"Munich?" Albov cocked his head as if a new bird note had issued from the woods. "What would you look for in Munich?"

"Boris Benz," Arkady said. He didn't use the woman's name because he wasn't sure of her identification.

In the silence Rodionov stiffened, like a man who had missed a step.

Albov looked down, around and finally raised a smile of astonishment mixed with admiration. "You know, it's in the blood," he told Rodionov. "When the Germans invaded and rolled to the gates of Leningrad and Moscow, and Stalin lost millions of men and the entire Red Army fell into disorder and retreat, one tank commander never stepped back. The Germans thought they had trapped General Renko. What they didn't understand was that he was happy behind their lines, and the bloodier and more confused the action, the better. The son is exactly the same. Is he trapped? No, he's here, there. God only knows where he will turn up next."

"There's a direct flight to Munich at seven forty-five tomorrow morning," Arkady said.

"You truly believe the prosecutor's office will let you leave the country?" Albov asked.

"I'm absolutely sure," Arkady said. He was, as soon as he saw Rodionov's reaction to Boris Benz's name, an instinctive flinch that had expressed the anger and fear of a stuck pig. Until then, the name could have meant nothing, but in an instant Arkady had ascertained, as Rudy might have put it, the high market value of Boris Benz.

"Even if the Ministry wanted to, it's not up to us," Rodionov said. "Foreign investigation is the responsibility of State Security."

"You were saying at Petrovka the other day that now we're members of Interpol, we work directly with foreign colleagues. I'll only have a carry-on bag. No inspection."

"*I* couldn't go tomorrow, if I wanted to," Rodionov said. "There's arranging an external passport and Ministry orders. It would take weeks."

"There are twelve rooms at the Central Committee. All they do is make up passports and visas on the spot. Lufthansa flight eighty-four," Arkady said. "Remember, Germans are punctual."

"There *is* a way," Albov said. "If you don't travel as an investigator, as an official of the prosecutor's office, but as a private individual. If the Ministry can generate a passport and if you had the American dollars or German marks, then you could simply buy a seat on the plane and take off. In fact, we've just opened a consulate in Munich; you could make contact and receive travel expenses there. The question is only where you'd get hard currency for the ticket."

"And the answer is . . . ?" Arkady asked.

"I could lend it to you. In Munich you could pay me back."

Arkady said, "The money has to come from the prosecutor."

Albov said, "Then, that's the way it will be done."

"Why?" Rodionov protested.

"Because this is a more delicate investigation than we were first aware of," Albov said. "Foreign investors, especially Germans, are sensitive to the messy scandals of the new Soviet capitalism. We want to clear everybody's name, even the names of people we've never heard of. Because, even though the investigator may be chasing phantoms, we don't want to place obstacles in his path. Besides, we don't know everything the investigator knows or what rash steps he thinks he has to take to preserve his independence."

"He never said what he knew."

"Because he's only desperate, he's not an utter fool. He stuffed your pocket with telegrams and you didn't even notice. I support Renko. More and more, I'm impressed by his adaptability. Still, I wonder," Albov said, turning toward Arkady. "I wonder if you've considered the fact that as soon as you step onto the plane you lose your authority. In Germany you'll be a common citizen—less, a Soviet citizen. To Germans you'll be nothing but a refugee, because to them all Russians are refugees. Secondly, you will lose your credibility here. You won't be a hero to your friends anymore. No one will believe any warnings, alarms or information that you left behind, because here too you will be regarded as a refugee. And refugees lie; refugees will say anything to get out. Nothing they say is considered the truth anywhere. The one thing I can promise you is that you'll be sorry you ever went."

"I'm only going for this case," Arkady said.

"See, already you're lying." Albov's eyes rested on Arkady sympathetically. He seemed to have to force himself to remember a less interesting man. "Rodionov, you'd better get to it. You have a great deal to do to make sure your investigator doesn't miss his flight. Necessary papers, funds, whatever, in a day." Turning to Arkady again, he asked, "What about flying Aeroflot?"

"Lufthansa."

"You want an airline where the seat belts work. I completely agree," Albov said.

Rodionov backed away, excluded, stealing glances, still watching for some other signal from Albov. Far down the road, Minin and his men had reassembled into a confused, forlorn group.

"Go," Albov said.

He opened a pack of Camel Lights and lit a match for himself and Arkady. He had a fastidious manner, saving the last lick of the flame for the cellophane, which he let burn and blow away on the morning breeze. Then he returned his attention to the gate. As the sun rose, the trees on either side seemed to grow, come into focus, turn even more green, shift through stages of ornate light and shade. The light that crept around the guard walk was white, as if on fire. Simultaneously, the gate itself fell into more shadow and by contrast loomed darker, reflecting the two men.

It occurred to Arkady what Albov had meant about being paid back. "You will be in Munich?"

"Some of my best friends are in Munich," Albov said.

II

MUNICH

∎

August 13–August 18, 1991

15

Federov, the consular aide who gathered Arkady at the airport, pointed out sights as if he had personally built Munich, poured the River Isar, gilded the Peace Angel and balanced the domes on the twin church spires of the Frauenkirche.

"The consulate here is new, but I was in Bonn, so this is pretty much old hat to me," Federov said.

It wasn't to Arkady. The world seemed to be spinning around him, full of traffic and unintelligible signs. Streets were so clean that they looked plastic. Bikers in shorts and summer tans shared the road without being mangled under the wheels of every passing bus. Windows were glass instead of crusted dirt. There were no lines anywhere. Women in short skirts carried not string bags but colorful sacks emblazoned with the names of stores; in full stride, legs and sacks moved with a purposeful, integrated rhythm.

"That's all you brought?" Federov was looking at Arkady's carry-on. "You'll have two suitcases on the way back. How long are you staying?"

"I don't know."

"Your visa's only good for two weeks."

He searched for some sign from his passenger, but Arkady was looking at walls of Bavarian yellow as smooth as butter, with balconies that had no weepy stains, stucco that was not cracked on brick lines, doors that did not wear graffiti and scars of abuse. In a pastry-shop window, marzipan pigs gamboled around chocolate cakes.

One moment Federov had the cautious attitude of a young man who had been sent to take delivery of dubious goods; the next he was consumed by curiosity. "Generally when someone like you arrives there's a welcoming committee and an official program. I want to warn you there's nothing laid on for you at all."

"Good."

Pedestrians waited like troops at red lights, whether traffic was coming or not. On green, cars swarmed ahead; it was like being in a hive of BMWs. The street spread into an avenue of stone mansions with steps that were guarded by iron gates and marble lions. Signs announced art galleries and Arab banks. The next square was lined by a row of medieval banners with corporate logos. Arkady saw a man who was dressed in lederhosen and high socks despite the heat.

"I just don't understand how you got a visa so fast," Federov said.

"Friends."

Federov glanced over again because Arkady didn't look like a man who had friends. "Well, however you did it, you landed in whipped cream," he said.

The consulate was an eight-story building on Seidlstrasse. A wood-paneled waiting room had chairs of bright chrome and black leather. Behind bulletproof glass was a reception desk with three television monitors. Federov slid Arkady's passport on a tray under the glass to a receptionist who looked Russian almost to her fingertips, which were long and polished like mother-of-pearl. When she started to push a book out, Federov blocked the tray and said, "He doesn't have to sign."

He led Arkady onto the elevator and up to the third floor, down a corridor of small offices, past a conference room with boxes and chairs still wrapped in blocks of plastic packing, and showed him through a metal door with a plaque that said in German CULTURAL AFFAIRS. Inside was a man with gray hair, a good Western suit and a frown. There were only two chairs in the room and he nodded for Arkady to take the other one.

"I'm Vice-Consul Platonov. I know who you are," he told Arkady. He didn't offer to shake hands. "That's all," he said to Federov, who could have been smoke, he was gone so fast.

Platonov had the forward hunch of a chess player. He looked like a man with a problem, something nasty but not too large, something he could resolve in a day or two. Arkady doubted this was his usual office. The walls still gave off the tang of fresh paint. A wide-angle photograph of Moscow at sunset leaned against the near wall. Against the far wall were posters: dancers of the Bolshoi and Kirov, treasures of the Kremlin Armory, a cruise boat on the Volga. The only other furnishings were a folding table, a phone and an ashtray.

"What do you think of Munich?" Platonov asked.

"It's beautiful. It's very rich."

"It was rubble after the war, worse than Moscow. That says a great deal about the Germans. You speak German?"

"A little."

"But you do speak German?" Platonov seemed to think he had a confession.

"In the Army I was stationed for two years in Berlin. I was monitoring Americans, but I did pick up some German."

"German and English."

"Not well."

Platonov was in his mid-sixties, Arkady guessed. A diplomat since Brezhnev? That took a man of both rubber and steel.

"Not well?" Platonov folded his arms. "Do you know how many years it has taken us to open a Soviet consulate here? This is the industrial capital of Germany. These are the investors we need to reassure. We're not even finished moving in and we have an investigator from Moscow? Are you after someone on the consulate staff?"

"No."

"I didn't think so. Usually we're ordered back to Moscow before we get bad news," Platonov said. "I asked if you were actually KGB, but they don't even want to see you. On the other hand, they're not stopping you."

"That's decent of them."

"No, that's suspicious. The last thing anyone wants is an investigator who is out of control."

"That's been my experience, too," Arkady had to admit.

"Aside from our staff, there aren't many Soviets in Munich. Factory directors and bankers training with Germans, a dance troupe from Georgia. Who are you interested in?"

"I can't say."

Arkady supposed that representatives of the Foreign Ministry were taught a wide stock of encouraging expressions and public grins, those little gestures that signified they were still human. Platonov, however, seemed content with a direct, hostile stare that never wavered while he opened a case and took out a cigarette for himself.

"Just so we understand each other, I don't care who you're after. I don't care if there's a family lying slaughtered in its blood back in

Moscow. No murderer is as important as the success of this consulate. The German people will not give hundreds of millions of Deutsche marks to murderers. We have fifty years of bad history to make up for. We want quiet, normal relations leading to loans and commercial agreements that will rescue *all* the families in Moscow. The last thing we want is Russians chasing each other through the streets of Munich."

"I can see that." Arkady tried to be agreeable.

"You have no official standing here. If you contact the German police, they will immediately call us and we will tell them you're simply here as a tourist."

"I've always been curious about Bavaria, the land of beer."

"We'll keep your passport. That means you can't travel somewhere else or register at a hotel. We have accommodations for you at a pension. In the meantime I will be working hard to have you recalled to Moscow—tomorrow, if possible. My suggestion is that you forget about any investigation. See the museums, buy some gifts, have your beer. Enjoy yourself."

THE PENSION WAS above a Turkish travel agency half a block from the train station. The accommodations were two rooms with bed, bare mattress, bureau, chair, two tables and a cabinet that opened to reveal a miniature kitchen. The toilet and shower were down the hall.

"Turks on the third floor," Federov said and pointed up. He pointed down. "Yugoslavians on the first. They all work at BMW. You could go join them."

The lights worked. The refrigerator light went on when Arkady opened the door and there were no cockroach eggs in the corners. Even the closet had a light, and he had noticed when they came into the building that the halls smelled of disinfectant instead of piss.

"So this is paradise. It's not all quite as great as you thought, is it?" Federov asked.

"It's been a while since you were in Moscow," Arkady said. He opened the rear window. The view was of the back of the train station and the tracks, steel ribbons shining in the sun. What was odd was that he felt as disoriented as if he were in a different time zone halfway around the world, when he had made only a four-hour flight.

Federov lingered at the door. "It occurs to me that you couldn't have a more inappropriate name than 'Renko'—for a visitor to Germany, I mean. I've heard about your father. He may have been a hero at home, he was a butcher here."

"No, he was a butcher at home, too."

"All I mean is that with a name like yours, maybe it would be wiser to stay right here and not go out at all."

"Key?" Arkady put his hand out when Federov started to leave.

With a shrug, Federov gave it to him. "I wouldn't worry, Investigator. One thing a Russian doesn't have to worry about in Germany is being robbed."

ALONE, ARKADY SAT on the windowsill and had a solitary cigarette. It was a Russian custom to sit before embarking on a trip, so why not on arrival? To take formal possession of a bare, unlocked room. Especially with a filthy Russian cigarette. Down on the tracks he saw a sleek red-and-black train inching toward the station. In the locomotive an engineer wore the gray cap of a general. He remembered the train he had seen in Kazan Station, with the man in the locomotive stripped to his waist and the way the forearm of the woman with him rested on his shoulder. He wondered where they were now. Pulling cars around Moscow? Rolling across the steppe?

He returned to the bed and opened his carry-on. From the pockets of his rumpled pants he disinterred Penyagin's handwritten list of three phone numbers, Rudy's fax and the identified still of Rita Benz. From a rolled jacket he took the videotape. The clothes, which represented his complete traveling wardrobe, fit on two hangers and in one bureau drawer. He slipped the numbers, fax and photo into the videotape case with the cassette. They were his treasure and shield. Then he counted the money he had squeezed out of Rodionov. One hundred Deutsche marks. How far would that take the usual tourist in Germany? A day? A week? It would take thrift and paranoia to survive much longer.

The cassette inside his shirt, Arkady went out and ran across a boulevard to the train station, which had the mammoth scale of a modern museum on the outside. Light filtered through frosted glass and pigeon netting on the inside. No gangs of Kazans in black jackets, no somnolently flipping television screen, no Dream Bar. Instead, bookstores, restaurants, wine shops, a theater with erotic films. A kiosk sold maps with translations in French, English, Italian, none in Russian. With the English version, Arkady headed back for the street and followed a crowd out the main entrance.

The smell of a café's good coffee and chocolate almost dropped him to his knees, but he was so unused to restaurants or even to eating at all that he kept moving forward in hopes of seeing an approachable ice cream wagon. He focused not on shop windows, but on the reflections in their glass. Twice he entered stores and immediately came back out to see if anyone was waiting for him. A tourist sees the sights. Arkady, however, had a tunnel vision that excluded crowds, fountains and statues for the sake of spotting a telltale Soviet face, rolling walk or habit, like wearing the wedding band on the right hand. The sound of German around him was a babble of surf. It was like waking up to notice that he had arrived in a wide plaza surrounded by handsome buildings patterned in brick, with stepped gables that climbed to spires of red tile. On one side of the square was a town hall of gray Gothic stone. Hundreds of people strolled or rested at tables with steins of beer or stared up at the hall's carillon of life-size clockwork dancers and musicians. Arkady turned around. Businessmen wore muted suits and silk ties. Women wore a stylish, not a grieving, black. Boys sported the T-shirts, shorts and backpacks of summer vacation. The volume of their voices swelled. There was a bookstore on a corner with three floors of books. Another shop had the sweet reek of tobacco. The yeasty bouquet of beer issued from this doorway and that. A golden Madonna looked down from a marble column.

He bought ice cream in a waffle cone, pantomiming his choice rather than testing his command of German. The ice cream was so rich that it tasted like frosting. He spent four marks on cigarettes. All the same, he had engaged with Munich now. He ran down into the plaza's subway station, bought a ticket and jumped onto the first train returning the way he had come.

Hanging on to the bar on either side of Arkady were a pair of Turks, each with a faraway gaze. Filling the seat before him was a woman holding a ham that rocked back and forth on her knees like a baby.

What were the chances of anyone following him? Not great, considering the difficulty of trailing someone in an urban setting. According to Soviet technique, to carry out surveillance of a cautious mobile target demanded five to ten vehicles and thirty to a hundred people. Arkady didn't know personally because he'd never had more than enough manpower and cars to follow someone around a room.

At the station stop, he returned to the same waiting hall where he had been an hour before. Some call boxes were in the open, but upstairs he found telephone cabinets and books for different cities on a stainless-steel counter. In Moscow, phone books were so rare they were kept in safes, but these weren't even chained.

The books were confusing because of the sameness and strangeness of German names, full of consonants in death throes, and the variety of advertisements that filled more than half the pages. Under "Benz," the only Boris had an address on Königinstrasse. There was no listing for any business called TransKom.

The phone cabinet had a rounded clear-plastic door. Arkady decided he knew just enough German to talk to an operator. He thought she said she had no number for TransKom. Then he called Boris Benz.

A woman answered, *"Ja?"*

Arkady said, *"Herr Benz?"*

"Nein." She laughed.

"Herr Benz ist im Haus?"

"Nein. Herr Benz ist in Ferien."

"Ferien?" On vacation?

"Er wird zwei Wochen lang nicht in München sein."

Away for two weeks? Arkady asked, *"Wo ist Herr Benz?"*

"Spanien."

"Spanien?" Two weeks in Spain? The news was just getting worse.

"Spanien, Portugal, Marokko."

"Nein Russland?"

"Nein, er macht Ferien in der Sonne."

"Kann ich sprechen mit TransKom?"

"TransKom?" The name seemed new to her. *"Ich kenne TransKom nicht."*

"Sie ist Frau Benz?"

"Nein, die Reinmachefrau." The housecleaner.

"Danke."

"Wiedersehen."

As Arkady hung up he thought that this was about as basic as a conversation could get without drawing pictures. So he had talked to a housemaid who said Boris Benz would be away on summer vacation for the next two weeks and who had never heard of TransKom. The only real information was that Benz had gone south for the Mediterranean sun. Apparently Germans did this. By the time he returned to Munich, Arkady would probably be back in Moscow. From the cassette, he pulled Rudy's fax and dialed the transmitting number shown on the top of the page.

"Hello," a woman answered in Russian.

Arkady said, "I'm calling about Rudy."

After a pause, "Rudy who?"

"Rosen."

"I don't know any Rudy Rosen." There was something slovenly about the voice, as if she wouldn't take a cigarette from her mouth.

"He said you were interested in Red Square," Arkady said.

"We're all interested in Red Square. So what?"

"I thought you wanted to know where it was."

"What is this, a joke?"

She hung up. In fact, she did what any normal person would, given such a stupid riddle, Arkady thought. Because he had failed was no reason to blame her.

On the same floor, he found a bank of self-operated luggage lockers for two Deutsche marks a day. He made another circuit of the hall before returning, putting coins in the slot, placing the cassette in an empty locker and pocketing the key. Now he could return to the flat or go back out on the street without fear of losing the evidence, which seemed a great accomplishment considering his state of confusion. Or a pitiful achievement considering how little time he had—according to Platonov, one day.

He returned to the phone-book counter, opened the Munich book, flipped to "R" and to "Radio Liberty–Radio Free Europe." When he called the number an operator answered only, "RL-RFE."

Arkady asked in Russian to speak to Irina Asanova, then waited for what seemed forever for her to come on the line.

"Hello?"

He had thought he was prepared, but he was so startled to actually hear her that he couldn't speak.

"Hello, who is this?"

"Arkady."

He recognized her voice, but, after all, he had been listening to her broadcasts. There was no reason for her to remember his.

"Arkady who?"

"Arkady Renko. From Moscow," he added.

"You're calling from Moscow?"

"No, I'm here in Munich."

The phone was so quiet, he thought that he might have lost the connection.

"Amazing," Irina said finally.

"Could I see you?"

"I heard they'd rehabilitated you. You're still an investigator?" She sounded as if her surprise was rapidly evaporating into irritation.

"Yes."

"Why are you here?" she asked.

"A case."

"Congratulations. If they let you travel, they must have a lot of faith in you."

"I've been listening to you in Moscow."

"Then, you know I have a broadcast in two hours." Papers rustled in the background to emphasize how busy she was.

"I'd like to see you," Arkady said.

"Maybe in a week. Give me a call."

"I mean soon. I won't be here long."

"This is a bad time."

"Today," Arkady said. "Please."

"I'm sorry."

"Irina."

"Ten minutes," she said, once she had made it clear that he was the last man on earth she wanted to see.

16

A taxi took Arkady to a park where the driver pointed out a path that led him to long tables, chestnut trees and a pagoda-shaped five-story wooden pavilion. "The Chinese Tower," Irina had told him to say.

In the shade of beech trees, diners carried giant steins of beer and paper plates that sagged under roast chicken, ribs, potato salad. Even the litter the breeze blew his way smelled good enough to eat. The lapping of the conversation and the steady pace of consumption had an unanticipated, sensual languor. Munich was still unreal to him. He had the sudden apprehension not that he was walking in a dream, but that he was someone's nightmare visiting the real world.

He had feared he might not recognize Irina, but there was no mistaking her. Her eyes were a little larger, seemingly darker, and she still possessed a quality that selfishly gathered light only for her. Her brown hair was redder and cut shorter, a starker frame to her face. She wore a gold cross over a black, short-sleeved sweater. No wedding ring showed.

"You're late." She gave Arkady a handshake.

"I wanted to shave," he said. He had bought a disposable blade and used it at the train station. Cuts on his chin tracked his haste.

"We were about to leave," Irina said.

"It's been a long time," Arkady said.

"Stas and I have a newscast to get ready." She didn't appear to be excited or nervous, just pressed by a heavy schedule.

"Not quite yet." A man, all bones wrapped in a loose sweater and baggy pants, with bright, tubercular eyes, arrived with three foaming steins of beer. He was Russian, Arkady knew immediately. "I'm Stas. Do I call you Comrade Investigator?"

"Arkady is fine."

The skeleton in the sweater sat by Irina and laid his hand over the back of her chair.

"May I?" Arkady took the chair facing them and said to Irina, "You look wonderful."

"You look good, too," she said.

"I don't think anyone is thriving in Moscow," Arkady said.

Stas raised his stein and said, "Drink up. The rats are leaving the ship now. Everyone's coming for a visit. Most of them are trying to stay. In fact, most of them are trying to get work at Radio Liberty; we see them every day. Well, who can blame them?" He watched a buxom girl collecting empties. "Waited on by Valkyries. What a life."

Arkady sipped for politeness' sake. "I heard you—"

"So, Arkady, you've had rather a checkered career," Stas interrupted. "Member of Moscow's Golden Youth, member of the Communist party, rising star of the prosecutor's office, hero who saved our dear dissident, Irina, years of Siberian exile atoning for that single act of decency, and now not only the prosecutor's pet but his ambassador to Munich, able to hunt down your lost love, Irina. Here's to romance."

Irina laughed. "He's just joking."

"I understand," Arkady said.

It was funny; in interrogation he had been naked, hosed down, insulted and hit, yet he had never felt as embarrassed as he did at this table. Besides being badly shaved, his stupid face was probably beet-red, he thought, because the evidence seemed to be that he was crazy. Evidently he had been crazy for years, imagining a connection between himself and this woman, who clearly shared no similar memory at all. How much had he imagined—their time hiding in his apartment, the shootings, New York? At the psychiatric isolator, when the doctors injected sulfazine into his spine, they used to say that he was crazy; now, over beer, it turned out that they had been right. He looked at Irina for any response, but she had the equanimity of a statue.

"Don't take it personally. That's just Stas." She lit one of Stas's cigarettes without asking. "Arkady, I hope you have some fun in Munich. I'm sorry I don't have time to do anything with you."

"That is too bad." Arkady drank to that.

"But you'll have friends at the consulate and you'll be busy with your case. You always were a dedicated worker," Irina said.

"A fool for work," Arkady said.

"It must be a heavy responsibility, representing Moscow. The prosecutor sent his human face."

"It's kind of you to say so." He was Rodionov's "human face"? Was that what she thought?

Stas said, "That reminds me, we ought to do an update on the crime rate in Moscow."

"On the deteriorating situation?" Arkady asked.

"Exactly."

"You work together?" Arkady asked.

Irina said, "Stas writes the newscasts, I only read them."

"Mellifluously," Stas said. "Irina is the queen of Russian émigrés. She has broken hearts from New York to Munich and all stations in between."

"Have you?" Arkady asked Irina.

"Stas is a provocateur."

"Maybe that's what makes him a writer."

"No," Irina said. "No, that's what got him beaten at demonstrations in Red Square. He defected to the Americans in Finland, for which the Soviet prosecutor general you work for pronounced him guilty of a state crime with a sentence of death. Amusing, isn't it? An investigator from Moscow can come here, but if Stas ever went back to Moscow he'd disappear. The same with me if I went back."

Arkady agreed. "Even I feel safer here."

"What is this case of yours? Who are you after?" Stas asked.

"I can't tell you," Arkady said.

Irina said, "Stas is afraid that I'm your case. Lately we've been seeing a lot of visitors in Munich. Family members, friends from before we left."

"Left?" Arkady asked.

"Defected," Irina said. "Dear old grandmothers and former soul mates who keep telling us everything is fine and that we can go home again."

Arkady said, "Nothing is fine. Don't go back."

"It's possible that at Radio Liberty we have a better idea of what's happening in Russia than you do," Stas said.

"I hope so," Arkady said. "People outside a burning house generally have a better view than the people inside."

Irina said, "Don't worry. I've already told Stas it hardly mattered what you said."

The sigh of a tuba marked the start of a waltz. Musicians in lederhosen had appeared on the first floor of the pavilion. Otherwise, Arkady saw little besides Irina. The women at other tables were beer-fed, slim, brunette, white-blond, in slacks and skirts, and all of a German sameness and safeness. With her wide Slavic eyes and self-possession, Irina was unique, an icon at a picnic. A familiar icon. Arkady could have traced in the dark the line from the lashes of her eye over the curve of her cheek to a corner in the softness of her mouth; yet she had changed, and Stas had put a name to it. In Moscow she had been a flame in the wind, so desperately outspoken that she was a danger to anyone near. The woman Irina had become was someone colder and in control. The queen of Russian émigrés was only waiting for Stas to finish his beer so she could leave.

Arkady asked her, "You like Munich?"

"Compared to Moscow? Compared to Moscow, rolling in broken glass is nice. Compared to New York or Paris? It's pleasant, but a little quiet."

"It sounds as if you've been everywhere."

"And you, do you like Munich?" she asked.

"Compared to Moscow? Compared to Moscow, rolling in Deutsche marks is nice. Compared to Irkutsk or Vladivostok? It's warmer."

Stas set down his empty stein. Arkady had never seen anyone so thin drain beer so quickly. At once Irina rose, in command, ready to hurry back to real life.

"I want to see you again," Arkady said in spite of himself.

Irina studied him. "No, what you want is for me to say that I'm sorry if you suffered on my account. Arkady, I *am* sorry. There, I said it. I don't think we have anything else to say." With that she left.

Stas lingered. "I hope you are a son of a bitch. I hate it when lightning hits the wrong man."

Because she was tall, Irina seemed to sail between tables, her hair back like a flag.

"Where did they put you up?" Stas asked.

"Across from the train station." Arkady mentioned the address.

"Sort of a dump," Stas said, surprised.

Irina finally disappeared into a crowd arriving on the other side of the tower.

"Thanks for the beer," Arkady said.

"Anytime." Stas hurried after Irina, maneuvering around tables with a limp that seemed more a gesture of determination than a handicap.

Arkady stayed seated because he didn't trust himself to walk. He felt he had come a long way to be run over by a truck. Tables were filling all the time, and he wanted the beer garden to close in over him. Here, beer had a sedative effect leading to calm, reasoned conversation. Couples young and old enjoyed civilized steins. Men with fierce eyebrows poured their concentration onto chessboards. The tower with the oompah band was about as Chinese as a cuckoo clock. No matter; he had wandered into a village where he was not known, neither welcome nor rejected. He would settle for invisible. He sipped the good beer.

What was really terrible, truly frightening, was that he did want to see Irina again. Humiliating though the experience had been, he realized he would accept more of it to be with her, which revealed a capacity for masochism that he had never known he had. Their encounter had been so grotesque as to be comic. This woman, this memory he had carried like an extra chamber of the heart and found after so long, seemed to barely recall his name. Well, there was a disproportion of emotion that was—to use her word—amusing. Or evidence of insanity. If he was wrong about Irina, perhaps he was wrong about the history he thought they shared. Reflexively he touched his stomach and felt the groove of scar tissue through the shirt. Though what did that prove? Maybe he had punctured himself with an umbrella one day on the way to school, or been pinned by a statute of Lenin as it fell. In half his statues Lenin pointed toward the future. It was a well-known dangerous finger.

"What's so hilarious?"

"Pardon?" Arkady came out of his reverie.

"What's so hilarious?" The place across the table had been taken by a large man with a florid face and crisp white shirt. A small wool hat perched on a head as bald as a kneecap. He held a beer in one hand and protected a whole roast chicken with the other. Arkady noticed that the entire table was elbow-to-elbow with people hoisting drumsticks, ribs, pretzels, golden beers.

"You're enjoying yourself?" the man with the chicken asked.

Arkady shrugged rather than unveil a Russian accent.

The man's eyes darted to his Soviet coat. He said, "You like the beer, the food, the life? It's nice. We worked forty years to have it so."

The rest of the table paid no attention. Arkady realized he hadn't eaten anything except an ice cream. The table was so awash in food that he almost didn't need to. The band slid from Strauss to Louis Armstrong. He finished the beer. Of course there were beer bars in Moscow, but there were no steins or glasses, so patrons filled cardboard milk cartons. As Jaak would have said, "Homo Sovieticus wins again."

Not that everyone recognized the fact. When Arkady opened a map, the man across the table nodded, suspicions confirmed.

"Another East German. It's an invasion."

RETREATING, ARKADY HEADED toward the nearest buildings over the tree-line, which proved to be offices for IBM and the tower of a Hilton. The lobby of the hotel could have been an Arab tent. Each chair and divan was occupied by a man in flowing white kaffiyeh and djellaba. Many were elderly, with canes, walkers and worry beads; Arkady assumed they had come to Munich for medical attention. Dark boys in Western slacks and button-downs played tag. Their sisters and mothers were in Arab dress; married women wore ornate plastic masks showing only their chins and brows and trailed perfume through the air.

In the hotel driveway, one young Arab was photographing another beside a new red Porsche. When the boy posing sat on a fender, the car's alarm erupted with a blaring horn and blinking lights. While the boys chased around the car and beat on the hood, the doorman and porter watched with expressively blank faces.

Arkady found the route he had come by cab, following the east side of the park to the museums on Prinzregentenstrasse. Cars flashed past under street lamps. The sky, however, was already darker than a Moscow summer night, and the classical façade of the Haus der Kunst looked almost two-dimensional.

It occurred to him that the west side of the park was bordered by Königinstrasse, where Boris Benz lived. The houses were appropriately grand for a "Queen's Street," stone mansions set behind gardens of aromatic roses and gates with plaques that warned VORSICHT! BISSIGER HUND!

Benz's address was between two enormous houses done in coquettish *Jugendstil,* the German answer to art nouveau. They looked like a pair of matrons peeping over fans. Squeezed in the middle was a garage that had been renovated as medical offices. The third-floor button was for Benz. Arkady pushed the button just in case. No answer.

On either side of the door was a panel of leaded glass for viewing visitors. Inside, on a side table, was a vase of dried cornflowers and three neat stacks of mail.

There was no answer when Arkady pushed the button for the office on the second floor. When he pushed the one for the first floor, a voice answered and Arkady said, *"Das ist Herr Benz. Ich habe den Schlüssel verloren."* He hoped he'd said that he had lost his key.

The door chimed and opened. Arkady sorted quickly through the mail for the doctors, medical journals and advertisements for car care and tanning salons. The only letter for Benz was from the Bayern-Franconia Bank. Someone named Schiller had handwritten his name above the return address.

Whoever had let Arkady in wasn't altogether trusting. The ground-floor door opened and a stern face in a nurse's cap looked out and demanded, *"Wohnen Sie hier?"* Her eyes were on the mail.

"Nein, danke." He backed out the door, surprised she had let him get as far as he had.

Arkady didn't know much about social customs in the West, but it struck him as odd that a housemaid would tell an unknown caller how long her employer would be away from home. Or that she would be so patient with the caller's primitive German. Why was she cleaning the apartment if Benz was gone? He wondered about the letter. In Moscow, depositors stood in line with bankbooks. In the West, banks mailed statements, but did the envelope usually come personally signed?

He walked a couple of hundred meters up Königinstrasse, crossed to the park and strolled back on a path overhung with oaks to sit on a bench with a view of Benz's house. It was the hour when Müncheners walked their dogs. They favored small ones—pugs and dachshunds not much larger than their beers. This parade was followed by a promenade of elderly, elegantly dressed couples, some with matching canes. Arkady wouldn't have been amazed to see carriages rolling down Königinstrasse behind them.

People went in and out of the house. The doctors drove away in long, somber cars. Finally the nurse of the dour countenance emerged, gave the street a parting look that put it on its good behavior and walked toward the other direction.

At a certain point, Arkady became aware that the lamps were brighter, the path darker, the night black. It was eleven P.M. All he was sure of was that Herr Benz had not returned.

It was one A.M. before he returned to the pension. If the rooms had been searched in his absence, he couldn't tell; they simply looked as barren as before. He remembered that he should have bought food. There were so many things he forgot to do. Here he was in the lap of luxury and it was as if he craved starvation.

He sat at the window with his last cigarette. The station was still. Red and green switches lit the yard, but no trains were moving. At one corner of the station was a bus terminal. It had shut down too. Empty buses lined the street. An occasional headlight went by, racing after . . . what?

What is the thing we crave most in life? The sense that someone somewhere remembers and loves us. Even better if we love them in turn. Anything can be endured if that idea holds fast.

What could be worse than discovering how fatuous, how ignorant, that assumption can be?

So, better not to seek.

17

In the morning, Arkady was visited by Federov, who flitted around the apartment like a maid on inspection.

"The vice-consul asked me to check on you yesterday, but you weren't around. Not last night, either. Where were you?"

Arkady said, "Sightseeing, walking around the city."

"Because you have no proper introduction to Munich police, no authority and no idea of how to conduct an investigation here, Platonov is concerned that you will get into trouble and make trouble for everyone else." He looked in the bedroom. "No blankets?"

"I forgot."

"I wouldn't bother, actually, if I were you. You won't be here long enough." Federov opened the closet and pulled out bureau drawers. "Still no suitcase? You're going to take back everything you buy in your pockets?"

"I haven't actually gone shopping yet."

Federov marched back to the kitchen and opened the refrigerator. "Empty. You know, you're such a typical Soviet cripple. You're so unused to food that you can't even buy it when it's all around you. Relax, it's real. This is Chocolateland." He shot a smile back at Arkady. "Afraid of being taken for Russian? It's true they despise us so much they're actually paying our army moving expenses to leave the DDR, building barracks for us in Russia just so we'll go. All the more reason to buy while you can." He shut the refrigerator door and shivered as if he had looked into a tomb. "Renko, you could be gone any minute. You should treat this like vacation."

"Like a leper on vacation?"

"Something like that." Federov tapped and lit a cigarette for himself. Arkady didn't necessarily want a cigarette first thing in the morning, but one thing he could say for Russians at home, even interrogators, was that they shared.

"This must be a bore for you, having to check on what I have for breakfast."

"This morning I have to take the Belorussian Women's Chorus to the airport, welcome a delegation of honored state artists of the Ukraine and get them situated, attend a lunch with representatives of Mosfilm and Bavarian Film Studios and then oversee a reception for the Minsk Folkloric Dance Group."

"I apologize for any complication I've caused." He offered his hand. "Please call me Arkady."

"Artur." Federov shook hands reluctantly. "Just as long as you understand what a pain in the ass you are."

"Do you want me to check in? I could give you a call later."

"No, please. Just do what's normal. Shop. Get some souvenirs. Be back here by five."

"By five."

Federov strolled to the door. "Have a beer at the Hofbräuhaus. Have a couple."

ARKADY HAD COFFEE at a stand-up cafeteria in the train station. Federov was right: outside Russia he didn't know how to conduct an investigation. He had no Jaak or Polina. Without official authority he couldn't enlist local police. Minute by minute, he felt more a stranger than at home. The counter was banked with apples, oranges, bananas, sliced sausage and pig's knuckles, all for sale, yet he found his hand starting to swipe a sugar packet. He stopped. It *was* the hand of a Soviet cripple, he thought.

At the end of the bar was a man almost identical to him, with the same pallor and disheveled jacket, except that he was stealing both sugar and an orange. The thief gave him a conspiratorial wink. Arkady looked around. At either end of the central hall was a pair of soldiers in gray uniforms with H&K submachine guns. Antiterrorist troops. Munich had its troubles, too.

He fell in with a group of Turks walking by the cafeteria toward the subway. At the steps, he turned and joined the crowd climbing up and hurrying to the station exits. Outside, he balanced on the plaza curb, waiting with all the good Münchners for the light to change, when he suddenly took off on his own against the red, through a gap in the traffic, to an island in the middle of the street, then raced, again alone, toward people who were lined along the far curb and watching him aghast.

Arkady made a detour through an arcade and came out on the pedestrian mall of the day before. He kept moving, checking each passing telephone booth without success for a directory, until at a side-street car park he found a yellow kiosk with a phone, bench and book. A tiny woman whose coat touched her toes stood by the kiosk and looked pointedly at her watch, as if Arkady were late. The phone rang and she glided by him to take possession of the booth.

A sign on the door indicated that this was one of the few German public phones that *accepted* calls. The woman's conversation was explosive but quick, ending with a decisive slap of the receiver on the hook. She slid the door open, announced, *"Ist frei,"* and walked away.

The telephone was his hope. In Moscow, public booths were gutted or out of order. Phones, when they rang, were usually ignored. In Munich, booths were maintained like bathrooms—better than bathrooms. When the phone rang, Germans answered.

Arkady looked up the Bayern-Franconia Bank and asked to speak to Herr Schiller. He imagined he would be stirring up some clerk, but there was a certain hush on the other end that let him know his call had gone to another level.

A different operator asked, *"Mit wem spreche ich, bitte?"*

Arkady said, *"Das Sowjetische Konsulat."*

He waited again. One side of the street was a department store whose window offered woolens, horn buttons, felt hats, the paraphernalia of Bavarian identity. On the other side, people headed to and from a garage. Cars rolled up and down the ramps, BMWs and Mercedeses bumper to bumper, steel bees in a giant beehive.

An authoritative voice came on the other end of the line and asked in Russian, "This is Schiller. Can I help?"

"I hope so. Have you ever been to the consulate?" Arkady asked.

"No, I regret . . ." By the sound of it, it wasn't a bottomless regret.

"We're fairly new here, as you know."

"Yes." A dry tone.

"We have some confusion at the consulate," Arkady said.

The answer mixed caution and amusement. "How so?"

"It may just be a misunderstanding or something lost in the translation."

"Yes?"

"We were visited by a certain firm that wants to engage in a joint venture in the Soviet Union. Of course that's good; that's what the consulate is here for. What is especially promising is that the firm claims it can produce financing in hard currency."

"Deutsche marks?"

"Quite a large sum of Deutsche marks. I was hoping you could give us some assurance that these funds are, in fact, available."

A deep breath at the other end suggested the effort necessary to explain finances to small children. "The firm may have a sufficient corporate budget, private funds, a loan from a bank or other institutions. There are many combinations, but Bayern-Franconia can only give you information if it is a partner in the venture. My advice is that you should study their credentials."

"Precisely what I was getting at. They led us to believe—or we misunderstood them to say—that their firm was associated with Bayern-Franconia, and that all the funding would come from you."

A new gravity issued from the other end. "What is the name of this company?"

"TransKom Services. It's engaged in recreational and personnel services—"

"This bank has no subsidiaries involved in the Soviet Union."

Arkady said, "I was afraid not. But the bank might have committed itself to such financing?"

"Unfortunately Bayern-Franconia does not believe the economic situation in the Soviet Union is stable enough to recommend investment at this time."

"Strange. He used the name of Bayern-Franconia freely at the consulate," Arkady said.

"Which is something we take seriously at Bayern-Franconia. Just who am I talking to?"

"Artur Federov. We would like to know, today if possible, whether the bank stands behind TransKom or not."

"I can reach you at the consulate?"

Arkady paused a suitable length of time to check a schedule. "I'll be out most of the day. I have a Belorussian chorus to meet at the airport, then Ukrainian artists, lunch with Bavarian film studios, then some dancers."

"You do sound busy."

"Could you call at five?" Arkady asked. "I will keep that time clear to speak to you. The best line to reach me on is 55 56 020." He was reading the number of the phone booth.

"What was the name of the representative of TransKom?"

"Boris Benz."

There was a pause. "I'll look into it."

"The consulate appreciates your interest."

"Herr Federov, my interest is in the good name of Bayern-Franconia. I will call at five exactly."

Arkady hung up. He assumed the banker would verify the call by immediately phoning the listed number of the consulate to ask for an Artur Federov, who should be safely bearing bouquets to the airport. He hoped the banker wouldn't be inquisitive enough to ask for anyone else at the consulate.

As he stepped out of the booth, he felt something change—a foot withdraw into a doorway or a shopper suddenly transfixed by a window display. He considered slipping back into the department store until he caught sight of himself reflected in the window. Was that him? This pale apparition in a shrinking jacket? In Moscow, he could pass as one scarecrow among many; among the robust sausage-eaters of Munich, he was frighteningly unique. He could no more lose himself among shoppers and tourists in the Marienplatz than a skeleton could hide by wearing a hat.

Arkady turned to the garage and walked up a ramp under a yellow-and-black sign that said AUSGANG! A BMW roaring down the chute squealed and rocked on its shocks while he pressed himself against the wall. The driver's beefy head swiveled and shouted, *"Kein Eingang! Kein Eingang!"*

On the first level, cars cruised among parked rows and concrete pillars in search of an empty slot. Arkady counted on an exit to the opposite street, but all the signs pointed to a central elevator with steel doors and a line of Germans dressed well enough to go to heaven. He found emergency stairs to the next floor, which was a similar scene of cars reverberating to the throaty urgency of gas engines and the deliberate ticking of diesels.

Fewer cars reached the next level. Arkady saw a number of parking places and a red door at the other end of the floor. He was halfway to it when a Mercedes rose from the ramp and coasted between open slots. The car was an older model, a white chassis crazed like old ivory, with the tinny resonance of a punctured muffler. It stopped in the dark under a missing light. Arkady walked with his hand on his pocket, in the manner of a man reaching for keys. As soon as he cleared the last car, he started to trot. He should have studied German more, he thought. The sign on the red door said KEIN ZUTRITT; "No admittance," he translated, too late. The jamb had a built-in digital lock that he fumbled with for a second before giving up and looking back for the Mercedes.

Which had vanished. But was not gone, because the walls echoed with its rheumatic tremor. Alone on this level, the sound seemed to be amplified. He could hear the knock of cylinders, the chime of a loose tailpipe. The driver had moved behind the elevator, he thought, or into one of the parking docks on the side. The docks were unlit, a good place to hide.

His return route to the emergency stairs crossed one open space where there were no pillars or parked cars to protect him. There was a different way out, down the "up" car ramp, defying the KEIN EINGANG prohibitions painted on either side. He slipped between cars and was at the head of the ramp before he realized his mistake. The white Mercedes was waiting. It had backed down the ramp to watch him.

Arkady raced the car to the stairs. He didn't know what sounded worse, his lungs or the car behind him, although the driver seemed to be keeping pace at Arkady's heels more than trying to run him over. At the first side dock filled by a car, Arkady dove in. The Mercedes stopped, effectively blocking the dock, and the driver got out.

On foot the odds were different. A fire extinguisher hung on the wall of the dock. Arkady lifted it from its hook and bowled it, making the driver jump in a particularly ungainly fashion. Arkady hit him on the way down. While the man tried to rise, Arkady ripped the rubber hose from the extinguisher, wrapped it around the driver's neck and dragged him out of the dock into the light.

Even with his neck squeezed up around his chin and ears, the driver was obviously Stas. Arkady unwound the hose and Stas sagged against a wheel.

"And a good morning to you." Stas felt his neck. "Talk about living up to your reputation."

Arkady squatted beside him. "I'm sorry. You scared me."

"*I* scared *you?* My God." He swallowed in a tentative manner. "That's what they say about Dobermans." He gagged and felt his chest.

At first, Arkady was afraid Stas was having a heart attack until he produced a pack of cigarettes. "Got a light?"

Arkady held out a match.

Stas said, "Fuck it. Take one for yourself. Beat me up, steal my cigarettes."

"Thanks." Arkady accepted the offer. "Why were you following me?"

"I was watching you." Stas cleared his throat. "You told me where you were staying. I couldn't believe they'd bring their favorite investigator all the way from Moscow to put him up in a hole like that. I saw that weasel Federov leave and followed you to the station. I wouldn't have kept up with you for long in the crowd, but you stopped at the phone. When I came back with the car, you were still there."

"Why?"

"I'm curious."

"You're curious?" Arkady noticed a woman who came out of the elevator and froze, bags swaying like pendulums, at the sight of two men sitting on the floor beside a car. "Curious about what?"

Stas shifted onto a more comfortable elbow. "About a lot of things. You're supposed to be an investigator, but you look to me like a man in trouble. You know, when that shit Rodionov, your boss, was in Munich, the consulate made a big fuss about him. He even visited the radio station and gave us an interview. Then you come and the consulate wants to bury you."

"What did Rodionov say?" Arkady asked in spite of himself.

" 'Democratization of the Party . . . modernization of the militia . . . sanctity of the investigator's independence.' The usual cock in the usual vigorously moving hand. How would *you* like to do an interview?"

"No."

"You could talk about what's happening with the prosecutor general's office. Talk about anything you want."

The elevator arrived again and the woman with the bags backed in with the briskness of someone going for the authorities.

"No." Arkady offered Stas a hand up. "I'm sorry about the mistake."

Stas stayed on the floor, as if he didn't mind being a heap of bones, as if he could win an argument from any position. "It's early. You can hit people this afternoon. Come to the station with me now."

"To Radio Liberty?"

"Wouldn't you like to see the world's greatest center of anti-Soviet agitation?"

"That's Moscow. I just came from there."

Stas smiled. "Just visit. You don't have to do an interview."

"Then why would I come?"

"I thought you wanted to see Irina."

18

Now that he was in Stas's Mercedes, Arkady couldn't believe that he had ever thought it was a German's car. The passenger seat was covered by a balding rug. The backseat was hidden under a nest of newspapers. With every curve, tennis balls rolled around his feet and with every bump volcanic clouds rose from the ashtray.

In a magnetic frame on the dashboard was a photo of a black dog. "Laika," Stas said. "Named after the dog Khrushchev sent into space. I was just a kid and I thought, 'Our first achievement in outer space is starve a dog to death?' I knew right then I had to get out."

"You defected?"

"In Helsinki, and I wet my pants I was so scared. Moscow claimed I was a master spy. The English Garden is full of spies like me."

"The English Garden?"

"You've already been there," Stas said.

When they emerged on a boulevard that ran by the psuedo-Greco museum of the Haus der Kunst, Arkady began to recognize where he was. Left was Königinstrasse, the "Queen Street" that Benz lived on. Stas turned right, and then along the park. For the first time Arkady noticed a sign that said ENGLISCHER GARTEN. Stas turned onto a one-way street with the red-clay courts of a tennis club on one side and a high white wall on the other. A dark row of beeches that grew along the wall screened whatever was behind it from the street. Bikes rested against a steel barrier that ran the length of the curb.

Stas said, "When I wake up in the morning, I ask Laika, 'What's the most perverse thing I can do today?' I think today will be one of my most interesting ones."

Parking was on the diagonal in front of the courts. Stas picked up a briefcase, locked the car and led Arkady across the street and through a gate of steel slats that was monitored by cameras and mirrors. Inside was a compound of white stucco buildings, with more cameras clinging to the walls.

Like anyone who had grown up in the Soviet Union, Arkady had two contradictory images of Radio Liberty. All his life the press had described the station as a front for the American Central Intelligence Agency and its loathsome collection of Russian stooges and traitors. At the same time, everyone knew that Radio Liberty was the most reliable source of information about Russia's missing poets and nuclear accidents. Still, though Arkady had himself been accused of treason, he felt uneasy about Stas and where they were headed.

He had half-expected American marines, but the guards in the station's reception foyer were German. Stas showed his ID and gave his briefcase to a guard, who pushed it into the leaded box of an X-ray detector. Another guard motioned Arkady to a desk protected by thick, lead-reinforced glass. The desk was bigger, the chairs plusher; otherwise there was a generic sameness to American and Soviet reception areas, an international design to accommodate the traveling pacifist and the bomb-heaving terrorist.

"Passport?" the guard asked.

"I haven't got it," Arkady said.

"His hotel is still holding it," Stas volunteered. "It's that fabled German efficiency we hear so much about. This is an important visitor. The studio is waiting for him right now."

Reluctantly the guard accepted the trade of a Soviet driver's license in exchange for a visitor's pass. Stas peeled off the backing and slapped it on Arkady's chest. A glass door buzzed, and they pushed through into a corridor of cream-colored walls.

Arkady stopped before they went any farther. "Why are you doing this?"

"Yesterday, I told you I didn't like it when lightning hit the wrong man. Well, you definitely have all the marks of a singed body."

"Aren't you going to get in trouble for bringing me in?"

Stas shrugged. "You're one more Russian. The station is full of Russians."

"What if I meet an American?" Arkady asked.

"Ignore him. That's what we all do."

The hall had a thick American carpet instead of a Soviet runner. At a half-march, half-limp, Stas led him by display cases that illustrated stories Radio Liberty had reported to the Soviet Union: Berlin airlift, Cuban missile crisis, Solzhenitsyn, invasion of Afghanistan, Korean airliner, Chernobyl, Baltic crackdown. All the photographs were captioned in English. Arkady felt he was gliding through history.

If the halls were tidy and American, Stas's office had the anarchy of a Russian repair shop: desk and rolling chair, anonymous furniture wearing a shawl, wooden filing cabinet, huge audiotape splicer and armchair. This was the bottom layer. The desk was covered by a manual typewriter, word processor, telephone, water glasses and ashtrays. On the shawl were two electric fans, two stereo speakers and a second computer monitor. A portable radio and spare computer keyboard stood on the cabinet. On the tape player were reels of tape, both loose and rolled. Everywhere—on desk, windowsill, cabinet, armchair—towered unsteady, ominous stacks of newsprint. A wall telephone drooped from an accordion extender. At a glance, Arkady knew that apart from the typewriter and desk phone, not a single item worked.

He leaned over the desk to admire pictures on the wall. "Big dog." It was the same dark and hairy beast who rode in the dashboard frame. Here Laika had been captured by the lens in a car, savaging a snowman, sprawled across Stas's lap. "What breed?"

"Rottweiler and Alsatian. Usual German personality. Make yourself comfortable." He cleaned newspapers off the armchair and followed Arkady's eyes around the room. "Well, they gave us all this electronic shit with useless software. I disconnected it, but I keep it around because it makes the bosses happy."

"Where does Irina work?"

Stas closed the door. "Down the hall. The Russian section of Radio Liberty is the largest. There are also sections for the Ukrainians, Belorussians, Baltics, Armenians, Turkics. We transmit in different languages for different republics. Then there's RFE."

"RFE?"

Stas folded himself into the desk chair. "Radio Free Europe, which serves Poles, Czechs, Hungarians, Rumanians. Liberty and RFE employ hundreds of people in Munich. The voice of Liberty to our Russian audience is Irina."

He was interrupted by a scratch at the door. A woman with bristling white hair, white brows and a black velvet bow waddled in with a handful of bulletins. Her body had gone to fat, but she scrutinized

Arkady's pinched suit with the slow-rolling eyes of an aged coquette. "Cigarette?" Her voice was lower than Arkady's.

From a drawer stuffed with cartons, Stas opened a fresh pack for her. "Ludmilla, you are always welcome."

When Stas lit the cigarette for her, Ludmilla leaned forward and closed her eyes. When she opened them, they were on Arkady. "A visitor from Moscow?" she asked.

Stas said, "No, the Archbishop of Canterbury."

"The DD likes to know who comes in and out of the station."

"Then he should be honored," Stas said.

Ludmilla gave Arkady a last sweep of her eyes and went out the door, leaving a vapor trail of suspicion.

Stas rewarded himself and Arkady with cigarettes. "That was our security system. We have cameras and bulletproof glass, but they don't compare to Ludmilla. The DD is our deputy director for security." He looked at his watch. "At two steps a second, thirty centimeters a step, Ludmilla will reach his office in exactly two minutes."

"You have security problems?" Arkady asked.

"The KGB blew up the Czech section a few years ago. Some of our contributors have died from poisoning and electrocution. You could say we have anxiety problems."

"But she doesn't know who I am."

"Undoubtedly she has seen the identification you left at the desk. Ludmilla knows who you are. She knows everything and understands nothing."

"I've put you in a difficult situation, and I'm in the way of your work," Arkady said.

Stas patted the bulletins. "Because of these? This is the daily budget of wire-service reports, newspapers and special monitoring reports. I'll also talk to our correspondents in Moscow and Leningrad. From this flood of information, I will distill about a minute of truth."

"The newscast is ten minutes long."

"I make up the rest." He added quickly, "Only joking. Let's say I pad. Let's say I don't want to put Irina in the position of telling the Russian people that their country is a rotting corpse, a Lazarus beyond resurrection, and that they should lie down and not even try to get up."

"You're not joking now," Arkady said.

"No." Stas leaned back to release a long sigh of smoke; he actually wasn't much wider than a bent chimney pipe, Arkady realized. "Anyway, I've got all day to trim the budget, and who knows what news-worthy disasters will happen between now and airtime?"

"The Soviet Union is fertile ground?"

"I must be modest. I only harvest, I do not sow." Stas fell silent for a moment. "Speaking of the truth, I can well believe that the bloodi-est, most cynical Soviet investigator could fall in love with Irina, jeop-ardize family and career, even kill for her. Afterwards, as I heard it, you received a Party reprimand, but the only punishment was a short tour in Vladivostok, where you had a soft job with the fishing fleet shuffling papers in an office. Then you were brought back to Moscow to help the most reactionary forces stifle business entrepreneurs. I heard that the prosecutor's office could barely control you because you were such a well-connected Party member. So when you joined us at the beer garden yesterday, you were not the plump apparatchik that I expected. I noticed something else." He rolled his chair forward; he moved more agilely on casters. "Give me your hand."

Arkady did so and Stas spread the hand to look at scars that crossed the palm laterally. "Those aren't paper cuts," he said.

"Trawl wires. The fishing equipment is old, so the wires fray."

"Unless the Soviet Union has changed more than I knew, hauling a bloody net is hardly the usual reward for a favorite of the Party."

"I lost the trust of the Party a long time ago."

Stas studied the scars like a palm reader. It struck Arkady that he had that heightened level of concentration that came from years of being either crippled or confined to bed. "Are you after Irina?" he asked.

"My business in Munich has nothing to do with her."

"And you can't tell me what that business is?"

"No."

The phone rang. Although dust seemed to rise with the clamor, Stas equably regarded the phone as if it were waving from a distant shore. He checked his watch. "That'll be the deputy director. Ludmilla has just told him that a notorious investigator from Moscow has infiltrated the station." He studied Arkady. "It just occurred to me that you're hungry."

THE STATION CAFETERIA was on the floor below. Stas led Arkady to a table, where a German waitress in a black-and-white dirndl took their

orders for schnitzel and beer. Young, fresh-faced Americans went outside to the garden. The tables inside were occupied by an older,
largely male émigré population that lingered under a haze of cigarette
smoke.

"Won't the director look for you here?" Arkady asked.

"In our own canteen? Never. I usually eat at the Chinese Tower;
that's where Ludmilla will head first." Stas lit a cigarette, gave a pre-
paratory cough and inhaled as he swept the room with his bright gaze.
"It makes me nostalgic to see the Soviet empire. Rumanians sit at
their own table there, Czech table there, Poles there, Ukrainians over
there." He nodded to Central Asians in white short sleeves. "Turkics
there. Turkics hate Russians, of course. The problem is that these days
they go ahead and say it."

"Things have changed?"

"For three reasons. One, the Soviet Union started falling apart. As
soon as the nationalities there started going for each other's throats,
the same thing happened here. Two, the canteen stopped serving
vodka. Now you can only have wine or beer, which is thin fuel. Three,
instead of the CIA, now we're run by Congress."

"So you're not a CIA front anymore?"

"Those were the good old days. At least the CIA knew what it was
doing."

The beer came first. Arkady took small, reverent sips because it was
so different from sour, muddy Soviet beer. Stas didn't so much drink
as pour it into himself.

He set down an empty glass. "Ah, the émigré life. Just among Russians there are four groups: New York, London, Paris and Munich.
London and Paris are more intellectual. In New York there are so
many refugees you can spend your life without speaking English. But
Munich is the group that's really trapped in time; this is where you
find the most monarchists. Then there's the Third Wave."

"What's the Third Wave?"

Stas said, "The Third Wave is the most recent wave of refugees. Old
émigrés don't want anything to do with them."

Arkady took a guess. "You mean the Third Wave is Jews?"

"Right."

"This is just like home."

Not exactly like home. Though Slavic conversation filled the cafeteria, the fare was pure German, and he felt solid food being instantly
transformed into blood, bone and energy. Better fed, he looked

around with more attention. The Poles, he noticed, had suits, no ties and the expression of aristocrats temporarily short of funds. The Rumanians chose a round table, the better to conspire. Americans sat alone and wrote postcards like dutiful tourists.

"You really had Prosecutor Rodionov here as a guest?"

"As an example of New Thinking, of political moderation, of the improved climate for foreign investment," Stas said.

"You *personally* had Rodionov here?"

"I personally wouldn't touch him with rubber gloves."

"Then, who did?"

"The station president is a great believer in New Thinking. He also believes in Henry Kissinger, Pepsi-Cola and Pizza Hut. These allusions are lost on you. That's because you've never worked at Radio Liberty."

A waitress brought Stas another beer. With her blue eyes and short skirt, she looked like a large, overworked girl. Arkady wondered what she made of her clientele of sunny Americans and contentious Slavs.

A large Georgian broadcaster with the curls and beak of an actor joined the table. His name was Rikki. He nodded abstractedly through an introduction to Arkady, then launched immediately into a tale of woe.

"My mother is visiting. She never forgave me for defecting. Gorbachev is a lovely man, she says; he would never gas demonstrators in Tbilisi. She has a little letter of remorse for me to sign so I can go home with her. She's so gaga she'd take me right to jail. She's having her lungs looked at while she's here. They should look at her brains. You know who else is coming? My daughter. She's eighteen. I've never seen her. She arrives today. My mother and my daughter. I love my daughter—that is, I think I love my daughter, because I've never met her. We talked on the phone last night." Rikki lit one cigarette from another. "I have pictures of her, of course, but I asked her to describe herself so I would recognize her at the airport. Growing children change all the time. Apparently, I am going to the airport to pick up a girl who looks like Madonna. When I started to describe myself, she said, 'Describe your car.' "

"This is when we miss the vodka," Stas said.

Rikki fell into a trough of silence.

Arkady asked, "Tell me, when you broadcast to Georgia, do you often think of your mother and your daughter?"

Rikki said, "Of course. Who do you think invited them here? I'm just surprised they came. And I'm surprised who they're turning out to be."

"Having a loved one come sounds like a combination of reincarnation and hell," Arkady said.

"Like that, yes." Rikki lifted his eyes to the clock on the wall. "I have to go. Stas, cover for me, please. Write something, whatever you want. You're a lovely man." He heaved himself up and plodded tragically toward the door.

" 'A lovely man,' " Stas muttered. "He'll go back. Half the people here will go back to Tbilisi, Moscow, Leningrad. What's crazy is that we, of all people, know better. We're the ones who tell the truth. But we're Russian, so we like lies, too. Right now we're in a state of special confusion. We had a head of the Russian section, very competent, highly intelligent. He was a defector like me. About ten months ago he went back to Moscow. Not just to visit; he redefected. A month later, he's a spokesman for Moscow appearing on American television, saying how democracy is alive and well, the Party is a friend of the market economy, the KGB is a guarantor of social stability. He's good; he should be, he learned here. He makes such a believable case that people at the station wonder: are we performing a real service or are we fossils of the cold war? Why don't we all march home to Moscow?"

"Do you believe him?" Arkady asked.

"No. All I have to do is look at someone like you and ask, 'Why is this man running?' "

Arkady left the question in the air. He said, "I thought I was going to see Irina."

STAS POINTED TO the lit red lamp above the door and ushered Arkady into a control booth. An engineer with a headset sat at the faint illumination of his console; otherwise, the booth was silent and dark. Arkady sat in back, below the turning reels of a tape recorder. Needles danced on volume meters.

On the other side of soundproof glass, Irina was at a padded hexagonal table with a central microphone and overhead light. Across from her sat a man in an intellectual's black sweater. Saliva sprayed like stoker's sweat when he talked. He joked, laughing at his own humor. Arkady wondered what he was saying.

Irina's head was slightly to one side, the pose of a good listener. Her eyes, in shadow, showed as deep-set reflections. Her lips, slightly open, held the promise of a smile, if not the smile itself. It was not a flattering light. The man's forehead bunched in muscles, his brows two hedgerows over the pits of his eyes. But the light flowed over Irina's even features and outlined in gold the corona of her cheek, her loose strands of hair, her arm. Arkady remembered the blue line that used to be under her right eye, a result of interrogation; the mark was faint now and she seemed flawless. An ashtray and a glass of water stood in front of her and the subject of her interview. She said a few words and the effect was like blowing on coals. At once the man became even more animated, waving his hand like an ax.

Stas leaned across the console and turned on the sound.

"That's my point exactly!" the man in the sweater burst out. "Intelligence agencies are always drawing psychological profiles of national leaders. It's even more necessary to understand the psychology of the peoples themselves. This has always been the province of psychology."

"Could you give us an example?" Irina asked.

"Easily! The father of Russian psychology was Pavlov. He's best known to the world for his experiments with associative reflexes, particularly his work with dogs, accustoming them to associate their dinner with the ringing of a bell, so that after a time they began to salivate just at the sound of the bell."

"What do dogs have to do with national psychology?"

"Just this. Pavlov reported that there were some individual dogs that he could not train to salivate at the sound of the bell; in fact, he could not train them at all. He called them atavistic, throwbacks to their wolf ancestors. They were useless in the laboratory."

"You're still talking about dogs."

"Wait. Then Pavlov expanded. He called that atavistic trait a 'reflex of freedom.' He said that this same reflex of freedom existed in human populations the same as in dogs, but to different degrees. In Western societies the reflex of freedom was pronounced. In Russian society, however, he said there was a dominant 'reflex of obedience.' This was not a moral judgment, only a scientific observation. And since the October Revolution and seventy years of communism, you can imagine how complete that reflex of obedience has become. So I'm simply saying that our expectations of any genuine democracy should be realistic."

"Define *realistic*," Irina said.

"Low." He exuded the satisfaction of a man describing the death of a reprobate.

The engineer broke in from the booth. "Irina, we get feedback when the professor gets close to the microphone. I'm going to play the tape back. Take a break."

Arkady expected to hear the conversation over again, but the engineer listened on his headset as sound continued to feed into the booth from the studio.

Irina opened a bag for a cigarette and the professor almost jumped the table to light it. As she shifted, her hair swayed, revealing the glint of an earring. The blue cashmere top was more elegant than Arkady would have thought she would wear in a radio station. When she thanked her guest with her eyes, he seemed content to squirm in them forever.

"That's a little harsh, don't you think? Comparing Russians with dogs?" she asked.

The professor folded his arms, still wrapped in self-satisfaction. "No. Think about it logically. Those individuals who wouldn't obey were all killed or left long ago."

Arkady saw contempt in her eyes, like the dilation of a flame. Or perhaps he was mistaken, because she responded with more amiable small talk. "I know what you mean," she said. "There's a different type leaving Moscow now."

"Precisely! The people who are coming today are the families who were left behind. They're stragglers, not leaders. This is not a moral judgment, merely an analysis of characteristics."

Irina said, "Not only families."

"No, no. Former colleagues I haven't seen for twenty years are popping up everywhere."

"Friends."

"Friends?" It was a category he hadn't considered.

Smoke had collected at the light and turned it into a nimbus around Irina. It was her contrast that was arresting. A mask with full mouth and eyes, dark hair cut severely but gently touching her shoulders. She glowed like ice.

Irina said, "It can be embarrassing. They're decent people and it's so important to them to see you."

The professor hunched forward, eager to commiserate. "You're the only one they know."

Irina said, "You don't want to hurt them, but their expectations are fantasies."

"They've lived in a state of unreality."

"They've thought about you every day, but the fact is that too much time has gone by. You haven't thought of them for years," Irina said.

"You've lived a different life, in a different world."

"They want to pick up where you left off," Irina said.

"They'd smother you."

"They mean well."

"They'd take over your life."

"And who knows anymore where you left off?" Irina said. "Whatever it was is dead."

"You have to be friendly but stern."

"It's like seeing a ghost."

"Threatening?"

"More pathetic than threatening," Irina said. "You just have to wonder, after all this time, why do they come?"

"If they listen to you on the radio, I can just imagine the fantasies."

"You don't want to be cruel."

"You're not," the professor assured her.

"It just seems . . . it seems to me that they actually would be happier if they stayed in Moscow with their dreams."

"Irina?" the sound engineer said. "Let's retape the last two minutes. Please remind the professor not to get close to the microphone."

The professor blinked, trying to look into the booth. "Understood," he said.

Irina twisted her cigarette into the ashtray. She took a drink of water, long fingers around the silvery glass. Red lips, white teeth. Cigarette bright as a broken bone. The interview started again at Pavlov.

Shamefaced, Arkady sank as far into his chair and as deep into shadow as he could go. If shadow were water he would have drowned happily.

19

The phone in the booth rang exactly at five.

"Federov here," Arkady said.

"This is Schiller at the Bayern-Franconia Bank. We spoke this morning. You had some questions about a firm called TransKom Services."

"Thank you for calling back."

"There is no TransKom in Munich. No local bank knows it. I spoke to several state offices and no TransKom is registered in Bavaria for workers' insurance."

"It sounds like you've been thorough," Arkady said.

"I think I've done all your work for you."

"What about Boris Benz?"

"Herr Federov, this is a free country. It is difficult to investigate a private citizen."

"Is he an employee of Bayern-Franconia?"

"No."

"Does he have a bank account with you?"

"No, but even if he did, there are safeguards of depositor confidentiality."

"Does he have a police record?" Arkady asked.

"I've told you everything I can."

"Someone who misrepresents an association with a bank has probably done so more than once. He could be a professional criminal."

"There are professional criminals even in Germany. I have no idea whether Benz is one. You told me yourself that you might have misunderstood what he said."

"But now the name of the Bayern-Franconia Bank is in the consulate reports," Arkady said.

"Remove it."

"It's not that simple. With such a major contract, there's sure to be an investigation."

"That sounds like your problem."

"Apparently Benz showed documents from Bayern-Franconia describing the bank's financial commitment. He took the papers with him, but Moscow will want to know why the bank is pulling out now."

The voice on the other end spoke as distinctly as possible. "There was no commitment."

"Moscow will wonder why Bayern-Franconia isn't more interested in Benz. If the bank is being unfairly implicated by a criminal, why isn't it more cooperative about finding him?" Arkady asked.

"We've cooperated with everything." Schiller sounded convincing, except there was that letter from him to Benz.

"Then, you don't mind if we send a man over to see you?"

"Send him. Please. Just so we can get this over with."

"His name is Renko."

THE THIRD FLOOR of the Soviet consulate was filled with women in such intricately embroidered blouses and full, brightly striped skirts that they looked like Easter eggs rolled pell-mell into the hall. Since each held a bouquet of roses, negotiating the corridor involved force and apologies.

Federov's desk stood among pails of water. He looked up from a stack of visas with a snarl that announced he had already fulfilled his day's quota of diplomacy. "What the devil are you doing here?"

"Nice," Arkady said. The office was small and windowless, the furniture modern and slightly miniature. Perhaps the occupant faced a subtle, nightmarish sense of growing larger every time he went to work. And getting wetter. A damp spot on the carpet showed where one pail had been kicked over. Arkady noted the dampness of Federov's pants and sleeves, pink petals on Federov's lapel and the way Federov's tie had become not looser but tighter and twisted to one side. "Like a florist shop."

"If we want to talk to you, we'll visit you. Don't come here."

Besides the passports, the desktop held sheets of consulate stationery, a pen-and-pencil set and a brace of phones, all new and shiny as a start-up kit.

"I want my passport," Arkady said.

"Renko, you're wasting your time. First of all, Platonov has your passport, not me. Second, the vice-consul is going to keep it until you get on the plane for Moscow, which will be tomorrow if all goes well."

"Maybe I could make myself useful. It looks like you have your hands full." Arkady nodded toward the hall.

"The Minsk Folkloric Chorus? We asked for ten, they sent thirty. They're going to have to sleep stacked like blini. I'll try to help them, but if they insist on tripling their visas they're going to have to suffer."

"That's what a consulate is for," Arkady said. "Maybe I can help."

Federov took a deep breath. "No. I think you're about the last person I would choose as my assistant."

"Maybe we could get together tomorrow, have lunch or tea, even dinner?"

"I'm on the run tomorrow. Delegation of Ukrainian Catholics in the morning, lunch with the folkloric chorus, catch up with the Catholics at the Frauenkirche in the afternoon, and an evening revival of Bertold Brecht. Full up. Anyway, you'll probably be flying home by then. Now, if you don't mind, I'm really busy. If you want to do me a favor, don't come back."

"Could I at least make a call?"

"No."

Arkady reached for the phone. "The circuits to Moscow are always busy. Maybe I could get through from here."

"No."

Arkady picked up the receiver. "It'll be quick."

"No."

As Federov grabbed the receiver, Arkady let go and the consular attaché stumbled backward, tipping over another pail of water. Arkady tried from the wrong side of the desk to catch him; instead, he swept all the passports from the desktop. Red booklets landed on the carpet, in puddles, in pails.

"You idiot!" Federov said. He scrambled around the pails to pick up passports before they sank. Arkady used handfuls of stationery to soak water from the carpet.

"That's useless," Federov said.

"I'm trying to help."

Federov blotted passports on his shirt. "Don't help me. Just go." A thought occurred to him as palpably as the squeal of a brake. "Wait!" Eyes on Arkady, he gathered all the passports onto his desk. Breathing hard, he counted them out carefully not once but twice and checked to be positive that the contents were, even if damp, still intact. "Okay. You can go."

"I'm very sorry," Arkady said.

"Just leave."

"On the way out, should I warn people below about the water?"

"No. Don't talk to anyone."

Arkady regarded the overturned pails, the floodplain of the carpet. "It's a shame, such a new office."

"Yes. Good-bye, Renko."

The door opened and a woman crowned by a felt hat draped with pearls peeped in. "Dear Artur Arturovich, what are you doing? When do we eat?"

"In a second," Federov said.

"We haven't eaten since Minsk," she said.

She took a brave position inside the door and other folkloric singers followed. As they flowed into the room, Arkady went in the opposite direction, squeezing past skirts and ribbons, dodging thorns.

IN A POLISH secondhand shop west of the train station, Arkady found a manual typewriter with spindly type bars, shabby plastic case and Cyrillic characters. He turned it over. On the base was a stenciled military number.

"Red Army," the shop owner said. "They're getting out of East Germany and what the bastards don't want to take, they sell. They'd sell the tanks if they could."

"May I try it?"

"Go ahead." The shop owner was already moving to greet a better dressed, more likely customer.

From his jacket Arkady took folded stationery and rolled a page into the machine. The paper was from Federov's desk. At the top was the embossed letterhead of the Soviet consulate, complete with hammer and sickle set in golden sheaves of grain. Arkady had considered trying to write in German, but he didn't trust his grasp of barbed

Gothic letters. Besides, for a certain roundness of style, only Russian would do.

He wrote:

Dear Herr Schiller,

This note is to introduce A. K. Renko, a senior investigator from the Moscow prosecutor's office. Renko has been assigned to inquire into questions concerning a proposed joint venture between certain Soviet entities and the German firm "TransKom Services," in particular the statements of its representative, Herr Boris Benz. Since the activities of TransKom and Benz may reflect badly on both the Soviet government and the Bayern-Franconia Bank, I hope we share a mutual interest in resolving this matter as rapidly and quietly as possible.

With every good wish,
A. A. Federov.

The close sounded grandly Federovian to Arkady. He pulled the sheet out and signed it with a flourish.

"So it works?" the shop owner called.

"Amazing, isn't it?" Arkady said.

"I can give you a good price. An excellent price."

Arkady shook his head. The truth was, he couldn't afford anything. "Do you have many buyers for a Russian typewriter?"

The owner had to laugh.

THE LIGHTS WERE still out in the Benz flat. At nine P.M. Arkady gave up. With a little planning, half his route back lay through parks: Englischer Garten, Finanzgarten, Hofgarten, Botanischer Garten. He wondered if this was the solace of rabbits—the whispered tread of paths, the soft arms of trees, the balm of shadows. From time to time, he stopped in the dark to listen. A student would wander by, nose in a book, hurrying to the light of the next lamp. Or a jogger at a serious, slow-motion pace. He heard no footsteps that abruptly stopped. It was as if when he had left Moscow he had stepped off the edge of the world. He had disappeared. He was in free-fall. Who needed to follow?

He emerged from the botanical garden a block from the train station. He was crossing the street to check the videotape in the station locker when he saw pedestrians scatter from a car making an illegal U-turn. The civil outcry was so great that he didn't see the car itself. He stayed on the boulevard's central island and hurried past the station and along the switching yard. It was not an example of good survival planning to be surrounded by a wide boulevard with fast-moving traffic. The approaching street was Seidlstrasse, with his room and, farther on, the Soviet consulate. As tires slowed behind him he turned to face a familiar, disheveled Mercedes. At the wheel was Stas.

"I thought you wanted to see Irina."

Arkady said, "I saw her."

"You took off before she even finished her interview. You were in the booth one second and the next second you were gone."

"I heard enough," Arkady said.

Stas ignored the HALTEN VERBOTEN signs, blithely waving on the cars backed up behind him in the fast lane. "I came looking for you because I thought something was wrong."

"At this hour?"

"I had work to do. I came when I could. How would you like to go to a party?"

"Now?"

"When else?"

"It's almost ten. Why would I want to go to a party?"

Drivers behind Stas shouted, honked and flashed their lights in a chorus wasted on him. "Irina will be there," he said. "You haven't actually talked to her yet."

"But I got her message. I got it twice in one day."

"You think she doesn't want to see you."

"Something like that."

"For a man from Moscow, you're very sensitive. Look, in a second we're going to be eaten alive by angry Porsches. Get in the car. We'll just drop in at the party."

"For another round of humiliation?"

"Have you got something better to do?"

THE PARTY WAS up four flights in an apartment full of what Stas called "Retro Nazi." The walls were checkered red-white-and-black with

Nazi flags. On the shelves were helmets, Iron Crosses, gas masks in and out of canisters, various-sized ammunition, photographs of Hitler, his dental mold, a picture of Hitler's niece wearing an evening gown and the wry smile of a woman who knows this is coming to no good end. The theme of the party was the first anniversary of the demolition of the Berlin Wall. Bits of the Wall—gray concrete with aggregate —were tied up with black crepe like birthday presents. People crowded the stairs, chairs and sofas, a mix of nationalities with enough Russians smoking enough cigarettes to make the eyes smart. Out of the haze, Ludmilla loomed like a long-lashed jellyfish, blinked at Arkady and disappeared.

Stas warned, "When you see Ludmilla, the deputy director is not far behind."

At the drinks table Rikki was pouring Coke for a girl in a mohair sweater. "Since I picked her up at the airport, my daughter and I have been doing nothing but shopping. Thank God the stores close at six-thirty."

She was about eighteen, wearing lipstick as red as an alarm sign, and had blond hair with dark roots. "In America, malls are open all night long," she said in English.

"Your English is good," Arkady said.

She said, "In Georgia no one speaks Russian."

"They're still Communists; they just play a new flute," Rikki said.

Arkady asked, "Was it an emotional moment for you, seeing your father after all this time?"

"I almost didn't recognize his car." She hugged Rikki. "Aren't there American bases around here? Don't they have malls?" Her eyes lit at the approach of a young, athletic American in a button-down shirt, bow tie and red suspenders, who included Arkady and Stas in an incriminating gaze. Ludmilla hovered at his back.

"This must be the surprise guest we had at the station today," he said. He gave Arkady a firm, democratic handshake. "I'm Michael Healey, the deputy director in charge of security. You know, your boss, Prosecutor Rodionov, visited the station. We gave him the red carpet."

"Michael is also the deputy director in charge of carpets," Stas said.

"That reminds me, Stas, isn't there a security directive that says official Soviet guests have to be cleared in advance?"

Stas laughed. "Station security is so thoroughly compromised that one more spy could hardly make a difference. Isn't tonight the perfect example of that?"

Michael said, "I love your sense of humor, Stas. Renko, if you want to visit the station again, just be sure to give me a call." He wandered off in search of white wine.

Stas and Arkady had scotch. "What's so special about tonight?" Arkady asked.

"Besides the first anniversary of the tearing down of the Wall? Rumor has it that tonight we will be joined by the former head of the Russian section. My former friend. Even the Americans loved him."

"This is the one who redefected to Moscow?"

"The same."

"Where's Irina?"

"You'll see."

"Ta-da!" The host of the party entered from the kitchen bearing a cake iced in black chocolate, with a candy Berlin Wall surrounded by burning red candles. He set the cake down. "Happy birthday, end of the Wall!"

"Tommy, you've outdone yourself this time," Stas said.

"I'm a sentimental fool." Tommy was the sort of fat man who had to keep tucking in his shirt. "Did I show you my Wall memorabilia?"

"The candles," Stas reminded him.

But the first note of the birthday song was interrupted by a commotion on the stairs, a wave of excitement that spread through the apartment, and a general movement to greet new arrivals. The first in the door was the professor that Irina had interviewed at the station. He unwrapped a scarf that looked like a hair shirt and kept the door wide for Irina, who seemed to float in on a bubble. Arkady could tell that she'd had good food and good wine at a good restaurant. Champagne and something better than borscht. She had probably gone straight from the station, which explained how overdressed she had seemed there. If her eyes noticed Arkady, they registered no interest or surprise. Following her was Max Albov, loose on his shoulders the same elegant jacket he had worn when Arkady had first met him at Petrovka. The three of them were laughing at a joke that had carried them up the stairs.

"Something Max said," Irina explained.

Everyone leaned toward them, wanting to share.

Max shrugged modestly. "All I said was, 'I feel like the Prodigal Son.'"

Immediately came protests of "No," explosive laughs, appreciative applause. Max's cheeks glowed from the exertion of the climb and the warmth of the reception. He put Irina's arm through his.

Someone remembered. "The cake!"

The birthday candles had burned themselves out. The candy Wall sank into a pool of wax.

20

The cake tasted like ashes and tar. The party, however, took on fresh life and became an event with Max Albov settled onto a sofa with Irina at the center. They reigned together, beautiful queen and cosmopolitan king.

"When I was here, people said I was CIA. When I went to Moscow, people said I was KGB. For some minds those are the only conceivable answers."

Tommy said, "Maybe you're an American television star now, but you're still the best damn head of the Russian section we ever had."

"Thanks." Max accepted a whiskey as a small token of esteem. "But those days are gone. I'd done what I could accomplish here. The cold war was over. Not only over, it was passé. It was time to stop being a cheerleader for Americans, friends though they might be. I felt that if I really wanted to help Russia now, it was time to go home."

"How did they treat you in Moscow?" Rikki asked.

"They wanted my autograph. Seriously, Rikki, you're a radio star in Russia."

"Georgia," Rikki corrected him.

"Georgia," Max conceded. He told Irina, "You're the most famous radio voice in Russia." He slipped into Russian. "What you're really asking is whether the KGB put the screws to me, whether I spilled any secrets that could have harmed the station or any of you. The answer is no. That time is past. I haven't seen the KGB or even met anyone from the KGB. Frankly, people in Moscow don't worry about us; they're too busy trying to survive, and they need help. That's why I went."

Stas said, "Some of us have death sentences waiting for us."

"Those old sentences are being taken off the books by the hundreds. Go to the consulate and ask." Max switched to English for the larger audience. "There's probably nothing worse waiting for Stas in Moscow than a bad meal. Or in his case, bad beer."

Arkady thought that Irina would be repelled by Max's touch, but she wasn't. With the exception of Rikki and Stas, they were all—Russians, Americans and Poles—if not persuaded, at least charmed. Had he suffered from his trip back into the Inferno? Obviously not. No singed hair. Instead, the healthy glow of a celebrity.

"In Moscow what exactly did you do to help the hungry Russian people?" Arkady asked.

"Comrade Investigator," Max acknowledged him.

"You don't have to call me comrade. I haven't been a member of the Party for years."

"More recently than I have been, though," Max said pointedly. "More recently than any of us in Munich has been. Anyway, *former* comrade, I'm glad you asked. Two things, in diminishing importance. One, creating joint ventures. Two, finding the hungriest, most desperate man in Moscow and arranging a loan so he could come here. You'd think that man would be more grateful. By the way, how is your investigation coming?"

"Slowly."

"Don't worry, you'll be home soon enough."

Arkady didn't mind so much being skewered like an insect on a pin as seeing his image in Irina's eyes. Look at this mosquito, this apparatchik, this ape at a civilized party! She listened to Max as if she had no independent memory of Arkady at all. She turned to Albov. "Max, could you give me a light?"

"Of course. You're smoking again?"

Arkady retreated from the circle of admirers and found himself back at the bar. Stas had followed. He lit a cigarette of his own and inhaled so deeply that his eyes seemed to glow. "You saw Max in Moscow?" he asked Arkady.

"He was introduced to me as a journalist."

"Max was an excellent journalist, but he can be what he wants to be, wherever he wants to be. Max is the next step in evolution: post–cold war Man. The Americans wanted someone who was knowledgeable about Soviet affairs. Actually, they wanted a Russian who sounded like an American, which is what he is. Why was Max interested in you?"

"I don't know." Arkady found vodka hiding behind bourbon.

Why do people drink? A Latin to be amorous, an Englishman to unbend. Russians were more direct, Arkady thought; they drank to be drunk, which was what he wanted to be now.

Ludmilla was already there. She emerged from the haze, all eyes and a velvet bow, and stole his glass away. "Everyone blames Stalin," she said.

"That does sound unfair." Arkady searched around the bottles and ice bucket for another glass.

"Everyone is paranoid," she said.

"Including me." There were no glasses anywhere.

Ludmilla lowered her voice, which was already a conspiratorial croak. "Did you know that Lenin lived in Munich under the name 'Meyer'?"

"No."

"You knew that it was a Jew that shot the czar?"

"No."

"All the bad things, the purge and the famine, were done by the Jews around Stalin to destroy the Russian people. He was the pawn of the Jews, their scapegoat. It was when he started to move against Jewish doctors that he died."

Stas asked Ludmilla, "Did you know that the Kremlin has exactly as many bathrooms as the Temple of Jerusalem? Think about it."

Ludmilla backed away.

Stas filled a glass for Arkady. "I wonder if she'll report that to Michael." He cast a consumptive's sardonic gaze around the room, not sparing anyone. "A mixed bag."

The party blossomed into arguments. Arkady took shelter on the stairs with another misanthrope, a German dressed in intellectual black. A girl sobbed at the bottom of the stairs. At any decent Russian party there were arguments and a girl crying at the bottom of the stairs, Arkady thought.

"I'm waiting to talk to Irina," the German said. He was in his twenties, with furtive eyes and nervous English.

"Me, too," Arkady said.

There was a silence, comfortable enough to Arkady, until the boy blurted out, "Malevich was in Munich."

"And Lenin," Arkady said. "Or was it Meyer?"

"The artist."

"Oh, the artist. *That* Malevich." The artist of the Russian Revolution. Arkady felt slightly stupid.

"There is a tradition of contact between Russian and German art."

"Yes." No one could argue with that, Arkady thought.

The boy examined his nails, which were bitten to the quick. "The red square symbolized the Revolution. The black square symbolized the end of art."

"Right." Arkady downed half his vodka in a swallow.

The boy giggled as if he had remembered something worth sharing. "Malevich said in 1918 that 'footballs of entangled centuries would burn out in the sparks of bubbling light waves.' "

"Bubbling light waves?"

"Bubbling light waves."

"Amazing." Arkady wondered what Malevich drank.

IRINA WAS NEVER alone long enough for Arkady to approach her. While he maneuvered between groups, he was snared by Tommy and led to an enormous map of Eastern Europe tacked to a wall, with German and Russian positions on the eve of Hitler's invasion marked by swastikas and red stars.

Tommy said, "This is terrific. I just learned who your father was. One of the great military minds of the war. What I'd love to do is mark exactly where your father was when the Germans rolled in. If you could point that out, it would be great."

It was a Wehrmacht map. Place names and rivers were in German. Widely spaced lines climbed the Ukrainian steppe, dashes warned of swamps in Bessarabia, swastikas were massed to sweep on separate fronts to Moscow, Leningrad and Stalingrad.

"I have no idea," Arkady said.

"Not a hint? Did he leave you any anecdotes?" Tommy asked.

"Only tactics." Max joined them. "Hide in a hole and stab your enemy in the back. Not bad tactics when you're overwhelmed and overrun." He turned to Arkady. "Are you feeling overwhelmed and overrun? Question retracted. What interests me, however, is that the father becomes a general and the son becomes an investigator. There's a similarity there, an inclination towards violence. What do you think, Professor? You're a medical man."

The psychologist who had arrived with Max was still tagging along. He ventured, "Perhaps a discomfort with normal society."

"Soviet society is not normal society," Arkady said.

"Then you tell us," Max said. "Explain to us why you are an investigator. Your father chose to kill people. That's why men become generals. To say a general hates war is to say that a writer hates books. You're different. You choose to arrive *after* the murder. You get the blood without the fun."

"Much like the victim," Arkady said.

"Then, what draws you? You live in one of the worst societies on earth, and then you choose the worst part of it. What is the morbid appeal? Picking over bodies? Sending one more hopeless soul to jail for the rest of his life? As my friend Tommy would say, what's in it for you?"

They weren't bad questions. Arkady had asked them about himself. "Permission," he said.

"Permission?" Max repeated.

"Yes. When someone is killed, for a short time people have to answer questions. An investigator has permission to go to different levels and see how the world is built. A murder is a little like a house splitting in half; you see what floor is above what floor and what door leads to another door."

"Murder leads to sociology?"

"Soviet sociology."

"Assuming people are honest. I would assume that people would lie."

"Murderers do."

Arkady noticed that Max's retinue had regrouped around them. Stas watched from a corner. Irina was in conversation in the hall that led to the kitchen, her back to this exchange. Arkady regretted ever opening his mouth.

"Speaking of honest answers, how long have you listened to Irina on the radio?" Max asked.

"About a week."

For the first time Max seemed genuinely surprised. "A week? Irina's been doing the newscast for a long time. I expected you to say you'd sat devotedly by the radio for years."

"I didn't have a radio." Arkady glanced toward the hall. Irina was gone.

"And a week ago you did? And here you are in Munich! At this very party! Now, that's an amazing coincidence," Max said. "Pure chance hardly explains that."

"Perhaps it was luck." Stas joined the conversation. "Max, we want to hear more about your new television career. What is Donahue really like? And about your joint venture. I always thought of you as an inspirational leader, not a businessman."

"But Tommy was going to tell me about his book," Max said.

Tommy said, "We were just getting to the interesting part."

Arkady ducked away. He found Irina in the kitchen, taking cigarettes from a carton open on the counter. Tommy was a haphazard chef; carrot shavings and celery greens spilled from chopping boards and around bright plastic appliances. A portable television sat on a shelf of cookbooks; a poster of an Aryan mother hung on the wall. The clock said two A.M.

Irina struck a match. Arkady remembered that the first time they had ever met, she had asked for a light, a test to see how he reacted. She didn't ask now.

That first time, he remembered, he had been unruffled. Now his mouth was dry, his breath stopped, without words. Why was he trying a third time? Was he intent on exploring how many levels of humiliation he could sink to? Or was he a kind of Pavlov's dog that insisted on being kicked?

What was strange was that Irina looked so much the same and yet not at all the same. She wasn't changed so much as an amalgam of someone he knew and of a total stranger who had moved into the familiar body, not recently but long ago. She folded her arms. The cashmere and gold she wore were a long way from the rags and scarves she used to sport in Moscow. The image of her he had carried with him still fit her, but only as a mask. Different eyes looked through it.

Arkady had been on Arctic ice. It wasn't as cold as this room. That was the trouble with knowing a woman intimately. When you're no longer welcome, you're banished to the dark. You spin around a sun that turns its back.

"How did you get here?" she asked.

"Stas brought me."

She frowned. "Stas? I heard he also took you to the station. I told you he was a provocateur. He's going a little far tonight—"

"Do you remember me?" Arkady asked.

"Of course I do."

"You don't seem to."

Irina sighed. Even to himself, he sounded pathetic.

"Of course I remember you. I simply haven't thought about you for years. It's different in the West. I had to survive, get a job. I met a lot of different people. My life changed, I changed."

"Don't be sorry," Arkady said. The way she described it, they were two tectonic plates moving in different directions. She was cold, analytical, correct.

Irina said, "I didn't set back your career too badly?"

"A Russian hiccup."

"Don't make me feel bad," she said, though there was no indication that he could.

"No. I had inflated expectations. Maybe my memory was playing tricks."

"To tell you the truth, I barely recognized you."

"I look that good?" Arkady asked. A feeble joke.

"I heard you were doing well."

"Who told you?" Arkady asked.

Irina lit a second cigarette from the first. Why do Russians need to burn a little all the time? he wondered. She stared at him, the smoke shifting, her face shrouded by her hair. He imagined holding her. No, it wasn't imagination; it was memory. He remembered the weight of her cheek against his hand, the smoothness of her brow.

Irina shrugged. "Max was a friend and support for years. It's wonderful to see him here again."

"I can tell he's popular."

"No one knows why he went back to Moscow. He helped you, so you have no reason to complain."

"I wish I'd been here," Arkady said.

If I stood and crossed the room, he thought. If I crossed the room and simply touched her, could a touch be the bridge? No, her face said.

"It's too late now. You never followed me. Every other Russian here emigrated or defected. You stayed."

"The KGB said—"

"I would have understood if you'd stayed for a year or two, but you stayed forever. You left me alone. I waited in New York; you never came. I went to London to be closer; you never came. When I found out where you were, you were doing exactly what you did before, being a policeman in a police state. Now here you are, finally, but not to see me. You're here to arrest someone."

Arkady said, "I couldn't come without—"

Irina asked, "Did you think that I'd help you? When I think of the time when I did want to see you and you weren't here, thank God Max was. Max and Stas and Rikki—everybody here had the nerve, one way or another, swimming, running or jumping from windows, to escape. You didn't, so you have no right to criticize any of them, or question any of them or even to be with them. As far as I'm concerned, you're dead."

She took a pack of cigarettes with her and left the kitchen as Tommy danced in, humming a polka, gathering olives and chips. His legs were drunk. On his head was a German helmet. In the helmet was a hole.

Arkady knew the feeling.

21

The Bayern-Franconia Bank was a Bavarian palace of limestone blocks under the practical hat of a red tile roof. The inside was all marble, dark wood and the discreet hum of computers calculating mysterious interest rates and currency exchanges. Led up an elevator and down a hall with rococo cornices, Arkady felt intimidated, as if he were trespassing in the church of a foreign rite.

There was something padded and posed about Schiller. He sat rigidly behind his desk, about seventy, with clear blue eyes in a pink face. Silver hair was brushed back from a narrow forehead. A linen handkerchief showed above the pocket of a dark young suit. A man in a windbreaker and jeans, with a tan that flowed into blond hair, stood at Schiller's side. His blue eyes and expression of restrained contempt were the same as the banker's.

Schiller scrutinized the letter that Arkady had typed on Federov's stationery. "You are what a senior Soviet investigator looks like?" he asked.

"I'm afraid so."

Arkady handed over his red identification book. He hadn't noticed before how much the corners were worn, the bindings torn. At arm's length Schiller scrutinized the picture. Even shaved, Arkady felt he looked as if he had sat on his clothes before dressing. He fought the impulse to pinch a crease in his pants.

"Peter, will you examine this?" Schiller asked.

"You don't mind?" the other man asked Arkady. It was the sort of courtesy extended to a suspect.

"Please."

Peter turned on the desk lamp. As he held a page under the light his jacket rode up to show a holster clip and pistol.

"Why didn't Federov come with you?" Schiller asked Arkady.

"He apologizes. He's with a church group this morning, then folk-singers from Minsk."

Peter gave back the ID. "Do you mind if I call?"

Arkady said, "Go ahead."

Peter used the phone while Schiller kept watch on his visitor. Arkady looked up. On the ceiling, fat cherubs with tiny wings were painted in mid-flutter against a plaster sky. Walls of Dresden blue colored the air a somber gray. Oil portraits of ancestral bankers hung between engravings of merchant ships. The good burghers looked embalmed, then painted. On a bookshelf were tomes on international law arranged by year and, in a crystal dome, a brass clock with a pendulum that wrapped itself around a pole. He noticed a black-and-white photograph of rubble and burned walls. A roof had collapsed like a tent on a skirt of bricks. A bathtub was set out on the street as a water trough. People huddled around the tub in the gray uniforms of displaced persons. "An interesting picture for a bank," he said.

Schiller said, "That *is* the bank. That's this building after the war."

"Very impressive."

"Most countries have recovered from the war," Schiller said drily.

Peter finally reached someone on the phone. "Hello." He checked the letter. "Is Federov there? Where could I find him? Could you tell me exactly when? No, no, thank you." He hung up and nodded to Arkady. "Some religious group and singers."

"Federov is a busy man," Arkady said.

Schiller said, "Your Federov is an idiot if he thinks the Bayern-Franconia Bank considers itself obligated to investigate a German citizen. And only a cretin could imagine Bayern-Franconia joining any venture with a Soviet partner."

"That's Federov," Arkady agreed, as if the attaché's antics were legend. "All I know is that I've been told to clear this up quietly. I understand that the bank is under no obligation to help."

Schiller said, "We have no inclination to help, either."

"I don't see why you should," Arkady said. "I told Federov he should inform the ministries and get it out in the open. Bring in Interpol, let it go through the courts, the more public the better. That's the way to protect a bank's reputation."

"The bank's name could be protected by simply removing it from the reports on Benz," Schiller said.

"True," Arkady agreed. "But the situation in Moscow being what it is, no one at the consulate is willing to take that responsibility."

"Could you?" Schiller asked.

"Yes."

"Grandfather, do you want my advice?" Peter asked.

"Of course," Schiller said.

"Ask him how much he wants to leave the bank alone. Five thousand Deutsche marks? If he splits with Federov, ten thousand? This whole story about TransKom, Benz and Bayern-Franconia—they've cooked it up. There are no reports, there's no connection. I look at him and I know he's lying. This is a protection racket. I suggest that we call other banks and ask whether they've been approached by Federov and Renko, whether they've heard a story about joint ventures and investigations. You should call the consul general right now, make an official protest, and then call a lawyer. What do you think of that?"

The banker's mouth had almost no lips at all, not enough to hold a smile. There was nothing old or weak about the eyes, though. They weighed Arkady as if he were small change.

"I agree," Schiller said. "You have probably never seen a less genuine-looking article in your life. On the other hand, Peter, you've never met a Soviet banker. It's true that the bank has no knowledge of or connection to any claims made by the individual whom the Soviet consulate has described. Certainly we feel under no obligation to give the consulate any assistance. However, if we've learned anything from history it is that mud makes good paint. Whether we deserve it or not, it never washes off entirely."

He fell silent, as if he had left the room for a moment. Then he gathered himself and looked at Arkady. "The bank will not participate in any inquiry, but purely as a courtesy to me my grandson Peter has volunteered to assist you, as long as this affair is kept absolutely quiet."

The outrage working in Peter's face showed less than wholehearted enthusiasm, Arkady thought.

"On an informal basis," Peter said.

"How can you help?" Arkady asked.

Peter produced a much nicer case than Arkady's. Authentic leather, gold tooling, with a color photo in green jacket and cap of Lieutenant

Schiller, Peter Christian, Münchner Polizei. This was more windfall than Arkady wanted. It was a trap of his own devising, though, because if he didn't accept the offer, the Germans would call the consulate again and again until they got through to Federov.

"I'd be honored," Arkady said.

PETER SCHILLER'S POLICE car was a green-and-white BMW, radio and phone under the dash, blue flasher on the backseat. He wore a seat belt and always used the turn indicator, yielding to bikers who left their lane, passing pedestrians massed in docile formations to wait for WALK signs at corners where there was no cross traffic in sight. He looked a little too big for the car. He also looked as if he would be happy to run down anyone who crossed against the light.

"I bet your radio and phone work," Arkady said.

"Of course they do."

Irrationally, Arkady yearned for Jaak's homicidal driving and for the suicidal dashes of Moscow pedestrians. Peter looked as if he kept in shape by lifting small oxen. His windbreaker was yellow. Arkady had noticed that yellow was the most popular color worn in Munich. A gold-mustard-diarrhea yellow.

"Your grandfather speaks Russian well."

"He learned it on the Eastern Front. He was a prisoner of war."

"Your Russian is good, too."

"I think all police should speak it," Peter said.

They headed south, toward the two bonneted spires of the Marienkirche in the center of the city. Peter downshifted to pass a trolley that was as well maintained as a toy. You had to work to keep Peter Schiller's kind of tan, Arkady thought. Ski in the wintertime, swim in the summer.

"Your grandfather said you'd volunteered. Volunteer something," he said.

Peter gave him a couple of level looks before responding. "Boris Benz has no criminal record. In fact, the only thing we have is that according to the Bureau of Vehicle Registration, Benz has blond hair, blue eyes, was born in 1955 in Potsdam, outside Berlin, and does not need glasses."

"Married?"

"To a Margarita Stein, a Soviet Jew. Her records are where? Moscow, Tel Aviv—who knows?"

"That's a start. Tax or employment records? Service or medical records?"

"Potsdam is in the DDR. *Was* in the DDR. Understand, we're all one Germany now, but many East German records have not been transferred to Bonn yet."

"What about telephone calls?"

"Tsk, tsk. Without a court order, telephone records are protected by law. We have laws here."

"I understand. You also have customs control. Did you check them?"

"Benz could be home, he could be anywhere in Western Europe. Since the EEC, there isn't any real passport control anymore."

"What kind of car does he drive?" Arkady asked.

Peter smiled, getting into the rhythm of the game. "A white Porsche is registered in his name."

"Plate number?"

"I don't think I'm allowed to share any more information."

"What information? Call Potsdam and order his records from there."

"For a private matter? That's absolutely against the law."

At an obelisk cars merged and separated with none of the nebular fury of a Moscow roundabout. There, particularly in winter, trucks and cars thundered into roundabouts with all the discipline of yaks. Here drivers, bikers and walkers seemed to have received their orders for the day. It was like a rest home the size of a city. Peter smiled like a man who could play all day.

"Many murders here?" Arkady asked.

"Munich?"

"Yes."

"Beer murders."

"Beer?"

"Oktoberfest, Fasching. Drunks. Not real murders."

"Not like vodka murders?"

"You know what they say about crime in Germany?" Peter asked.

"What do they say about crime in Germany?"

"It's against the law," Peter said.

Arkady recognized the trees of the Botanischer Garten. As soon as the BMW stopped at a light, he got out and reached back to stuff a piece of paper into Peter's jacket. "That's a Munich fax number. Find out who it belongs to, if that's not against the law. On the other side is a phone number. You can call me there at five."

"Your number at the consulate?"

"I won't be there. It's a private number." My private minute at the booth, Arkady thought.

"Renko!" Peter shouted as Arkady reached the sidewalk. "Stay away from the bank."

Arkady kept walking.

"Renko!" Peter added another warning. "Tell Federov what I said."

ARMED WITH SOAP and string, Arkady returned to the pension, washed his clothes and hung them up to dry. From the floor below came the sweet smell of spiced lamb. He wasn't hungry. Such lethargy came over him that he could barely move. He stood by the window looking down the street and toward the railroad yard at the trains sluggishly moving in and out. The rails were as silvery as snail tracks, perhaps fifty parallel lines and as many switches shunting an engine from this line to that. How easily, without noticing, a man finds himself parallel to the life he meant to have, then arrives, years later, to find the band gone, flowers dead, love past. He should be ancient, bent and bearded, disembarking with a cane instead of merely being too late.

He dropped onto his bed, and at once fell into a black sleep. He dreamed he was in a locomotive. He was the engineer, stripped to the waist and sitting at a cockpit of gauges and controls. Blue sky sped by the window. A woman's hand rested lightly on his shoulder. He didn't look back for fear that she might not be there. They were running along the seashore. Somehow, without tracks, the engine plowed through the beach. Faraway waves reflected rows of sunlight, nearer waves curled lazily over each other and collapsed on the sand, perfect gulls plunged into the water. Was it her hand or the memory of her hand? He was happy not to look and keep the train moving by sheer will if necessary. But the wheels ground to a stop. The sun was sinking. Waves mounted in towering black walls that carried along dachas, cars, militiamen, generals, Chinese lanterns and birthday cakes.

In panic, Arkady opened his eyes. He was in bed in the dark. He looked at his watch. Ten P.M. He had slept ten hours, right through the call to the booth from Peter Schiller—if he had ever called.

Someone was knocking at the door. Getting up, he brushed aside the drying shirts and pants hanging in his way.

He didn't recognize the visitor, a heavyset American with stringy hair and a tentative smile.

"I'm Tommy, remember? You came to a party at my place last night."

"The man in the helmet, yes. How did you know where to find me?"

"Stas. I bugged him until he told me; then I just knocked on every door here until I found you. Can we talk?"

Arkady let him in and searched for a shirt and cigarettes.

Tommy wore a corduroy jacket stressed at the buttons. He bounced on his toes and his hands hung in soft fists. "I told you last night that I was a student of World War Two. 'The Great Patriotic War' to you. Your father was one of the outstanding generals on the Soviet side. Naturally I'd like to talk some more about him with you."

"I don't think we talked about him at all." Arkady sat down to pull on socks.

"That's what I mean. The truth is, I'm writing a book about the war from the Soviet side. I don't have to tell you about the sacrifices the Soviet people made. Anyway, that's one reason I work at Radio Liberty—for the information. When someone interesting comes through, I interview them. I heard you might be leaving Munich pretty soon, so I came over."

Arkady searched for his shoes. He wasn't following Tommy closely. "You interview them for the station?"

"No, just for me, for the book. I'm interested in more than military tactics; I'm also interested in the clash of personalities. I was hoping you could give me some insight into your father."

Out the window, the rail yard was a field of signal lights. Arkady saw flashlights running around flatcars and heard the heavy grip of couplers engaging. "Who told you I was leaving soon?" he asked.

"People said."

"Who?"

Tommy rose on his toes. "Max."

"Max Albov. You know him well?"

"Max was head of the Russian section. I'm in the Red Archives. We worked together for years."

"The Red Archives?"

"The greatest library of Soviet studies in the West. It's at Radio Liberty."

"You were friends with Max?"

"I'd like to think we're still friends." Tommy held up a tape recorder. "Anyway, what I wanted to cover to begin with was your father's decision, despite being overrun, to stay behind the German lines and wage guerrilla warfare."

Arkady asked, "Do you know Boris Benz?"

Tommy leaned backward and said, "We met once."

"How?"

"Right before Max went to Moscow. Of course no one knew he was going. He was with Benz."

"You haven't seen Benz since?"

"No. It was purely by chance. Max and I were surprised to see each other."

"You met Benz only once and yet you remember him?"

"Under the circumstances, yeah."

"Who else was there?"

As Tommy squirmed, his shirttail showed under his jacket. "Employees, customers. No one I've seen since. Maybe this isn't a good time for an interview."

"It's the perfect time. Where did your encounter with Benz and Max take place?"

"Red Square."

"In Moscow?"

"No."

"Munich?"

"It's a club."

"Would it be open now?"

"Sure."

"Show me." Arkady picked up a jacket. "I'll tell you all about the war and you tell me about Benz and Max."

Tommy gulped down a brave breath. "If Max was still with Liberty, you couldn't get a word—"

"Have you got a car?"

"Sort of a car," Tommy said.

ARKADY HAD NEVER ridden in an East German Trabant before. It was a fiberglass tub with tail fins. The sound of its two cylinders was a syncopated popping. Fumes flowed not only from the exhaust but from a kerosene heater that sat on the car floor between his feet. They drove with the front windows rolled down; the rear windows were glued shut. Every time an Audi or Mercedes passed, the Trabant bobbed in its wake.

"What do you think?" Tommy asked.

"It's like being on the road in a wheelchair," Arkady said.

"It's more an investment than a car," Tommy said. "The Trabi is a piece of history. Except for being slow and dangerous and polluting, it's probably the most efficient piece of technology in the world today. It goes fifty miles an hour and it'll run on methane or coal tar— probably even on hair tonic."

"Sounds more Russian."

In truth, however, the Trabant made Arkady's Zhiguli look like luxury. It made a Polish Fiat look good.

"Ten years from now this will be a collector's item," Tommy promised.

They had reached the outer city, a black plane where stakes of light led to different autobahns. When Arkady twisted to see whether anyone was following, the seat almost snapped beneath him.

"The whole German-Russian thing is so incredible," Tommy said. "Historically, with the Germans always moving east and the Russians always moving west, and then you add Nazi racial laws, making all Slavs into *Untermenschen* only good for slaves. Hitler on one side, Stalin on the other. Now, that was a war."

His face was creased with a new grin of pride and camaraderie. He was a lonely man, Arkady realized. Who else would ride around late at night with a Russian investigator? When a tank truck approached in the passing lane, engulfed the air and roared by, the Trabi vibrated violently in the shock wave and Tommy glowed with pleasure.

"I got to know Max best before I came to the Red Archives, when I ran the Program Review section. I didn't create programs; I had a separate staff that reviewed them for content. Radio Liberty has guidelines. Our strongest anti-Communists, for example, are monarchists. Of course we're supposed to be pushing democracy, but sometimes a little anti-Semitism creeps in, sometimes a little Zionism. It's a balancing act. We also translate programs so that the station president knows what we're putting on the air. Anyway, my life was easier because Max was head of the Russian desk. He understood Americans."

"Why do you think he went back to Moscow?"

"I don't know. We were all amazed. Obviously he had to be in contact with the Sovs before he went back, and they played it as a feather in their cap when he showed up in Moscow. But nobody here suffered. He wouldn't have been welcome at the party if anyone had."

"How do the Americans at the station feel about him?"

"To begin with, President Gilmartin was upset. Max was always the favorite. It was a shock to think that the KGB had penetrated Liberty. You met Michael Healey at my party. He's deputy director. He tore the station apart looking for moles. Now it looks like Max went back just to make money. Like a capitalist. You can't blame him for that."

"Did Michael talk to Benz about Max?"

"I don't think Michael knew about Benz. You don't want Michael messing with your life. Anyway, it all turned out okay. Max came back smelling like a rose." Tommy made his point stronger: "He's been on CNN."

Arkady turned in his seat to look behind them again. If something was impinging on his consciousness, there was nothing in sight but the haze of the city.

Ahead, the road forked north toward Nuremberg, south to Salzburg. Tommy turned right, and as soon as they came off the curve and through an underpass Arkady saw what appeared to be a pink island in the dark. He didn't know what he had expected—Kremlin walls or St. Basil's domes rising like phantoms by the autobahn? Whatever, something more than a one-story building of white stucco framed in red neon, with a square red light bleeding into the air beside a sign that said RED SQUARE and, in more demure cursive, SEX CLUB. As he got out of the Trabi he thought that nothing you dream is as strange as what you see.

THE INSIDE OF the club was so washed in red lights that it was difficult to focus, but Arkady did notice women in garter belts, black stockings, push-up bras and corsets. The theme was established by brass samovars on the tables and fluorescent stars on the walls.

"What do you think?" Tommy scooped his shirt back into his belt.

"Like the last days of Catherine the Great," Arkady said.

It was interesting how intimidated men were at a house of prostitution. They had the money, the choice, the chance to leave. Women were servitors, slaves, mattresses. Yet the power, at least before sex, was inverted. The women, ogled in their lingerie, sprawled on love seats as comfortably as cats; the men betrayed the tics of the un-dressed. American soldiers stood at a horseshoe bar. Approached by a prostitute, they nervously played out a charade of charm and seduc-tion while she maintained a face so slack and bored that she could have been asleep. What amazed Arkady was that the women actually were Russian. He heard it in their accents and whispers to each other, saw it in the pallor of their skin, the tilt of their eyes. He saw a woman in pink silk as broad-shouldered as a farm girl from the steppe who might have wandered west in her underwear. She whispered to a more delicate friend with huge Armenian eyes and a body stocking of black lace. When he looked at them he couldn't help wondering why. How did imported Russian prostitutes differ from German ones? In wing-spread, submissiveness, the ability to heal? They pointed to him. They could spot it; he was Russian, too. He asked himself how desperate he was for love, or at least for a facsimile of it. Did the need shine from him or did he look as dead as a charred match?

He reminded Tommy, "You said that Max Albov came back to Mu-nich smelling like a rose."

Tommy said, "If anything, I think we respect Max more. I bet he'll make a million."

"Doing what? Did he say?"

"Television journalism."

"He mentioned a joint venture."

"Properties, assets. He says a man who can't make money in Mos-cow couldn't find flies on shit."

"Sounds inviting. Maybe everyone should go back to Moscow."

"That was the idea."

Tommy couldn't take his eyes off the women. He looked red-faced and overheated just by proximity, pressing his shirt against his belly, raking his hair with thick fingers, signs of an excitement Arkady did not share. Love was the mountain breeze, sunrise and nirvana, sex was a roll in the leaves, paid sex was the taste of worms. But it had been so long since he had known either sex or love, who was he to judge? One man imagines paid sex to be coarse and deadening, the next man finds it simple and direct. Does the second man have less imagination or more money?

Every race has its catalog of features. A Tatar heritage of narrowed, upward-slanting eyes. Slavic oval outline and rounded brow. Small lips, skin pale as snow. None of the women looked like Irina, though. Her eyes were broader and deeper, more Byzantine than Mongol, both more open and more hidden in their look. Her face was less oval, lighter in the jaw, her mouth fuller, more articulate. It was curious—in Moscow he heard Irina five times a day. Here, silence.

Sometimes he thought of normal, alternative lives he and Irina could have led. Lovers. Husband and wife. The ordinary way people live and sleep and wake together. Perhaps even grow to hate each other and decide to leave, but in a normal fashion, not with lives cut in half. Not with a dream that degenerated into obsession.

The woman in pink came over with her friend and asked for champagne.

"Sure." Everything seemed like a good idea to Tommy.

The four of them took a table in the corner. The woman in pink was Tatiana; her friend in the body stocking was Marina. Tatiana had dark roots and an elaborate blond ponytail; Marina wore black hair brushed over a bruised cheek. Tommy, playing host, introduced "My pal Arkady."

"We knew he was Russian," Tatiana said. "He looks romantic."

"Poor men are not romantic," Arkady said. "Tommy is much more romantic."

"We could have fun here," Tommy suggested.

Arkady watched a woman walk, hips slowly marching toward another battle as she led a soldier through a beaded curtain to the back rooms. "Do you see many Russians here?" he asked.

"Truck drivers." Tatiana made a face. "Usually we have a more international clientele."

"I like Germans," Marina said in a reflective mood. "They wash."

"That's important," Arkady said.

Tatiana lowered her champagne under the table to reinforce it from a flask and generously did the same for the other three glasses. Vodka once again subverting the system. Marina leaned over her glass and whispered, *"Molto importante."*

"We speak Italian," Tatiana said. "We toured Italy for two years."

Marina said, "We were with the Bolshoi Piccolo Ballet Company."

"Not necessarily connected to the original Bolshoi Ballet." Tatiana giggled.

"We did dance." Marina sat straighter to emphasize a sinewy neck.

"Small towns. But so much sun, such music," Tatiana recalled.

"There were ten other so-called Russian ballet companies in Italy when we left, all copying us," Marina said.

"I think we can say we spread a love of dance," Tatiana said. She poured Arkady a second shot. "Are you sure you don't have any money?"

"She's always attracted to the wrong men," Marina said.

"Thanks," Arkady said to both of them. "I'm looking for a couple of friends. One named Max. Russian, but better dressed than me, speaks English and German."

"We never saw anyone like that," Tatiana said.

"Or Boris," Arkady said.

"Boris is a popular name," Marina said.

"His last name was something like Benz."

"That's a popular name here, too," Tatiana said.

"How would you describe him?" Arkady asked Tommy.

"Big, good-looking, friendly."

"Does he speak Russian?" Tatiana asked.

"I don't know. He only spoke German around me," Tommy said.

Benz was such a nebulous creature, nothing but a name on a registration form in Moscow and on a letter in Munich, that Arkady found himself relieved to meet anyone who might have met the man in the flesh.

"Why would he speak Russian?" Arkady asked.

"The Boris I'm thinking of is very international," Marina said. "I'm only saying that his Russian is very good."

"He's German," Tatiana said.

"You haven't been to bed with him."

"Neither have you."

"Tima was. She commented on it."

" 'Commented on it'?" Tatiana affected a prissy accent.

"We're friends."

"What a cow. I'm sorry," Tatiana added when she saw that Marina was hurt. She told Arkady, "He's a Polish sausage, what can I tell you?"

"Is Tima here?"

"No, but I can describe her to you," Tatiana said. "Red, four-wheel drive, also answers to the name 'Bronco.' "

"I know where she means," Tommy said, excited to get back into the conversation. "It's right down the road. I'll take you."

"I wish you did have money," Tatiana told Arkady. Under the circumstances he thought it was the biggest compliment he could expect.

■ ■ ■

A DOZEN JEEPS, Troopers, Pathfinders and Land Cruisers sat in a highway turnout, a prostitute waiting behind the wheel of each car. Clients parked on the shoulder to shop. Once a price was set, the woman turned off the red lamp that announced her availability, the client climbed in and they drove to the far side of the turnout, away from the passing lights of the road. Twenty off-the-road vehicles stood there already, on the verge of a black field.

Tommy and Arkady walked by the lit cars and then down the center of the turnout, stepping aside as a Trooper eased by. Tommy was becoming a more eager guide all the time. "They worked out of camping trailers in the city until residents complained about the late-night traffic. There's less visual impact here. They're safe; doctors check them once a month."

The back windows of the far cars all had drawn curtains. A Jeep jiggled from side to side as if it were running in place.

"What does a Bronco look like?" Arkady asked.

Tommy pointed out one of the larger models, but it was blue. They were all high off the ground, what a person would want to set off across the tundra in.

"What do you think?" Tommy asked.

"They all look good."

"I mean the women."

Arkady caught a different drift. "Tommy, what do you *really* mean?"

"I mean, I could lend you some money."

"No, thanks."

Tommy shifted from foot to foot, then held out his car keys. "Do you mind?"

"You're serious?" Arkady asked.

"Since we're here, we might as well enjoy it." Tommy talked in gusts, gathering bravado. "Christ, it will only take a few minutes."

Arkady was stunned, and felt stupid for being so. Who was he to judge anyone else? In another second, Tommy would be pleading. He took the keys. "I'll be in the car."

The Trabi was parked across the highway. From it he saw Tommy head directly to a Jeep, agree instantly to a price and run around to the passenger side. The Jeep backed away into the dark.

Arkady lit a cigarette and found an ashtray, but no radio. What a perfectly Socialist car, designed for bad habits and ignorance, and he was its perfect driver.

Headlights swung on and off the road, creating an ad hoc junction. Perhaps it wasn't so much a matter of there being no crime in Germany as how crime was defined. In Moscow prostitution was against the law. Here it was a regulated trade.

A Trooper pulled into the slot that the Jeep had abandoned. The driver turned on her red light, primped her curls in the rearview mirror, made up her mouth, adjusted her bra, pushed up her breasts like muscles and then picked up a paperback. The woman in the car ahead stared with eyes that looked as if they were painted on her lids. Neither of them looked like a Tima. Arkady assumed the name was short for Fatima, so he searched for someone vaguely Islamic. At this distance the lights were softened to candle glow. Each windshield looked like a separate icon with a separate virgin bored to distraction.

After twenty minutes he began to get nervous about Tommy. An image of the cars on the far side of the turnout shone in his mind. A car rocking harder and harder on its springs, its curtain closed tight. If ever there was a place where sex and violence could be confused, this was it. The sound of someone being throttled and beaten? From the outside, that could sound like love.

It was an unreasonable fear, but he was relieved to see Tommy darting nimbly back across the road. The American dove into the car and squeezed behind the steering wheel. Breathing hard, he asked, "Was I gone long?"

"Hours," Arkady said.

Tommy pressed himself back into his seat to tuck in his shirt and button his jacket. The smell of perfume and sweat invaded the small car with his return, like the aroma of a trip to an exotic land. He was so proud of himself, Arkady wondered how often he got up his nerve to approach a prostitute.

"Definitely worth the money. Sure you won't change your mind?" he asked.

"I'll take your word for it. Let's go."

Arkady's door opened. Peter Schiller had to crouch to be on a level with them. "Renko, you didn't answer your phone."

■ ■ ■

PETER'S BMW STOOD in the dark far back from the highway. Arkady spread-eagled, leaning against the side of the car while Peter patted him down. They had a clear view of the turnout, of the cars off the road and of Tommy heading back to Munich alone in his Trabant.

"Moscow's a mystery to me," Peter said. He ran his hands around the small of Arkady's back, the inside of his thighs, along his wrists and ankles. "I've never been there and never hope to be there, but it seems to me that a senior investigator shouldn't have to work out of a public phone booth. I checked out the number when you didn't answer."

"I hate staying by a desk."

"You don't have a desk. I went by the consulate and talked to Federov. I pried him away from some singers. He doesn't know anything about your investigation, he never heard of any Boris Benz and I think it's fair to say he wishes he never heard of you."

"We never did develop a rapport," Arkady conceded.

When he tried to turn, Peter pushed his face against the roof of the car. "He told me where to find the pension. Your lights were out. I waited and thought about how to deal most effectively with you. It was obvious you picked Bayern-Franconia out of the blue to run a protection racket on. It's also clear you were doing it alone, to make a few Deutsche marks during your holiday. A little Russian free enterprise. I considered the usual protests to different ministries and Interpol until I remembered how sensitive my grandfather is to any publicity attached to the bank. It's a merchant bank, not for the public, and it doesn't need publicity, least of all the kind you'd give it. So then I considered just taking you out someplace and beating you until you were a bloody pulp."

"Isn't that against the law?"

"Beating you so badly you'd be afraid to tell anyone what happened."

"Well, you can always try," Arkady said.

Arkady didn't have a gun and Peter had a pistol, a Walther from the glimpse he'd had at the bank. He was pretty sure that Peter Christian Schiller wouldn't shoot, at least not until he ordered Arkady away from the BMW, because a bullet could go right through soft tissue and spread glass and gore all over the interior of his handsome car. If Peter wanted to hit him, Arkady didn't know whether he would resist. At this point what would a little blood or loose teeth matter? He straightened up and turned around.

Peter's yellow jacket was whipping around him in a breeze that came off the field. He held his pistol low. "Then who should show up but your friend in the Trabi. I thought, here's a poor bastard from East Germany. No one drives a Trabi anymore if they can avoid it. Sometimes you see them near the old border, but not here. Ten minutes later he comes out of the pension with you. It made more sense that you had an Ossie as an accomplice."

"An 'Ossie'?"

"East German. He picks the victim, you show up with a phony letter from the consulate. I called in the plate number, but the car belongs to a Thomas Hall, American national, Munich resident. Why would an American drive a Trabi?"

"He says it's an investment. You followed us?"

"It wasn't difficult. Nothing else was as slow."

"So what are you going to do?" Arkady asked.

The wonderful thing about a German face was that the agony of thought played so clearly on it. Even in the dim light from the highway, Peter looked torn by fury on one side and by curiosity on the other. "You're a good friend of Hall's?"

"I never met Tommy before last night. I was surprised to see him tonight."

"You and Hall went to a sex club together. That sounds friendly."

"Tommy said he'd seen Benz there. The women at the club said we should look here."

"You never talked to Hall before last night?"

"No."

"You never communicated with him before last night?"

"No. What are you getting at?" Arkady asked.

"Renko, this morning you gave me a fax number to find. I did. The machine belongs to Radio Liberty. It's in the office of Thomas Hall."

There were surprises left in life after all, Arkady thought. Here he had spent the evening with an apparent innocent, only to discover his own stupidity. Why hadn't he checked the Liberty numbers himself? How many other pieces of information had he brushed off his lap?

"Do you think you can catch up with Tommy?" Arkady asked.

Peter wavered, and Arkady watched with interest to see which way he would go. The German stared back so intently that Arkady thought of the old stage routine of one man pretending to mirror the other.

Finally Peter said, "Right now, the only thing I'm certain of is that I can catch a Trabi."

■ ■ ■

THEY RETURNED BY the same route Tommy had taken but at a different speed. Peter wound the BMW up to two hundred kilometers, as if he were driving on a familiar racetrack in the dark. He kept glancing at Arkady, who wished he would keep his eyes on the road.

"You never mentioned Radio Liberty at the bank," Peter said.

"I didn't know Liberty was involved. It may not be."

"We don't need a Russian civil war here. We'd rather you all went home and killed yourselves there."

"That's a possibility."

"If Liberty's involved, Americans are involved."

"I hope not."

"You've never worked with Americans?"

"You've worked with Americans," Arkady assumed from Peter's tone.

"I trained in Texas."

"As a cowboy?"

"For the air force. Jet fighters."

On a curve, a sign shot by. Arkady thought there was nothing like high speed to make a man appreciate the camber of a road. "For the German air force?"

"Some of us train there. There's less to hit if we crash."

"That makes sense."

"Are you KGB?"

"No. Did Federov say I was?"

Peter produced a sardonic laugh. "Federov swore you weren't KGB. God forbid. But if you aren't, why are you interested in Radio Liberty?"

"Tommy sent a fax to Moscow."

"Saying?" Peter demanded.

" 'Where is Red Square?' "

They drove in silence until a pink spot emerged ahead.

"We have to talk to Tommy," Arkady said. He held up a cigarette. "Do you mind?"

"Roll down the window."

Air whistled in and with it came an acrid smell that made his throat close.

Peter said, "Someone's burning plastic."

"And tires."

The pink spot grew, vanished and reappeared, larger and deeper in color. It disappeared, then came into sight again at the abutment of a cross ramp, a torch at the base of thick, roiling smoke that leaned away from the wind. Closer, the torch was a meteor furiously trying to burrow its way into the earth.

"Trabi," Peter said as they went by.

They walked back from the downwind side, hands covering their noses and mouths. The Trabant was a small car, now compacted even more by its impact with the base of the ramp. Yet the flames were enormous, red scalloped with chemical blue and green, and the smoke was black as oil. The Trabi didn't just burn from the inside; it was all on fire at once, plastic walls, hood and roof melting as they burned so that flames rained onto the seats. The tires burned as spectral rings.

They circled the wreck as best they could in case Tommy had crawled free.

Arkady said, "I've seen this kind of fire before. If he isn't out now, he's dead."

Peter retreated. Arkady tried to get closer, crawling on all fours below the smoke. The heat was too intense, a breath that made his jacket steam. When the wind shifted he saw in the car the kind of portrait a scissors artist cuts out of black paper. It was burning, too.

Peter returned in the BMW, backing up past the fire and searching the road with his spotlight until he found skid marks. He stopped, got out and set a blue flasher on the roof. He was probably a good policeman, Arkady thought.

Too late for Tommy. In violet hues, a plastic door peeled away. As the plastic roof curled back, a stronger updraft made flames swirl like a passionate flower folding and unfolding.

22

You know, in the old days we would have gassed you, tied you and shipped you home in a crate. We don't do things that way anymore. Now that our relations with the Germans have improved, we don't need to," Vice-Consul Platonov said.

"No?" Arkady asked.

"The Germans do it for us. First I remove you from these premises." Platonov pulled a shirt off the line strung across the room, surveyed a map of Munich spread on the table, the roll and juice by the sink, and then deposited the shirt in Federov's hands. "Renko, I know it feels like home to you, but since the consulate rents this room, we can do what we want. Right now I want to report you as a vagrant, which is what you are because I have your passport and without it you can't register anywhere else."

Federov unzipped Arkady's carry-on into a yawning mouth and tossed in the shirt. "Germans deport foreign vagrants, especially Russian vagrants."

"It's a matter of economics," Platonov said. "It's bad enough, they think, taking care of East Germans."

"If you're thinking about political asylum, forget it." Federov emptied the bureau drawers and bustled around the room like the energetic assistant he was. "That's out of date. No one wants defectors from a democratic Soviet Union."

Arkady hadn't seen the vice-consul since his first welcome to Munich, but Platonov had not forgotten him. "What did I tell you? See the museums, buy some gifts. You could have made a year's salary just buying here and selling when you got back. I warned you that you had no official status, and not to contact the German police. So what did you do? You not only went right to the Germans, but you also involved the consulate."

"Have you been to a fire?" Federov sniffed a jacket.

Arkady had washed the clothes he had worn the night before, and had showered too, but he doubted that his hair or his jacket would ever be completely free of smoke.

Platonov said, "Renko, twice a week I have tea with Bavarian industrialists and bankers to convince them that we are civilized people they can do business with and safely lend millions of Deutsche marks to. Then you show up and start twisting arms and demanding protection money. Federov tells me he had a difficult time convincing a lieutenant of the Polizei that he was not part of a conspiracy to defraud German banks."

"How would you like to be visited by the Gestapo?" Federov asked. He poured wallet, change purse, toothbrush and toothpaste into the bag. The locker key and Lufthansa ticket he confiscated and put into his pocket.

"Did he mention any bank in particular?" Arkady asked.

"No." Federov looked into the refrigerator and found it empty.

"Did the Germans make an official protest?"

"No." Federov folded up the map and threw it into the bag.

"Have you heard from the police since?"

"No."

Not even since the car wreck? That was interesting, Arkady thought. "I'll need my airplane ticket," he said.

"Actually, you won't." Platonov dropped an Aeroflot ticket on the table. "We're sending you home today. Federov will put you on the plane."

"My visa is good for another week," Arkady said.

"Consider your visa canceled."

"I'd need new orders from the prosecutor's office. Until then I can't leave."

"Prosecutor Rodionov is a hard man to reach. I have to ask myself why he sent an investigator on a tourist visa, giving you no real authority. The whole affair is too odd." Platonov wandered to the window and looked out toward the rail yard. Over the vice-consul's shoulder, Arkady saw trains slide across the tracks, morning commuters poised on the steps. Platonov shook his head in admiration. "Now, there's efficiency."

"I'm not going," Arkady said.

"You have no choice. Either we put you on the plane or the Germans will. Think how that would look on your record. I'm giving you the easy way out," Platonov said.

"All because I'm evicted?"

"As simple as that," Platonov said, "and absolutely legal. I really have to appreciate good diplomatic relations."

"I've never been evicted before," Arkady said. Arrested and exiled, but never simply evicted. Life was getting subtle, he thought.

"It's the coming thing." Federov swept the rest of the wash off the line and into the carry-on.

The door opened. Standing in the hall was a black dog that Arkady assumed was part of the eviction process; the animal had eyes as dark as agate and, by its size and density of hair, looked crossbred from a bear. It walked in confidently and regarded the three men with equal suspicion.

Unequal footsteps followed from the hall and Stas looked in. "Going somewhere?" he asked Arkady.

"Being sent."

Stas entered, ignoring Platonov and Federov, though Arkady was sure he knew who they were; he had studied Soviet apparatchiks all his life, and a man who studies worms all his life recognizes worms. Federov started to drop the bundle in his arms, but when the dog turned he held on to the clothes.

"I sent Tommy around last night. Did you see him?" Stas asked Arkady.

"I'm sorry about Tommy."

"You heard about the accident?"

"I saw it," Arkady said.

"I want to know what happened."

"So do I," Arkady said.

Stas's eyes shone a little more than usual. When he glanced at Platonov and the burdened Federov, the dog followed suit. He looked at the open carry-on again. "You can't leave," he said as if it were a decision.

Platonov spoke up. "It's German law. Since Renko has no place to stay, the consulate is expediting his return home."

"Stay with me," Stas told Arkady.

"It's not that simple," Platonov said. "Invitations to Soviet citizens have to be submitted in writing and approved in advance. His visa has been canceled and he already has his new ticket to Moscow, so it's impossible."

Stas asked Arkady, "Can you go now?"

Arkady removed his locker key and Lufthansa ticket from Federov and said, "Actually, I'm almost packed."

STAS JOINED THE traffic milling around the center of town. Though it was a gray summer day, the windows were down because the dog's breath condensed on the glass. The animal filled the rear seat of the car, and Arkady had the feeling that he would be allowed in front with his bag only as long as he moved slowly. When he had left, Platonov and Federov had looked like a pair of pallbearers whose corpse was walking out the door.

"Thanks."

"I did have some questions," Stas said. "Tommy was a silly man and he drove a stupid car. The Trabi wouldn't go more than seventy-five kilometers per hour and never should have been on a highway, but I don't understand how he could lose control and hit an abutment so hard."

"I don't either," Arkady said. "I doubt there's enough left of the car to tell the police anything. It burned down to an engine block and axle."

"It was probably that idiotic heater. A kerosene heater on a car floor? A death trap."

"Tommy didn't suffer long. If the crash didn't kill him, the smoke did. We see the flames, but they die of fumes first."

"You've seen this kind of thing before?"

"I saw a man in Moscow die in a car fire. It just took a little longer because it was a better car."

Thinking about Rudy made Arkady remember Polina. Also Jaak. He thought that if he got back to Moscow alive he would be a less critical person, more appreciative of friendship and deathly cautious of all cars and fires. Stas, on the other hand, drove recklessly. At least he watched the road, content to let the dog keep watch on Arkady.

"Did Tommy take you to Red Square?"

"You know about that place?"

"Renko, there are not many reasons to be on that road at that time of night. Poor Tommy. A case of fatal Russophilia."

"Then we went to a parking lot, sort of a mobile brothel."

"A wonderful place if you're looking for a wasting disease. German law says the women are checked for AIDS every three months, which means they're more scientific about the beer they drink than the women they sleep with. Anyway, trying to have sex in a Jeep can give you a hunchback and I have enough disabilities as it is. I thought the two of you were going to talk about famous battles of the Great Patriotic War."

"We did for a little while."

"Americans always want to talk about the war," Stas said.

"Do you know Boris Benz?"

"No. Who's he?"

There wasn't a hint of deception or a pause for thought. Children performed clownish, wide-eyed lies. Adults gave themselves away with small gestures, casting the eyes toward memory or couching the lie with a smile.

"Could you stop at the train station?" Arkady asked.

When Stas pulled in among the buses and cabs at the north side of the station, Arkady hopped out, leaving his bag behind.

"You're coming back?" Stas asked. "I have this feeling that you travel light."

"Two minutes."

Federov had brains of stale bread, but he might recognize a station locker key when he saw one, and it was even possible that he could remember the number. Arkady's original deposit had expired and he had to pay the attendant an extra four Deutsche marks to open the locker and retrieve the videotape, which left him with seventy-five Deutsche marks for the rest of his vacation.

When he went outside, a traffic policeman was trying to move Stas's shabby Mercedes out of the way of an Italian tour bus. The bus was polished like a gondola and had a furious musical horn. The more the bus honked and the policeman shouted, the louder the dog barked back. Stas himself sat behind the wheel and enjoyed a cigarette. "Not opera," he told Arkady, "but close."

ARKADY WAS GETTING his bearings. He knew when Stas turned north toward the museums and east toward the Englischer Garten. He noticed that a white Porsche he had seen at the station was half a block behind them.

"So, who is Boris Benz?" Stas asked.

"I don't really know. He's an East German who lives in Munich and travels to Moscow. Tommy said he'd met him. That's who we were looking for last night."

"If you and Tommy were together, why weren't you in the crash? Why didn't you die too?"

"The police picked me up. I was coming back in a police car when we saw the fire."

"They didn't mention that you were along."

"There was no reason to. An accident report is a short, simple form."

Peter had identified Arkady as a "witness who observed the deceased consuming alcohol at a roadside erotic club." A brief but pungent description, he thought. He added, "Especially a single-car accident where the car has burned so badly it almost disappears. There's nothing left to report."

"I think there's more. What did this Benz do in Moscow? Why aren't you investigating on a more official level? Where did Tommy meet Benz? Who introduced them? Why would the police take you out of Tommy's car? Was it an accident?"

"Did Tommy have any enemies?" Arkady asked.

"Tommy didn't have many friends, but he had no enemies at all. Why do I have this foreboding that anyone who helps you immediately acquires enemies? I shouldn't have sent him to you. He couldn't protect himself."

"You can?"

Although he didn't catch any signal from Stas, Arkady felt a hot canine breath at the back of his neck.

"Her name is Laika, but she's very German. Loves leather and beer, distrusts Russians. She makes an exception in my case. We're almost there." He waved toward a building that was a vertical garden of geraniums. "Every balcony a beer garden. Bavarian heaven. Actually, the balcony with cactus is mine."

"Thanks, but I won't be staying," Arkady said.

Stas swung in front of the building and killed the engine. "I thought you needed a place."

"I needed to get away from the consulate. You're generous. Thanks," Arkady said.

"You can't just walk off. Look, the truth is that you don't have a place to sleep."

"Right."

"And you don't have much money."

"Right."

"But you think you can survive in Munich?"

"Right."

Stas said to the dog, "He's so Russian." He told Arkady, "You think some special destiny is protecting you? Do you know why Germany looks so neat? Because every night the Germans pick up Turks, Poles and Russians and put them in sanitary jails until they're shipped home."

"Maybe I'll be lucky. You showed up when I needed you."

"That's different."

Stas got no farther before the Porsche eased alongside. The sports car moved back and forth, eyeballing Arkady and Stas. An electrically controlled window slid down, revealing a driver wearing dark sailing glasses with a red cord. His smile seemed to have more than two rows of teeth.

"Michael," Stas said.

"Stas." Michael had the kind of American voice that cut through the sound of a car engine. Arkady recalled a cool introduction to the station's deputy director at Tommy's party. "Have you heard about Tommy?"

"Yes."

"Sad." Michael observed a moment of silence.

"Yes."

Michael became more businesslike. "I was just coming to ask you about it."

"You were?"

"Because I heard that your friend, the visiting Investigator Renko from Moscow, was with our Tommy last night. And who do I see here but Renko himself?"

"I was just leaving," Arkady said.

"Good, because the station president would really like to have a few words with you." Michael pushed open the passenger door of the Porsche. "I just want you, not Stas. I'll bring you back, I promise."

Stas said to Arkady, "If you think Michael is any kind of salvation, you're insane."

∎ ∎ ∎

MICHAEL DROVE THE Porsche with one hand and used a cellular phone with the other. "Sir, I have Comrade Renko in tow." He gave Arkady a wink. "In tow, sir, in *tow*. We hit a gap between radio receivers. These phones work on line of vision." He cupped the phone on his shoulder to shift. "Sir, we'll be there in a second. I wish you'd wait until I get there. In a second." He dropped the phone into a sleeve between bucket seats and offered another glimpse of his dark glasses and bright smile. "Fucking technical incompetent. Well, Arkady, I've been checking up on you and you're an interesting guy. From what I hear, you're a maverick. I found you in Irina's file. It's safe to say that now you're in Tommy's file too. Does trouble just follow you, or what?"

"Were you following Stas?"

"I admit I was, and he led me right to you. The side trip to the train station gave me a scare. What did you take out of the locker?"

"A fur hat and an Order of Lenin."

"It looked like a little plastic box. A familiar kind of box. I can't place it and it's driving me crazy. You know, as deputy director for security I have excellent relations with the local police. I can find out in a roundabout way what you and Tommy were doing last night, or else you can simply tell me. Only one way gets you extra credit."

"Extra credit?"

"Let me put it more simply: money. What we can't afford is any mystery about one of our employees being killed. We hoped that the bad old days of the cold war were behind us. I'm betting they are."

"Why? You might lose your job; they might shut the station."

"I'm looking ahead."

"So is Max Albov."

"Max is a winner. He's a star. Like Irina, if she polished her English a little more and chose her friends a little better." He glanced over. "President Gilmartin is going to ask you about Tommy. Gilmartin is head of Radio Liberty and Radio Free Europe. He's the frontline voice of the United States and he's a busy man. So if you're cute, then fuck you and you can eat dog food. If you're honest, then there's a bonus for you."

"It pays to be honest?"

"Exactly!"

The Porsche surged ahead of the traffic like a speedboat, and Michael smiled as if Munich were tossing in his wake.

THEY CROSSED TO the east side of the city and the largest houses, short of palaces, that Arkady had ever seen. Some of them were modern, stark Bauhaus plaster and steel tubing. Others looked almost Mediterranean, with glass doors and potted palms. A few were either miraculously surviving or painstakingly reconstructed examples of *Jugendstil,* mansions covered with playful, vinelike façades and curving eaves.

Michael pulled into the driveway of the grandest of the mansions. On the front lawn a man was setting up a combination umbrella and table.

Michael led Arkady across the grass. Although no drops were falling, the man was dressed in a raincoat and rubber boots. About sixty, with a noble brow and jowls, he regarded Michael's arrival with a mixture of exasperation and relief.

"Sir, this is Investigator Renko. President Gilmartin," Michael said.

"A pleasure." Gilmartin gave Arkady a firm sportsman's hand and then sorted through a toolbox on the table for the shiniest pair of pliers. A wrench and screwdriver had already spilled onto the lawn.

Michael pulled off his sunglasses and let them hang from the cord. "I wish you'd waited for me, sir."

"The goddamn Germans are always complaining about my dish. The grief. I have to have a dish, and this is the only place with a clear sight of satellites unless I put it on the roof, and then would the Heinies scream."

Now that Arkady looked, he saw that the umbrella was actually camouflage, striped fabric over a satellite dish three meters wide. Dish and table were bolted to the ground.

"The boots are a good idea," Michael said.

"I've been around broadcasting long enough to know better safe than sorry," Gilmartin said. He told Arkady, "I was with the networks for thirty years until I decided I didn't like the direction the medium was going. I wanted to have an impact."

"Tommy," Michael reminded him.

"Yes." Gilmartin fixed Arkady with a stare. "Dark Ages, Renko. We've had trouble in the past. Murders, break-ins, bombings. You blew up our Czech section a few years back. Tried to stab our Rumanian chief to death in his garage. Electrocuted one of our nicest Russian contributors. But we never lost an American, and those were the days when we were admittedly CIA. Prehistoric. We're funded by Congress now."

"We're a private corporation," Michael said.

"Delaware, I believe. My point is, we're not secret agents."

"Tommy was an inoffensive guy," Michael said.

"The most inoffensive guy I ever met," Gilmartin said. "Besides, the days of rough stuff are supposed to be over, so what were you, a Soviet investigator, doing with Tommy when he died?"

Arkady said, "Tommy had a historical interest in the war against Hitler. He asked some questions about people I knew."

"There's more to it than that," Gilmartin said.

"There's a lot more to it," Michael agreed.

"The station is like a family," Gilmartin said. "We watch out for each other. I want to know the whole unvarnished story."

"Such as?" Arkady asked.

"Was there sex involved? I don't mean you and Tommy. I mean, were there women?"

Michael said, "The president means that if Washington goes through Tommy's laundry, are they going to find dirt?"

Gilmartin said, "It doesn't matter to them that prostitution is legal in Germany. American standards are set in Peoria. Even a hint of scandal here always brings accusations of corruption and high living."

"And reductions in funding," Michael said.

"I want to know everything you and Tommy did last night." Gilmartin said.

Arkady took a moment to choose his words. "Tommy came to the pension where I was staying. We talked about the war. After a while I said I'd like some fresh air, so we got into his car and drove around. We did see a group of prostitutes on the highway. At that point I left Tommy and he drove alone back to the city. On the way he had an accident."

"Did Tommy have sex with a prostitute?" Gilmartin asked.

"No," Arkady lied.

"Did he talk to a prostitute?" Michael asked.

"No," Arkady lied again.

"Did he talk to any Russians besides yourself?" Michael asked.

"No," Arkady lied a third time.

"Why did you separate?" Gilmartin asked.

"I *did* want to see a prostitute. Tommy refused to stay."

Michael asked, "How did you get back to Munich?"

"The police picked me up on the side of the road."

"A sorry night on the town," Gilmartin said.

"None of it was Tommy's fault," Arkady said.

Michael and Gilmartin exchanged looks that made a silent conversation; then the president lifted his eyes and considered the sky. "It's awfully thin."

"But if Renko sticks to it, it's not bad. He's Russian, after all. They're not going to have a year to boil it out of him. And remember, Tommy drove an East German Trabant, not a very roadworthy car. That's what we zero in on: the car was a death trap." Michael patted Arkady on the back. "You're probably lucky to be alive."

"Losing Tommy must be a blow," Arkady said to Gilmartin.

"More a personal tragedy. He wasn't in any decision-making role. Research and translations, right?"

"Yes, sir," Michael said.

"Though they're important," Gilmartin hastened to add. "Michael's Russian is better than mine, but I think it's fair to say that without our able translators the Russians on the staff would run amok."

Gilmartin's attention moved to his other concern. He pointed his pair of pliers at loose bolts that had rolled into a fold of the diagram. "Know anything about satellite dishes?" he asked Arkady.

"No."

"I'm afraid I may have moved something out of alignment," Gilmartin confessed.

"Sir, we'll think about wind load, check the signal and make sure you didn't damage any cable," Michael said. "Looks like a good job."

"Think so?" Reassured, Gilmartin stepped back for a better view. "You know, this would be even more convincing if we brought chairs out and got people to really use this as an umbrella."

"Sir, I don't think you'd actually want people drinking lemonade under a microwave receiver."

"No," Gilmartin said. He scratched his chin with the pliers. "Maybe just the neighbors."

23

Stas lived alone . . . and not alone. Moving through the hall meant elbowing Gogol and Gorky. Poets Pushkin through Voloshin resided in a closet. The elevated thoughts of Tolstoy filled shelves above a Swedish sound system, CDs and television set. Newspapers and magazines were stacked by year. The least slip, Arkady thought, and a man could die under an avalanche of stale news, music, fantasy, romance.

Stas said, "I don't like to think of it as messy. I prefer to think of it as life lived at full tide."

"It looks like full tide," Arkady said.

"Hotels are lacking in soul," Stas said.

Laika sat by the door. Arkady could barely see her eyes through her fur, though he felt them following his every move.

"Thanks, I have someplace to go," he said.

After the visit to the station president, Arkady had spent the rest of the day watching Benz's house. It was dusk now and light was seeping from the room. He had decided to ride the subway until it shut down, or to buy a cheap ticket for an early-morning train so he could wait at the station. That way he would at least be more migrant than vagrant. He had come to Stas's place only for his bag.

One question kept forcing itself to the front of Arkady's mind. It was so obvious that it was hard work not asking. "Where is Max staying?"

"I don't know. One drink before you go," Stas said. "I suspect you're in for a long night."

Before Arkady could protest or get around the dog and out the door, his host was in the kitchen and back with two water glasses and a bottle of vodka. The vodka was iced. "Fancy," Arkady said.

Stas filled the glasses halfway. "To Tommy."

The cold vodka gave Arkady's heart a brief squeeze on the way down. Alcohol didn't seem to affect Stas; he was a frail reed that stood up to the flood. He refilled the glasses. "To Michael," he offered. "And the snake that bites him."

Arkady drank to that and set the glass on a stack of papers out of Stas's reach. "I'm just curious. You go out of your way to annoy the Americans. Why don't they fire you?"

"German labor law. The Germans don't want any foreigners on their welfare rolls, so once one has a job it's almost impossible to dismiss him. There are meetings between the American management and the Russian staff at the station. By law, the reports are written in German. It drives the Americans crazy. Michael tries to fire me once a year. It's wonderful, like starving a shark. Anyway, I put good programs on the air."

"You like to embarrass him?"

"I'll tell you what real embarrassment is—when the Jews on the staff accused the station of anti-Semitism, took it to a German court and *won*. That's embarrassment. I don't want Michael to forget episodes like that."

"When Max defected back to Moscow, wasn't that embarrassing?"

Stas took a deep breath. "It was embarrassing to me and to Irina. Actually, it was embarrassing to everyone. We'd had security problems before."

"Michael said so. An explosion?"

"That's why we have the gates and big walls now. But to have the head of the Russian section defect back to Moscow is a security problem on a different level."

"I'd think that Michael would hate Max even more than he hates you."

"You'd think so." Stas looked at his empty glass. "I've known Max for ten years. I was always struck by how he could get along with the Americans and us. He changed, depending where he was and who he was with. You and I are Russians. Max is liquid. He changes shape. He fills the container whatever the container is. In a fluid situation, he's king. He came back from Moscow more of a businessman than he was before. The Americans can't help believing Max because he's like a mirror. To them he looks like another American."

"What kind of business is he involved in?"

"I don't know. Before he left he used to say a fortune could be made out of the collapse of the Soviet Union. He said it was like any huge bankruptcy; there were still assets and property. What's the biggest landowner in the Soviet Union? Who owns the biggest office buildings, the best resorts, the only decent apartment houses?"

"The Party."

"The Communist party. Max said that all it had to do was change its name, call itself a company and restructure. Dump the shareholders, keep the goods."

ARKADY WASN'T AWARE at what point he had set his bag down, but he discovered himself sitting on the couch. Bread, cheese and cigarettes were on the table. A floor fixture pointed light in three directions. The balcony door was open to street sounds and night air.

Stas filled the glasses again. "I wasn't a spy. The KGB called demonstrators and defectors either spies or mentally ill. Russians understand that. The part I didn't expect was that the Americans would think that it was a KGB plot to insert the dangerous Stas into the unsuspecting West. Some of the CIA believed it. *All* of the FBI believed it. The FBI doesn't believe *any* defectors. Jesus could ride an ass out of Moscow and they'd open a file on him.

"There were real heroes. Not me. Men and women who crawled through minefields into Turkey or ran through gunfire to reach an embassy yard. Who threw away careers and lost their families. For what? For Czechoslovakia, Hungary, God, Afghanistan. Which doesn't mean that they weren't compromised. You understand, but Americans don't. We grew up with informers; among our friends and families there always were informers. Even among heroes there were informers. It's complex. A woman, an old lover from Moscow, visits Munich. Michael demands to know why I see her when everyone knows she's an informer. But that doesn't mean I don't still love her. We have a writer at Liberty whose wife worked at an army base teaching the Russian language to American officers, screwing them and getting information for the KGB so she could live like a decent Western woman. She spent two years in jail. That doesn't mean her husband didn't take her back. We all talk to her. What are we going to do, pretend she's dead?

"Or we arrive compromised. An artist, a friend of mine, was called in by the KGB before he left Moscow. They said, 'We never put you in a camp, so no hard feelings. All we hope is you don't slander us to the Western press. After all, we think you're a wonderful artist and you probably don't realize how difficult it is to survive in the West, so we'd like to give you a loan. In dollars. We won't tell anyone and you don't need to sign a receipt. After a few years you pay it back with interest or no interest, when you can, just between us.' Five years later he publicly sent them a check and demanded a receipt, but it took him that long to realize how cheaply he'd been compromised and canceled out. How many other loans are out there?

"Or we go crazy. There's the writer who went to Paris. A famous writer who survived the gulag and wrote under the pen name of 'Teitlebaum.' It was revealed that he informed for the KGB. He wrote a defense and said, no, no, it wasn't him who informed, it was Teitlebaum!

"And occasionally," Stas said, "we're killed. We open a letter bomb or get jabbed with the tip of a poisoned umbrella, or drink ourselves to death. Even so, at one time we were heroes."

Laika stretched like a sphinx in the middle of the floor. Arkady couldn't see the dog's eyes as much as feel their force. Her ear might turn toward the sound of a particularly noisy car on the street four stories down, but her focus remained on him. He said, "You don't have to explain yourself to me."

"I do because you're different. You aren't a dissident. You saved Irina, but everyone wants to save Irina, that's not necessarily a political act."

"It was more personal," Arkady admitted.

"You stayed. People who knew Irina knew about you. You were the ghost. She tried to reach you once or twice."

"Not that I know of."

"What I'm trying to say is that we made a sacrifice to be soldiers on the right side. Who knew that history was going to change? That the Red Army would end up as camps of beggars in Poland? That the Wall was going to fall? They thought the Red Army was a danger? Now they're worried about two hundred and forty million Russians eating their way to the English Channel. Radio Liberty isn't quite the front line anymore. We're not jammed, we have correspondents now in Moscow, we regularly interview people in the Kremlin."

"You won," Arkady said.

Stas killed the bottle and lit a cigarette. His narrow face was wan, his eyes two bright matches. "Won? Then why only now do I feel like an émigré? Say you leave your native land because you were forced out, or because you thought you could help more from the outside than in. Democrats of the world applaud your noble effort. But it wasn't because of any effort of mine that the Soviet Union dropped to its knees and stretched out its long neck. It was history. It was gravity. The battle isn't in Munich, it's in Moscow. History has marooned us and gone in a different direction. We don't look like heroes anymore; we look like fools. Americans look at us—not Michael and Gilmartin, they're concerned about their jobs and keeping the station alive—but other Americans read headlines about what's happening in Moscow and look at us and say, 'They should have stayed.' It doesn't matter whether we were forced out or risked our lives or wanted to save the world; now Americans say, 'They should have stayed.' They look at someone like you and say, 'See, he stayed.'"

"I didn't have a choice. I made a bargain. They'd only leave Irina alone if I stayed. Anyway, that was long ago."

Stas peered into his empty glass. "If you'd had the choice, would you have left with her?"

Arkady was silent. Stas leaned forward and waved smoke away to see him more clearly. "Would you?"

"I was Russian. I don't think I could have gone."

Stas was silent.

Arkady added, "*My* staying in Moscow certainly had no effect on history. Maybe *I* was the fool."

Stas stirred, went to the kitchen and returned with another bottle. Laika kept her attention on Arkady in case he produced a bomb, a gun or a sharpened umbrella against her master.

"Irina had a difficult time in New York. She was in films in Moscow?" Stas asked.

"She was actually a student until she was thrown out of the university. Then she got work at Mosfilm as a wardrobe mistress," Arkady said.

"In New York she did stage costumes and makeup, fell in with an artistic crowd and worked in art galleries, first there and then Berlin, all the time defending herself from saviors. The pattern was always the same: an American would fall in love with Irina and then rationalize it as a political good deed. I think Radio Liberty must have been a relief. To give him credit, Max was the one who recognized how good she was. She wasn't a regular at first, just filling in, but he said there was a quality in her voice on the air, as if she were speaking to someone she knew. People listened. I was skeptical at first because she had no professional training. He gave me the job of teaching her how to hit her marks and watch the clock. People have no idea how fast they talk. Irina could run through a script once and almost have it memorized. With training, she was the best."

Stas opened the bottle. "So there we were, Max and I, two sculptors working on the same beautiful statue. Naturally we both fell in love with Irina. We did everything together—Max, Stas and Irina. Dinners, skiing in the Alps, musical side trips to Salzburg. An inseparable trio, neither Max nor I ever gaining an edge on the other. I didn't actually ski. I read down in the lodge, secure in the knowledge that Max was making no romantic headway on the slopes because, in fact, our trio was really a quartet." He poured the vodka. "There was always that man in Irina's past. The one who saved her life and stayed, the one she was waiting for. How could anyone beat a hero like that?"

"Maybe no one needed to. Maybe she just got tired of waiting," Arkady said.

They drank at the same time, like two men chained to the same oar.

"No," Stas said. "I'm not talking about long ago. When Max went to Moscow last year I thought I was in command of the field. But I was outmaneuvered to a degree I never anticipated, in a manner that only proves Max's genius. Because you see what Max did?"

"No," Arkady admitted.

"Max came back. Max loved her and he came back for her. It was what I couldn't do and what you never did. Now he's the hero and I'm demoted to mere 'dear friend.' "

Stas's eyes looked fueled by vodka. Arkady wondered if he had ever actually seen the man *eat*. He swirled the vodka in his own glass so that it rolled around like mercury. "What was Max before he ever came to the West?"

"He was a film director. He defected at a film festival. Hollywood, however, was not interested in his work."

"What kind of films had he done?"

"War epics, killing Germans, Japanese, Israeli terrorists—the usual. Max did have the tastes of a famous director: custom suits, fine wine, beautiful women."

"Where is he staying in Munich?" Arkady asked again.

"I don't know. What I'm trying to say is that my last hope is you."

"Max has outmaneuvered me, too."

"No, I know Max. He only attacks when he has to. If you weren't a threat he'd be your best friend."

"Not much of a threat. As far as Irina is concerned, I'm dead." That was the word she had used in Tommy's kitchen, like a knife she'd found on the table.

"But did she tell you to go?"

"No."

"So she hasn't really made up her mind."

"Irina doesn't care whether I come or go. I don't think she even sees me."

"Irina hasn't smoked for years. The first time she saw you she asked for a cigarette. She sees you."

Laika's head turned toward the balcony and she rose to her fore-paws, then stood, ears sharp. Stas motioned for Arkady to be quiet, then reached for the light fixture and turned it off.

The room was black. Outside was the percussive noise of Volkswagens and the sound of a bell chasing someone from a bike lane. Closer, Arkady heard the toeholds of rubber soles, the easing of a rail, the soft landing of a big man onto the balcony. Laika was invisible, but Arkady located her by an anticipatory growl in the darkness. As a step crossed the balcony he felt the dog coil to attack.

There was an audible intake of breath and a voice in pain. "Stas, please! Stas!"

Stas turned the lights on. "Sit, Laika. Good girl, sit, sit."

Rikki staggered through the door. Arkady had met the Georgian actor-become-broadcaster in the station cafeteria and at Tommy's party. Each time Rikki had appeared distraught, or at least histrionic. Now he was again. The back of one hand was covered in spines. "The cactus," he moaned.

"I rearranged them," Stas said.

Arkady turned on the outdoor light. Under a hanging lamp was a metal table, two chairs, a pail of empty beer bottles and a semicircle of potted cacti, some of them pincushions with short spines and some that resembled serrated bayonets.

"It's an alarm system," Stas said.

A shock wave went through Rikki with each needle that Stas pulled out. "Everyone else has geraniums on their balcony. I have geraniums. The geranium is a lovely flower," he said.

"Rikki lives upstairs." Stas plucked the final spine.

Red puncture marks dotted Rikki's hand. He looked at them mournfully.

"Do you always visit this way?" Arkady asked.

"I was trapped." Remembering, he pulled Stas and Arkady away from the balcony. "They're at my door."

"Who?" Stas asked.

"My mother and my daughter. All these years waiting to see them and now they're here. My mother wants to take the television. My daughter wants to drive back in the car."

"Your car?" Stas asked.

"*Her* car, once she gets to Georgia." Rikki explained to Arkady, "In a moment of weakness, I said she could. But I have a new BMW. What is a girl going to do with that in Georgia?"

"Have fun," Arkady said.

"I knew this would happen. These people have no control. They're so greedy it makes me ashamed." Rikki's face fell tragically.

Stas said, "Don't answer your door and they'll go away."

"Not them." Rikki's eyes lifted to the ceiling. "They'll wait me out."

"You can go down the stairs from here," Arkady said.

Rikki said, "I told them to wait a minute. I can't simply disappear. I have to open the door sometime."

Stas asked, "Then, why come here?"

"Do you have any brandy?" Rikki examined his hand, which was already starting to swell.

"No. Vodka," Stas offered.

"It will have to do." He allowed himself to be helped to a chair and given a glass. "This is my plan: let her take a different car."

Stas said, "You picked her up at the airport. She knows your car. She loves your car."

"I'll say it's yours—that I borrowed it from you to impress her."

"Ah. And what car are you going to let her take?" Stas asked.

"Stas." Rikki batted his eyes. "Stas, we're close friends. Your Mercedes is ten years old, bought used—a dog bed, if I may speak frankly. My daughter is a woman of some taste. She'll take one look at your car and will refuse to touch it. I was hoping we could trade keys."

Stas poured two more vodkas and said to Arkady, "You wouldn't know it now, but Rikki once swam the Black Sea. He had a wet suit and a compass. He dove through nets and swam under patrol boats. It was a heroic escape. Now here he is, hiding from his daughter."

"You won't trade?" Rikki asked.

"Life has caught up with you. I think your daughter's going to make you pay for years," Stas said. "The car is only a beginning."

The vodka seemed to stick in Rikki's throat. He drew himself up with dignity, walked out to the balcony and spat over the rail. "Damn her! And you!" he told Stas. He set the glass on the balcony table and hoisted himself up on the waterpipe that ran down the front of the building. For a man his size he was still agile. Arkady saw his legs swing to the upper balcony. As he thrashed, geranium petals rained.

ARKADY AWOKE ON the sofa. It was two A.M. by his watch. There is no hole deeper than two in the morning, the hour when fear rules the world. Stas had avoided the question twice. Where was Max staying?

By nature, Russians did not like hotels. Visitors stayed with friends. Other friends knew where. The idea that Max was lying beside Irina made Arkady stare into the bluish dark of the room. He could almost see them in bed, as if it were just on the other side of the living-room table. See Max's arm locked around her; hear Max breathe the perfume of her hair.

He lit a match. Chairs, desk and bookshelves crept out of the dark and toward the flame. He threw off his blanket. On the desk he had seen the telephone. Feeling around the top, he found a small address book. He lit another match clumsily with one hand, opened the front of the book and found "Irina Asanova" and her number. The flame was at his fingers. He pinched it out and picked up the phone. Would he say he was sorry to wake her, but they had to talk? She'd already made it clear she had nothing to say to him, especially if Max was lying next to her. Arkady could warn her. How jealous and inept that would sound, with Max right there.

Or when she answered he could ask for Max. That would let her know he was aware of how things stood. Or if she asked who was calling, he could say, "Boris," then see how she reacted to that.

Arkady punched her number, but when he started to lift the phone to his ear, his wrist was clamped. Damp teeth held the hand and phone down. When he made the slightest effort to raise the phone, the jaws tightened. He moved his other hand to the phone and a growl resonated through his arm.

On the other end of the line he heard the characteristic two rings of a German phone. "Hello?" Irina said.

Arkady tried to wrench his arm free and the jaws closed.

"Who is this?" Irina asked.

The whole weight of the dog hung from his arm.

A click was followed by a dial tone.

As Arkady let his arm fall, the jaws relaxed. When he replaced the phone on the cradle, the teeth let go. He felt the dog waiting to make sure he left the phone alone.

Save me, Arkady thought. Save me from myself.

24

The secret was that Stas did all his eating at breakfast: liver, smoked salmon, potato salad and pots of coffee. He also had the VCR and enormous television of an unmarried man.

With a remote control, Arkady played the videotape. On Fast Forward, the television screen raced through monks, Marienplatz, beer garden, modern traffic, beer hall, swans, opera, Oktoberfest, Alps, beer garden. Stopped. He rewound to the start of the last scene. It was a sun-dappled garden in a wall of honeysuckle tended by bees. Diners sat exhausted by the effort of heavy lunches, all but the woman at one table. He froze the frame where she raised her glass.

"Never seen her before," Stas said. "What shocks me is that I've never been in this beer garden. I thought I'd been in them all."

The screen came back to life. She raised her glass higher. Blond hair swept back almost ferociously, gold necklace bedded on black cashmere, cat-eyed sunglasses that expressed amusement, red nails and lips that promised in Russian, "I love you."

Stas shook his head. "I'd remember her."

"Not at Radio Liberty?" Arkady asked.

"Hardly."

"Around Tommy?"

"Possibly, but I've never met her."

Arkady tried a different tack. "I'd like to see where Tommy worked."

"The Red Archive? The next time I try to sign you in, the guards will call Michael. I don't mind annoying him, but he'll just tell the guards not to give you a pass."

"Is Michael always at the station?"

"No. Between eleven and twelve he plays tennis at the club across the street. But he takes his phone everywhere."

"You'll be at the station?"

"I'll be at my desk until noon. I'm a writer. I turn the decline and fall of the Soviet Union into bite-sized words."

WHEN STAS LEFT, Arkady neatened the couch, washed the dishes and ironed the clothes that Federov had squashed into the bag the day before. His wrist was ringed with bruises, but the skin wasn't broken; Stas had seen the marks and said nothing. Every step he took, from sofa to sink to ironing board, he was followed by Laika. So far, she found his behavior acceptable.

While he ironed, Arkady ran the tape again. As the camera panned, he realized he might be looking at a restaurant patio rather than a beer garden. There was indoor dining, though the light outside was too intense to see through the windows.

What did he know about her? She might at one time have been a Moscow *putana* called Rita. She could be the globetrotting Frau Benz. The only hard evidence of her existence was this tape. This time he noticed that her table was set for two. She had an almost theatrical presence. The gold necklace was Teutonic, but the angles of her face were distinctly Russian. Thick makeup—that was more Russian, too. He wished that just once she would take off her glasses. Slowly her lips formed a smile and said to Rudy Rosen, "I love you."

Laika whined, walked toward the television set and sat again.

Arkady rewound and froze every other frame. Backward from her glasses. Retreat from her table. Turn from the diners. Embroidery of vines and bees. Sidecart of linen, utensils, water carafes. Stucco. Honeysuckle. Window with one pane that reflected the person with the camera standing before a solid wall of green. That was another question: who took the pictures? A man with distinctively broad shoulders in a sweater that was red, white and black. Marlboro colors.

He played it forward again. Motes floated in the sunlight. Bees stirred and diners came back to semilife. The woman in the glasses repeated, "I love you."

■   ■   ■

AT THE LUITPOLD garage, an elongated Mercedes with a red car phone was parked by the attendant's booth. Remembering the Arabs at the Hilton, Arkady climbed the ramp to the next level, chose a BMW that looked light on its feet and gave it a firm shove. The car woke at once with blinking lights and a sounding horn. He heaved into Mercedeses, Audis, Daimlers and Maseratis until the entire level reverberated with an orchestra of alarms. When he saw the attendant come racing up the ramp, he ran down the stairs.

In the booth were ticket punch, register, car tools and a long shiv for opening locked car doors. The shiv demanded patience that Arkady didn't have time for. He took a lug wrench. As he broke the window of the Mercedes, the limousine's alarm joined the woodwinds, but in five seconds he was walking out the garage exit with the phone.

In Moscow, he was a senior investigator of the city prosecutor's office; here, after less than a week in the West, he was a thief. He knew he should feel guilty; instead, he felt alive. Even smart enough to turn off the phone.

It was after eleven by the time he got to Radio Liberty. Across the street, and hidden by parked cars and wire fences, were a clubhouse, patio tables and steps leading down to clay tennis courts where players in whites and pastels patrolled the baselines and traded top spin. What a delightful world, Arkady thought. Imagine having the leisure in the middle of the day to pull on shorts, chase a fuzzy ball, work up an athletic sweat. He looked into Michael's Porsche. Its red cellular phone, the plastic scepter, was gone.

Michael was on a court near the clubhouse. He wore shorts and a V-necked sweater and played with the indolent ease of someone who had been given his first tennis ball in the crib. His opponent, whose back was to Arkady, swung wildly and moved as unsteadily as a man on a trampoline. Behind him and directly in Michael's line of sight was a table with the phone, its antenna fully extended. The other tables were empty.

While Arkady considered an approach, he noticed that life offered its own distractions. Michael's opponent hit balls left and right and over Michael's head to the screen. Other times he missed the ball completely. Sometimes he got tangled up in his shorts. The game seemed not just foreign to him, but from a planet with a different gravity.

During a conference at the net, Arkady was surprised to overhear his own name. As the opponent returned to the baseline, he got a good look. Federov. The consular aide's next serve flew over the screen and bounced into a far court where two women were playing. They wore short skirts that displayed scissory, tanned legs, and they regarded the ball as a breach of form. Michael strolled to the fence and apologized with a tone that suggested his empathy. Waving his racquet and making too much noise for a tennis court, Federov ran to join him. By then Arkady had walked by the table and switched phones.

On the far side of the clubhouse were two recycling bins, orange for plastic, green for glass. Arkady tossed the phone into the orange one, then walked back past the tennis courts, through the station gates, under the cameras, by the guard booth in the parking lot and up the steps to the reception area.

Summoned, Stas came to the desk, a little astonished to see him, while the guards tried to call Michael. "It's ringing."

Stas said, "We haven't got all day."

The guard hung up, welcomed Arkady with a glare and a visitor's pass. After a buzz at the door he was back in the cream-carpeted hallway of Radio Liberty. The bulletin boards were changed, a sign of a well-run organization. Glossy photographs showed President Gilmartin leading a tour of Hungarian broadcasters and applauding the folkloric dancers from Minsk. Technicians with audiotape trafficked up and down the corridor. Ludmilla's gray bangs bobbed in and out of a doorway.

"Did you come to bomb the director's office or Michael's? How much trouble am I in?" Stas asked.

"Which way is the Red Archive?"

"The stairs are between the soda and the snack machine. Bomb away."

WHEN TOMMY BOASTED about the Red Archive being the greatest library of Soviet life outside Moscow, Arkady had pictured the lamps and musty stacks of the Lenin Library. As usual, he was unprepared for reality. There were no lamps in the Red Archive, only the aquarium glow of room-length fixtures. No books either, only microfiche files, motorized steel cabinets that glided on tracks. Instead of a reading room there was a machine that enlarged microfiche to legible size. Arkady ran a hand over a file in awe. It was as if Ancient Rus, Peter and Catherine the Great and the storming of the Winter Palace had been reduced to the head of a pin. He was relieved to see something as primitive as a wooden box with file cards in Cyrillic.

All the researchers scribbling away at desks were Americans. A woman with a blouse full of bows was delighted to see a Russian.

"Where was Tommy's desk?" Arkady asked.

"The *Pravda* section." She sighed and pointed to another door. "We miss him."

"Of course."

"There's so much information coming these days," she said. "There used to be none and now there's too much. I wish it would just slow down."

"I know what you mean."

The *Pravda* section was a narrow room made smaller by shelves of bound copies of *Pravda* on one side and *Izvestia* on the other. At the end of the room a VCR was taping from a color television set. The station had to have a satellite dish because, though the sound was low, Arkady realized that he was watching Soviet news. On the screen, a crowd in shabby clothes was pushing over a truck. When it landed on its side, they swarmed into the back of it. A close-up of the driver showed his bloody nose. A different angle on the truck displayed the name of a cooperative for rendering tallow. People climbed out of it waving bones and black meat. Arkady realized how much he had been conditioned by a few days of ample German beer and food. Was it this bad, he asked himself? Was it really this bad?

Behind the set was Tommy's desk, covered by newspapers, coffee rings and machine-gun bullets used as paperweights. In the middle drawer were soft pencils, staplers, memo pads, paper clips. In the side drawers, Russian-English and German-English dictionaries, cowboy paperbacks, heavier books on military history, manuscripts and rejection letters. There was not even a phone jack for a fax.

Arkady returned to the file room and asked the woman at the file cards, "Did Tommy have a fax when he worked at Program Review?"

"Possibly. The Review section is in a different part of town. He could have used one there."

"How long was he here?"

"A year. I wish we had a fax here. That's one of the executive perks. Privileges," she said brightly, as if describing awards. "We do have information here. Anything about the Soviet Union. Any subject."

"Max Albov."

She took a deep breath and played with the bows on her collar. "Well, that's close to home. Okay." She started away, stopped. "Your name is?"

"Renko."

"You're visiting?"

"Michael."

"Then . . ." She lifted her hands. The sky was the limit.

Max was a vein of gold that seemed to work its way through cabinet after cabinet of microfiches. Arkady sat at the enlarger and scrolled through years of *Pravda, Red Star* and *Soviet Film* describing Max's career in cinema, his treacherous defection to the West, his service with Radio Liberty—the CIA's mouthpiece of disinformation—his pangs of conscience, his return to the motherland and his recent incarnation on American television as a respected journalist and commentator.

An early item in *Soviet Film* caught Arkady's attention. "For director Maxim Albov, the most important part of the story is the woman. 'Get a beautiful actress, light her properly and your film is already halfway a success.' "

His films, however, had all been of the action variety, extolling the daring and sacrifices of the Red Army and border guards against Maoists, Zionists and mujaheddin.

Another item read, "One effect of an Israeli tank on fire was particularly difficult because the film crew didn't have the blasting caps or plastic explosives they had requested. The successful shot was improvised by the director himself.

"Albov: 'We were filming outside Baku, near a chemical complex. Filmgoers don't know that my initial schooling was in chemistry. I was aware that by combining seemingly innocent ingredients we could create a spontaneous explosion without a fuse or a cap. Since the question was timing we tested forty or fifty samples before filming, which we did with a remote camera behind a Plexiglas screen. It was a night shot and the effect when the Israeli tank erupts into flame is spectacular. Hollywood couldn't do better.' "

Arkady's head snapped up as the archive door slammed open and Michael and Federov entered. Still in tennis shorts, Federov's legs were a fluorescent white. He carried a racquet. Michael held a phone. They were accompanied by the guards from the reception desk and by Ludmilla, who glowered like a vicious pug.

LUDMILLA SAID, "USE my office. It's next to yours. That way your secretary won't log him in. He just disappears."

Michael liked the suggestion. They crowded into a room with black furniture and ashtrays set out like urns of the recently departed. On the walls were photographs of the famous poet Tsetaeva, who had emigrated to Paris with her husband, an assassin. Even by Russian standards it had been a troubled marriage.

The guards pushed Arkady down onto an ottoman. Federov sank into the sofa and Michael perched on the edge of the desk.

"Where's my goddamn phone?"

"In your hand?" Arkady asked.

Michael let the receiver drop on his desk. "This is not mine. You know where mine is. You changed the fucking phones."

"How could I change your phone?"

"That's how you got past the front desk."

Arkady said, "No, they gave me a visitor's pass."

"Because they couldn't reach me on the phone," Michael said. "Because they're idiots."

"What does your phone look like?"

Michael practiced even breathing. "Renko, Federov and I got together today to talk about you. You seem to cause problems across the board."

"He refused an order from the consul to go home." Federov was happy to be included. "He has a friend here at the station named Stanislav Kolotov."

"Stas! I'll interrogate him later. He sent you to the archive?" Michael asked Arkady.

"No, I just wanted to see where Tommy worked."

"Why?"

"He made his work sound interesting."

"And the files on Max Albov?"

"He sounded fascinating."

"But you told the head researcher that you'd come to see me."

"I did come to see you. Yesterday, when you took me to President Gilmartin you promised me money."

Michael said, "You fed Gilmartin horseshit."

"Renko does need money," Federov said.

"Of course he needs money. Every Russian needs money," Ludmilla said.

"Are you sure that's not your phone?" Arkady asked.

"This is a stolen phone," Michael said.

"The police should check it for prints," Arkady said.

"Well, it's got my fingerprints on it now, naturally. The police will be here soon enough. The point is, Renko, that you like to stir things up. It's my job to keep things smooth. I've come to the decision that things here will run a lot smoother if you're back in Moscow."

Federov said, "That's the feeling at the consulate, too."

When Arkady shifted, he felt a guard's hand leaning on each shoulder.

Michael said, "We've decided to put you on the plane. Consider that done. The communiqué my friend Sergei here sends to Moscow will depend in large part on your attitude, which so far is piss-poor. He could describe your work here as so successful that you went home early. On the other hand, I would guess that an investigator who's sent back for harming relations between the United States and the Soviet Union, for abusing the hospitality of the German republic and for stealing the property of this station will get a cold reception. Do you want to clean a latrine in Siberia for the rest of your miserable life? That's your choice."

"I'd like to help," Arkady said.

"That's better. What are you looking for in Munich? Why have you been poking around Radio Liberty? How is Stas helping you? Where's my phone?"

"I have an idea," Arkady suggested.

"Tell me," Michael said.

"Call."

"Call who?"

"Yourself. Maybe you'll hear a ring."

There was silence for a moment. "That's it? Renko, you're worse than an asshole, you're a suicide."

Arkady said, "You can't send me back. This is Germany."

Michael hopped off the edge of the desk. He had the springy step of an athlete, a faint sunglass mask around his eyes and a tarry smell of

sweat and after-shave. "That's why you're going. Renko, you're a refugee. What do you think the Germans do with people like you? I think
you know Lieutenant Schiller."

The guards pulled Arkady to his feet. Quick as a dog, Federov
jumped up.

An ashtray, phone and facsimile machine furnished Ludmilla's
desk, and as Michael strode across the room and opened the door for
Peter Schiller, Arkady saw that next to its Transmit button, the fax had
the number that had called Rudy Rosen and asked, "Where is Red
Square?"

Peter said, "I hear you're going home."

"Look at that fax," Arkady said.

This seemed to be an occasion that the lieutenant had waited for.
He bent Arkady's arm behind his back and screwed his wrist so that he
rose to the balls of his feet. "Everywhere I go, you are making a
mess."

"Take a look."

"Theft, trespass, resisting police. Another Soviet tourist." Peter
swung Arkady toward the door. "Bring the phone you found, please,"
he told Michael.

"We're dropping charges to speed the repatriation process," Michael said.

Federov followed. "The consulate rearranged his visa. We have a
seat for him on the flight today. This can all be done quietly."

"Oh, no," Peter said. He held Arkady like a prize. "If he has broken
German law, he's in my hands."

25

The cell was like a Finnish bathroom: fifteen square meters of white tile floor, blue tile walls, a bed facing a bench, a toilet in the corner. For cleanliness' sake, on the other side of the stainless-steel bars lay a coiled hose. Arkady's belt and shoelaces were in a box by the hose. A uniformed policeman little older than a Young Pioneer came by every ten minutes to make sure he wasn't hanging himself by his jacket.

A pack of cigarettes arrived in mid-afternoon. Oddly enough, Arkady wasn't smoking as much as usual, as if food had cut down the appetite of his lungs.

Dinner came on a compartmentalized plastic tray: beef in brown sauce, dumplings, carrots with dill, vanilla pudding, plastic utensils.

Ludmilla had been the voice on the other end when he called the fax number from the train station. Even if she had known Rudy, though, she didn't know he was dead when she asked, "Where is Red Square?"

The Soviet quota of living space was five square meters, so this holding cell was a veritable suite. Also, a Soviet cell was a manuscript. Plaster walls were scribbled with personal messages and public announcements. "The Party Drinks the People's Blood!" "Dima Will Kill the Rats Who Turned Him In!" "Dima Loves Zeta Forever!" And drawings: tigers, daggers, angels, full-bodied women, freestanding cocks, heads of Christ. But the tiles here were glazed, highly fired and unscratchable.

Aeroflot had taken off by now, he was sure. Did Lufthansa have an evening flight?

As he made a pillow of his jacket, Arkady found a wadded envelope in an inner pocket and recognized the shaky, needle-fine writing of his own name. It was the letter from his father that Belov had given him and that he had carried around for more than a week, from a Russian grave to a German cell, like a forgotten poison capsule. He crumpled the paper into a ball and threw it toward the bars. Instead of passing through, it hit one and rolled to the drain in the middle of the floor. He tossed it again, and again it bounced back and rolled to his feet.

The paper rustled. What would the parting words of General Kiril Renko be? After a lifetime of curses, what final curse? In the war between father and son, what last blow?

Arkady remembered his father's favorite phrases. "Titcalf" when Arkady was a small boy. "Poet," "queer," "shitpants" and "eunuch" were heaped upon the student. "Coward," naturally, when Arkady refused officer's school. "Failure," of course, from then on. What extra accolade had been saved? The dead had a certain advantage.

He hadn't talked to his father for years. At this low point in his career, in this tiled hole, was this the right time to allow his father a posthumous stab? There was something funny about the situation. Even dead, the general still had the instincts of an executioner.

Arkady flattened the envelope on the floor. He tugged open the corner of the flap, inserted a finger and cautiously tore open the end, because he wouldn't have been surprised if his father had left a razor. No, the letter itself would be the razor. What were the most hateful, damaging words he could hear? What was worth hissing from the grave?

Arkady blew into the envelope and his breath lifted a half-sheet of onionskin. He smoothed the paper and held it to the light.

The handwriting was so faint and palsied that it was more a wave from the deathbed than a letter, written with a hand that could barely hold a pen. The general had managed only one word: "Irina."

26

Night traffic on Leopoldstrasse was a sinuous flow of headlights, glass, sidewalk cafés, chrome.

Peter lit a cigarette while he drove. "Sorry about the cell. I had to put you someplace where Michael and Federov couldn't get at you. Anyway, you screwed them good. You should be proud. They can't figure out how you switched phones. They kept showing me: car, tennis court, car."

He downshifted and snaked in front of cars. Sometimes Arkady got the impression that Peter barely controlled the urge to drive on the sidewalk to get ahead.

"Apparently Michael's phone was special. It had a scrambler for security. He was upset because he would have to get a new one from Washington."

"He found his phone?" Arkady asked.

"This is wonderful. This is the *Schlag,* the whipped cream on the cake. He took your advice. After Federov left, Michael put on long pants and called his own number and walked up and down the streets until he found his phone ringing just so softly inside a garbage bin. Like finding a kitten."

"So there are no charges?"

"You were seen leaving the garage where the first phone was stolen, but by the time I was finished with him, the attendant didn't know if you were short or tall, white or black. With better prompting, he might give a more accurate description. The main thing is, you're still here and you have me to thank."

"Thank you."

Peter showed a crescent smile. "See, that wasn't hard. Russians are so touchy."

"You feel unappreciated?"

"Ignored. It's nice that Russians and Americans get along so well, but that doesn't mean they can ship you back to Moscow when they want."

"Why didn't you look at Michael's fax when I told you to?"

"I already knew. After your friend Tommy died, I called the number. The woman answered herself. I'm that way, when someone is killed I become more curious, not less." He handed Arkady the pack of cigarettes. "You know, I enjoyed your game with the phones. We must be alike. If you weren't such a liar, we could be a good team."

ON THE HIGHWAY, Peter shifted into overdrive, where he was happiest. "You admit you made up the story about Bayern-Franconia and Benz. Why did you choose my grandfather's bank? Why call *him*?"

"I saw a letter he wrote to Benz."

"Do you have the letter?"

"No."

"Did you read the letter?"

"No."

Kilometer marks flashed by. Overpasses roared above them.

"Don't you have a partner back in Moscow? Couldn't you give him a call?" Peter asked.

"He's dead."

"Renko, do you ever feel like the plague?"

Peter must have been keeping track of where they were because suddenly he downshifted and braked to the footing of a black ramp shaded into ash-white. Tommy's Trabant was gone.

Peter let the BMW roll back slowly. "You can see the concrete is not just burned, it's chipped. I asked myself, how could a feeble little Trabi hit with that kind of force? Doors folded, locked shut. Steering wheel bent. There are only tire prints of the Trabi and no sign of any broken glass or taillights. But as we come back onto the road, see the skid marks."

Two dark apostrophes tailed away from the road toward the ramp.

"Did you test them?"

"Yes. Poor-quality carbon rubber. You can't even recap tires like that, can't burn them or recycle them. Trabi tires. The investigators think Tommy fell asleep and lost control. Fatal one-man, one-car accidents are always the most difficult to reconstruct. Unless it was a two-car accident, and a larger vehicle came from behind and smashed the Trabi into the ramp. If Tommy had any family or any enemies, the investigation would still be open."

"It's closed?"

"Germany has so many highway accidents, terrible accidents on the autobahn, we can't investigate them all. If you want to kill a German, do it on the road."

"Were there any flash marks in the car, any sign of arson?"

"No."

Peter raced in reverse, and with no more than a tap of the brake snapped the car around so that it followed its nose. Arkady remembered that he had flown jets. In Texas, where there was less to hit.

"When Tommy was burning you shouted that you saw a fire like that before. Who?"

"A racketeer." Arkady corrected himself. "A banker named Rudik Rosen. He burned up in an Audi. Audis burn well, too. After Rudy died he got a fax from the machine that we saw at the station."

"The sender thought he was alive."

"Yes."

"What kind of car fire was it? Electrical? Collision?"

"Different from this. It was arson. A bomb."

"Different? I have another question. Before this Rosen died, were you in his car with him?"

"Yes."

"Why is that the first thing I completely believe? Renko, you're still lying about everything else. There's more than Benz involved. Who else? Remember, there's a plane leaving for Moscow tomorrow. You could still be on it."

"Tommy and I were looking for something."

"What?"

"A red Bronco."

Ahead, taillights lined the shoulder of the highway. On the turnout were the taller outlines of off-the-road vehicles. Peter swerved up among them and coasted to a stop. Figures jumped out of the way, arms shielding their eyes. From the dashboard he took flashlights for Arkady and himself. When they got out, they were accosted by men angry about the intrusion into turnout privacy. Peter stiff-armed one and snarled convincingly enough at another to send him backpedaling between fenders. There seemed to be two sides of Peter Schiller, Arkady thought: the Aryan ideal and the werewolf—nothing in between.

Peter worked the women waiting for customers while Arkady moved along vehicles that had pulled back to the far side of the turnout to consummate business. Since he didn't know what a Bronco looked like, he had to read the name on each vehicle. Wasn't a bronco a bucking horse? No, that wasn't the sound. It was more like the beating of a damp drum or, in the shells of the vehicles, the mating of turtles.

There were no red Broncos, but Peter returned from the other side of the turnout to say that one had just left with a driver named Tima. He didn't seem discouraged. Maybe he drove a little faster getting back onto the highway.

Arkady imagined the night trailing behind them like a scarf. The rest of Munich lived quietly on a schedule, ate its muesli, biked to work, paid for sex. Peter moved as if he lived at a higher rpm.

"I think when you were in the Trabi waiting for Tommy, somebody saw you. Then poor Tommy started home and someone followed him. It wasn't an accident. It was murder, but they thought they were killing you."

"You want to drive around until someone tries to kill us?"

"To clear my head. Are you following someone from Moscow? Or has someone followed you?"

"At this point I'd follow anything. I'd pick out one star and aim at that."

"Like my grandfather?"

"Maybe your grandfather is connected and maybe he's not. I honestly don't know."

"Have you ever met Benz?"

"No."

"Have you talked to anyone who met Benz?"

"Tommy. Slow down," Arkady said. Walking on the shoulder of the road was a girl in a red-leather jacket and boots, and as they went by he saw that she had black hair and a round Uzbek face. "Stop!"

She was angry and not in the mood for a lift. Her German was a dialect of Russian.

"That *Arschloch* threw me out of my car. I'll kill him."

"What did your car look like?" Arkady asked.

She stamped her boot. "*Scheisse,* everything I have is in there."

"Maybe we can find it."

"Pictures and personal letters."

"We'll look for it. What kind is it?"

She looked off toward the dark and reconsidered. Uzbekistan is a long way off, Arkady thought. Her legs looked thin and cold. She said, "Never mind. I'll take care of it myself."

Peter said, "If someone stole your car, you should report it to the police."

She studied him and the BMW, with its extra aerial and spotlight. "No."

"What's Tima short for?" Arkady asked.

"Fatima." Immediately she added, "I never said my name was Tima."

"Did he take the car two nights ago?"

She crossed her arms. "Have you been watching me?"

"Do you come from Samarkand or Tashkent?"

"Tashkent. How do you know so much? I'm not talking to you."

"How long ago tonight did he take the car?"

She set her face and starting walking again, wobbling on her heels. Uzbeks had once been the Golden Horde of Tamerlane that had swept from Mongolia to Moscow. This was the end, stumbling on the autobahn.

THEY DROVE INTO the Red Square parking lot and cruised through. There was no red Bronco. A contingent of businessmen were trooping loudly from vans into the sex club.

"Slumming," Peter said. "The Stuttgart set. They'll only touch the beer here and then they'll go home and fuck their wives silly." He shot a little gravel at them as he swung by.

Back on the road, Peter was calmer, as if he had reached some internal decision. Arkady relaxed, too, more in tune with the speed.

The city spread as it approached, not like wildfire, more like a battlefield of moths.

■ ■ ■

A RED BRONCO sat in front of Benz's flat. The apartment was dark. They drove by twice, parked on the next block and returned on foot.

Peter stayed in the shadow of a tree while Arkady walked up the steps and pushed the button to the flat. No voice came over the intercom. No window lit upstairs.

Peter joined him. "He's gone."

"The car is here."

"Maybe he went for a walk."

"A midnight walk?"

Peter said, "He's an Ossie, how many cars can he have? Renko, let's act like detectives and see what we can find."

He gave Arkady a flashlight, led him to the Bronco and opened the tweezers of a combination knife. The chrome on the front bumper was untouched, but its rubber guard sparkled in the flashlight's beam. Peter squatted and teased from the rubber what looked like threads of glass.

"One reason it's almost impossible to reprocess a Trabi is that the fiberglass body breaks up into such sharp splinters." He dropped pieces into a paper envelope. "Dead or alive, a Trabi is very difficult to handle."

PETER RADIOED IN the Bronco's plate. While they waited for an answer he shook pieces from the envelope into the ashtray, then turned the flame of his lighter directly on the threads. They lit like yellow kindling; strings of black ash rose on brown smoke, and a familiar, noxious aroma filled the car.

"Pure Trabi." Peter blew out the flame. "Proving nothing. There's not enough left of Tommy's Trabi to match to this, but even a lawyer would have to say the Bronco hit something."

The radio spoke rapid German. Peter wrote on a pad "Fantasy Tours" and the address of Boris Benz.

Arkady said, "Ask how many cars are registered in Fantasy's name."

Peter asked, then wrote on the pad the number 18. Also, "Pathfinders, Navajos, Cherokees, Troopers, Rovers."

He put the phone back in its sleeve. "You said you never met Benz."

"I said that Tommy met Benz."

"You said that you and Tommy were on the highway because you were looking for Benz. You went to the sex club first."

"Tommy saw him there a year ago."

"Who was the connection? How did they meet?"

Arkady had succeeded in keeping Max's name from Peter because Max was only one step away from Irina. It would be a bitter outcome, he thought, if he had come all this way just to drag her into Peter's investigation.

Peter said, "Why would they meet? Tommy wanted to talk to Benz about the war?"

"I'm sure Tommy told him about it. He was interviewing people for a book about the war. He was obsessed with it. His apartment is a museum of the war."

"I was there."

"What did you think?"

Peter's eyes looked energized, as if they had picked up electricity from the radio. From his jacket he produced a key. "I think we should visit this museum again."

SWASTIKAS STRETCHED ACROSS two walls. The Wehrmacht map covered a third. On the shelves were Tommy's collection of gas masks, tin panzers, a hubcap from Hitler's touring car, assorted ammunition, Goebbels's reinforced shoe. A clock in the shape of an eagle said twelve A.M.

Peter said, "I was here earlier. In and out. Normally we don't search the apartments of traffic victims."

On the table where the birthday cake for the Berlin Wall had melted, a typewriter was set up with notes, paper and file cards. Peter wandered about, focusing field glasses, trying on an armband and an SS cap, like an actor let loose in a prop room. He lifted a helmet, the one Tommy had worn at the party.

"Alas, poor Jürgen, I knew him well."

He laid down the helmet and picked up a dental mold. "Hitler's teeth," Arkady said.

Peter opened the mold. *"Sieg heil!"*

The short hairs on Arkady's neck rose.

"Do you know why we lost the war?" Peter asked.

"Why did you lose the war?"

"It was explained to me by an old man. We were hiking in the Alps. We were on a high meadow surrounded by wildflowers when we stopped to eat. The subject of the war came up. He said the Nazis had committed 'excesses,' but the real reason Germany lost the war was because of sabotage. There were workers in the munitions factory who deliberately degraded the gunpowder in the shells to make our weapons ineffective. Otherwise we would have been able to hold out for an honorable peace. He described the grandfathers and boys fighting in the ruins of Berlin, stabbed in the back by those saboteurs. It was years later when I learned that those saboteurs were Russians and Jews, slave labor being starved to death while they worked. I remembered the flowers, the wonderful view, the tears in his eyes."

He put the mold down, joined Arkady at the table and flipped through the file cards, notes and pages. "What are you looking for?" Arkady asked.

"Answers."

They searched the drawers of the desk and night table, folders that were stuffed into cabinets, address books discovered under the bed. Finally, next to the phone in the kitchen, numbers without names were penciled on the wall. Peter gave a laugh of dark amusement, nailed one number with his finger and dialed the phone.

Considering the hour, the other end answered quickly. Peter said, "Grandfather, I'm coming over with my friend Renko."

THE ELDER SCHILLER padded around in a silk robe and velvet slippers. His living room was covered in Oriental carpets. His lamps had shades of stained glass.

"I was awake anyway. The middle of the night is the best time to read."

The banker seemed to make a firm distinction between work and personal life. Bookshelves accommodated not tomes on banking regulations but art books that ran from Turkish rugs to Japanese ceramics. Objets d'art—a Greek bronze of a dolphin, Mexican skulls of sugar and jade, a Chinese alabaster dog—sat under spotlights arranged by someone who had taken great care to display eclectic pieces of modest size but unusual quality. A dark icon of a Madonna was in the traditional place, high in a corner that would have been the "beautiful corner" of a pre-Revolutionary peasant house. Its thick wood was split and the Madonna's face was shrouded by smoke, which made her eyes seem all the more luminous.

Schiller poured tea into a gilded cup. He wore a brace under his bathrobe, Arkady realized, and leaned stiffly, marble from the waist up.

"I'm sorry, I don't have any jam. I remember that Russians love their tea with jam."

Peter paced back and forth.

"Walk," his grandfather told him. "It's good for the rug." He turned to Arkady. "When he was a boy, Peter would march a kilometer on that carpet, back and forth. He always had too much energy. He can't help it."

"Why did the American have your number?" Peter asked.

"His book, his moronic book. He's the sort who lurks in graveyards and thinks he has a career. He kept pestering me, but I refused to be interviewed by him. I suspect he gave my name to Benz."

"The bank was not involved?" Arkady asked.

Schiller allowed himself the thinnest suggestion of a smile. "Bayern-Franconia would no more invest in the Soviet Union than in the far side of the moon. Benz approached me personally."

Peter said, "Benz is a pimp. He runs a string of prostitutes on the autobahn. What would he approach you about?"

"Real estate."

"It was business?" Arkady asked.

Schiller sipped his tea. The cup was porcelain with a gilded rim. "Before the war, we had our own bank in Berlin. We're not Bavarian." He cast a concerned eye on his grandson. "That's Peter's problem; he's not bred to be a drunken lout. Anyway, the family lived in Potsdam, outside the city. We also had a summer home on the coast. I've described them to Peter many times. Beautiful places. We lost them all. Bank and houses, everything ended up in the Soviet sector and then in the Democratic Republic of Germany. We lost them first to the Russians and then to the East Germans."

Arkady said, "With reunification I thought private property was being returned."

"Oh, yes. The former East Germany is haunted now by Jewish ghosts. But we weren't helped because the new law excluded properties confiscated from '45 to '49, which was when we lost ours. Or so I thought until Benz appeared at my door."

"What did he say?" Arkady asked.

"He represented himself as some sort of real estate agent. He informed me that there was some question about exactly when the Potsdam house had been seized. When the Russians were in charge, many estates simply stood empty for years. Records had been lost or burned. Benz said he might be able to provide me with the proper documentation to help my claim." Schiller turned stiffly in his chair. "It was for you, too, Peter. He said he might be able to help us with the summer house, too. They could all be ours again."

"For how much?" Peter asked.

"No money. Information."

"Bank information?"

Schiller was offended. "Personal history." The banker shook off his slippers. His feet were mottled blue, with yellowed nails. Two toes were missing. "Frostbite. I should live in Spain. Peter, you know where the brandy is. I feel a chill."

Arkady asked, "What did you do on the Eastern Front?"

Schiller cleared his throat. "I was with a special detachment."

"How special?"

"I understand what you're saying. Other special detachments rounded up Jews. I did nothing like that. My detachment gathered art. My father wanted to keep me out of the front line, so he got me attached to a group of SS who followed the advance. I was a boy, younger than either of you. He told me that I could protect art. He was right; without us, thousands of paintings, pieces of jewelry and irreplaceable books would have disappeared into knapsacks, been burned, melted down or completely disappeared. We were literally rescuing culture. The lists were already drawn up. Göring wrote one list, Goebbels another. We had teams of carpenters, packers, our own trains. The Wehrmacht had orders to keep the tracks open just to send our cargo back. It was an enormously busy fall. When winter came we stalled outside Moscow, and that was the war right there, though we didn't know it."

With brandy, the tea was better. The banker shifted in his chair. It occurred to Arkady that for the older man every movement involved pain.

"This is what Tommy wanted to ask you about?" Arkady asked.

"Some of the same questions," Schiller said.

Peter said, "You told me you were captured outside Moscow and spent three years in a camp. You said you surrendered when your rifles froze."

"My feet froze. To tell the truth, when I was captured I was hiding in a boxcar. The SS men were shot on the spot. I would have been shot, too, if the Russians hadn't opened some cases and found icons inside. There was some interrogation of me, which was not delicate. I agreed to make lists of what we'd taken. Then the whole war went in reverse. I was never in camp, not for a day. I traveled with the Red Army, first searching for what the SS had shipped. Then, as we moved further west, I was as an adviser to special troops from the Soviet Ministry of Culture, helping to locate and send German works of art to Moscow. Stalin made a list, Beria made a list. We sent even more because we found what the SS had taken from different countries— the Koenigs drawings from Holland, the Poznan paintings from Poland. We stripped the Dresden Museum, the Prussian Royal Library, museum collections from Aachen, Weimar, Magdeburg."

"In other words, you collaborated," Peter said.

"I served history. I survived. I was hardly the only one. When the Russians arrived in Berlin, where do you think they went? While the city burned, while Hitler was still alive, they were in the museums. Rubenses, Rembrandts, the gold of Troy disappeared, treasures that have never been seen again."

"Were you there?" Arkady asked.

"No, I was still in Magdeburg. When we were done there, the Russians gave me a vodka. We'd been together for three years. I even wore a Red Army coat at that point. They took the coat off, marched me a few steps to an alley, shot me in the back and left me for dead. See, Peter, personal history."

"What was Benz most interested in?" Arkady asked.

"Nothing in particular." Schiller reconsidered. "Actually, I had the feeling he was checking his list against mine. At heart he was a crude man, a real barracks bastard. In the end, all we talked about was how to build crates. The SS enlisted carpenters from the Berlin firm of Knauer, the most expert art transporters of the time. I drew him diagrams. He was more interested in nails and woods and documentation than in art."

"What do you mean, 'barracks bastard'?"

Schiller said, "It's commonplace. How many German girls have had babies by foreign soldiers stationed here?"

Arkady said, "Benz was born in Potsdam. You're saying his father was Russian?"

"That's what he sounded like," Schiller said.

Peter said, "All the stories you told me about defending Germany. You were a thief, first on one side and then on the other. Why didn't you tell me all this before? Why tell me now?"

The banker eased his feet into his slippers. He turned as completely to Peter as he could. He had that deadly combination of age: eggshell frailty and brutal honesty. "It didn't concern you. The past was gone. Now it does. Everything has a price. If we can get our house and property back, if we can go home, Peter, this is the price for you."

PETER DROPPED ARKADY off at Stas's apartment and tore off into the dark.

Arkady unlocked the door with the house key Stas had given him. Laika sniffed him quietly and let him in. He went to the kitchen and made a late dinner of hard biscuits for the dog, and tea, jam and cigarettes for himself.

Steps shambled up the hall. Stas leaned against the doorjamb in mismatched pajama top and bottom and regarded Laika and the biscuits. "Slut."

"I woke you," Arkady said.

"I'm not awake. If I were awake, I'd be asking where the devil you've been." At a sleepwalker's pace he staggered to the refrigerator and took out a beer. "Obviously you think of me as the hall porter, the concierge, the elf who polishes your shoes. So where *have* you been?"

"With my new German partner. He has become wildly enthusiastic. In return, I've misled him as best I can."

Stas sat down. "You cannot mislead a German any more than you can lead a German."

Nevertheless, Arkady had misled Peter by omission, by not mentioning Max because of Irina. By now Peter was convinced that his grandfather was the only connection between Tommy and Benz. "I traded on his sense of national guilt."

"If you can find a German with guilt, you should trade on it. Generally I have found this to be a country of widespread amnesia, but if you have found a guilty German, I can guarantee that no one on earth has ever had a larger sense of guilt. Correct?"

"Close enough."

Stas tipped the bottle back so that it seemed to balance on his lips, then set it down empty. "I was awake anyway. I was thinking that if I'd stayed in Russia, I probably would have died in a camp. Or maybe I only would have been pressed as flat as a blini."

"You were right to get out."

"As a result of which I've had enormous influence on world events. I make fun of the station, but Liberty's budget is less than the cost of a single strategic bomber."

"Is that so?"

"Not to mention this is a tax-free situation for me."

"That sounds good."

Stas stared at the kitchen clock. The second hand dropped in audible clicks, a sound like a key turning over and over in a lock. Laika moved close to him and laid her shaggy head on his lap.

Stas said, "Maybe I should have stayed."

27

In the morning a heavy fog brought out headlights. Bicycles appeared and disappeared as wraiths.

Irina lived a block from the park, on a street that mixed town houses, artists' studios and boutiques. All the buildings were dressed in fey *Jugendstil* except hers, which was plain and modern. Though her windows were set back, Arkady located her balcony, a chrome rail before a wall of vines, lush and bright in the wet. He stood at a bus stop at the end of the street, the most logical and least conspicuous place to wait.

Did the balcony lead directly to the kitchen? He could imagine the warmth of lights, the smell of coffee. He could also imagine Max having an extra cup, but he had to eliminate Max from the picture in his mind or slide into crippling jealousy. Irina might drive to the station. Worse, she might leave with Max. He focused on the hope that she was alone, was drying a cup and saucer, was putting on her raincoat, would take the bus.

A delivery truck parked in the middle of the block. The driver climbed down from the cab, opened the rear doors, brought racks down to street level with a hydraulic lift and rolled them into a dress shop. The truck's windshield wipers kept time, though rain wasn't falling so much as hanging in the air in fine droplets. Traffic had a sheen. Arkady stepped off the curb for a better view of Irina's house when a bus arrived and chased him back. Passengers boarded and canceled their own tickets in an automatic punch box. Every single one of them—that was the amazing thing.

The bus pulled away and the delivery truck drove off. It took

Arkady a minute to notice that the vine-covered wall on Irina's balcony was a darker green, which meant that the lights of her apartment
were off. He watched her door for another minute before he realized
that she had left while the truck had been blocking his view. He had
expected her to use the bus in this weather; instead she'd gone in the
other direction toward the park and he'd missed her.

Arkady ran the length of the street to the park. In the foreshortened view that accompanies emotion, umbrellas bobbed on either
side. A Turk wearing a conical hat of newspaper biked between the
bumpers of limousines. Across the street the Englischer Garten began
as a wall of giant beeches. Farther down the street, a woman in a white
raincoat entered a park gate.

He darted between cars. The radio station lay diagonally across the
park. Where he entered the gate, paths twisted left and right. The
Englischer Garten was called the "green lung" of Munich. It had a
river, streams, forests, lakes—all veiled now by mist, giving the park a
cold, close breath that made Arkady gather his jacket at his neck.

He could hear her, though; at least, he heard someone walking. Did
he remember how she walked? Long strides, always sure of herself.
She hated umbrellas, she hated crowds. He hurried after the echo,
aware that any hesitation put her farther ahead. If she was ahead. The
path kept trying to turn away. Overhead, beeches were monkey bars in
a cloud. Oaks were shorter, as bent as beggars. Where the path
crossed a streambed, steam rose from the water, a ghostly flood tide.
A creature resembling a large caterpillar sniffed around wet leaves.
Closer, it became a wire-haired dachshund. Its owner crept behind, a
yellow slicker with a scoop and bag.

Beyond, Irina had disappeared—if it was Irina. Over the years, at a
distance, how many women had he dressed in her features? This was
the illusion of his life, the nightmare.

Arkady had the park to himself. He heard the slow condensation of
mist on leaves, the thud of nuts from the beeches onto sodden earth,
the dash of unseen birds. Where shadows faded, he found he had
reached the edge of a wide meadow, completely lost in a circle of
green. For a moment on the far side he saw a flash of white.

Running over the grass, he had the labored breath and heavy feet of
a farm horse. When he reached the spot where the brief sight of white
had been, she was gone again. Now, though, he knew the direction. A
path led along a russet screen of maples and the languid vapor of
another stream. He heard steps again and, where the maples ended,

saw her, a bag over her shoulder. Her coat was actually more silver than white, with a reflective quality. Her hair was uncovered, darker in the rain. She looked back and then continued walking, faster than before.

They walked at the same pace, ten meters apart, down a dark avenue of firs. Where the path narrowed to a strip that threaded a stand of birches, she slowed, then stopped and leaned against the white, papery column of a birch for him to catch up.

They walked on together in silence. Arkady felt like a man who had approached a deer. The single wrong word, he thought, and she would bolt for good. When she glanced at him he didn't dare try to hold her eyes or read them. At least they were walking side by side. In itself, that was a victory.

He was sorry that he looked so bad. His shoes were flecked with grass, his clothes damp and molded to his back. His body was too thin, and probably his eyes had the glower of the chronically starved.

They came to the edge of a lake. The water was black and still. Irina looked down at their reflections, at the man and woman looking up from the water, and said, "That's the saddest thing I ever saw."

"Me?" Arkady asked.

"Us."

BIRDS COLLECTED. THE park was rich in them: velvet-headed mallards, wood ducks, wigeons and teal appeared out of the mist, breaking the surface of the water into spoons of light. Shearwaters flew as acrobatically as signatures, geese dropped like sacks.

They sat on a bench.

She said, "There are people who come here every day to feed the birds. They bring pretzels the size of wheels."

It was cool enough for their breath to condense.

"I sympathize with these birds," she said. "The difference is that you never came. I will never forgive you."

"I can tell."

"And now that you're here, I feel like a refugee all over again. I don't like that feeling."

"No one does."

"But I've been in the West for years. I've earned the right to be here. Arkady, go home. Leave me alone."

"No. I won't go."

He half-expected her to rise and leave the bench. He would follow her; what else could he do? She stayed. She let him light another cigarette for her. "A bad habit," she said. "Like you."

Despair saturated the air. Cold penetrated his thin jacket. He heard his heart echo across the water. A walking collection of bad habits was what he was. Ignorance, insubordination, lack of exercise, dull razors.

So many birds arrived, some dropping wholesale in flocks, others wheeling individually out of the mist, that Arkady was put in mind of the factory ship he had spent part of his exile on, and how gulls had mobbed the air above the stern for the overflow and refuse from the nets. He remembered standing in the breeze above the stern ramp fieldstripping a cigarette and a gull snatching the paper from the air and carrying it away as its prize. "Find the Russian duck," he said.

"Where?"

"The one with dirty feathers and a crooked bill smoking a cigarette."

"There is no such thing."

"But you looked, I saw you. Imagine when Russian ducks really do hear about this lake, a lake with pretzels, they'll come here by the millions."

"The swans too?"

A line of swans glided imperiously through the ducks. When a mallard resisted, the lead swan stretched out its long and creamy neck, opened its bright, yellow bill and snorted like a pig.

"Russian. He's already infiltrated," Arkady said.

Irina sat back to study him. "You do look terrible."

"I can't say the same for you."

She bent the light her way. Mist sat on her hair like jewels. "I heard you were doing so well in Moscow," she said.

"Who did you hear that from?"

She hesitated. "You're not what I expected. You're what I remembered."

THEY WALKED SLOWLY. Arkady was aware that she walked a critical millimeter closer and that their shoulders occasionally grazed.

"Stas was always curious about you. I'm not surprised you're friends. Max says you're both artifacts of the cold war."

"We are. I'm like a piece of marble you find in an ancient ruin. You pick it up, turn it around in your hand and ask, 'What was this? Part of a horse trough or part of a noble statue?' I want to show you something." He took out an envelope, opened it and showed her the paper and the one word scribbled inside.

"My name," she said.

"It's my father's writing. I hadn't heard from him in years. This must have been almost the last thing he did before he died. You actually talked to him?"

"I wanted to reach you without causing trouble so I tried your father."

Arkady tried to imagine this. It sounded like a dove flying into a furnace, though his father had been a fairly cold furnace in his last years.

"He told me what a hero you were, how they tried to break you but that you forced the prosecutor's office to take you back, that they gave you the most difficult cases and that you never lost. He was proud. He went on and on. He said he saw you often and that you'd write me."

"What else?"

"That you were too busy for women, but women were always chasing you."

"None of this rang a false note?"

"He said the only problem with you was that you were a fanatic and that sometimes you put yourself in God's place. That some things only God could judge."

"If I were General Kiril Renko, I wouldn't have been so eager to see the face of God."

"He said he thought about you more and more. Did you have women?"

"No. I was in psychiatric cells for a while, then I was in Siberia on the move, and then I was fishing. There was limited opportunity."

She stopped him. "Please, I remember Russia. There's always opportunity. And when you got back to Moscow, you must have had a woman there."

"I was in love. I wasn't looking for women."

"In love with me?"

"Yes."

"You *are* a fanatic."

They walked along a pond that bore snowy down and fine drops of rain like pearls. Was it the same lake as before?

"Arkasha, what are we going to do?"

THEY LEFT THE park for a university café that had stainless-steel machines hissing into pots of milk and posters of Italy—ski slopes of the Dolomites, colorful tenements in Naples—on the walls. The other patrons were students with open books and bowl-sized cups of coffee. They took a table by the window.

Arkady talked about working his way across Siberia, from Irkutsk to Norilsk to Kamchatka to the sea.

Irina talked about New York, London, Berlin. "Theater work in New York was good, but I couldn't join the union. They're like Soviet unions—worse. I waited on tables. In New York, waitresses are fantastic. So hard and so old you think they waited on Alexander the Great or the pharaohs. Hard workers. An art gallery. They wanted someone with a European accent. I was part of the gallery ambience, and I started getting involved in art again. What no one was interested in then was the Russian avant-garde. You know, you expected to see me in Russia and I expected to see you walk into an art gallery on Madison Avenue, dressed in a proper suit, good shoes, tie."

"Next time we should coordinate dreams."

"Anyway, Max was visiting the Liberty office in New York. He produced a show on Russian art and happened to interview me and said if I was ever in Munich and needed work to call him. A year later I did. I still do some work for Berlin galleries. They're always looking for pieces of Revolutionary art because now the prices are phenomenally high."

"You mean the art of our defunct and discredited Revolution?"

"Is auctioned at Sotheby's and Christie's. Collectors can't get enough. You're in trouble, aren't you?"

"I *was* in trouble. Not now."

"I mean with your work."

"Work has its difficult moments. The good people die and the wrong people walk away with the spoils. My career seems to be in a shadow, but I'm thinking of taking a holiday, a vacation from professional pursuits."

"And do what?"

"I could become a German. Transitionally, of course. First I'd turn into a Pole, then an East German, finally a fully mature Bavarian."

"Seriously."

"Seriously, I will wear different clothes every day and walk into your life until you say, 'This is just what Arkady Renko should look like; this is the proper suit.'"

"You wouldn't let go?"

"Not now."

ARKADY DESCRIBED HOW the breath of a reindeer herd crystallized and fell like snow. He talked about salmon runs on Sakhalin, the white-headed eagles of the Aleutians and waterspouts that danced around the Bering Sea. He'd never thought before of what a catalog of experiences his exile had brought to him, how unique and beautiful they were, what clear evidence that on no day could a man be sure he should not open his eyes.

They had a lunch of microwaved pizza. Delicious.

He told her how the first wind of the day approaching through the taiga made the million trees shiver like black birds taking flight. He talked about oil field fires that burned year-round, beacons that could be seen from the moon. He described walking from trawler to trawler across the Arctic ice. Sounds and sights not afforded most investigators.

They had red wine.

He talked about workers on the "slime line," the dark hold where fish were gutted in a factory ship, and how each individual was a separate mind with a fantasy unconfined by gunwales or decks—a defender of the Party who had taken to the sea in search of romance, a botanist who dreamed of Siberian orchids, each person a lamp on a separate world.

After finishing the wine, they had brandy.

He described the Moscow he had found on his return. Center stage, a dramatic battlefield of warlords and entrepreneurs; behind it, as still as a painted backdrop, eight million people standing in line. Yet there were moments, the occasional dawn when the sun was low enough to find a golden river and blue domes, and the entire city seemed redeemable.

■ ■ ■

THE WARMTH OF patrons and the steam of the machines had produced a film of condensation on the window that diffused the light and color of the street. Something caught Irina's eye and she wiped the glass. Max was outside. How long had he been looking in?

He entered and said, "You two seem to be getting on like a pair of conspirators."

"Join us," Arkady offered.

"Where have you been?" Max asked Irina. His manner was alarmed, relieved, alarmed, in three rapid steps. "You haven't been at the station all day. People were worried about you; we were out searching for you. You and I were supposed to go to Berlin."

"Talking to Arkady," Irina said.

Max asked, "Are you finished?"

"No." Irina took one of Arkady's cigarettes and lit it. She made it a drawn-out gesture of unconcern. "Max, if you're in a hurry, go to Berlin. I know you have business there."

"We both have business there."

"My business can wait," Irina said.

Max was absolutely still for a moment, reevaluating Irina and Arkady together, then dropped his brusque manner as easily as his hat, which he shook free of rain. Arkady remembered Stas's description of him as liquid, the master of a changing situation.

Max smiled, pulled up a third chair, settled and gave Arkady a nod of acknowledgment. "Renko, I'm amazed you're still here."

Irina said, "Arkady has been telling me what he was doing the last few years. It's different from what I'd heard."

Max said, "He was probably modest. People claim he was the darling of the Party. A well-earned status, I'm sure. Who knows what to believe?"

"I know," Irina said. She blew smoke Max's way.

He brushed it aside, considered his hand as if he had caught a cobweb and raised his eyes to Arkady. "So how is your investigation going?"

"Not well."

"No arrests imminent?"

"Far from it."

"And you must be running out of time."

"I was thinking of abandoning the entire case."

"And?"

"Staying."

"Really?" Irina said.

"You're joking," Max said. "You came all the way to Munich to give up? Where's your patriotic duty, your sense of pride?"

"I have very little country left and I certainly have no pride."

"Arkady doesn't have to be the last man in Russia," Irina said.

"You know, some people are going back, some people see opportunities," Max pointed out. "This is a time to contribute, not run away."

Irina said, "That's interesting, coming from someone who has run twice."

"It's hilarious," Stas said. He closed the café door and fell back against it, a rain-soaked mime of collapse. "Irina, the next time you vanish, leave a forwarding address. This is the most exercise I've had since Laika learned to fetch."

His clothes looked wrung, body and all, but he stayed on his feet and concentrated his attention on Max.

"Are you all right?" Irina asked.

"I may throw up. Or maybe I'll have a beer. Max, you were lecturing on political morality? I'm sorry I missed that. Was it a short lecture?"

Max said, "Stas doesn't forgive me for going home. He hasn't accepted that the world has changed. It's sad. Sometimes intelligent men cling to simple answers. Even the fact that you're in Munich proves how things have changed. You don't claim to be a political refugee, do you?" He tilted toward Irina. "Let Renko come or go, I don't see what it has to do with us."

Irina said nothing. Like a man who senses a growing gulf, Max edged his chair closer and lowered his voice. "I want to know what kind of wild stories Renko has been entertaining you with. All of a sudden he seems to have assembled an audience here."

"They were probably happier without us," Stas said.

"I only want to remind you that Renko is no unsullied hero. He stays when he should go; he goes when he should stay. He's the master of bad timing."

"Unlike yours," Irina said.

"I also want to point out," Max said, "that your hero probably just came to you because he was frightened."

"Why would he be frightened?" Irina asked.

"Ask him," Max said. "Renko, weren't you with Tommy when he

suffered his fatal accident the other night? Weren't you with him right before it?"

"Is this true?" Irina asked Arkady.

"Yes."

Max said, "Stas and Irina and I have no idea what kind of disagreeable business you're involved in. But isn't it possible that Tommy is dead because you dragged him into it? Do you really think you should drag Irina into it, too?"

"No," Arkady admitted.

"I'm only suggesting," Max said to Arkady, holding up his hand to stifle Stas's protests, "I'm only suggesting that you came to Irina simply because you want to hide."

Stas said, "Max, you really are a shit."

Max said, "I want to hear the answer."

Water dripped from Stas's chin. Max looked unmeltable. For a moment the only sound was the ring of china on the counter and the slow release of steam.

Arkady said, "I heard Irina on the radio in Moscow. That's why I came."

Max said, "You're a devoted fan. Get an autograph. Go home to Moscow and you can hear her five times a day."

Irina said, "We can take him to Berlin."

Max's voice went flat. "What?"

She said, "If you're right, Arkady should get out of Munich. No one connects us to him. He'll be safe with us."

"No," Max said in disbelief. Arkady saw that he had come to a totally different conclusion; he had carefully and confidently built a seamless, logical argument with only one way out, a perspective of Arkady disappearing over the horizon. Irina had ignored all of it. "No, I am not taking Renko to Berlin."

"Then, go without me," Irina said. "Arkady and I will do fine here."

Max said, "We're not staying at a hotel. We'll be in the new apartment."

"It's a big apartment," she said. "You can have it all to yourself if you want."

Max reassembled his composure, but for a moment Arkady recognized one reason why the man had returned from Moscow. The worst of reasons.

Love curls around like a snake and crushes two men at the same time.

III

BERLIN

■

August 18–August 20, 1991

28

Max drove a Daimler, a sedan with the woodwork of an antique cabinet and the sound of a muted trumpet. His attitude was friendly, as if they were off on a lark, as if becoming a threesome had been his idea.

The German landscape lay under folds of rain. Sitting in front, Irina was the tangible warmth in the car. She propped her back against the door to include Arkady when she talked, almost as if to exclude Max.

"You'll like the show. It's a Russian show, but some of the pieces have never been seen in Moscow, not publicly."

"Irina wrote the catalog," Max said. "She really should be there."

"It's just about the provenance of the painting, Arkady, but the painting itself is beautiful."

"Are critics allowed to use the word *beautiful*?" he asked.

"In this case," she promised him, "it's perfect."

Arkady enjoyed hearing about this other life of hers, this new and independent mix of knowledge and opinions. He was now, as a benefit of experience, a skilled hauler of nets and gutter of fish. Why shouldn't she be an expert on the arts? Max seemed just as proud.

From the backseat, he couldn't tell at what point they crossed what had been the old East German border. As the highway narrowed they slowed for farm equipment that lunged in and out of the mist. When the road cleared, they raced ahead again, as if the three of them were in a bubble caught in a river fed by the rain.

There was a sense of suspended time in the situation. Part of it was Max's self-control. Arkady thought Max had wanted to kill him in Moscow; instead he had let him escape to Munich. He was sure Max had wanted him dead in Munich, yet here he was driving him to

Berlin. On the other hand, Arkady couldn't touch Max. With what authority? As a refugee? He couldn't even ask questions without Irina accusing him of using her again, without losing her a second time.

Max said, "Since Irina is going to be busy tomorrow, let me take you around the city. You've been to Berlin before?"

"In the army. He was stationed there," Irina answered for Arkady. He was surprised she remembered.

"Doing what?" Max asked.

Arkady said, "Listening to the American command, translating for the Soviet command."

Irina said, "Like you at Radio Liberty, Max."

More and more she was given to sarcastic attacks on Max, and the walls of the bubble would tremble. Yet it was Max's luxurious car they rode in, his destination they drove to. "I'll show you the new Berlin," he told Arkady.

WHEN THEY REACHED the city late at night, the rain had stopped. They entered on the Avus, the old raceway through the Berliner Woods, then drove directly onto the Kurfürstendamm. Instead of the homogeneous affluence of Munich's Marienplatz, the Ku'damm was a chaotic collision of West German shops and East German shoppers. For block after block, crowds in Socialist off-colors milled around display cases of silky Italian scarves and Japanese cameras. Their faces had the tight, poutish look of poor relations. A phalanx of skinheads marched in leather jackets and boots. Street lamps hung on ornate Nazi-era poles. Tables sold pieces of the Wall, with graffiti and without.

"It's terrible, it's a mess, but it's alive," Irina said. "That's why the art market had always been here. Berlin is the only international city in Germany."

Max said, "The city between Paris, Moscow and Istanbul." He pointed to a sidewalk vendor with a rack of uniforms. Arkady recognized the gray chest and blue shoulders of a Soviet Air Force colonel's greatcoat. The vendor himself was covered with Soviet military medals and ribbons from his collar to his belt. "You should have kept your uniform," Max said.

Stas had forced a hundred Deutsche marks on Arkady before he left Munich; he had never been richer or felt poorer.

They passed the Kaiser Wilhelm Church's shattered, floodlit brow.

Looming behind it was a glass tower topped by a Mercedes star. Max left the boulevard and followed a dark, arterial route along a canal. All the same, Arkady's internal compass began to function. Before they even reached Friedrichstrasse, he knew they were in what used to be East Berlin.

Max turned down the ramp of a garage. As they drove in, the garage lights automatically went on. A smell of wet cement hit their nostrils like the chlorine of a pool. Electrical junction boxes hung by wires from the walls.

"How new is this building?" Arkady asked.

Max said, "It's still under construction."

Irina said, "Believe me, no one will know you're here."

Max unlocked the elevator with a key. Inside, it had crystal sconces and an unscratched parquet floor. He toted Irina's overnight bag. Holding his own carry-on, Arkady felt like a workman with a sackful of tools.

They stopped on the fourth floor, where Max opened a door to a two-story living room and loft. "Just a studio. I'm afraid it's not furnished, but the electricity and plumbing are in and the rent is free." Ceremoniously he handed the door key to Arkady. "We'll be two stories up."

Irina said, "The main thing is that you'll be safe."

"Thanks," Arkady said.

Max gathered Irina into the elevator. He had her, which was thanks enough.

THE KEY HAD freshly stamped, sharp serrations, perfect to unlock the heart, Arkady thought, if you worked diligently in between the ribs.

No bed, bedding, chairs or bureau. Dry walls angled seamlessly into hardwood floors. The bathroom was all tiles gleaming like teeth. The kitchen had a stove but no utensils. If he'd had food, he could have held meat in his hands above the flame.

Steps echoed out of proportion to every move he made. He listened for sounds from two stories above. In Munich he had dreaded the possibility that Irina was sleeping with Max. Now, overhead, he had the certainty. What was Max's apartment like? Extrapolating, Arkady pictured the finish on the walls, the polish on the floors. He could imagine the rest.

He asked himself if he should have stayed in Munich.

Choice was the luxury of casting a vote, trying on shoes, lingering over a menu and deciding between red caviar and black.

He'd had to come to Berlin. If he hadn't he would have lost Irina, not to mention Max. This way he had them both. Like a man who is proud he wears so much rope around his neck.

THE ELEVATOR WAS locked. Arkady took the emergency stairs down to the garage, where he wedged the door open and stepped out onto the street. Though Friedrichstrasse was a major thoroughfare, its street lamps were as dim as curb lights. Except for himself, the sidewalk was empty. Anyone awake was in the West.

He spotted the point of a television tower and immediately knew that Alexanderplatz was to his right, West Berlin to his left. The mental map he had was out of date by a decade or so, but no major city in Europe was as unchanged as East Berlin in the last forty years. The advantage of the Soviet model was that construction and upkeep were kept to a minimum, so Soviet memories tended to be excellent.

Munich had been new territory to Arkady. Not Berlin. Day after day, his military assignment had been to monitor British and American radio patrols as they drove through the Tiergarten to Potsdamer Platz, along Stresemann to Checkpoint Charlie, then on to Prinzenstrasse and back. He followed them from the moment they left their motor pool. It was his own daily ride.

It didn't matter how fast Arkady walked. Jealousy stayed with him, a shadow that walked ahead in giant steps, shrank at the next lamp, then jumped out again.

On Unter den Linden, office buildings were massive and fragile in the same way Soviet architecture was. The hugest structure was, in fact, the Soviet embassy. Trabis were parked nose in. Figures shifted under the lime trees. A man stepped out and hoisted a hand and a cigarette like a question mark. Arkady hurried by, surprised he looked good to anyone.

He was approaching the floodlights of the Brandenburg Gate and the familiar outline of Victory in her chariot when the city opened up into a sudden expanse of stars and grass. It wasn't a park, but a wide ridge of green hillocks that stretched north and south. Over them a breeze lifted waves of insect calls. His first impulse was to step back.

This is where the Wall had been, he realized, which was like saying, "This is where the pyramids were."

Actually, around the Gate there had been two Walls, stranding it like a piece of Greece in the middle, so that it was not a gate but a terminus, with the view on either side brought to a halt. The Wall had been a white horizon four meters high. There had also been a flattened no-man's-land of watchtowers both round and rectangular, trip wires, sapper charges, tank traps, dog tracks, brushed fields of antipersonnel mines and seasonal brambles of concertina wire. Everywhere, lights had crackled like an electric charge.

The void left by the destruction of the Wall and all this attendant apparatus was more immense than its presence had been. An image returned that was more connection than memory. He had been at this same point one summer night long ago. Nothing special had happened except that he had noticed a handler with a brace of dogs that were trotting excitedly along the base of the inner wall. The handler was East German, not Soviet, and the way he kept the dogs encouraged but in check was exactly the same way the charioteer up on her pedestal lightly reined her horses. The dogs had sniffed the ground, then turned, straining on their leads, in Arkady's direction. He had had the irrational fear—he was a young officer who had done nothing wrong —that they were tracking him, that they could smell his treasonous lack of fervor. He had stood his ground and the dogs had turned aside before they came near. From then on, though, he had never looked at the Gate without seeing in the chariot's silhouette a handler and dogs.

Arkady moved into the lights and crossed in long, cautious steps. On the other side was the Tiergarten, a park of well-behaved flowerbeds and well-illuminated avenues. It took him twenty minutes to walk the length of the Tiergarten and around its zoological garden to Zoo Station. There the subway emerged to ride above the street. It was the only train stop that West Berliners had been allowed to use to go east. It was also the station where Soviets had been delivered when they went west.

At street level, much of what Arkady remembered was covered with spray paint. Currency-exchange windows were shuttered, though a late-night drug trade flourished in the doorways. Overhead, though, less had changed. The same narrow-gauge tracks ran by the same elevated platforms under the same glass roof. Lockers were still available twenty-four hours a day. He stowed the videotape he had brought from Munich.

Phones were lined up on the street under the station. Arkady unfolded a wad of paper and called the number Peter Schiller had given him.

Peter answered on the eighth ring, sounding irritable. "Where are you?"

"Berlin. And you?" Arkady asked.

"You know I'm in Berlin. You called this afternoon to say I had to drive in the damn rain all day to be here. You know this is a Berlin number. Who are you with?"

A train came into the station. The sound traveled down through the girder that supported the phone. "Good," Arkady said. "Then, I'll try you tomorrow at noon at this same number. Maybe I'll know more then."

"Renko, if you think you can lead—"

Arkady hung up. It was a comfort to know that Peter was raging somewhere close by, nearer than Munich but farther than arm's reach.

He took the same route back through the park. Again he anticipated the sight of a cement barrier so intensely lit that it rose like a wall of ice. Again he crossed nothing but rubble covered by springy grass and nodding heads of flowers.

He told himself he should have more faith.

29

The morning was bright, dry, not a cloud in the sky. Arkady and Max strolled the same route he had taken the night before. Irina was at the gallery, helping with the installation of the show.

Max was the sort of animal that basked in the sun. He wore a suit the color of butter. In the windows they passed he looked as if he were being importuned by his companion for loose change, a meal, a business opportunity. Then he would put his hand on Arkady's arm as if to say, "Look at this raffish friend I have in tow." Their eyes would meet, and in the small black center of his irises Arkady could read that Max had not slept with Irina during the night, and that his bed had been no more comfortable than Arkady's bare floor.

"It's a developer's dream," Max said. "This side of Berlin always had the grandeur. University, opera, cathedral, the great museums were always in East Berlin. We Soviets built as many monstrosities as we could, but we never had the money or the energy of capitalist developers. West Berlin has shops with the highest real estate value in the world. Imagine the value of East Berlin. See, without knowing, we Russians saved it. This is literally metamorphosis, this is East Berlin crawling out of its cocoon."

Friedrichstrasse was different in the daylight. In the dark, Arkady hadn't seen how many government offices were gutted. One was a wooden front with painted windows around the foundation of a Galeries Lafayette that was taking its place. Another was swaddled in five stories of heavy canvas. Though the street was relatively empty compared to the Ku'damm, from every direction came the sound of a hidden traffic of earthmovers, pile drivers, cranes.

Arkady asked, "Do you own the building we stayed in last night?"

Max laughed. "You're too suspicious. I look for vision, you look for fingerprints."

There were still Trabis under the lime trees, but they were outnumbered by VWs, Volvos, Maseratis. Out of open buildings floated the dust of Sheetrock and the whine of electric drills. Whitewashed windows bore announcements of future offices of Mitsubishi, Alitalia, IBM. Across the street at the Soviet embassy, the steps were empty and the windows were dark. On a side street, a café had set white chairs and tables on the sidewalk. They sat and ordered coffee.

Max checked his watch, a diver's chronometer with gold links. "I have an appointment in an hour. I'm the agent for the building you slept in. For a former Soviet, real estate is almost the redemption of life. Do you have any investments?"

"Aside from books?" Arkady asked.

"Aside from books."

"Aside from a radio?"

"Aside from a radio."

"I inherited a gun."

"In other words, no." Max paused. "Something can be arranged. You're intelligent, you speak English and a little German. With decent clothes you'd be presentable."

A coffeepot came with poppy-seed rolls and strawberry jam. Max poured. "The problem is, I don't think you appreciate how much the world has changed. You're a specimen from the past. It's as if you'd arrived from ancient Rome, chasing someone who offended Caesar. Your idea of a criminal is, to say the least, out of date. To stay, you'd have to let go of all that, to erase it from your mind."

"Erase it?"

"Like the Germans. West Berlin was leveled, so they started fresh and built it into a showcase of capitalism. Our response? We built the Wall, which of course was a pedestal for West Berlin."

"Why don't you invest in West Berlin?"

"That's thinking in the past. Frankly, West Berlin is nothing. It's an island, a club for freethinkers and draft dodgers. But a united Berlin will be the capital of the world."

"That does sound visionary."

"It is. Forgive me for saying so, but the Wall was an even larger reality than your investigation. Now the Wall is gone and Berlin is finally free to bloom. Think of it: over two hundred kilometers of Wall erased, an extra thousand square kilometers in the center of Berlin to be developed. It's the greatest real estate opportunity in the second half of the twentieth century."

There was such conviction in Max's eyes that Arkady realized he had encountered a salesman. Max was selling the idea of the future, and it was compelling. Evidence of the future lined the street. Urgent sounds of it echoed everywhere. The only silent building was the Soviet embassy hulking like a mausoleum above the trees.

Arkady said, "Does Michael share this vision of yours? For a man who is the radio station's deputy director for security, he welcomed you back pretty quickly."

"Michael is a little desperate. If the Americans drop the station, he'll be left with a European life-style and no particular skills. He doesn't have a graduate degree in business administration; he simply has a Porsche. If he can adapt to a new situation, so should you."

"How would I?"

"Your investigation got you here. What you do from this point on is an entirely different question. Do you go forward or do you turn back?"

"What do you think?"

"I'll be honest," Max said. "It wouldn't matter to me except for Irina. Irina is part of Berlin. She stands to benefit. Why do you want to take that away from her? She's never had a chance to enjoy money."

"She can do that with you, enjoy money?"

"Yes. I don't describe myself as a completely innocent person, but fortunes are not made with 'thank you' and 'please.' I bet that when the wheel was invented, it rolled over someone." Max wiped his mouth. "I understand the hold you have on Irina. Every émigré feels guilty about somebody."

"Really? Who do you feel guilty about?"

A good salesman was not discouraged by rudeness. Max said, "It's not a matter of morality. It's not even a matter of you or me. It's just that I have the capacity to change and you don't. Maybe you're a heroic investigator, but you're a figure from the past. There's nothing for you here. I want you to be honest and ask yourself what's best for Irina, going forward or going back?"

"That's up to Irina."

"See, Renko, that's an admission that you *do* know the right answer. Of course the decision is up to Irina. The point is, you and I know what's best. We just came from Moscow. We both know that even if she goes back, I can protect her better than you. I doubt you'd survive a day back there. So, we're speaking of an emotional regression, aren't we? The two of you as poor but loving refugees? With the Soviet embassy trying to deport you? I think you'd need an influential sponsor and, frankly, no one comes to mind but me. The moment you decide to stay you'd have to drop your investigation. Irina would leave you in an instant if she thought you'd stayed for anything else but her."

"If you know that, why haven't you told her I was after you?"

Max paid homage with a sigh. "Unfortunately, Irina still has a high opinion of your abilities. She might think you were right. We're on the horns of a dilemma—you on one horn, me on the other. We're coexisting. That's why morality is so beside the point. That's why we'll have to work out some arrangement."

After Max paid the check and left, Arkady went alone through the trees to the Brandenburg Gate, where Victory wore her daytime tint of verdigris. Swifts circled around her, feeding on insects. He slipped among tourists to the meadow. Although his shoes and cuffs were damp, a summer warmth radiated from the ground. The grass had tassels of white flowers and miniature ripples of insects escaping from each footfall. Bees rushed between balls of clover, making up for the downtime of wet weather. A bike path had been laid out; bikers in helmets and skintight outfits rode in single file, flying like flags on a motorcade. Were they aware that they were trespassing on the site of Max's New Berlin?

SINCE HE HAD time, Arkady walked along the Ku'damm to Zoo Station. He felt as if he had fallen into an army of East Berliners who had invaded in good order but had fallen apart at the first sidewalk display of running shoes. West Berliners retreated behind the railings of cafés, but even there they were pursued by Gypsies with tambourines and babies. A pair of Russians pushed a rack of uniforms. Arkady picked over an assortment of pieces of the Wall with documents attesting to their authenticity. On another table he found an autopilot and altimeter from a Red Army helicopter. He supposed he might find the entire helicopter if he went up and down the Ku'damm long enough. He arrived at Zoo Station right at noon and called Peter's number. This time there was no answer.

Overhead, a train had arrived, releasing yet more regiments of Ossies down the steps to the street. Out of indecision, Arkady was swept up by the crowd and marched across the street to the base of the memorial church, gray and shattered as a tree trunk struck by lightning, where backpackers sprawled on the stairs to watch a street magician. A tour bus aimed a broadside of cameras.

The old Berlin had been divided in half and ruled essentially by Russians and Americans. He hardly saw an American tourist now. Maybe he could stay as a statue, he thought: "The Last Russian," posed as if he were trying to sell a pin of Lenin.

ARKADY WAS RETURNING over the meadow when he saw four sections of the Wall left standing like gravestones. So Max was wrong, he thought; not everyone wanted to erase the Wall and turn without pause to the money till. Someone thought a memorial was appropriate.

Next to the section was a construction crane with a double jib for tall buildings. About seventy meters up, at the crown of the top jib, the block and tackle held a square basket. Against the sky Arkady saw a figure climb over the edge of the basket and jump. Arms and legs spread, he plunged through the air and disappeared behind the sections.

Arkady walked over quickly. Closer, the sections were each four meters square and elaborately spray-painted with every color of peace symbol, and airbrushed with Christs, gnostic eyes, prison bars, names and messages in different languages. Behind the cement slabs people sat at tables set on gravel. A sign said JUMP CAFÉ.

A truck offered sandwiches, cigarettes, sodas and beer. The customers were bikers, some older couples with dogs leashed to their chairs, a pair of businessmen dark enough to be Turks and a circle of teenagers, the sun sparkling on the rivets of their jackets.

The jumper, a boy in a tank top and fatigues, was swaying upside down a few feet in the air. Arkady realized that he had never hit and that he was connected by elastic cords running from his ankles to the top of the crane. The jib lowered to let him settle on the earth, hands first. He released the cords and staggered dizzily to his feet to applause from the bikers and tribal whoops from his friends.

Arkady was interested in the two businessmen. Their suits were good, but they had massed bottles of beer on their table in a gluttonous volume. They had thick bodies and slouched with their heads tucked in a familiar attitude. Though they sat looking away from him, one of them had memorably ugly hair, long in the back, short on the sides, with an orange fringe on top. Though they didn't clap, they watched with close attention.

A second figure was still in the cage high above the tables. He pulled in the loose cords and seemed to sit down. A moment later, he climbed onto the edge of the cage and balanced himself with one hand on a cable. A schnauzer yapped and its owner plugged its mouth with wurst. The figure on the cage looked like he was trying to pick a place to land.

"Dvai!" shouted the man with the bad hair, fed up with waiting. Come on! The way fishermen shout when someone is slow pulling in a net.

The figure jumped. He dropped with his arms and legs windmilling. This time Arkady saw cords playing out loosely behind. He assumed that careful calculations took into account the weight of the jumper, the distance to the ground, the full extension of the cords. The face hurtling down was white, eyes first, mouth peeled open. Arkady had never seen anyone so full of second thoughts. He heard an audible chord as the elastic went taut, then the diver was rising in reverse, a quarter of the way back up. He bounced lower, more slowly and more crazily. Now his face was red and the oval of his mouth resumed human shape. Two girls in leather jackets ran forward to help their hero down. Everyone else applauded except for the two businessmen, who laughed so hard they coughed. The one with the hair leaned back to catch his breath. He was Ali Khasbulatov.

Arkady had last seen Ali with his grandfather Makhmud at the South Port car market in Moscow. Ali smacked the table with his hand like a body hitting the ground and started to roar all over again. When an empty bottle rolled off the table onto the gravel, Ali didn't deign to pick it up. The other man at the table was also Chechen, older with eyebrows brushed like fans. The kids in leather jackets found the laughter offensive, but after some cautious glances left the two men alone. Ali spread his arms like wings, pretended to flutter, then to drop. Waved away praise for his acting from the man across the table. Lifted his glass and lit a cigarette with satisfaction.

No one else wanted to jump for Ali's entertainment. After fifteen minutes, he and the other Chechen left and walked to Potsdamer Platz, where they got into a black VW Cabriolet and drove away.

Arkady couldn't follow on foot, but he turned back in the direction of the Ku'damm with a freshened eye.

In front of the KaDeWe department store he found two Chechens resting on the fender of an Alfa Romeo. Up the Ku'damm, outside the great glass rectangle of the Europa Center, four Lyubtersy mafiosos were squeezed together in a Golf. A side street called Fasanenstrasse had elegant restaurants with French doors and wine stands, and also small, hairy Chechens tucked in a booth of one of them. On the next block a Long Pond mafioso patrolled the boutiques.

Arkady hit Zoo Station again. The telephone books and the operator had no listings for TransKom or Boris Benz. There was a number for a Margarita Benz. Arkady called.

On the fifth ring Irina answered, "Hello?"

"This is Arkady."

"How are you?"

"I'm fine. I'm sorry to bother you."

"No, I'm glad you called," Irina said.

"I was wondering when this event was tonight. And how formal it is."

"At seven. You'll come here with Max and me. Don't worry about formality. Do what German intellectuals do: when in doubt, wear black. They all look like widows. Arkady, are you sure you're all right? Is Berlin completely confusing?"

"No, actually it's starting to look familiar."

THE ADDRESS FOR Margarita Benz was only two blocks away on Savigny Platz. On the way Arkady passed a commercial section of electronics stores with notices in Polish. Polish cars were parked in front. Men unloaded aromatic bags of cheap Socialist sausage and loaded VCRs.

He found the address at a genteel doorway just off Savigny. The legend below the third-floor button was GALLERIE BENZ. He hesitated, then turned away.

Savigny Platz itself was a square with two matching miniparks, each surrounded by a tall box hedge. A formal garden was laid out with marigolds and pansies. Set deep into the hedges were arbors designed for trysts.

Something about the neatly trimmed palisade of the hedge made him walk through the park and to a corner. Across the street were the outdoor tables of a restaurant under a filigree of shade lent by a beech. As he crossed, he heard the chatter of cutlery. A waiter poured coffee at a sideboard framed by honeysuckle grown over a yellow wall. Four tables were occupied, two by executive types efficiently eating, two by students resting, heads in hands. The tables inside were hidden by reflections of the street. In the windowpanes the box hedge of the park looked like a solid wall of green.

It was the Bavarian beer garden from Rudy's tape. Arkady had thought it was in Munich because it had been inserted into a travelogue of the city, an assumption so stupid in retrospect that it made his stomach hurt.

A waiter was staring at him. *"Ist Frau Benz hier?"* Arkady asked.

The waiter checked the end table, the same one she sat at in the tape. Her regular table, obviously.

"Nein."

Why insert Margarita Benz into the tape? The only reason Arkady could think of was identification if she had never met Rudy before and didn't want to give him her name. But she was the sort of woman who had her own table at an attractive restaurant on a stylish plaza in Berlin. What business could a Moscow money changer have with her?

The waiter was still staring. *"Danke."* Arkady backed away, catching his own image in the glass, as if he had stepped into the tape too.

ON THE WAY back to the apartment, Arkady bought blankets, towel, soap and a pullover in intellectual black. At six-thirty P.M. he was collected by Max and Irina on their way down to the garage.

"You're thin; you can wear something like that," Max said. Covered by a jacket with brass buttons, he looked as if he had stepped off a yacht.

Irina wore an emerald outfit that accented the red in her hair. She was so nervous and excited that in the elevator she was like an extra light.

Arkady was fascinated by this whole new life she had. He said, "This is a big affair. You don't want to tell me what it is?"

"It's a surprise."

"Do you know anything about art?" Max asked Arkady as if including a child.

Irina said, "Arkady will recognize this."

They drove in the Daimler along the Tiergarten to Kantstrasse. Irina turned around to Arkady, her eyes huge in the shell-like gloom of the sedan. "You are all right? It worried me when you called."

Max asked, "He called?"

"I'm looking forward to this, whatever it is," Arkady said.

Irina reached back and took his hand. "I'm glad you came," she said. "It's perfect."

They parked at Savigny Platz. Walking to the gallery, Arkady became aware that he was approaching a cultural event of some size. Men so distinguished that they could have been the kaiser escorted matrons draped in beads and jewels. Academics in black marched with wives in knit coats. There were even berets. Photographers crowded around the nondescript entrance to the gallery. Arkady slipped in while Irina endured a short bath of flashes. Inside, a line had formed at a brass elevator. Max led the way to the stairs and pushed along the banister past people inching up.

On the third floor, a throaty voice called out, "Irina!" Arrivals showed invitations at a desk, but Irina was waved forward by a woman with a broad Slavic face and dark eyes that contradicted a mane of golden hair. She wore a long purple dress that looked like the vestment for a cult. Her makeup shifted when she smiled.

"And Max." She kissed him three times, Russian style.

"You must be Margarita Benz," Arkady said.

"I hope so, or I'm at the wrong gallery." She let Arkady touch her hand.

He considered mentioning that they had met before, car to car, she with Rudy and he with Jaak. No, he would be a good guest, he told himself.

The doors were opened. The gallery was a loft with a high ceiling and movable partitions stationed to create an open section on one side, a theater on the other, and to lead the eye in between. Arkady was aware of Irina, Max, waitresses, the alert faces of security guards, the anxious faces of employees right and left.

On a stand in the middle of the gallery was a weathered, rectangular crate of wood. Though the corners were chipped, it was obvious that it was well constructed. Through stains, Arkady could see a blurred stamp of the eagle, wreath and swastika of the postal authority of the Third Reich.

However, his attention had gone to the painting that hung alone on the far wall. It was a small square canvas painted red. There was no portrait or landscape or "picture" in it at all. There was no other color, only red.

Polina had painted six almost like it to blow up cars in Moscow.

30

Arkady also recognized it as "Red Square," one of the most famous paintings in the history of Russian art. It wasn't large and it wasn't a true square either, because the upper right-hand corner rose in a disorienting manner. And it wasn't just red; as he approached, he saw that the square floated on a white background.

Kazimir Malevich, the son of a sugar maker, was perhaps the greatest Russian painter of the century, and certainly the most modern, even though he died in the thirties. He was attacked as a bourgeois idealist and his paintings were hidden in museum cellars, but with the perverse pride that Russia took in the quality of its victims, everyone knew the images of Malevich. Like every other student in Moscow, Arkady had dared to paint a red square, a black square, a white square . . . and produced junk. Somehow Malevich, who did it first, had created art, and now the world genuflected to him.

The gallery filled rapidly. A separate room was hung with other artists of the Russian avant-garde, the brief cultural explosion that had started with the last days of the czar, heralded the Revolution, was stifled by Stalin and was buried with Lenin. There were examples of sketches, ceramics and book jackets, though none of the gum wrappers that Feldman had mentioned. The room was almost empty because everyone was drawn to the simple red square on a white field.

Irina said, "I promised you the show would be beautiful." In Russian, the word for "beautiful" has the same root as the word for "red." "What do you think?"

"I love it."

"You said the right thing."

The painting reflected Irina. She radiated.

"Congratulations." Max arrived with glasses of champagne. "This is a coup."

"Where did it come from?" Arkady asked. He couldn't imagine the Russian State Museum lending one of its most valuable possessions to a private gallery.

"Patience," said Max. "The question is, what will it bring?"

Irina said, "It's priceless."

"Only in rubles," Max said. "The people here have Deutsche marks, yen and dollars."

THIRTY MINUTES AFTER the doors were opened, security guards herded everyone into the theater section, where the video artist Arkady remembered from Tommy's party was waiting beside a VCR and a parabolic rear-projection screen. There weren't enough chairs, so people sat on the floor and crowded the walls. From the back Arkady overheard some of their comments. They were devotees and collectors, far more knowledgeable than he, but one thing even he knew: there was not supposed to be any "Red Square" by Malevich outside Russia.

Irina and Margarita Benz went to the front of the theater while Max joined Arkady. Only when the room was absolutely still did the gallery owner speak. She had a hoarse voice with a Russian accent, and though Arkady's German wasn't good enough to catch every word, he understood that she was placing Malevich at the level of Cézanne and Picasso as a founder of modern art, perhaps a little higher as the most relevant and challenging artist, *the* genius of his age. As Arkady recalled, Malevich's problem had been that there was another genius residing at the Kremlin, and *that* genius, Stalin, had decreed that Soviet writers and artists should be "engineers of the human soul," which in the case of painters meant producing realistic pictures of the proletariat building dams and collective farmers reaping wheat, not mysterious red squares.

Margarita Benz introduced Irina as the author of the catalog, and as she stepped forward Arkady saw her looking over the seated rows at him and Max. Even in his new pullover he was aware that he looked more like an uninvited guest than a patron of the arts, while Max was the opposite, practically a host. Or were he and Max bookends, meant to be a pair?

The lights went out. On the screen was "Red Square," four times its actual size.

Irina spoke in Russian and German. Russian for him, Arkady knew; German for everyone else. "Catalogs will be available at the door and they will go into much greater detail than anything I say now. It's important, however, that you have a visual understanding of the study this painting has undergone. There are some details you can see on a screen that you wouldn't be able to find if we allowed you to pick up the painting and examine it by hand."

It was both comforting and odd to hear Irina's voice in the dark. It was like hearing her on the radio.

The red square was replaced on the screen by a black-and-white photo of a dark man with serious brows, fedora and topcoat standing before an intact Kaiser Wilhelm Church, the one that was now a war memorial on the Ku'damm.

Irina said, "In 1927 Kazimir Malevich visited Berlin for a retrospective exhibit of his paintings. He had already fallen into disfavor in Moscow. Berlin at that time had two hundred thousand Russian émigrés. Munich had Kandinsky. Paris had Chagall, the poet Tsetaeva and the Ballet Russe. Malevich was considering his own escape. The Berlin show contained seventy Malevich paintings. He also brought with him an undetermined number of other works—in other words, half of his entire life's output. However, when he was summoned back to Moscow in June, he returned. His wife and small daughter were still in Russia. Also, the Communist party's Central Committee's agitation and propaganda section was putting artists under more pressure and Malevich's students appealed to him to protect them. When he boarded the train for Moscow, he left instructions that none of his art be returned to Russia.

"At the end of the 1927 Berlin show, all the works were crated by the art-transport firm of Gustav Knauer and sent for storage at the Provinzialmuseum in Hanover, which waited for further instructions from Malevich. Some works were exhibited there, but when the Nazis came to power in 1933 and denounced 'degenerate art,' which included, of course, avant-garde Russian art, the Malevich paintings were returned in their Knauer crates and hidden in the museum cellar.

"We know that they were still there in 1935, when Albert Barr, the director of the Museum of Modern Art in New York, visited Hanover. He purchased two paintings and smuggled them out of Germany rolled in his umbrella. The Hanover museum decided that possession of the rest of the Malevich collection was too dangerous and shipped them back to one of Malevich's original hosts in Berlin, the architect Hugo Haring, who hid them first in his house and then, during the Berlin air raids, in his hometown of Biberach in the south.

"Seventeen years later, the war over and Malevich dead, curators of Amsterdam's Stedelijk Museum traced the route of the Knauer crates to Haring, who was still alive in Biberach, and acquired the paintings that now comprise the largest collection of Malevich work in the West. But from photographs of the Berlin show, we know that fifteen major paintings are missing. We also know from the quality of the Amsterdam collection that some of the finest paintings Malevich brought to Berlin were not exhibited in the Berlin show at all. How many of those private works are missing we will never know. Did they burn during the Berlin Blitz? Were they destroyed in transit by a zealous postal inspector who had discovered 'degenerate art'? Or in all the confusion of the war, were they simply crated, stored and forgotten in Hanover or in the East Berlin warehouse of the Gustav Knauer transport firm?"

Malevich was replaced on the screen by a battered box covered with stamps and yellowed documents. It was the one standing in the gallery. Irina said, "This crate came to the gallery a month after the Wall came down. The wood, nails, style of construction and bills of lading are consistent with the Knauer crates. Inside was an oil on canvas painting, fifty-three by fifty-three centimeters. The gallery knew at once that it had found either a Malevich or a masterful fraud. Which?"

The crate faded and on the screen the painting reappeared in its actual size, a hypnotic beacon. "There are less than a hundred and twenty-five oil paintings by Malevich in existence. Their rarity, as well as their importance in the history of art, accounts for their extraordinarily high value, especially such masterpieces as 'Red Square.' Most of the Malevich paintings were suppressed in Russia for fifty years as 'ideologically incorrect' art. They're still being released now, like political hostages finally seeing the light of day. The situation is complicated, however, by the number of counterfeits flooding the Western art market. The same forgers who once produced counterfeit medieval icons now produce counterfeit works of modern art. In the West, we rely on provenance—exhibition catalogs and bills of sale that provide the dates when art was shown, sold and resold. The situation was different in the Soviet Union. When an artist was arrested, his work was confiscated. When his friends heard of his arrest, they hastened to either hide or destroy whatever works of his they had. The artworks of the Russian avant-garde that exist today are survivors, with the unlikely stories that survivors have of being stuffed in false bottoms or hidden behind wallpaper. Many genuine works have no provenance at all in the Western sense. To demand the usual Western provenance from a survivor of the Soviet state is to deny its survival at all."

On videotape, hands in rubber gloves gently turned "Red Square" over and delicately peeled off a chip, which was analyzed and found to be of German manufacture from the correct time period; Irina pointed out that Russians always used German art materials when they could.

There were paintings within paintings. Under X ray, "Red Square" was a negative that revealed a rectangle painted over. Under fluorescent light, the border's lower layer of zinc white paint softened to a creamy hue. Under ultraviolet light, the brushwork of lead white turned to blue. Under oblique light, magnified brush strokes were rapid horizontal commas with variations—a cloud of strokes here, a tidal swell of strokes there in a varying sea of different reds, broken by a crazing called "craquelure," where red paint had not bonded to the yellow paint hidden underneath.

Irina said, "While the work is unsigned, every brushstroke is a signature. Brushwork, choice of paints, repainting, lack of signature, even the 'craquelure,' are characteristic of Malevich."

Arkady liked the word *craquelure*. He suspected that under the proper light he might show some "craquelure" of his own.

The screen went white again, moving over a magnified weave of canvas and primer thrown into relief by oblique light to the telltale grain of a fingerprint faintly discernible through the paint. Irina asked, "Whose hand left this mark?"

A face with deep-set, sorrowful eyes filled the screen. The camera pulled back to show the blue tunic and sorrowful face of the late General Penyagin. Hardly a person whom Arkady had expected to meet again, least of all in artistic circles. With a pen the general pointed to similar whorls and deltas in the enlargements of two fingerprints, one lifted from the gallery's "Red Square" and the other from an authenticated Malevich in the Russian State Museum. An off-camera voice translated. It occurred to Arkady that a German forensic technician would have been faster, but a Soviet general was more impressive. By now he had recognized the off-camera voice as Max's. It asked, "Would you conclude these prints are from the same man?"

Penyagin stared straight into the camera and worked up forceful-ness, as if he sensed how short his starring role would be. "In my opinion," he said, "these prints are absolutely those of the same indi-vidual."

As the lights of the room came up, the most kaiserlike guest in the audience rose and asked angrily, "Did you pay a *Finderlohn*?"

"Finder's fee," Max translated for Arkady.

Margarita answered the question. "No. Though a *Finderlohn* is per-fectly legal, we dealt directly with the owner from the start."

The man said, "Such fees are notorious ransoms. You know that I'm referring to the fees paid in Texas for the Quedlinburg treasure, which was stolen from Germany by an American soldier after the war."

"No Americans are involved." Margarita almost smiled.

"Only one of numerous examples of German art despoiled by the occupying forces. Like the seventeenth-century painting stored in Reinhardsbrunn castle and stolen by Russian troops. Where is it now? On the auction block at Sotheby's."

Margarita assured him, "There are no Russians involved, either, except for Malevich. And, of course, I have some Russian background myself. You must be aware that it is absolutely against the law to export art of this period and quality from the Soviet Union."

The art lover was mollified, though not without a parting shot. "So it came from East Germany?"

"Yes."

"Then it's one of the few good things that did."

He drew general agreement.

Was the painting a Malevich? Arkady wondered. Forget the ama-teur performance by Penyagin. Could the story of the crate be true? It was a fact that most of the Malevich works in existence had been hidden or smuggled to reach the museums where they now reigned. He was the outlaw artist of the century.

What provenance did Arkady have to show for himself? Not even a Soviet passport.

MARGARITA BENZ PLAYED a strict but generous hostess, keeping people at arm's length from the painting, forbidding cameras, steering her guests toward a table of caviar, smoked sturgeon, champagne. Irina circulated from guest to guest, answering questions that sounded like hostile inquisitions. That was the German language to an outsider, Arkady thought; if this audience was unhappy, it would have left. All the same, watching her he was put in mind of a white stork walking among crows.

A pair of Americans in black tie and pumps communed over the plates of food. "I didn't like that crack about the States. Remember, the Sotheby's sale of Russian avant-garde was a big disappointment."

"Those were all minor works and mostly fakes," the other American said. "A major piece like this could stabilize the whole market. Anyway, if I don't get it, I still will have had a nice trip to Berlin."

"Jack, this is what I wanted to warn you about. Berlin has changed. It's definitely dangerous."

"Now that the Wall's down, it's dangerous?"

"It's full of—" He glanced up, took his friend by the arm and whispered, "I'm thinking of moving to Vienna."

Arkady looked around for what could have scared them. There was no one but him.

AN HOUR LATER, a continuing high noise level and a thick cigarette haze signaled the success of the show. Arkady retreated to the video theater and watched a tape of prewar Berlin that was part footage of horse-drawn trolleys on Unter den Linden, part photographs of Russian refugees. He played with the machine, running the tape forward and back. The figures on the screen were the most exotic and attractive refugees of their time, of course. All of them—writers, dancers and actors—gave off a hothouse fluorescence.

He thought he was alone until Margarita Benz asked, "Irina was good tonight, didn't you think?"

"Yes."

The gallery owner stood in the doorway of the theater with a drink in one hand, a cigarette in the other. "She has a wonderful voice. You found her convincing?"

"Totally," Arkady said.

She slipped inside. He heard her shoulder graze the wall as she approached. "I wanted to get a good look at you."

"In the dark?"

"You can't see in the dark? What a bad investigator you must have been."

Her manner was a strange mix, coarse and imperious at the same time. He remembered the two contradictory identifications Jaak had made on her pictures: Mrs. Boris Benz, German, staying at the Soyuz, and Rita, hard-currency prostitute, emigrated to Israel five years ago. She dropped her cigarette into her glass, set it on the VCR and gave Arkady matches so that he could light another for her. The tips of her nails were as hard as tines. When Arkady had first seen her in Rudy's car, he had said to himself, a Viking. Now he thought, a Salome.

"Did you make a sale?" he asked.

"Max should have told you that a painting like that isn't sold in a minute."

"How long?"

"Weeks."

"Who owns the painting? Who's the seller?"

She laughed on the exhale. "What rude questions."

"This is my first show. I'm curious."

"Only the buyer needs to know the seller."

"If it's Russian—"

"Be serious. In Russia no one knows who owns what. If it's Russian, whoever has it owns it."

Arkady accepted the rebuff. "How much do you think you'll get?"

She smiled, so he knew she would answer. "There are two other versions of 'Red Square.' They're each valued at five million dollars." The number seemed to roll in her mouth. "Call me Rita. My close friends call me Rita."

Malevich appeared on the screen in a self-portrait, with a high collar, black suit and anxious shades of green.

"Do you think he was actually going to leave?" Arkady asked.

"He lost his nerve."

"You can tell that?"

"I can tell."

"How did you get out?"

"Dear, I fucked my way out. I married a Jew. Then I married a German. You have to be willing to do that sort of thing. That's why I wanted to see you, to see what you're willing to do."

"What do you think?"

"Not enough."

Interesting, Arkady thought. Maybe Rita was a better judge of character than he was. He said, "I had the idea from some of your guests that they've seen too many Russians since the Wall came down."

Rita was scornful. "Not too many Russians, too many other Germans. West Berlin used to be like a special club, now it's just a German city. All those East Berlin kids grew up hearing about Western life-styles, so now they come over and want to be punks. Their fathers are unregenerate Nazis. When the Wall came down, they poured in. No wonder West Berliners are lifting their skirts and running."

"Are you thinking of running?"

"No. Berlin is the future. This is what Germany is going to be. Berlin is wide open."

THEY SAT, A foursome, around a late dinner on the patio of the restaurant on Savigny Platz. Max was enjoying the slow dissipation of excitement the way a director of a theatrical production savors an opening night, and was as doting and admiring of Irina as if she were his star. She carried the glow of celebration; she seemed to be circled by candles and crystal. Rita was in the same chair she had sat in on the videotape. As she looked at Max, Irina and Arkady, she seemed concerned over a basic problem of arithmetic.

For Arkady, Max and Margarita kept fading away; all he could see was Irina. Their eyes would meet as palpably as a touch, so he kept up his part of the conversation even in silence.

The waiter set down his tray next to Max and nodded toward two men in shiny suits approaching along the park. They moved slowly, as if they were walking a dog, but there was no dog.

"Chechens. Last week, they broke up a restaurant down the block, the quietest street in Berlin. They killed a waiter with an ax in front of the customers." He rubbed one arm. "With an ax."

"What happened afterwards?" Arkady asked.

"Afterwards? They came back and said they would protect the restaurant."

"Outrageous," Max said. "Anyway, you're already protected, aren't you?"

"Yes," the waiter was quick to agree.

The Chechens crossed over to the restaurant. Arkady had seen one eating with Ali at the Jump Café, and the other was Ali's younger brother, Beno, who had the size and swagger of a jockey. "You're Borya's friend, aren't you? We heard you had a place here."

"Do *you* have a place here?" Max acted amazed.

"A whole suite." Beno had inherited his grandfather's shrewd eyes and force of concentration, Arkady realized: this was the next Makhmud, not Ali. The way he focused on Max, Arkady doubted that he noticed anyone else at the table. "You're having a party? Can we join?"

"You're not old enough."

"Then, we'll get together later."

Beno led the older Chechen down the street, two world travelers at their ease.

WHEN RITA STARTED to sign the dinner check, Max insisted on paying the bill for generosity's sake, and also to demonstrate that he was in control. He wasn't in control, though, Arkady thought. Nobody was.

31

In the middle of the night he woke, aware that Irina was in the room with him. She was in a raincoat, her feet bare in the thin milk of moonlight that covered the floor. She said, "I told Max I was leaving him."

"Good."

"It's not. He says he knew as soon as you came to Munich this could happen."

Arkady sat up. "Forget about Max."

"Max has always treated me well."

"We'll go someplace else tomorrow."

"No, you're safe here. Max wants to help. You don't know how generous he can be."

Her presence was overwhelming. On her shadow he could have drawn her face, eyes, mouth. He smelled her and tasted her in the air. At the same time he knew how tenuous his hold on her was. If she caught his slightest suspicion about Max, he would lose her in a moment.

"Why don't you like Max?" she asked.

"I'm jealous."

"Max should be jealous of you. He's always been good to me. He helped with the painting."

"How?"

"He brought the seller to Rita."

"Do you know who the seller is?"

"No. Max knows a lot of people. He can help you if you let him."

"Whatever you want," Arkady said.

She stooped and kissed him. Before he could stand, she was gone.

ORPHEUS HAD DESCENDED into the underworld to save Eurydice. According to Greek legend, he found her in Hades and led her through endless, slowly rising caverns toward the surface. The only stricture laid by the gods on Orpheus for this second chance was that he not look back until they had reached the surface. On the way, he felt her start to change from a wraith to a warm, living body.

Arkady thought about the logistical problems. Orpheus, obviously, had gone first. As they maneuvered along the ledges of their subterranean route, had he held her hand? Tied her wrist to his as if he were stronger?

Yet when they failed the fault wasn't Eurydice's. Even as they approached the light of the mouth of the cave through which they could make their final escape, it was Orpheus who turned, and with that backward glance condemned Eurydice to death again.

Some men had to look back.

32

At first Arkady couldn't tell whether Irina's visit had been real, because outwardly nothing seemed changed. Max led them to breakfast at a hotel on Friedrichstrasse, praised the renovation of the restaurant, poured the coffee and laid out newspapers by importance of reviews.

"The timing was good and the show made both *Die Zeit* and the *Frankfurter Allgemeine*. Two cautious but positive reviews, harking back to the long-standing debt that Russian art owes to German support. A bad review in *Die Welt*, which doesn't like modern art or Russians. A worse one in *Bild*, a right-wing rag that prefers news events about steroids or sex. It's a good start. Irina, you have interviews this afternoon with *Art News* and *Stern*. You do better than Rita with the press. More important, we're having dinner with some Los Angeles collectors. Americans are only the beginning; the Swiss want to speak to us next. The nice thing about the Swiss is that they don't flaunt the art they buy; they prefer it in a vault. Which reminds me, we'll pull the painting off public exhibition by the end of the week to make it more accessible for serious people."

Irina said, "The show was supposed to run a month so the public could see it."

"I know. It's a matter of insurance. Rita was afraid to show the painting at all, but I told her how strongly you felt."

"What about Arkady?"

"Arkady." Max sighed to indicate this was a lesser subject. He wiped his mouth. "Let's see what we can do. When does your visa run out?" he asked Arkady.

"In two days." He was sure Max knew.

"That's a problem because Germany doesn't accept political refugees from the Soviet Union anymore. There's nothing political to be afraid of." He turned to Irina. "I'm sorry, there really isn't. You can go back anytime you want to. Even if there's a charge of treason against you, nobody cares. At the worst they won't let you in. If you were with me, there'd be no problem at all." He returned to Arkady. "The point is, Renko, that you can't defect, so you'll have to get an extension of your visa from the the German Foreign Police. I'll take you. You'll also need a work permit and a resident's permit. This is all assuming, of course, that the Soviet consulate will cooperate."

"They won't," Arkady said.

"Oh, then, that's a different story. What about Rodionov back in Moscow? Doesn't he want you to stay longer?"

"No."

"Strange. Who are you after? Can you tell me that?"

"No."

"Have you told Irina?"

"No."

Irina said, "Max, stop it. Someone is trying to kill Arkady. You said you were going to help."

"It's not me," Max said. "It's Boris. I talked to him on the phone and he's very unhappy about you and the gallery getting involved with someone like Renko, especially when we're about to see the culmination of all our work."

"Boris is Rita's husband," Irina told Arkady. "A typical German."

"Have you ever met him?" Arkady asked.

"No."

Max seemed pained. "Boris is afraid that your Arkady is in trouble because he's involved with the Russian mafia. A hint of that and the show would be a disaster."

"I have nothing to do with the gallery," Arkady said.

Max went on. "Boris thinks Renko is using you."

"To do what?" Irina demanded.

She *had* come during the night, Arkady thought; it wasn't a dream. She watched Max for the least little misstep. New lines had been drawn and Max retreated over them as carefully as he could.

"To stay, to hide—I don't know. I'm only telling you what Boris thinks. As long as you want Renko here, I'll do my best to keep him here. That's a promise. After all, it seems that as long as I have him, I'll have you."

THEY PLAYED AT being a Western couple. Their names could have been George and Jane. Tom and Sue. They shopped, buying a sport shirt for Arkady that he wore from the store. Wandered through the Tiergarten to the zoo, where they ignored the lions and watched the pony carts. Saw no Chechens or art collectors. Neither tried to say anything exceptional. Normalcy was a spell too easily broken.

At two, Arkady delivered her to the gallery, then went to Zoo Station and put more coins in his locker. He tried calling Peter, but there was no answer. Peter was fed up or had lost interest. Either way Arkady had lost contact.

As soon as he put the phone back on the hook it rang. Arkady stepped back. Along the sidewalk, Africans were selling Ossies what appeared to be French luggage. Backpackers with long hair queued sleepily at the currency exchanges. No one came forward to answer the phone. He picked it up.

Peter said, "Renko, you'd make a terrible spy. A good spy never calls from the same place twice."

"Where are you?"

"Look across the street. See the man in the nice leather jacket talking on the phone? That's me."

IN GOOD WEATHER, the drive out of the city was like a summer jaunt. They went south through the evergreens of the Grunewald, then by the waters of the Havel and hundreds of small boats, their sails catching as much sun as breeze, at a distance looking like gulls.

"There are some benefits to being German. In the middle of your first call I heard a train on your end of the line. Being efficient people, the transport organization was able to tell me at what subway and surface stations around the city trains were arriving at exactly that time. I narrowed the list to Zoo Station because, of course, you're Russian. Zoo was the one station you were sure to know. You were bound to head to familiar places."

"You're brilliant. It's undeniable."

Peter didn't argue the point. "When you called yesterday from Zoo Station I was there waiting for you. I followed you around Berlin. You noticed the city has changed?"

"Yes."

"When the Wall came down there was such intensity of celebration. East and West Berlin back together. It was like a wild night of love-making. Afterwards was like waking in the morning and finding this woman you had yearned for so long was going through your pockets, your wallet, taking the keys to your car. The euphoria was gone. That's not the only change. We were ready for the Red Army. We weren't ready for the Russian mafia. I was behind you yesterday. You saw them."

"It's like Moscow."

"That's what I'm afraid of. Compared to your gangsters, German criminals are a Salzburg choir. German killers clean up after themselves. Russian mafias just shoot each other on the streets. Boutiques are keeping doors locked, hiring private guards, moving to Hamburg or Zurich. It's bad business."

"You don't seem upset."

"They haven't reached Munich yet. Life was boring until you came along."

Arkady felt that once again Peter had taken flight, and all that he could do was see where he would land. He didn't know how long Peter had followed him, and waited to hear the names of Max Albov, Irina Asanova, Margarita Benz.

Somewhere in the woods, among the cottages and country lanes, the highway crossed the former East German border and Potsdam came into view. At least the part of Potsdam that was proletariat housing and might have appeared promising in an architectural rendering, but in reality was ten stories of anonymous balconies with fractured cement.

Old Potsdam was hidden in a canopy of beech trees. Peter parked on a leafy boulevard in front of a three-story town house. This was the kaiser's kind of mansion, a wrought-iron gate and portico wide and high enough for a carriage, marble stairs to double doors, classical stone facing, carved scrollwork above the windows that were high enough to show coffered ceilings, an artist's tower rising above a tiled roof. Except that so much of the facing had fallen off the bricks that a makeshift scaffolding covered the second floor. A wooden ramp ran down one side of the stairs; the other side was broken. Some windows were bricked in, some boarded up. A stunted tree and tall grass grew from the caved-in turret of the tower. The grounds were long abandoned to rubble and weeds of opportunity. A ferrous powder compounded of rust, soot and the dust of decaying bricks covered the gate. But the building was inhabited; from head to foot, the balconies and surviving windows wore boutonnieres of red geraniums, and dim lights and slow movement showed through the glass. By the gate was a sign that said MEDICAL CLINIC.

"The Schiller house," Peter said. "This is it. This is what my grandfather sold out for, this ruin."

Arkady asked, "Has he seen it?"

"Boris Benz brought him a photograph of it. Now he wants to move back in."

On both sides, the block was lined with mansions similar in design and disrepair to the Schiller house. Some worse. One was as masked by ivy as an ancient tomb. Another was posted VERBOTEN! KEIN EINGANG!

Peter said, "This used to be Banker's Row. Every morning they would all go to Berlin, every evening return. These were cultured, intelligent people. They had a modest portrait of the Führer. They closed their eyes when the Meyers disappeared from this mansion over here or the Weinstein family vanished from that house over there. Later, they could get those houses for a good price. Well, you can't tell where the Jews lived today, can you? Now my grandfather wants us to trade with the devil again for this."

A balcony door opened and a woman in a white cap and apron backed out with a wheelchair that she turned around. She put on the brake and sat down for a cigarette, mistress of all she surveyed.

"What are you going to do?" Arkady asked.

Peter pushed open the gate. "I should take a look, don't you think?"

The driveway had once been laid in cobblestones and led to a reception arch of pillars. Now two ruts cut through the weeds, and one of the pillars had long since suffered a collision and been replaced by a standing sewer pipe. The front door had a red cross and a RUHIG! sign for quiet, but it was open and the sound of radios and the smell of antiseptic drifted out. There was no reception desk. Peter's inspection tour took them down a hall of dark mahogany to a ballroom turned into a mess hall and an enormous kitchen divided by cinder blocks into a small kitchen with steaming vats of soup and a second area of tiled baths and toilet stalls.

Peter tried the soup. "Not bad. They have good yellow potatoes in East Germany. I was in Potsdam last night, but I didn't get here."

"Where were you?"

"In the archives of the Potsdam City Hall, looking for Boris Benz." He let the ladle drop and moved on. "There's not enough of him," he said. "I tap into the federal computer and I see his driver's license, Munich residence, marriage license. I see his registered ownership of a private company called Fantasy Tours, with work, insurance and medical records in order, because his employees are examined for venereal disease once a month by law. What does not show up is his local education or work history."

"You told me that Benz was born here in Potsdam and that many East German records weren't transferred yet."

Peter bounded up the stairs. "That's why I came here. But there are no records at all here for Boris Benz. It's one thing to plug a name into a computer file; you're only adding one more blip to the screen. It's more difficult to insert a name on an old, meticulously written school roll. As for work or military records, they don't matter if you're not looking for work or a loan from the bank. It only proves that Boris Benz has more money than personal history. Ah, this must have been the master bedroom."

They looked into a ward with five cots on a side. Some of the beds were occupied by patients attached to IVs. Family photographs and crayon drawings were taped to the walls. The sheets looked clean and the parquet floor was mopped to a shine. Four elderly women in housecoats were playing cards. One of them looked up. *"Wir haben Besuch!"* Visitors!

Peter nodded approvingly at each resident. *"Sehr gut, meine Damen. Schöne Fotos. Danke."* They beamed as he waved and backed away.

The other bedrooms had also been turned into wards and more zinc-lined baths. Cigarette smoke traveled out the open transom of an office. They climbed to the third floor. In the ceiling of the stairwell where a chandelier had once hung was a fluorescent ring.

Peter said, "I asked myself, if Benz didn't grow up here, how would he know about my grandfather or what he did in the war? Only the SS or Russians knew. So there are two answers: he's Russian or German."

"Which do you think it is?" Arkady asked.

"German," Peter said. "East German. To be more precise, the Staatssicherheitsdienst. Stasi. Their KGB. For forty years Stasi created identities for spies. Do you know how many people worked for them? Two million informers. More than eighty-five thousand officers. Stasi owned office buildings, apartment houses, resorts, bank accounts in the millions. Where did all the agents go? Where did the money disappear to? In the last weeks before the Wall came down, the agents at Stasi were furiously creating new identities for themselves. When people stormed its offices, they were empty and the master files had evaporated. One week later Boris Benz rented his apartment in Munich. That's when he was born."

The third floor was servants' quarters turned into medicine closets and nurses' rooms. Panties were drying on a line that ran from corner to corner.

Peter said, "Where could the Stasi go? If they were important, they were going to be put in jail. If they were unimportant, with 'Stasi' on their papers no one would hire them. They couldn't all rush to Brazil like a second wave of Nazis. Russia doesn't want thousands of German agents. What's this?"

A narrow stairway was blocked by pails. Peter moved them aside, climbed the stairs and tried the knob of a door built into the ceiling. A sash snapped and dust cascaded down the steps as he pushed the door open.

They pulled themselves up into the tower. The casement windows were buckled, parts of the roof fallen in, and from one corner grew a stunted linden tree, a lifelong prisoner of the tower. The view was wonderful: lakes and rolling hills reaching to Berlin, green country in every other direction. Two stories below was the balcony with the nurse in the wheelchair. She had pushed off her sandals and rolled down her stockings to her calves. She raised the leg rests and angled the chair for more direct exposure to the sun, then lolled back like Cleopatra, the cigarette in her mouth an exclamation point to total ease.

Peter said, "Ask yourself, where does an Ossie find the money to buy eighteen new cars? Or live in Munich? For a man with no history, Benz was born with impressive connections."

"But why bother your grandfather?" Arkady asked. "What did he get except war stories?"

"Stasi was more than spies; they were thieves. They targeted people with valuable goods. People weren't just arrested; their savings were taken as 'reparations to the state,' and their paintings and coin collections ended up in the apartment of a Stasi colonel. Maybe when Benz disappeared, he took something and doesn't know quite what. There's so much still hidden in this country. So much."

Peter's was a perfectly German, exquisitely logical answer to the identity of Boris Benz. It wasn't Arkady's answer, but he admired it nonetheless.

Peter asked abruptly, "Who is Max Albov?"

"He's given me a place to stay in Berlin." Surprised, Arkady tried to go on the offensive. "That's why I was calling you. You have my passport and I can't stay in a hotel without it. Also, I want to extend my visa."

Peter tested a post before leaning against it. "Your passport is the leash I have on you. I'd never see you again if I give it back to you."

"Is that so bad?"

Peter laughed, then cast his eyes over the trees. "I can imagine myself growing up here. Running in the hall, climbing the roof, breaking my neck. Renko, I worry about you. I followed you to that apartment on Friedrichstrasse yesterday. Albov arrived before I left for Potsdam and I identified him by his license. From the checking I've done, he's a slippery type. A defector twice, no doubt connected to the KGB, an ersatz businessman. What could possibly bring the two of you together?"

"I met him in Munich. He offered to help."

"Who's the woman? She was with him in the car."

"I don't know."

Peter shook his head. "The correct answer is 'What woman?' I see now that I shouldn't have left; I should have camped on Friedrichstrasse and watched. Renko, are you safe?"

"I don't know."

Peter accepted that. He took a deep breath. "Berlin air. It's supposed to be good for you."

Arkady lit a cigarette. Peter took one. From the balcony below came audible snoring mixed with the garden sound of flies. "The Workers' State," Peter said.

"What about the house?" Arkady asked. "Are you going to be a landowner, are you going to move in?"

Peter leaned on one railing, then another. He said, "I like to rent."

33

The day was fading when Peter dropped Arkady at Zoo Station. Over the city was a momentary hush, a pause between afternoon and evening. Minute by minute, Arkady was learning what he would do to stay with Irina. The answer seemed to be *anything*.

She would be going to dinner with American collectors. Arkady bought flowers and a vase and walked through the Tiergarten in the direction of the Brandenburg Gate, its columns and pediments as high as a five-story building. He saw how impressive a promenade this could be, a boulevard that ran the length of the western half of the city and continued through the Gate into the old imperial squares of the east. He had it practically to himself. When the Wall was up, this hundred meters of blacktop had been the most carefully observed spot on earth—from one side by watchtowers, from the other by tourists who climbed a platform to gawk.

At the base of the columns was a white Mercedes and a man bouncing a soccer ball on his head. Wearing a camel's-hair coat tied as casually as a bathrobe, he balanced the ball on his forehead, dropped it to knee, to instep, tipped the ball to his other foot and flipped it up again. A professional player like Borya Gubenko didn't lose his skills if he kept in shape. He bounced the ball from knee to knee.

"Renko!" He waved Arkady closer, keeping the ball in steady motion.

While Arkady came closer, Borya kicked the ball high into the air. Arms out like a tightrope walker, he caught it on his foot, cradled it on his instep and flipped it up to his head. "I've been doing more than just hitting golf balls in Moscow," he said. "What do you think? Think

I'm ready to run back out there out and defend the goal for Central Army?"

"Why not?"

When Arkady was close enough, Borya stepped back to let the ball drop, then stepped forward and kicked it full force into his stomach. Arkady dropped. As he landed, he heard the vase break. His legs went different ways. The ground spun and he couldn't get his balance even lying down. There was a ring around his vision and spots in the sky.

Borya knelt and put a gun to his ear. An Italian pistol, Arkady thought. "I owe you a lot more than that," Borya said.

The gun wasn't necessary. He rose, opened the passenger door of the Mercedes, lifted Arkady by the collar and the back of his belt—the same way drunks were toted out of football games—and threw him into the front seat, put the ball in back and slid behind the wheel. The car's acceleration shut Arkady's door.

BORYA SAID, "IF it were up to me, you'd be dead. You never would have left Moscow. If people saw us kill you, so what? We'd pay them off. I think there's a self-destructive streak in Max."

Arkady breathed shallowly. He hadn't had the wind knocked out of him for so long that he had forgotten the utter helplessness. Flowers and vase were lost. His stomach still felt concave. He was aware that Borya was taking a scenic route along the River Spree, more or less in the direction of the sunset, maintaining just enough speed so that Arkady wouldn't jump. Borya could have killed him by now.

Borya said, "Sometimes smart people overcomplicate. Great plans, no execution. What's the classic example?" He snapped his fingers. "In that play."

Arkady said, *"Hamlet?"*

"Hamlet, perfect. You don't admire the ball forever, you kick it."

"Like you kicked the Trabi off the road in Munich?"

"It could have solved our problems. It should have. When Rita told me you were still alive and that Max had brought you here, I honestly couldn't believe it. What's going on with you and Max?"

"I think he wants to prove he's the better man."

"No offense, but Max has everything and you have nothing." Borya broke into a smile. "In the West that's how it's scored. He's the better man."

Arkady asked, "Who's the better man, Borya Gubenko or Boris Benz?"

Borya's smile spread into the grin of a boy caught stealing cookies. He fished out Marlboros and gave one to Arkady. "As Max says, we have to be new men for new times."

Arkady said, "You needed a foreign partner for the joint venture and it was easier to create one than find one."

Borya stroked the wheel. "I like the name Benz. It has a more reassuring sound than Gubenko. Benz is a man people want to do business with. How did you figure it out?"

"Obvious things. You were Rudy's partner, but on paper Benz was Rudy's partner. Once I knew Benz was a paper identity, you were the most likely candidate. It struck me as odd that the clinic at your Munich house believed me for a second and let me in the door when I claimed I was you. I don't sound very German. Then you made the mistake of videotaping a restaurant window when you were taping Rita. Your reflection wasn't a perfect portrait because you were holding the camera, but on a big screen an old football hero still stands out."

"The tape was Max's idea."

"Then, I should thank him."

Heading south toward the Ku'damm, they passed a service station with signs in Polish. Borya said, "What the Poles do is, they steal a car, a nice car, cut it off the motor, drop the car on a legal motor, maybe a piece of junk that barely runs, and drive to the border. The border guards check the number on the motor and they let it through. It's like a joke: how many Poles does it take to steal a car? If you have any money, you just pay the guard and drive through."

"Getting a painting across the border, is that more difficult?" Arkady asked.

"You want to know the truth? I like that painting. It's a rare work of art. But we don't need that painting. There's a difference of opinion here. We were doing very well with the slot machines, the girls—"

"That's the personnel part of TransKom, bringing prostitutes from Moscow to Munich?"

"It's legal. It's an opportunity. The world's opening up, Renko."

"Then why smuggle the painting?"

"It's democracy. I was outvoted. Max wants the painting and Rita loves the idea of being Frau Margarita Benz, gallery owner, instead of a madam, which is what she was. After I missed you in the Trabi, I wanted to hit you here. I was outvoted again. I have nothing against you, but I wanted to leave Moscow behind. When I heard you were here, I exploded. Max says you're going to be quiet, you have a personal involvement and you're not going to get in the way. That you're on the team. I'd like to believe it, but when I follow you I see you jump in a car with the German police and go for a day trip to Potsdam. Put me anywhere in the world and I recognize the local militia. You're twisting our pricks, Renko, and that's a mistake. This is a new world for both of us and we should take advantage instead of tearing each other down. We can't be Neanderthals the rest of our lives. I'm happy to learn from the Germans or the Americans or the Japanese. The problem is the Chechens. They're going to spoil Berlin the way they spoiled Moscow. They pick on Russian businesses. It's a shame that they bring down their own people. Walking around with automatic weapons as if they were home, kicking their way into restaurants, busting up shops, kidnapping children—horrible stories. So far the German police don't know what to do because they've never seen anything like it. They can't infiltrate because none of them can pass for Chechen. Not close. But it's shortsighted on the part of the Chechens because they have so much money that if they invested it here legally they could make a fortune. I could show them how to get into the positive side of business. Rudy was an economist, Max is a visionary, but I'm a businessman. I can tell you from experience that business is based on trust. At the golf range I trust that my suppliers are selling me good liquor, not poison. The suppliers trust that I'll pay them in real money, not rubles. The most civilizing idea in the world is trust. If Makhmud would just listen, we could live in peace."

"That's all you want?"

"That's all I want."

They drove through the now-familiar hordes of the Ku'damm, under neon grails of AEG, SIEMENS, NIKE and CINZANO below a sky of pale lavender. The ruins of the Kaiser Wilhelm Church looked out of place because it was the only building in sight that wasn't new. Hard behind it stood the glass wall of the Europa Center, starting to blaze with office lights. Borya parked in the Center's garage.

In its shopping area, the Europa Center had more than a hundred shops, restaurants, cinemas and cabarets. Borya led Arkady past the entreaties of sushi bars, first-run westerns, cultured pearls, Swiss watches and nail salons. His eye had a speculative glint, as if he were considering expanding on his golf range.

"Makhmud trusts you. With you along, he might listen."

"He's here?" Arkady asked.

"It's one thing for Max to say that you're as good as on the team. If you do this for me, this little thing, then I'll know you're okay. He's right upstairs. You know how he is about his health."

They climbed three flights. Arkady had expected that any meeting with Makhmud Khasbulatov would take place in the back of a car or in the corner of a dimly lit restaurant, but at the top of the stairs was a brightly illuminated carpeted foyer and a counter lined with a selection of organic shampoos, sunglasses and chelated vitamins. For sixty Deutsche marks the clerk issued them towels, rubber slippers and metal-bead chains with locker keys.

"A bathhouse?" Arkady asked.

"A sauna," Borya said.

The changing room had lockers, showers, hair dryers, complimentary mousse. Arkady hung his miserable few clothes on hangers, locked up and slipped the chain over his hand like a bracelet. Borya had to stuff his wardrobe in. Most men when they stripped looked misshapen or diminished. An athlete like Borya Gubenko had undressed before other people all his life. He wore physical ease. Arkady looked starved alongside him.

"Makhmud comes here?" Arkady asked.

"Makhmud is a health nut. Wherever he is, here or Moscow, he spends an hour a day in a sauna."

"How many other Chechens are here?" At the South Port car market, Makhmud never had less than half a dozen.

"A few. Relax," Borya said. "I just want you to talk to Makhmud face-to-face. For whatever reason, he likes you. Also I want you to see that everything I do here is legitimate."

"This is a public place?"

Borya pushed open the sauna door. "It couldn't be more public."

Arkady was used to utilitarian bathhouses, to pale Russian torsos and the smell of alcohol working its way out as sweat. This was different. A veranda with a tropical forest of plastic plants opened onto a circular indoor swimming pool surrounded by marble steps. Swimming, floating, stretched across chaise longues were naked bodies so pink they looked as if they had just rolled in snow. Male, female, boys and girls. The scene would have been hedonistic if it hadn't been so serious. They looked as fit as Olympians and as stiff as mummies, some with the embellishment of a towel, some not. A man with a goatee and a belly of gray hair walked up the steps as gravely as a senator. Chechens were easy to find. Two of them leaned on the balustrade watching a woman swim slowly back and forth in bathing cap and goggles, nothing else. Although Chechens would never allow their wives to go naked in public, they had no objection if Germans wanted to.

Toddlers with hair as fair as goose down ran out of a dining area, their shrieks echoing off the copper baffles above the pool. Arkady heard the bang of dominoes being slapped on a dining table. Probably more Chechens there.

Borya took Arkady the other way, past two smaller sitting pools and through the wooden door of a dry sauna. Inside was the senatorial German. They climbed benches to the warmest air. The German paid them no attention. He sat by a wall thermometer and rubbed sweat like soap over his body. Every few seconds he checked the temperature. Sweating seemed to take all his concentration. The metal beads of Arkady's chain were already hot. The sauna was well insulated. He could hear no pool sounds at all.

"Where's Makhmud?"

"Somewhere here," Borya said.

"Where's Ali?" If Makhmud was nearby, so was his favorite bodyguard.

Borya put a finger to his mouth. He could have been a sculpture except for the dew of sweat starting to appear on his temple, upper lip, the hollow where his neck sank into the armature of muscle that was his chest. He whispered, "Dry heat takes too long. Let's try the Russian bath."

He climbed down and Arkady followed. Outside, the Chechens at the balustrade watched the swimmer dry herself by the near edge of the pool. She wasn't young, but from the back she had a hard, athletic body to be proud of and she turned toweling down into an elaborate process. She pulled off her cap, releasing thick blond hair that she swung round to rake fiercely with her fingers, then brush back wet from a face that was broad, Slavic, not the least German, with eyes that were so bold and diffident they summed up and dismissed both the Chechens and Arkady at the same time. It was Rita Benz.

Borya pushed through a door labeled RUSSISCH DAMPFBADEN and Arkady followed, plunging into an aromatic cloud. The bench on his side was empty. He sat, put his hand out and touched a limestone rim. A fountain. The only light rose as a smoky glow from four glass floor tiles around the fountain's base. He couldn't see Borya on the other side.

A sauna was an oven that slowly baked the sweat out; a Russian bath was so saturated by moist steam that perspiration bloomed in an instant. The scent of cypress helped open the pores. Sweat flowed down Arkady's forehead, ran over his chest, accumulated between his toes, filled every crevice of his body; he felt like one great conduit of sweat. He thought about Rita and the first time he had seen her in Rudy's car. The way she had looked at him now was the way she had looked at him then.

"Ali?" Makhmud's voice came out of the corner.

Arkady was already moving toward the door when Borya hit him. His head bounced off the wall and he toppled off the bench and to the floor.

He didn't so much lose consciousness as pass through a brief eclipse. Then his eyes were open and he half-crawled, half-swam off the floor and perched unsteadily on the edge of the bench. Aside from his poor balance and a compression problem in his ears he was in one piece. The question that victims of concussions always asked was, what happened? A second ago he had been in the Russian bath with Borya and Makhmud. Now he seemed to be alone.

The steam was pink. To Arkady that meant his head was cut and blood was running into his eyes. He found a knot on his scalp, but no cut. He wiped his face with a towel. The bath was still a cube of rose-colored steam.

Arkady looked down. The glass tiles on the floor were red. As he maneuvered around the fountain he saw a red foot dangling from the opposite bench. The foot led to a body that he pulled toward the light.

Makhmud seemed to be eating a towel. So many puncture marks bled from his neck and chest that he looked as if he had been the target of an automatic weapon, but the taped grip of a knife stuck out of his withered stomach. Arkady remembered that he had worn a towel tied prudishly around his waist. Borya had carried his towel in his hand. Arkady felt his wrist. The chain and key were gone.

There was a knock on the door. When Arkady didn't answer, the door opened and Ali stepped halfway in. Steam rushed out. He looked fat and strong and his hair hung in ringlets around his eyes. "Granddad, don't you think you've been in here long enough?"

Arkady said nothing. He felt the fact register in Ali's mind that steam should be white. Ali moved all the way in and shut the door. His pudgy hand groped through the mist. Arkady stood on the bench so that his feet wouldn't be visible in the light and walked around to the other side.

"Where are—"

For a moment there was nothing but the sound of water running over the rims of the fountain. Then he heard Ali lift the dead man and the suction as he pulled out the knife. With Makhmud off the glass tiles there was more light in the bath. Arkady saw Ali's feet turn around. "Who's here?" Ali asked.

Arkady was silent. Two more Chechens were outside the door, more at different areas around the spa, he thought. Ali had only to call. "I know you're here," he said:

There was a flurry in the mist, a flutter of water particles spinning as Ali slashed at steam. He was partially impeded by the fountain. Arkady tried to slide by toward the door and felt a hot line draw across his back. He retreated. Ali had also felt contact. His next move was a thrust into the wood by Arkady's hand.

Arkady kicked out and Ali rocked. The fountain shifted, too. A hand grabbed Arkady's foot and dragged him down onto the bench, then to the floor. Ali took a handful of hair and pulled Arkady's head back, but the motion made him slip on the slick floor and lose the knife. Arkady heard it rattle on the far side of the bath.

They crawled over each other toward the sound. Ali had enough weight to force Arkady down and reach ahead. He got to his feet, a red Buddha rising through clouds, with the knife in his hand. It was a boning knife with a long, narrow blade. Arkady hit him. Ali slid back and came forward again. Arkady feinted another punch and Ali leaned forward to keep his momentum. When the punch didn't come, he started to slide. He swung the knife and grabbed Arkady on the way down. They skated clumsily together for a second and landed under the fountain.

Ali heaved free and sat against the bench. He looked down, where his stomach was sliced open on a curve from his left hip to his right rib. He tried to hold his stomach together, but it was running out like a spilled cup. Ali sucked air. He couldn't get enough to talk. He had the expression of a man who had willingly jumped from a height to find to his horror and disbelief that this time there was no safety cord. He thought Arkady was helping him up, but Arkady was taking the key chain off his wrist.

Arkady gathered his towel and slippers and left the bath. The two

Chechens had moved down to the pool, though Rita was gone. He was aware he was covered in blood. He dove into the nearest sitting pool, which was frigid, and climbed out, leaving red curls unraveling in the water. He rinsed in the second, heated pool and dried himself as he went to the changing room.

Ali's locker contained his shiny suit and a Louis Vuitton bag with a machine pistol, three clips and a Vuitton wallet fat with high-denomination Deutsche marks. Arkady dressed at normal speed and on the way down the stairs passed office workers who were hurrying up for after-hours relaxation and didn't seem to find it unusual how badly a Russian's clothes could fit. He returned his slippers to the cashier on the way out.

34

At Friedrichstrasse the garage door was still wedged open. Arkady climbed the stairs to the fourth floor. He left the lights off while he found his carry-on and changed clothes. Ali's shoes pinched; he would have to get new ones tomorrow.

Timing was everything. If Borya heard that two bodies had been found in the bath, he'd be reassured. If he heard both were Chechen, he'd be warned. The police would put together a description of the man who had left in Ali's suit. Beno and the other Chechens would already be looking for him.

Arkady was no expert on small arms, but he recognized the machine pistol as a Czech Skorpion, an automatic with a snout sticking out of an oversized slide. The clips held twenty rounds each, which the pistol could empty in two seconds. Perfect Ali fireworks; with a Skorpion, no one needed to aim.

When the door opened behind him, Arkady pushed home a clip and turned to fire.

Irina was in the doorway, so frozen in place she balanced between the light of the hall and the dark of the room. Arkady looked to see whether anyone else was in the hall, then pulled her in by the wrist and shut the door.

"I thought I heard you," she said. Her voice came out as small as a prerecorded tape.

"Where's Max?"

"Why do you have a gun?"

"Where is Max?"

"Dinner was over early. The Americans had to catch a plane. Max went to the gallery to see Rita. I came here to see you." She pulled her wrist free. "Why is it dark in here?"

When she tried to reach the switch, he pushed her hand away. She tried to open the door and he kicked it shut.

"I can't believe this, Arkady. It's happening again. You didn't come back for me, you came for someone else. You used me again."

"No."

"Yes, you did. Who are you after?"

Arkady was silent.

"Who else?" she asked.

He said, "Max. Rita. Boris Benz, except that his real name is Borya Gubenko."

He felt her pull away. She said, "I used to think that the day I left you was the worst day of my life. This is worse, though. You've come back and outdone yourself. I've wasted my life on these two days."

"You—"

"Five minutes ago I was yours. I ran down here. What do I see? Investigator Renko."

"They killed a money dealer in Moscow."

"What do I care about Soviet laws?"

"They murdered my partner."

"Why should I care about Soviet police?"

"They killed Tommy."

"People around you get killed. Max wouldn't hurt me. He loves me."

"I love you."

She hit him. First with the flat of her hand as hard as she could, then with her fists. He stood like a man leaning into the wind and let the pistol hang. He let it slide down his leg to the floor.

"I want to see your face," Irina said.

She found the switch and turned it on. At once he could see something was wrong from the shock in her eyes. He put his hand up and felt a tender swelling from his temple to his brow. It had ballooned since he had left the bathhouse.

She looked at Ali's shirt on the floor. The back was soaked through, red as a flag. She unbuttoned the shirt he was wearing. He pulled it off and she turned him around to look. He heard her breath stop. "You're cut."

"It's not deep."

"You're still bleeding."

They turned on the bathroom light. In the cabinet mirror Arkady saw that Ali had slashed him from the right shoulder blade down to his belt. Irina tried to swab the blood from his back, but a washcloth was inadequate. Arkady set the pistol in the basin of the sink, undressed and stepped into the shower. She set the water on cool and cleaned him around the long red slice.

His muscles bunched and shook from the temperature of the water, then eased at the touch of her hand on his back. Her fingers found a scar on his rib, and as if tactilely remembering, went to a puckered mark on his leg and then up to a slick ridge in the middle of his stomach, as if he were a map with four limbs.

Arkady turned off the water. He emerged from the shower while she pulled off her skirt and slipped in two steps from her pants. He lifted her up. She held on to his neck, wrapped her legs around his waist and arched herself so he could enter.

She opened herself even as she held him tight. Her mouth was hot. Her eyes were wide, as if afraid to close. Outside they were locked. Inside he traveled to the heart of her. They rocked, his back against the wall.

She cried with sharp intakes of breath. In the mirror, he saw the wall wiped with his blood. They looked as if they were climbing together from a black pit to the light, on one pair of legs that had never been so strong before. She held on, her fingers curling in his hair.

"Arkasha!" She leaned back while inside he drove closer to a yielding core. She held on as desperately, her mouth on his again, on his cheek and against his ear whispering with a voice as hoarse as his until the last inner resistance dissolved.

As his legs failed, they dropped slowly to their knees to the tiles of the floor, then he on his back and she astride.

There was a moment of softness. She pulled her blouse up over her head. Her breasts were bare, the tips dark and hard. He felt himself grow large again.

He filled his mouth with her breast. Her hair hung in a curtain around her face. Her tears sluiced down her neck and between her breasts to him, a mixed taste of salt and sweet. And forgiveness. This was the absolution from and for herself. When she threw her head back, he saw below her right eye a delicate blue flaw, her own Moscow scar. As she rode, her eyes closed as if he were rising inside along her spine up to her throat.

She twisted to be beneath him and spread to take him even farther in, her legs high, in flight. He drove her along the tiles. Inside, she carried him deeper, as if they could shed their bodies, shed the lost years, shed the pain. Save each other. Two persons in one skin.

THEY LAY ON the bathroom floor as if in bed, her head pillowed on his chest, her leg resting over his so that he felt her brush of hair against his thigh, a subtle contract of trust. So what if their flanks were red from the blood on the tiles? If Orpheus and Eurydice had emerged intact from hell, what would they look like?

EVEN IN SHADOW, Irina looked exhausted. "I think you're wrong. Max isn't a killer. He's smart. As soon as reforms started in Russia, he said it wasn't reform, it was collapse. He was unhappy because our relationship hadn't developed the way he'd hoped. He wanted to come back a hero."

"By defecting again?"

"By making money. He said the people in Moscow needed him more than he needed them."

"He must have been right." If he had been wrong, Max never could have returned to Germany.

"He wants to prove he's smarter than you."

"He is."

"Oh, no, you're brilliant. I said I'd never let you be close to me again, yet here I am."

"You think Max and I can work out our misunderstanding?"

"He helped you get to Munich, he helped you get to Berlin. He'd help again if I asked. Just wait."

THEY SAT ON the floor by the living-room window with the lights off. They were classic refugees, Arkady thought, he in pants, Irina in his shirt. Dried, the cut on his back looked like a zipper.

Where could they go? The police were searching for Makhmud and Ali's killer. Assuming their guidelines were like the militia's, the Germans would broadcast his description, watch the airport and train stations, alert hospitals and pharmacies. Meanwhile, Borya's people and the Chechens would search the streets. Of course the Chechens would also be hunting Borya.

After midnight there was little traffic. Before Arkady saw cars down on the street he could identify their voices. The asthmatic rattle of Trabis, the clockwork ticking of diesel cabs. A white Mercedes went by at the speed of a trolling boat.

"Do you want to help?" he asked.

"Yes."

"Get dressed and go up to your floor." He gave her Peter's telephone number. "Tell the person who answers where we are, then stay there until I come up."

"Why don't we go up together? You can call."

"I'll be with you in a minute. Just keep calling until you get an answer. Sometimes he doesn't pick up right away."

Irina didn't argue. She pulled on her skirt and went barefoot into the hall. The brief glimpse of light was blinding.

Below, the white Mercedes passed by again. Arkady heard the organ note of the Daimler before he saw it slowly approaching from the other direction. Max and Borya had to protect each other from Chechens as much as hunt for him. Max would be the one coming up, but Irina was right, he wouldn't hurt her.

The two cars passed each other in front of the building and drove on.

In a few years, when developers were done, Friedrichstrasse would be pulsing like a regular artery with department stores, fast-food outlets and espresso bars. Arkady felt he was keeping watch in the graveyard of the old East Berlin.

The two cars appeared again from the same directions as before. They must have circled the block. The Mercedes parked across the street while the Daimler swung into the building garage.

There wasn't a lot of protection in an unfurnished apartment. Arkady set his carry-on directly in front of the door so that anyone opening it would focus first on the bag. He lay down on the far side of the floor facing the door to present as small a target as possible. Through the floorboards, Arkady felt the elevator engage. He doubted Max would be alone. The crystal sconces in the elevator cab were bright. Arkady wanted the irises of Max's and any friends' eyes dazzled, tight as pins.

The pistol came with a folding wire stock that Arkady straightened and put against his shoulder. He pushed the safety-rate selector to full automatic and laid the three other ammo clips in front of him like extra cards. The hall light edged the black rectangle of the door. In this frame the door seemed to vibrate.

In the hall, the elevator stopped. He heard the doors of the car slide open, pause, then shut. The elevator went on up to the sixth floor.

There was a knock. Irina slipped in and shut the door behind her. Her eyes found Arkady. "I knew you weren't coming up."

"Did you call?"

"A machine answered. I left a message."

"You're missing Max," Arkady said. "He's going up right now."

"I know. I used the stairs. Don't try to make me leave without you. I did that before. That was my mistake."

Arkady didn't take his eyes from the door. Max might be temporarily confused to discover Irina gone, he thought. The elevator stayed on the sixth floor for ten minutes, though, longer than made sense unless Max was quietly coming down the stairs. But when the elevator activated again it went straight down to the garage and seconds later Irina said she saw the Daimler leave, with the Mercedes following.

35

Irina said, "I always imagined who you were with. I saw someone very young, for some reason. Small and dark, bright, passionate. I thought of places you would walk, what you'd talk about. When I wanted to torture myself, I imagined an entire day at the beach—blankets, sand, sunglasses, the sound of waves. Evening in a cabin. She tunes a short-wave radio looking for romantic music when she happens to hear me. She stops, because the station is Russian, after all. Then she moves the dial and you let her; you don't say a word. So I imagined my revenge. She gets a trip to Germany. By coincidence we share the same compartment of a train, and as it's a long trip we talk, and naturally I discover who she is. We usually end up on an icy platform in the Alps. She's a nice woman. I push her off the platform anyway for taking my place."

"You kill her, not me?"

"I'm mad, I'm not crazy."

FROM THE APARTMENT floor, the street had a sound like surf. A wash of headlights moved across the ceiling.

Arkady saw a car park one block north on Friedrichstrasse. He couldn't tell the make, though he could see that no one got out. A second car parked a block south.

■ ■ ■

AS THE HOURS passed, he told her about Rudy and Jaak, about Max and Rodionov, about Borya and Rita. To him it was an interesting tale. He remembered his walk with Feldman, the art professor describing the Revolutionary Moscow that had been. "The squares will be our palettes!" We ourselves are palettes, Arkady thought. Possibilities. Inside Borya Gubenko was a Boris Benz. Inside an Intourist prostitute known as Rita was the Berlin gallery owner Margarita Benz.

Irina said, "The question is, who can we be? If we get out alive. Russian? German? American?"

"Whatever you want. I'll be putty."

"Putty is not what comes to mind when I think of you."

"I can be American. I can whistle and chew gum."

"Once you wanted to live like the Indians."

"Too late for that now, but I can live like a cowboy."

"Rope and ride?"

"Drive cattle. Or stay here. Drive on the autobahn, climb the Alps."

"Be a German? That's easier."

"Easier?"

"You can't be American unless you stop smoking."

"I can do that," Arkady said, although he lit another cigarette. He exhaled and watched the smoke.

He screwed the cigarette out on the floor, put his finger to her lips and motioned her to move away. It had taken him a moment to realize that the shift in the smoke was air stirring under the door. Stairwells produced suction, though he wouldn't have felt the draft if he hadn't been lying down.

He put his ear to the floor. See, he *could* live like an Indian. He heard the easing of shoes in the hallway.

Irina stood against a wall, not trying to hide or get small.

Around his carry-on bag, Arkady saw the light at the bottom of the door, a white bar fading at one end.

He pressed his stomach into the floorboards. If he were any flatter he could slide under the door himself. He glanced at Irina. Her eyes watched him like hands keeping a man from falling off a cliff.

The door swung open. Light fanned in and a familiar bulk stepped across the threshold.

"You could get killed that way, Peter," Arkady said.

Peter Schiller kicked the bag aside. He snorted at the sight of Arkady. "Is this a shooting range?"

"We were expecting other people."

"I'm sure you were." Peter saw Irina, who returned his stare undiminished. "Renko, we have Russians running all over Berlin. We have two dead mafiosos at the Europa Center, cut up by someone who looked like you. What happened to your back?"

"I slipped." Arkady got to his feet and shut the door.

"Arkady was with me," Irina said.

"How long?" Peter asked.

"All day."

"Lies," Peter said. "This is a gang war, isn't it? Benz is connected to one of them. The more I know about the Soviet Union, the more it sounds like one endless gang war."

"In a way," Arkady conceded.

"This afternoon you said you didn't even know this woman. Tonight she's your witness." Peter walked around the room. He had the size and vigor of a Borya, but more Wagnerian, Arkady thought. A Lohengrin who had stumbled into the wrong opera.

"Where is Benz?" Arkady asked.

"Gone," Peter said. "He boarded a plane to Moscow an hour ago."

It wasn't a bad time to leave Berlin. Maybe Borya was abandoning the entire Benz identity, Arkady thought. After this Boris Benz might never be seen again. Eliminating Makhmud was certainly a more important accomplishment than hanging on to the German asset of Fantasy Tours. All the same, he was surprised; Borya wasn't the type who settled for less than everything.

Peter said, "Benz boarded the plane with Max Albov. They're both gone."

"Max was coming here," Irina said.

Arkady remembered how the elevator had paused on his floor before continuing to the sixth. Max must have been packing. "Why would he go to Moscow?"

"They got on a charter flight," Peter said.

"How could they get on a late-night charter flight at the last minute?"

"There were lots of seats available at the last minute," Peter said.

"Why?"

Peter looked at both Arkady and Irina. "You haven't heard? You don't have a radio or a television here? You must be the only ones in the world who don't know. There's been a coup in Moscow."

Irina laughed softly. "It finally happened."

"Who took over?" Arkady asked.

"A so-called Emergency Committee. The army rolled in. That's all anyone knows."

A coup was the predicted catastrophe, the long-due sum of Russian fears, the Moscow night that followed day, yet Arkady was stunned. Stunned to find himself stunned. Max and Borya must have been surprised, too.

"With all that confusion, why would Max go back?" Arkady asked.

Irina said, "It doesn't matter as long as they aren't coming here."

"So you don't need this anymore." Peter took the machine pistol away from Arkady, scooped the clips off the floor and stuffed them in his belt.

"We're safe," Irina said.

"Not quite," Peter said. He motioned with the pistol for them to move to a corner. Arkady had put the safety on; now Peter pushed it off.

The room was still dark. Peter could see them against the glow of the glass better than they could see him, but Arkady caught the gesture for them not to move. In the hall the elevator door opened. Irina took Arkady's hand. Peter motioned for them to lie down, then turned around and fired through the wall.

The Skorpion wasn't a particularly loud weapon, though its 7.62-mm heads went through Sheetrock as if it were paper. Peter walked along the wall, sawing waist-high, reloading as he went. A couple of rounds sparked off studs and nails. Shouts of outrage and confusion answered from the hall. Peter sprayed the second clip at knee level. Someone in the hall finally understood what was happening and fired back. A saucer-sized chunk of the wall exploded into the room. Peter used the shining hole as a target. He turned his back to the wall, disengaged the empty clip and inserted the last. An arc of holes answered through the walls. Peter walked to the high point of the arc, aimed low and fired, standing as close as a carpenter to the wall, surrounded by shafts of light. He moved to the side when a single shot responded, took his stance again, put the barrel in the hole and widened it with four more shots. He set the rate to manual and listened for moans, then placed a shot straight through the wall at his feet. Reset to automatic and finished the clip in a spray. In ten seconds Peter had put eighty rounds through the wall. On his way to the door, he let the Skorpion fall and reached around to the holster at the back of his belt for his own gun in case he needed it.

He didn't. Four Chechens lined the hall. Covered in blood and lime, they seemed to have suffered an industrial accident. Peter sorted through them, holding a cautionary gun to each head with one hand while he checked the carotid pulse with the other. A couple of the dead men held Skorpions of their own, for all the good it did them. Arkady recognized Ali's friend from the Wall café staring up through a layer of dust. He didn't see Beno.

"They were parked outside when I got here," Peter said. "Two in each car."

"Thank you," Arkady said.

"Bitte." Peter relished the word, like a mouthful of satisfaction.

PEOPLE ARE CONFUSED when they wake to the sound of automatic fire. In an area of the city with so much construction, the first reaction is bourgeois outrage that anyone would break the law and drive a nail before dawn.

On the street, Arkady saw blue police lights floating far off down Friedrichstrasse, approaching without sirens since it was the middle of the night. He and Irina followed Peter around a corner to his car. As he started to drive, Peter monitored the police radio.

The responding officers had to locate the right address, then search four floors to find the bodies. There were no witnesses in the building. Arkady knew that possibly someone in an apartment across the street had noticed them leaving the building, but what was there to describe except two men and a woman seen from hundreds of feet away at an angle in the dark?

Peter said, "There's nothing we can do about your finger- and foot-prints, they're all over the apartment, but they won't be easy to match. Your friend says she has no criminal record in Germany and there are no prints on you at all."

"What about you?"

"I wiped the pistol and the clips, and I didn't use my own gun."

"That's not what I meant. What about *you*?"

Peter drove for a while before he said, "There's an official review every time you use a firearm. I don't want to explain why I shot four men that I didn't formally identify and warn. Through a wall? They could have been four visitors asking directions, collecting for Greenpeace or Mother Teresa."

There was dust on Peter's fingers. He wiped them on his shirt. "I don't necessarily want to explain how I was helping my grandfather. This is a Russian gang war, I'm not going to let it turn into a public scandal about him."

"If they do trace this to me, Federov knows your name," Arkady said.

"With the coup, I think the consulate in Munich has more on its mind than me or you."

On the police band, a dispatcher ordered ambulances to Friedrichstrasse. The urgency of the voice contrasted with the calm of the Tiergarten, the park's rounded massing of shadow under morning stars.

Peter said, "You've lied to me from the start, but I have to admit that I've found out more from your lies than the lies I heard before. What is it about you, I wonder? I still expect the truth."

Arkady said, "If we go to Savigny Platz, I might be able to show it to you."

WHILE ARKADY SAT on an arbor bench, his back tightened. He needed aspirin or nicotine, but he had no pills and didn't indulge the telltale glow of a cigarette because the hedges around him stayed dark as the sky slowly lightened to gray. From the bench he couldn't see Peter and Irina, parked a block away. He could see the lights of the gallery, which looked as if they had burned through the night.

In Moscow, under the same roof of clouds, tanks were rolling through the streets. Was it a military putsch? Was the Party reclaiming its role as the vanguard of the people? Had the work of national salvation begun in earnest, with both hands? Just as the Party had protected Prague, Budapest and East Berlin before? There should at least be a rumble of distant thunder.

Except on Friedrichstrasse, the Germans seemed to have slept soundly through the night. German television had closed its eyes at its accustomed time. Arkady assumed that the planners of the coup would, at minimum, detain a round thousand of the leading reformers, take control of Soviet television and radio, close the airports and telephone lines. He had no doubt that City Prosecutor Rodionov deplored the necessity of a coup, but as every Russian knew, grim tasks were best done quickly. What Arkady did not understand was why Max and Gubenko had rushed back. How could an international flight land if the airports were closed? This would be a good time to listen to Radio Liberty. He wondered what Stas was saying.

A fine sprinkling of rain arrived. Then the rustling of unseen birds in the hedges, like the excitement of extras in the wings. Over the hedges spread the window lights of early risers, a sea sound of traffic, the browsing of street cleaners.

The two/two time of high heels passed on the other side of the hedge. Rita came into view, in matching poppy-red slicker and hat, walking briskly between the garden squares that made up the plaza, hand in her right pocket. Arkady had seen her at least start to sign a dinner check; he knew she was right-handed. When she unlocked the ground-floor door, she kept her hand in the pocket and looked back at the street before she entered.

Ten minutes later an armed guard came out, yawned and stretched and went off with loggy steps in the opposite direction.

After another ten minutes, the gallery lights went out. Rita reappeared, locked the door and started back across the plaza, holding a canvas bag by the handles with her left hand.

Arkady caught up with her on the bag side in the middle of the plaza and said, "That's no way to treat a five-million-dollar painting."

She was startled enough to stop. He appreciated the purity of her first reaction, which was fury. The contents of the bag were wrapped in plastic. "I hope that's waterproof," he said.

When Rita started walking again, he grabbed a handle of the bag. "I'll shout for the police," she said.

"Shout. I hear the life of the German policeman is incredibly boring —at least it would be without Russians. The police would love to hear a story about you and Rudy Rosen, though the details might not help your business much. So Max and Borya left you all alone?"

Arkady liked Rita's resilience. She was used to dealing with men. A softer, more reasonable expression came over her. "I'm not going to wait around for Chechens to show up." She offered a neutral smile. "Can we talk out of the rain?"

He thought of slipping into an arbor, but Rita led him across the street to patio tables sheltered by an awning. It was the same restaurant as in the videotape, and she went to the same table at which she had raised her glass and said, "I love you." The inside of the restaurant was black. They had the patio and plaza to themselves.

Despite the early hour, Rita's face was made up in a mask that was ferocious and exotic. The red slicker she wore had an oily quality that went well with her lips. Arkady unzipped her coat.

Rita asked, "Why did you do that?"

"Let's say that you're an attractive woman."

They sat, each with a hand on the bag under the table. Because her coat was open, the pockets hung straight down, out of her immediate reach.

Arkady asked, "Do you remember a Russian girl called Rita?"

Margarita said, "I remember her well. A hardworking girl. One thing she learned was that she could always do business with the militia."

"And Borya."

"The Long Pond people protected the girls in the hotel. Borya was a friend."

"But to make real money Rita had to get out of Russia. She married a Jew."

"No crime."

"You didn't get to Israel."

Margarita held up her right hand to show her long nails. "Do you see these building a kibbutz in the desert?"

"And Borya followed."

"Borya had a perfectly legal proposition. He needed someone to help him recruit girls to come and work in Germany, and he needed someone to watch over them while they were here. I had the experience."

"There's more to it than that. Borya bought papers that created a Boris Benz, which was convenient when he went searching for a foreign partner in Moscow. This way he could be both. When you married Boris Benz, that let you stay here, too."

"Borya and I have a special relationship."

"And if the wrong person called, you could play his maid and say that Herr Benz was vacationing in Spain."

"A good whore is a good mimic."

"Do you think the Boris Benz identity was a good idea? It was a weak point. Too much depended on it."

"It worked fine until you came along."

Arkady looked around at the empty tables without taking his hand from the bag. "You made a videotape here and sent it to Rudy. Why?"

"Identification. Rudy and I had never met. I didn't want to give him a name."

"He wasn't a bad character."

"He was helping you. After Rodionov told us, it was just a matter of how to get rid of Rudy to the best effect. He knew about the painting. We let him think if he got it authenticated he could make his own sale. I gave him a slightly different painting. Borya said that with a big enough explosion we could get rid of Rudy and give Rodionov a reason to wipe out the Chechens, both at the same time."

"Did you think Borya was going to stay here at some point and become Boris Benz for good?"

"Where would you rather be, Moscow or Berlin?"

"So in the videotape when you said, 'I love you,' you were saying it to Borya."

"We were happy here."

"And you were willing to do things for Borya that his wife never would, like going back to Moscow and delivering a firebomb to Rudy. I had to ask myself why an obviously well-to-do tourist would stay someplace as shabby and far out of the city as the Soyuz Hotel. The answer was that it was the hotel closest to the black market and the shortest ride with a firebomb that didn't have a fuse. You were brave, taking a chance you wouldn't blow up too. That's love."

Rita wet her lips. "You're so good at questions, could I ask you one?"

"Go ahead."

"Why don't you ask about Irina?"

"Like what?"

Rita leaned forward as if she were whispering in a crowd. "What Irina got out of it. Do you think Max paid for her clothes and all her little gifts because she made good conversation? Ask yourself what she was willing to do for him."

Arkady felt his skin start to heat.

"They were together for years," Rita said. "Practically man and wife, like Borya and me. I don't know what she's telling you now. I'm just saying that what she's doing for you she did for him. Any woman would."

His ears burned. A hot meridian spread across his face. "What are you really trying to say?"

Rita's head rested sympathetically to one side. "It sounds as if she hasn't told you everything. I've known men like you all my life. Somebody has to be a goddess, and everyone else is a whore. Irina slept with Max. He bragged about what she would do." Rita invited him to lean toward her and lowered her voice even more. "I'll tell you and you can compare."

As soon as he felt the tension on the handle ease, Arkady lifted the canvas bag. "Shoot now and you'll put a hole through the painting. I don't think it's insured for that," he said.

"You prick."

Arkady grabbed the pistol when she brought it over the table. It was Borya's .22. He bent her wrist and twisted the gun free.

"You fuck," Rita said.

Borya had betrayed her, run to Moscow and abandoned her with this puny gun. Arkady removed the rounds from the breech and clip and tossed the empty pistol in her lap. "I love you, too," he said.

36

At an airport souvenir shop, Arkady bought a beer tray and a cotton shawl embroidered with the rats of Hamelin. In a bathroom stall, he covered the painting with the shawl, wrapped the tray in bubble plastic, put it in Rita's canvas bag, and then rejoined Peter and Irina in a corner of the transit lounge.

Arkady said, "Think of all the paintings and manuscripts confiscated from artists and writers and poets for seventy years, hidden away by the Ministry of the Interior and the KGB. Nothing is thrown away. Poets may get a bullet in the back of the head, but the poem is stuffed in a box and buried in a cellar. Then, at a magical moment, when Russia joins the rest of the world, all that evidence becomes valuable assets."

"But they can't sell it," Irina said. "Art more than fifty years old cannot legally be taken from the Soviet Union."

"But it can be smuggled out," Peter suggested.

Arkady said, "Bribes will do. Armored tanks, railroad trains and crude oil have been moved across the border. To bring a painting out is relatively easy."

"Even so," Irina said, "the sale isn't valid if Russian law is broken. Collectors and museums don't like to be involved in international disputes. Rita couldn't sell 'Red Square' if it came from Russia."

Peter said, "Maybe it's a fake from Germany. There were fantastic forgers in East Berlin, all out of work now. Has this painting really been examined?"

Irina said, "Completely. It's been dated, X-rayed and analyzed. It even has Malevich's thumbprint."

"All of that can be faked," Peter said.

"Yes," Irina admitted, "but it's a curious thing about fakes. They can be the best forgeries on earth, with the correct wood, paints and technique, but they don't look right."

Peter said, "This is becoming spiritual."

Irina said, "It's like knowing people. After a while you learn the fake from the real. A painting is an artist's idea, and ideas can't be forged."

"How valuable did you say the painting is?" Peter asked.

"Perhaps five million dollars. That's not much here," Arkady said, "but in Russia it's five hundred million rubles."

"Unless it's fake," Peter pointed out.

Arkady said, " 'Red Square' is real and it's from Russia."

"But they found it in a Knauer crate," Irina said.

Arkady said, "The crate is fake."

"The crate?" Peter sat up. Arkady could see him mentally rearranging. "I hadn't thought from that direction before."

Arkady said, "Remember, Benz wasn't interested in the art your grandfather stole. He had his own. He was interested in the crates your grandfather built—with Knauer carpenters, if you remember."

"That's good," Peter said appreciatively. "That's very good."

Arkady laid the shawl on Peter's knees. Peter sat up straighter. "What are you doing?"

"The cultural atmosphere is a little unsettled in Moscow right now."

"I don't want it."

"You're the only person I can leave it with," Arkady said.

"How do you know I won't disappear with it?"

"There's a kind of justice in making you a guardian of Russian art. Besides, it's a trade." Arkady patted the jacket pocket with the passport and visa that Peter had returned to him and the ticket he had bought with Ali's money.

There had been no difficulty in getting on the regular Lufthansa flight to Moscow. There was nothing like a military coup at a destination for decimating a passenger list. What Arkady still didn't understand was why leaders of the new Emergency Committee were allowing planes to land at all.

■ ■ ■

STAS LIMPED OFF the Munich flight with a tape recorder and a camera. He was full of perverse good cheer. "Such a glorious idiocy. The Emergency Committee didn't arrest any of the democratic leaders. Now it's a standoff. The tanks are in Moscow, but they just keep circling around. Standards for oppression have really dropped."

"How do you know what's happening?" Arkady asked.

"People are calling us from Moscow," Stas said.

Arkady was amazed. "The telephone lines are open?"

"That's what I mean about idiocy."

"Does Michael know you're going?"

"He tried to stop me. He says it's a security risk and an embarrassment to the station if we're caught. He says Max called from Moscow to say that it's business as usual and there's nothing for me to be so excited about."

"Does he know Irina's going?"

"He asked. He doesn't know."

Though boarding had started, Arkady dove into a telephone booth. A recorded message on the phone repeated over and over that the international circuits were busy. The only way he could get through was to call continuously. As he was about to give up, he noticed a fax center.

Polina had said she would take Rudy's fax machine. At the desk, he wrote her telephone number and the message, "Looking forward to seeing you. If you have a painting of Uncle Rudy's, could you bring it with you? Drive very carefully." He added his flight number and arrival time and signed the message, "Arkady." Then he asked for a fax directory and wrote a second message to Federov: "Followed advice. Please inform City Prosecutor Rodionov of return today. Renko."

The clerk's eyes opened as wide as a doll's. "You must be anxious to get home," she said.

"I'm always anxious when I go home," Arkady said.

Irina waved him to the gate, where Stas and Peter Schiller were regarding each other like examples of different species.

Peter grabbed Arkady and pulled him aside. "You can't leave me with this."

"I trust you."

"My short experience with you suggests that's a curse. What am I going to do with it?"

"Hang it someplace with a constant temperature. Be an anonymous donor. Just don't give it to your grandfather. You know, the story about Malevich wasn't a lie. He did bring his paintings to Berlin to keep them safe. For the time being, do what he did."

"It seems to me that Malevich's mistake was going back. What if Rita calls Moscow and says you took the painting? If Albov and Gubenko know you're coming, they'll be waiting for you."

"I hope so. I wouldn't be able to find them, so they have to find me."

"Maybe I should go with you."

"Peter, you're too good. You'd scare them away."

Peter shifted reluctantly.

Arkady said, "Life can't all be fast cars and automatic weapons. You finally have a task worthy of you."

"They'll kill you at the airport or on the way in. Revolutions are for settling scores. What's an extra body? At least here I can throw you in jail."

"That sounds inviting."

"We can keep you alive and extradite Albov and Gubenko."

"No one has ever successfully extradited anyone from the Soviet Union. And who knows what government will be in place tomorrow? Max might be Minister of Finance and Gubenko might be Minister of Sport. Besides, if there's a decent investigation into Ali and his friends, I think you'll be glad I'm far away."

A soft gong announced the last boarding call. Peter said, "Germany goes straight downhill every time Russians show up."

"And vice versa," Arkady said.

"Remember, there's always a cell waiting for you in Munich."

"Danke."

"Be careful."

Peter scanned the boarding line as Arkady joined Stas and Irina. From halfway down the ramp, Arkady could see Peter's head over the crowd, still carrying out the duty of a rear guard. At last glimpse, Peter took a firm grip on the shawl and slipped away.

THE CANVAS BAG fit in the overhead compartment. Arkady sat on the aisle, Stas by the window, Irina in between. When they lifted off, Stas's face took on an even more ironic expression than usual. Irina held on to Arkady's arm. She looked exhausted, blank, not unhappy. Arkady thought the three of them resembled refugees so confused that they were going the wrong way.

A number of passengers seemed to be journalists and photographers burdened with carry-on gear. No one wanted to spend two hours at a baggage claim while a revolution was going on.

Stas said, "The Emergency Committee starts off by saying Gorby's sick. Three hours later, one of the ringleaders drops from hypertension. This is a strange coup."

"You don't have visas. What makes you think they'll let you off the plane?" Arkady asked.

Stas said, "You think any reporter here has a proper visa? Irina and I have American passports. We'll see what happens when we get there. This is the biggest story of our lives. How could we pass it up?"

"Coup or no coup, you're on a list of state criminals. So is she. You could be arrested."

"You're going," Stas said.

"I'm Russian."

Though Irina's voice was soft, it possessed finality. "We want to go."

Germany stretched below, not the straight roads and quilted farms of the West, but narrower, more winding lanes and shabbier fields the farther east they flew.

IRINA RESTED ON Arkady's shoulder. The feel of her hair cushioned against his cheek was so normal it was overpowering, as if he were briefly traveling through an alternative life he had missed. He never wanted to come down.

Stas talked nervously, like a radio at low volume. "Historically, revolutions kill the people at the top. And usually Russians overdo it. The Bolsheviks killed the ruling class and then Stalin killed the original Bolsheviks. But this time the only difference between Gorby's government and the coup is that Gorby isn't in it. Did you hear the complete statement of the Emergency Committee? They're seizing power to protect the people from, among other things, 'sex, violence and glaring immorality.' Meanwhile, troops keep moving into Moscow and people are erecting barricades to protect the White House."

The White House was the Russian Parliament building on the river at the Red Presnya embankment. Presnya was an ancient neighborhood given the honorific "Red" for building barricades against the czar.

Stas said, "That won't stop tanks. What happened in Vilnius and Tbilisi were rehearsals. They'll wait until night. First they'll send in Internal troops with nerve gas and water cannons to disperse the crowd, and then KGB troops will storm the building. The Moscow commandant has printed three hundred thousand arrest forms, but the Committee doesn't want to use them. They expect people to see the tanks and slink away."

Irina asked, "What if Pavlov rang a bell and his dogs ignored him? They'd change history."

"I'll tell you what else is strange," Stas said. "This is the longest I've ever seen so many journalists stay sober."

POLAND SPREAD AS dark as an ocean floor.

Food carts blocked the aisles. Cigarette smoke circulated along with theories. The army was moving already, to offer the world a fait accompli. The army would wait until dark to carry out its attack so that there would be fewer photographs. The Committee had the generals. The democrats had the Afghan vets. No one knew which way the young officers just back from Germany would lean.

"By the way," Stas said, "in the name of the Committee, City Prosecutor Rodionov has been rounding up businessmen and confiscating goods. Not all businessmen, just those against the Committee."

When Arkady closed his eyes, he wondered what kind of Moscow he was returning to. It was a rare day that offered so many possibilities.

Stas said, "It's been so long. I have a brother I haven't seen in twenty years. We call once a year, at New Year's. He called this morning to tell me he was going to the Parliament building to defend it. He's a fat little man with kids. How is he going to stop a tank?"

"Do you think you can find him?" Arkady asked.

"He told me not to come. Can you imagine that?" Stas stared out of the window for a long while. Vapor had condensed into balls of water between the double panes. "He said he'd wear a red ski cap."

"What is Rikki doing?"

"Rikki went to Georgia. He put his mother, daughter, TV and VCR in his new BMW and they went tootling off. I knew he would. He's a lovely man."

THE CLOSER THEY got to Moscow, the more Irina looked like the girl who had left it, like someone returning to a fire with a particular glow. As if the rest of the world were an unlit, interim place. As if she were coming back with a vengeance.

Arkady thought he could be swept up by her and follow. Happily, once he was done with Borya and Max.

How much of all this was his private score, to atone in some small measure for Rudy, Tommy and Jaak? The dead aside, how much was because of Irina? Dealing with Max wouldn't erase the years she had known him. He could call them émigré years, but seen from a height Russia was a nation of émigrés, inside and out. Everyone was compromised to some degree. Russia had a history of such confusion that when a few moments of clarity arrived, everyone naturally rushed to the event.

In any case, Max and Borya were more likely to be the thriving specimens of a new age than he was.

AS THEY CROSSED into Soviet airspace, Arkady expected the plane to be ordered to turn around. When they approached Moscow, he thought it would be directed to a military base, refueled and sent home. When seat-belt signs lit, there was a general, last-second extinguishing of cigarettes.

Out the window were the familiar low woods, power lines and gray-green fields that led to Sheremetyevo.

Stas held his breath like a man diving.

Irina held Arkady's hand as if she were the one bringing him home.

IV

MOSCOW

■

August 21, 1991

37

Arrival in Moscow was never a rose-strewn path, but this morning even the normal bleakness was accentuated. After Western lights, the baggage area was dark and cavernous, and Arkady wondered whether there had always been as much numbness in the faces, such a closed-down look to the eyes.

Michael Healey was waiting at the customs booths with a colonel of the Frontier Police. Radio Liberty's deputy director wore a trench coat of many belts and watched passengers through dark glasses. The Frontier Police was KGB; they wore green tunics with red tabs and faces screwed to perpetual suspicion.

Stas said, "The winged shit must have taken the direct flight from Munich. Damn."

"He can't stop us," Irina said.

"Yes, he can," Stas admitted. "One word and the best that can happen to us is being put back on the plane."

Arkady said, "I'm not going to let him take you back."

"What are you going to do?" Stas asked.

"Let me talk to him. Just get in line."

Stas hesitated. "If we do get through, there's a car waiting to take us to the White House."

"I'll meet you there," Arkady said.

"You promise?" Irina asked.

In this setting, Irina's Russian seemed different, softer, with more dimensions. This was why beautiful icons had plain frames.

"I'll be there."

Arkady walked ahead to Michael, who followed his approach like a man pleased to find gravity working in his favor. The colonel seemed to be primed for more prosperous targets; he gave Arkady only passing notice.

Michael said, "Renko. Good to be home? I'm afraid that Stas and Irina won't be able to stay. I have their tickets for the flight back to Munich."

"You'd really point them out?" Arkady asked.

"They're ignoring orders. The station has paid them, fed them, housed them. We can demand a little loyalty. I just want to make it clear to the colonel that Radio Liberty refuses any responsibility for them. They aren't assigned to this story."

"They want to be here."

"Then they're on their own and they can take their chances."

"Are you going to cover the story?"

"I'm not a reporter, but I've been around reporters. I'll help."

"You know Moscow?"

"I've been here before."

"Where is Red Square?" Arkady asked.

"Everyone knows where Red Square is."

Arkady said, "You'd be surprised. A man here in Moscow got a fax just two weeks ago asking him, 'Where is Red Square?'"

Michael shrugged.

Ahead of Stas and Irina, photographers top-heavy with gear and carry-on bags clattered forward. Stas slipped fifty-Deutsche-mark notes into his passport and Irina's.

Arkady said, "The fax came from Munich. In fact, it came from Radio Liberty."

"We have a number of facsimile machines," Michael said.

"The message came from Ludmilla's machine. It was sent to a black-market speculator who happened to be dead, so I was the one who read it. It was in Russian."

"I suppose it would be, a fax between two Russians."

"That's what fooled me," Arkady said. "Thinking that it was between two Russians and that it was about Red Square."

Michael seemed to have found something to chew on. His dark glasses maintained a smooth gaze, but his jaw was busy.

Arkady said, "But just when you least expect it, Russians can be exact. For example, the fax asked where was 'Krassny Ploschad'? Now, in English a square can be a place or a geometric figure, but in Russian, the geometric figure is a *kvadrat*. In the English language,

Malevich painted 'Red Square.' In Russian, he painted 'Krassny Kvadrat.' I didn't understand the message until I saw the painting."

"What are you getting at?"

" 'Where is Red Square the place?' makes no sense. 'Where is "Red Square" the painting?' makes a great deal of sense when you're asking a man who thinks he will have the painting to sell. Ludmilla couldn't use the wrong word, no Russian could. Her office is next to yours, as I remember. In fact, she works for you. How is your Russian, Michael?"

Siberians killed rabbits at night with flashlights and clubs. The rabbits would sit up and stare red-eyed at the beam until the club came down. Even through glasses, Michael had the transfixed attention of a rabbit. He said, "All that proves is that whoever sent the fax thought the person on the other end was alive."

"Absolutely," Arkady agreed. "It also proves that they were trying to deal with Rudy. Did Max put you and Rudy together?"

"There's nothing illegal about sending a fax."

"No, but in your first message you asked Rudy about a finder's fee. You were trying to cut out Max completely."

"It doesn't prove anything," Michael said.

"Let's leave that up to Max. I'll show him the fax. It has Ludmilla's number on it."

The customs line shuffled forward again and Stas Kolotov, state criminal, stared directly through the glass at the officer, who compared eyes, ears, hairline, height to the picture in the passport, then riffled through the pages.

Arkady said, "You know what happened to Rudy. It's not as if you'd be safer in Germany. Look what happened to Tommy."

Stas got his passport back. Irina pushed her passport through the slot and presented a glare so defiant it invited arrest. The officer never noticed. After a professional frisk of the pages, her passport was returned and the line moved forward.

"Michael, I don't think this is a time to call attention to yourself," Arkady said. "This is a time to ask, 'What can I do for Renko, so that he won't tell Max?' "

Despite Stas's urging, Irina stopped at the far side of the booths. Arkady mouthed the word "Go," and he and Michael watched Stas lead her through the exit.

It turned out that Michael did have something to say. "Congratulations. Now that you got her in, she'll probably be killed. Just remember, you brought her back."

"I know."

A German television crew was negotiating the price of bringing in a video camera. The Emergency Committee, a colonel of customs informed them, had only that morning banned the transmission of video images by foreign reporters. The colonel accepted an informal bond of a hundred Deutsche marks to ensure that the crew didn't violate the Committee's laws. The other camera crews ahead of Arkady all had to make their own financial arrangements with customs and then race to their cars. Arkady's Soviet passport was a disappointment, a no-sale. Like a cashier, the customs officer just waved him through.

An open double door led to the waiting hall and a reception line of emotional families waving cellophane-wrapped bouquets. Arkady watched for dry-eyed men with heavy athletic bags. Since Sheremetyevo's metal detectors were haphazardly manned, the only persons sure to be unarmed and unprotected were arriving passengers. He held the canvas bag to his chest and hoped that Rita's call saying that he had the painting had gotten through.

Arkady recognized a small figure in a raincoat sitting alone in a row of chairs halfway down the waiting hall. Polina was reading a newspaper—*Pravda* by the look of it. Not a difficult guess, he admitted, since most papers had been banned the day before. He stopped for a cigarette by the flight board. Amazing. Here was an entire nation that could go about its business and keep its eyes down. Maybe history was nothing but a microscope. How many people had actually stormed the Winter Palace? Everyone else was searching for bread, trying to stay warm, or getting drunk.

Polina pulled her hair away from her eyes to give Arkady a sharp glance, dropped her newspaper and marched out. Through the window, he watched her join a male friend who was sitting on a scooter at the curb. The friend came to attention and moved to the rear saddle. Polina sat in front, stomped the starter pedal with more fury than weight and drove off.

Arkady walked up the hall, took the seat she had left and looked at the newspaper, which said, "The measures that are being taken are temporary. They in no way signal a renunciation of the course aimed at profound reforms. . . ."

Under the newspaper were car keys and a note that said, "White Zhiguli license X65523MO. You shouldn't have come back." Translated from Polina-ese, this meant, "Welcome home."

The Zhiguli was parked in the front rank of the terminal lot. On its floor was a square canvas covered in red paint. Arkady removed the beer tray from the plastic wrap, replaced it with the painting and put it into Margarita's bag.

He took the highway south to Moscow. As he reached the dark of an underpass, he rolled down the passenger window and sailed the beer tray out.

At first the road seemed normal. The same unrepaired cars rolled at high speed over the same potholes, as if he had been gone for a single morning. Then, set back from the highway behind a row of alders, he saw the dark outline of a tank; once he spotted one, he saw more tanks like dark watermarks on a screen of green.

There were no tanks on the highway, in fact, no sign of the military at all until the side road at Kurkino, where an endless line of armored personnel carriers filled the slow lane. Soldiers wearing campaign caps rode in open hatches. They were boys with eyes tearing in the wind. Where the highway crossed the Ring Road and became the Leningrad Road, the caravan exited and headed into the city.

Arkady sped up and slowed down while a sleek metallic-blue motorcycle with two riders stayed a steady hundred meters behind him. They could simply put a bullet in his head as they drove by. Except for the painting, on which they wouldn't want a scratch.

A light rain cleaned the street. Arkady looked on the dashboard shelf. No wipers. He turned on the radio and after Tchaikovsky heard instructions on how to remain calm. "Report the agitation of provocateurs. Allow responsible organs to carry out their sacred duty. Remember the tragic events of Tiananmen Square, when pseudo-democratic agents provoked unnecessary bloodshed." The accent seemed to be on *unnecessary*. He also found a station operating from the House of Soviets that denounced the coup.

At a red light, the motorcycle pulled up behind him. It was a Suzuki, the same model he and Jaak had admired outside a cellar in Lyubertsy. The driver wore a black helmet, leather jacket and pants sculpted like armor. When Minin hopped off the back, raincoat flapping, hand on hat, Arkady floored the accelerator, raced through the cross traffic and left the bike behind.

The Voikovskaya metro station was surrounded by Muscovites who had emerged from rush-hour trains to study the clouds, arrange their raincoats and gather resolve for the dash home. Calmer souls loitered at the entrance to buy roses, ice cream, piroshki. The scene was surreal because it was so normal that Arkady began to wonder whether the coup was taking place in another city.

Cooperatives no bigger than shacks had set up business behind the station. He got in line at one that sold Gauloises, razor blades, Pepsi and canned pineapples, and bought himself a bottle of carbonated mineral water and a tall lavender aerosol can of "Romantic" deodorant. He went on to a secondhand store that sold watches without hands and forks without tines and bought two collections of odd keys on wire loops. He tossed the keys and kept the wires, which he added with the water and deodorant to the canvas bag.

Back in his car, Arkady returned to the avenue and cruised until he picked up the motorcycle again outside Dynamo Stadium. Traffic was becoming more difficult. When the Sadoyava Ring was blocked by a procession of armored personnel carriers, he made a left and followed them until he could slip through at Fadayeva. First he smelled, then saw, the black exhaust of tanks idling in Manege Square along the west wall of the Kremlin. Crossing Tverskaya, he had a glimpse of Red Square, its brow of cobblestones blocked by lines of Internal troops spaced like hedgerows.

Shoppers emerged from Children's World bearing stuffed animals. On the sidewalk women held up pantyhose and used shoes for sale. A coup? It might be happening in Burma, darkest Africa, the moon. The majority of people were too exhausted. If there was shooting in the streets, they would still stand in line. They were sleepwalkers, and at this sunset Moscow was the center of sleep.

Across the square from the toy shop, the Lubyanka looked equally somnolent. However, in the back of the building, a line of vans rolled out of the truck bay.

ARKADY DROVE INTO his courtyard, squeezed the Zhiguli between the vodka cases around the church and opened the gate to the wood-cart alley that ended on a bluff overlooking the canal. Carrying Rita's bag, he entered the back door of an apartment house and climbed the stairs to the fourth floor, where he had a view of the courtyard and the blue motorcycle lurking behind a delivery truck a block away.

Arkady sympathized with Minin. On any other day, he would have cars and radio communications. What did he remember about his assistant? Impatience, a tendency to rush ahead. Minin got off the motorcycle, his face folded with doubt. He was followed by the driver, who pulled off his helmet to release long black hair. It was Kim, looking for Arkady now.

He went out the back door and across an overgrown lot that dwindled down to a dirt path threading between the back walls of workshops and brought him to the street on the far side of the motorcycle. Looking toward his house, he saw Minin push the buttons of the code box.

The Suzuki leaned on its kickstand, front wheel at an angle. The motorcycle had a blue plastic body that swept from the windshield to the exhaust like the cowling of a jet engine. Access to the exhaust pipes was tight; on the other hand, anything added wouldn't easily be seen. Arkady got on his back and felt the long scab on his back crack under his weight. The Suzuki had a four-into-two-into-one exhaust system running from header pipes to muffler. When he shook the water bottle and sprayed them, the pipes spat back. Although he emptied the bottle on the pipes first, he still burned his fingers when he reached in, ran the wires around them and attached the deodorant can. Nevertheless, he twisted the wires tight. Jaak would have been proud.

By the time Arkady got to his feet, Minin and Kim had disappeared. He wiped his hands on his jacket, shouldered the canvas bag and followed their trail to the house. He saw the curtains in his window shift.

Minin had composed a grin. He let Arkady enter the apartment and close the door before popping out of the bedroom hall with the huge Stechkin he had waved outside Rudy's apartment. A Stechkin was a machine pistol like a Skorpion but not as ugly. In fact, it was the best-looking part of Minin.

The closet opened at Arkady's back and Kim stepped out. He had a face as flat as a jack of spades, and he had a Malysh, the same weapon he had carried to protect Rudy so long ago. He must have had it tucked inside his leather jacket. Arkady was impressed. It was like facing artillery.

Minin said, "Give me the bag."

"No."

Minin said, "Give it to me or I'll kill you."

Arkady held the bag to his chest. "The painting inside is worth millions of dollars. You don't want to put holes in it. It's fragile. If I even fall on it, it will be trash. How would you like to explain that to the city prosecutor? Also, I don't want to undermine your authority, Minin, but I can't think of anything more stupid than putting a target between two automatic weapons." He asked Kim, "Can you?"

Kim moved to the side.

"This is your final warning," Minin said.

Arkady kept the bag cradled to his chest while he opened the refrigerator. Something like moss had grown out the top of the kefir bottle. He shut the door on the smell.

"I'm curious, Minin. How do you think getting this painting will safeguard the Party's sacred mission?"

"The painting belongs to the Party."

"So much does. Are you going to pull the trigger or not?"

Minin let the gun hang. "It doesn't matter whether I shoot you. As of today you're dead."

"You're working with Kim. Aren't you a little embarrassed to be riding around with a homicidal maniac?" When Minin didn't answer, Arkady turned to Kim. "Aren't you embarrassed to be riding with an investigator? One of you ought to be." Kim smiled, but Minin was actually sweating with hate. "I've always wondered, Minin, what do you have against me?"

"Your cynicism."

"Cynicism?"

"About the Party."

"Well." Minin had a point.

"I thought, 'Senior Investigator Renko, son of General Renko.' I thought you'd be a hero. I thought it would be a great experience to work shoulder to shoulder with you, until my eyes came clear and I saw the sort of corrupt individual you were."

"How?"

"We were supposed to be investigating criminals, but you always turned the investigation against the Party."

"It just worked out that way."

"I watched to see if you took money from the mafias."

"I didn't."

"No. You were more corrupt because you didn't care about money."

Arkady said, "I've changed. Now I want money. Call Albov."

"Who's Albov?"

"Or I will walk out with the painting and you will have lost five million dollars."

When Minin said nothing, Arkady shrugged and took a step to the door.

"Wait," Minin said. He went to the wall phone in the hall, dialed and walked the receiver into the living room. Arkady examined his bookshelf and pulled out *Macbeth*. The gun that should have been behind Shakespeare was gone.

Minin had a moment of satisfaction. "I was up here while you were in Germany. I searched everything." Someone came on the line because Minin spoke rapidly into the receiver and explained Arkady's lack of cooperation. He looked up. "Show me the painting."

Arkady lifted the painting out of the bag and pulled it halfway out of the plastic wrap.

"There's been a mistake," Minin said to the phone. "There's no painting, just a canvas. It's red." His forehead squatted. "That's it? You're sure?" He held the phone out to Arkady, who took it only after slipping the painting back into the bag.

"Arkady?"

"Max," Arkady said, as if they hadn't seen each other for years.

"I'm glad to hear your voice, and I'm certainly pleased you brought the painting with you. We spoke to Rita, who was upset and sure you were going to turn her over to the German police. You could have stayed in Berlin. What brought you back?"

"I would have stayed in jail. The police were searching for me, not Rita."

"True. Borya did set you up. I'm sure the Chechens would also love to know where you are. It was very shrewd of you to return."

Arkady asked, "Where are you?"

Max said, "The situation being what it is, I don't want to broadcast that. Frankly, I'm worried about Rodionov and his friends. I hope they have the resolve to finish this business quickly, because the longer they wait, the bloodier it will be. Your father would have wiped out the defenders at the White House already, wouldn't he?"

"Yes."

"I understand that you want to make some sort of arrangement about the painting. What?"

"A British Air ticket to London and fifty thousand dollars."

"A lot of people are trying to leave town. I can give you any amount of rubles, but foreign currency is tight right now."

"I'm giving the phone back to Minin."

As soon as he had handed over the phone, Arkady took a serrated knife from a drawer by the sink. While each act was reported by Minin, he opened the window and pulled the wrapped painting out of the bag. The wrap's plastic bubbles started popping as Arkady sawed.

"Wait!" Minin said and offered the phone to Arkady again.

Max was laughing. "I get the point. You win."

"Where are you?"

"Minin will bring you."

"He can lead me. I have a car."

"I'd better talk to him," Max said.

Minin listened grimly before he returned the receiver to the hall. "You don't have to lead me," Arkady said. "Just tell me where he is."

"There's going to be a curfew tonight. In case there are any road-blocks, it's better if we all go."

Kim broke into a grin bursting with personality. "Hurry up. I want to come back and find the girl on the scooter." It was the first time he had opened his mouth and it wasn't what Arkady wanted to hear.

"We saw Polina," Minin said. His tone was judicial, though his tongue left a brief dab on his lips. "You look like shit. You look like you've been rolling on the ground. They didn't treat you too well in Germany."

"Travel is wearing," Arkady said. Switching the bag from hand to hand, he slipped out of the soiled jacket. The back of his shirt was black with old blood and red with new. Kim sucked in an audible breath. From the closet, Arkady selected a wrinkled but cleaner jacket, the one he had worn to the cemetery. From its pocket, he pulled his heirloom, his father's revolver, the Nagant, an ancient fire-arm with a hammer and wooden grip as curved as apostrophes. The four rounds, thick as silver nuggets, were in the pocket, too. One arm through the handle of the bag, he swung open the cylinder and loaded it. He said, "How many times have I told you, Minin? Don't just check the closets, check the clothes too."

MININ AND ARKADY waited in the courtyard while Kim went for the motorcycle. The sky was dark. Lamplight and rain intensified the blue of the church and lent the windows of the house a pastel oiliness.

Arkady wondered whether the television hypnotist was on tonight. He said, "I have a neighbor who collects my mail and puts food in my refrigerator. There was no mail and no food."

Minin said, "Maybe she knew you were away."

Arkady let the inadvertent admission gape for a while. The church gutters were stopped up, as usual, and the overflow fell in bright threads. He said, "She lived right below me. She always heard me walking around, and she probably heard you."

Minin's face played in and out of the shadow of his hat.

"Why don't you just say you're sorry?" Arkady asked. "She had a bad heart. Maybe you didn't mean to scare her."

"She interfered."

"Pardon?"

"She overstepped. She knew she was sick, I didn't. I take no responsibility for the consequences of her own actions."

"You mean you're sorry?"

Minin put the barrel of the Stechkin where the bag covered Arkady's heart. "I mean shut up."

"Do you feel left out?" Arkady asked more softly. "That I'm depriving you? That they're having a revolution without us, you or me?"

Minin tried to be silent, but he shifted with the feet of an ardent spear-carrier. "I'll be there when the action starts."

Kim arrived on his motorcycle and followed them through the low arch of the alley. At the car, Minin jumped in on the passenger side. "I'm not going to let you slip away again. And I'm not going to ride with that lunatic anymore."

Arkady considered compromises. If he refused to go, he wouldn't find Albov. Also, he had pressed Minin about as far as he could. "Put the gun in your left hand," he said.

When Minin did as he was told, the selector catch of the Stechkin was above his top knuckle. Arkady reached across and turned the catch down from automatic to safe. He said, "Keep your left hand where I can see it."

The Zhiguli had a manual shift. Arkady rested the canvas bag by his left foot and laid the Nagant on his lap.

KIM LED THE way up Tverskaya in the central, official lane. Rain had chased most shoppers off the sidewalk. At Pushkin Square, a crowd carried banners in the direction of the Parliament building. Many were kids, of course, but an unusual number were Arkady's age or older, men and women who had been children during the Khrushchev era, had been allowed the heady oxygen of that short-lived reform, but had said nothing when Soviet tanks invaded Prague, and had lived in shame ever since. That was the essence of collaboration. Silence. They wore woolen caps over thinning hair, but they had miraculously discovered their voices.

In Mayakovsky Square, the traffic stopped for tanks moving to the Parliament building by way of the Sadoyava Ring. "The Taman division," Minin said approvingly. "They're the toughest. They'll roll right up the Parliament steps."

But Moscow was such a big stage that most people seemed unaware of any coup. Couples walked hand in hand toward the Cinema House. A kiosk opened its shutters and, oblivious to the rain, a line of customers formed.

Tracks wove in and out of shining macadam. Tverskaya became Leningrad Prospect, which turned onto the Leningrad Road. Kim raced ahead. At speed, at least, Arkady wasn't afraid of Minin shooting him. "We're taking the airport road?" he said.

Minin said, "You're falling behind. I don't want to miss the fireworks."

Along Chimki Lake was a sudden calm, a shadow among the urban lights, the monotone of drops on the water. A line of slitted headlights appeared, more tanks moving at a walking pace. Beyond them was the horizontal haze of the Ring Road.

The motorcycle began to trail sparks, as if it were dragging its muffler. The can Arkady had wired to the exhaust pipes was one-third propane gas, which expanded twenty-one hundred times. Ignited, it expanded like a blowtorch. Flames fanned up the plastic sides and through the ports and over the rear tire in jets of fire that seemed to drive the bike forward. Arkady saw Kim looking at his rearview mirror, where the light would first appear to be coming from, then from side to side, then finally down, where the entire plastic sheath was igniting like a meteor around his legs and boots. The bike oscillated from lane to lane. That must be an impulse, Arkady thought, to try to outrun fire. Though the road was crossing an arm of the lake and there was no place to turn off, Kim jumped the shoulder of the road.

"Stop! Stop the car!" Minin pushed his gun against Arkady's head.

The motorcycle touched a side rail and rolled like a tumbling flame. Kim stayed with it through a long slide, then the bike spun again, spewing a helmet from the blaze. As Arkady accelerated by, Minin pulled the trigger. The Stechkin didn't fire. He remembered the safety and switched hands, but Arkady picked up the Nagant and held it on him.

"Get out." He slowed to fifteen kilometers, enough to knock Minin off his feet when he landed. "Jump."

Arkady leaned, opened the passenger door and pushed Minin. But as the door swung wide, Minin swung with it and hung on to the outside of the door, pressed against the glass. He broke the window with the Stechkin, got his elbows in and aimed. Arkady tapped the brake. As Minin fired, the side window behind Arkady exploded. The door swung out and Minin's hat flew off. The motorcycle burned far behind, the lights of the Ring Road overpass appeared ahead. Arkady kicked the door open again with his right foot and with his left pushed the gas pedal all the way down. Minin's weight and the force of air resistance forced the door back in. Minin began firing as soon as the door swung inward, spraying the rear and side windows as Arkady steered across the shoulder of the road and hit the corner of the overpass.

The dark under the ramp was enormously quiet. When the Zhiguli came out the other side, the passenger door hung like a broken wing and Minin was gone.

Arkady had no guide left, but he was fairly certain by now that he was returning to a place he knew. He brushed glass off the bag. Air tunneled sideways through the hanging door and out the shattered windows.

Arkady remembered that Soviet cars always evolved, doing with fewer and fewer luxuries.

This was the new model.

38

The first time Arkady came through the village, women were selling flowers on the side of the road. Not tonight. The place seemed abandoned, its windows dark, as if the houses themselves were trying to hide. Sunflowers bobbed in the rain. A cow, startled by his headlights, bolted from a garden.

On the road, water was pooling in tread tracks. Tanks had kneaded mud to a soft consistency, and where they had moved two abreast, they had rolled over fences and fruit trees. The Zhiguli had front-wheel drive, and Arkady plowed ahead in low gear as if he were steering a boat.

The fields on the other side of the village were flatter and the way was straighter, though more chewed up. Half a kilometer on, the right shoulder of the road was crushed by tracks emerging from a field. Mud stood stacked like bricks, showing how the tanks had maneuvered onto the road, advancing one tread to pivot on the other. It would have looked like a military parade, Arkady thought, except that it had started from a potato field, with as few witnesses as possible.

The rest of the way was smooth enough for him to use only running lights. Fields stretched in rows from gray to black, and with the rain the road looked like a causeway between bodies of water.

There were no bonfires this time to guide him. Coasting between animal pens into the yard of the Lenin's Path Collective, he saw the rusting tractors and reapers waiting like so many theatrical props, the garage where he had discovered General Penyagin's car, the butchering house, the shed full of consumer goods. In the middle of the yard the lime pit in which he had found Jaak and Penyagin was swollen by the rain.

Arkady got out, pushed the revolver under his jacket into the back of his belt and held the bag chest-high. With every step, milk that was a combination of rainwater and septic lime filled his shoes.

On the far side of the yard, past the barn and shed, were headlights. Closer, he saw the car was a Mercedes and that the lights were aimed at a figure climbing out of one of the command bunkers, the one that had been locked during his first visit. Borya Gubenko struggled under the weight of a flat, rectangular wooden case. His shoes were encased in mud, his camel's-hair coat was hemmed with mud. He lifted the case up to the back end of a Lenin's Path truck, the same one that had sold Jaak a shortwave radio.

On the truck bed, Max arranged the case against others standing on end. "You almost missed us," he called to Arkady. "We were packing to go."

Borya seemed less pleased. He was drenched, his hair stuck to his brow, as if he'd played a full day of goal in foul weather. He looked past Arkady. "Where's Kim?"

"Kim and Minin had road problems," Arkady said.

Max said, "I'm sure. I would have been disappointed if they had made it. Anyway, I knew you'd come."

"I have to get more." Borya gave both Max and Arkady a hard look and trudged back to the bunker. The case that had just been loaded bore fading stamps: FOR REFERENCE ONLY and CONFIDENTIAL MATERIALS OF THE ARCHIVES OF THE USSR MINISTRY OF THE INTERIOR.

"How is Irina?" Max asked.

"She's happy."

"What I'd forgotten about Irina was her impulse for martyrdom. How could she resist you?" Max seemed bemused, a little distracted. "I didn't get a chance to say a proper good-bye in Berlin because Borya was in a rush. He's unromantic. Once a pimp, always a pimp. He's still hanging on to his prostitutes and slot machines. He wants to change, but the criminal mind is so limited. Russians don't change."

"Where is Rodionov?" Arkady asked.

"He's keeping the prosecutor's office in line for the Emergency Committee. The Committee is such a collection of Party hacks and all-out drunks that Rodionov shines by comparison. Of course the Committee will win because people always recognize the crack of a whip. The trouble is that the coup is so unnecessary. Everyone could have been rich. Now we're going to go back to a system of counting crumbs."

Arkady nodded at the crates. "Those aren't crumbs. Why are you moving them if the Committee will win?"

"In the wildly remote unlikelihood that the attack fails, people are going to trace the route of the tanks very quickly. Once they're here, they'll go right to the bunkers and we'd lose everything."

Arkady looked in the direction Borya had gone. "I'd like to see."

"Why not?" Max jumped off the truck, happy to oblige.

The space inside the bunker was narrow, designed for a dozen men to sweat out a nuclear holocaust and live like apes around a vented generator so that they could radio troops that had been crisped in the field. The generator, throbbing like a Trabi, powered red emergency lights. Borya was covering a painting with an oilcloth.

"It's tight," Max said. "We had to get rid of the radiation counters. They didn't work anyway."

He played a flashlight. The eye imagines a mine with veins of malachite, lapis or gold twisting into the ground. This was even brighter. Some of the paintings were crated, but most were not, and the beam lit a canvas covered with the primal stripes of Matiushin, in colors as fresh and vivid as the day they were painted. Max moved the beam across a palm tree by Sarian, Vrubel's swans, radiant suns of Iuon, an angelic cow by Chagall. An ogre by Lissitzky overlapped erotic sketches by Annenkov. Above a kaleidoscope by Popova was a fighting cock, all whirling feathers, by Kandinsky. Arkady felt he had stepped into a mine of images, as if a culture had been buried.

Max shared his pride. "This is the greatest collection of Russian avant-garde art in the world, outside of the Tretyakov Gallery. Of course the Ministry didn't know what they were confiscating because the militia doesn't have any taste. The people they stole from did, however, and that's what matters, right? First the Revolution confiscated all the private collections. The revolutionaries themselves wanted the most revolutionary paintings. Then Stalin purged his old friends and the militia got its second harvest of great art. And it kept on harvesting, right through Khrushchev and Brezhnev, hiding it all away beneath the Ministry. That's how great collections are built. Let's give Rodionov credit because when he was given the task of cleaning up the Ministry archives he recognized 'Red Square' and it led him to all these, which are great art but not in the class of 'Red Square.' He also had the sense to know that while he could smuggle the painting out himself, he needed someone more sophisticated to both get it out and legally put it on the market. You have the painting?"

Arkady said, "Yes. Do you have the money and the ticket?"

Borya looked around with the experience of a man who knew how complicated transactions could be. "It's crowded here. We need more room."

Max led the way into the butchering house. The flashlight picked butcher blocks, meat grinders and waist-high tallow pots out of the dark. The pig still hung on the wall hook, exuding an odor of swamp gas.

Max shared cigarettes. "I'm not surprised to see you. What I do find hard to believe is that you're willing to make an arrangement. That simply isn't like you."

"Yet here I am and here's the painting," Arkady said.

"So you say. I think that fifty thousand dollars is high, considering there's no one else you can sell it to. You don't have the provenance or the Knauer crate."

"You agreed."

"Tonight of all nights, it's difficult to get money together," Max said.

Borya stared out at the rain. "Take the painting."

Max said, "You're always in a hurry. We can work this out between intelligent men."

"What is it with the two of you?" Borya asked. "I don't get it."

"Renko and I have a uniquely intimate relationship. We're practically partners already."

"Like last night in Berlin? When you came down from the apartment, you said Renko and the woman weren't there. I'm starting to think I should have been the one to go up. Now that I think about it, I've done all the work."

"Don't forget Rita," Arkady reminded him. "She must have overwhelmed Rudy."

Borya's shrug became a smile. "Rudy wanted to get into the art business with us, so we let him. He thought someone was coming from Munich with a fabulous picture for him to authenticate. He didn't know who Rita was because he didn't have a real active sexual life."

"Unlike Borya," Max said. "Some people might call Borya indiscriminate. Bigamous, at the least."

"So Rita brought him one," Borya said. "Max painted it. He called it a 'special effect,' like in the movies."

Max said, "Kim added his own incredibly crude bomb because Borya demanded that everything in the car burn up."

Borya said, "Kim can do all kinds of things with blood."

"Such a rich life Borya has had," Max said. "Rita and Kim. In TransKom we had a venture that could have become a true multinational company if we'd just stayed away from gambling and whores. It's the same with this Emergency Committee. They could have all been real millionaires, but they couldn't tolerate even the least reform. It's like having a partner who's in the last stage of syphilis, when it attacks the brain. Now we're just salvaging what we can."

"I had a friend named Jaak, a detective. I found him here in a car. What happened?" Arkady asked.

"Bad timing," Borya said. "He ran into Penyagin. The general was checking the communications in the other bunker, and your detective asked why there was a battalion of tanks and troops sitting in the field. He thought it was going to be like Estonia all over again, there was going to be a coup, and he was going to go back to Moscow to sound the alarm. It was lucky I was around. I was checking a shipment of VCRs in the shed, and I stopped him before he got to the car. But Penyagin was in a dither."

Max said, "Borya doesn't like grandstand critics."

"Penyagin was supposed to be head of CID. You'd think he'd seen a body before," Borya said.

"He was a desk man," Arkady said.

"I guess so. Anyway, Minin was supposed to investigate, but you showed up first." Borya stared at the lime pit. Like a man who can't trust his good fortune, he said, "I can't believe you came back."

"Where is Irina?" Max asked.

"Munich," Arkady said.

"Let me tell you where I'm afraid she is," Max said. "I'm afraid she came back with you and went to the White House, where she'll probably be gassed and shot. The Committee may be a collection of Party nobodies, but the troops know their job."

"When is the attack?" Arkady asked.

"At three A.M., the middle of the night. They'll use tanks. It will be fast but messy, and they won't be able to spare reporters even if they wanted to. Do you know what would really be ironic? If this time I saved Irina." Max let a moment pass. "Irina's here. Don't deny it. You still have a little glow. She wouldn't let you come back without her."

Strangely, Arkady couldn't deny it, though a lie would have served. As if a word could make her disappear.

"Now do you know what you wanted to know?" Borya asked Max, who nodded. "Let's see the painting." He snatched the bag away and opened it while Max played the flashlight through the plastic wrap. "Just like Rita told us."

Max lifted the painting out. "It's heavy."

Borya protested, "It's the painting."

Max unwound the wrap. "It's wood, not canvas, and it's the wrong color."

"It's red," Borya pointed out.

"Red is all it is," Max said.

Arkady thought it looked like one of Polina's better efforts—vibrant crimson instead of dark maroon, with more consistent brush strokes.

"I think it's a fake, but what's your opinion?" Max turned the flashlight directly into Arkady's eyes.

Borya kicked Arkady's legs out from under him, then, with no loss of momentum, moved in and planted a second kick in his chest. Arkady rolled into the dark. On his side, he freed the Nagant from the back of his belt. Faster, Borya produced a pistol and fired into the floor, spraying Arkady with cement.

Arkady shot. Max had been standing in the black behind the flashlight. Now he held a shield of phosphorescent white brilliant enough to light the entire butchering house. Polina's canvas had ignited as the slug passed through and Borya squinted, stupefied by the blaze. When he understood what was happening, he turned back to Arkady and fired wildly four more times.

Arkady shot and Borya dropped to his knees, into the soft folds of his coat. The breast of his coat showed a bright rosette. Arkady fired a second time in the same place. Borya swayed, rose and lined his eye on the sight. His eye wavered. As he started to topple, he put his hands on the floor, still clutching his gun, trying to keep the world from spinning. His head rolled and he relaxed and slumped across the floor at full length, as if he were diving for a penalty kick.

On the floor, the canvas produced a white light that broke into noxious smoke against the ceiling. Max's sleeve was on fire. He was framed in the doorway for a moment, a man attached to a torch. Then the doorway went dark as he ran.

The house filled with a chemical cloud that made Arkady's eyes tear. Flames ran down the blood grooves of the floor. His chest stung, though he didn't feel particularly hurt. Borya's first kick had folded his knees in a new way and his legs were numb. He dragged himself over the floor to retrieve his jacket and Borya's gun, a little TK pistol that was empty. He crawled to the door, pulled himself up so that he could exit erect, staggered out and leaned as stiff as a ladder against the wall until sensation returned.

Except for the glow from the butchering house and the headlights of the car, the yard was black. The surface of the lime pit seemed to seethe, but it could have been an effect of raindrops. There was no sign of Max, not even smoke.

The Mercedes switched to high beams and Arkady's shadow jumped the pit. He stepped back and started to slide, so he stood his ground and fired the Nagant's last shot, though his eyes were so overloaded he could barely see his hand, much less the car. The lights swung to the side, raced across the yard and onto the road that led through the pens toward the village. Taillights danced from rail to rail until they disappeared.

More on one foot than two, Arkady made it to the step of the truck. His knees still felt rearranged. When he opened his shirt, he could see that his stomach was pocked by cement, no worse than bird shot. He wished he had a cigarette.

He buttoned his shirt and pulled on his jacket, then removed the ignition keys from the truck and locked its back doors. Hobbling to the bunker, he closed it against the rain.

In the last glimmer from the fire, Arkady staggered across the yard to the Zhiguli. The car had the gaping windows and crumpled fender of an abandoned wreck. Max had a head start. On the other hand, the Zhiguli was made for Russian roads.

39

The radio picked up nothing. He might have been traveling cross-country in Antarctica.

He would have seen more in Antarctica. Snow reflected light, potato fields absorbed it. Man didn't have to search for black holes in the universe when there were potato fields.

By the time he was on the highway, his leg had stiffened so much from Borya's kick that he no longer knew whether he had the clutch in or out.

The Ring Road was a starry line of lamps. Above the city, tracers dotted the sky. He tried the radio again. Tchaikovsky, of course. And a warning that a curfew was in effect. Arkady turned the radio off. The air rushing through the broken windows made him feel as if he were reentering earth.

On the Leningrad Road, armored personnel carriers stopped pedestrians but let cars drive through, so that there were long spaces of sparse traffic and empty sidewalks, then crossing spotlights and military vehicles proceeding slowly on a circular road. The Zhiguli, bent door and all, drew no attention. At night a driver noticed that Moscow was a series of concentric rings, and how much the city was orbits of light in a void.

The metro and buses were shut down, but people started to reappear out of the dark singly or in groups of ten or twenty, heading south. Troops were nonexistent at one corner, massed at another. In the Red Presnya district, Belovaya Street was blocked by tanks; the idling of their engines sounded like deep thought. Regular militia was off the street.

Arkady parked and joined the sidewalk traffic. A stream of men and women poured toward the river. Obviously some knew each other because there was quiet murmuring. Mostly they were silent, as if everyone were saving their breath for the walk, and as if that breath, visible in the rain, were enough communication. No one mentioned or looked askance at Arkady's bloody shirt. To his relief, his leg functioned, knee and all.

Arkady let himself be swept forward. As the pace quickened, he found himself running with the crowd down a side street that had been turned into a dead end by army trucks parked bumper to bumper. But the canvas cover of one truck was pulled back and people helped each other up, as if climbing a country stile.

On the other side of the truck, the wide Red Presnya embankment road curved between the river and the White House. It was a relatively new building, a four-story marble box, with two arms that seemed to float lightly in the glow of thousands of people carrying candles. Arkady's group squeezed single file between buses and bulldozers that had been set up as a barricade.

Along the way, he heard every rumor. The Kremlin was ringed by tanks ready to move down Kalinin Prospect to the White House. Riot troops were stationed outside the Bolshoi. The Committee was bringing gas canisters by barge to the embankment. Commandos had found tunnels to the White House. A helicopter assault would land on the roof. KGB agents inside the building would machine-gun the defenders at a secret signal. It would be like China or Rumania, but worse.

People hovered over small warming fires of trash, and around votive candles stuck into makeshift altars of wax. These were people who in all their lives had gone to no public demonstration that hadn't been organized and herded. Yet their feet had brought them here.

There weren't many ways to reach the White House because the bridge over the river was barricaded at both ends. Arkady spotted Max among people arriving from Kalinin Prospect. From a distance he didn't look much the worse. He nestled one hand in his jacket pocket but moved with an assurance that parted the crowd.

At a corner of the White House a tank that had come to its defense was festooned with flowers. The soldiers on board were boys with the hollowed eyes of determination and fear. The turrets swung toward Kalinin Prospect, where Arkady heard the drumming of automatic fire.

Students played guitars and sang the kind of sappy songs about birches and snow that usually drove Arkady insane. Around another fire, rockers took sustenance from a tape of heavy metal. Ancient veterans linked their arms and puffed up the ribbons on their chests. A battalion of street cleaners, women in black coats and scarves, stood like a row of witnesses.

Arkady maneuvered to keep Max in sight since he seemed to know better which way to go. He skirted a barricade being assembled from construction timbers, mattresses, iron fences and benches. Its builders were men with attaché cases and women with shopping bags who had come directly from offices or bakeries to the battle line. A girl in a raincoat scaled the makeshift palisade to tie a Russian tricolor to the highest plank. Polina looked down from her vantage point without seeing Arkady in the crowd below. Her cheeks were flushed, her hair free, as if she were riding the crest of a wave. Her friend from the airport climbed after her, more carefully, as the sound of weapons fire resumed.

Max moved toward the White House steps. As Arkady tried to catch up, he saw there was a defense plan of sorts. Within the barricades, women had established themselves as an outer ring that soldiers would have to break through first. Then came shock troops of unarmed citizens, a mass that water cannon or armor would have to dislodge. Behind them, younger and stronger men were organized in divisions of about a hundred. At the bottom of the White House steps Afghan vets stood in groups of ten. Above them was an inner cordon of men wearing dark ski masks over their faces and shouldering weapons. At the top of the steps strobe lights popped around microphone booms and still and video cameras.

"You?" A heavyset militiaman grabbed Arkady's arm.

"I'm sorry." Arkady didn't recognize him.

"You almost ran me over last week. You caught me taking money."

"Yes." Arkady remembered; it had been after the funeral.

"See, I'm not just someone who stands in the street and takes bribes."

"No, you're not. Who's in the ski masks?"

"A mix—private guards, volunteers." The officer's concern, however, was Arkady. He gave his full name, insisted that Arkady repeat it and shook his hand. "You never know another man until a night like tonight. This is the drunkest I've ever been and I haven't touched a drop."

Everywhere was a common look of astonishment, as if they had all ventured individually to drop their lifelong masks and show their faces. Middle-aged teachers, muscular truck drivers, wretched apparatchiks and feckless students wandered with expressions of recognition. As in *I know you*. And among all these Russians, not a bottle. Not a one.

Afghan vets with red bandannas around their arms patrolled the perimeter. Many still had their fatigues and desert caps, some held radios, others carried sacks of Molotov cocktails. Everyone had said how they had gone to Afghanistan, become dope addicts and lost the war. These were the ones who had lost their friends in the dust of Khost and Kandahar, fought on the long retreat on the Salang Highway, and avoided the anonymous ride home in zinc-lined coffins. They seemed very competent tonight.

Max's hair and one ear looked singed and he had changed jackets, but he seemed remarkably untouched after having had one arm on fire at the collective. He stopped by worshipers huddled around a priest who was blessing crucifixes at the base of the White House steps, then turned and saw Arkady.

A bullhorn announced, "As attack is imminent, we are observing a blackout. Extinguish all lights. Those with gas masks, prepare to put them on. Those without should tie wet cloths over their noses and mouths."

Candles disappeared. In the sudden dark there was a stir of thousands of people slipping on goggles and tying scarves and handkerchiefs over their faces. Undeterred, the priest pronounced blessings through a gas mask. Max had slipped away.

The bullhorn appealed, "Please, reporters, do not use your flashes!" But someone stepped out of the White House door and the response at the top of the steps was an explosion of strobes and spotlights. Arkady saw Irina among the reporters and Max climbing toward her.

The embankment was blacked out, but the scene at its center was an illuminated theatrical production. The steps spilled over with lights and journalists trading shouts in Italian, English, Japanese and German. There were no official press passes for a coup, but reporters were professionals used to mayhem and Russians were accustomed to disorder.

Max was stopped halfway up by two men in ski masks. Half an eyebrow was gone and his neck had a raw sheen, yet he seemed unruffled and in control. Cameramen rushed up and down the steps on either side. He enlisted the guards in conversation, employing a confidence that commanded any situation, an ability to flow around any obstacle.

". . . you can help me," Arkady heard him say as he caught up. "I was on my way here to join my colleagues from Radio Liberty when my car was deliberately run off the road. In the explosion one man was killed and I sustained injuries." He turned and pointed to Arkady. "There is the driver of the other car. He followed me."

The guards had cut eyeholes in woolen ski caps that were a contrast to their satiny suits. One was hulking and the other small, but they both had sawed-off rifles that they held casually in Arkady's direction. He didn't even have his father's gun, and by now he was so exposed he couldn't retreat.

"He's not from the press. Ask for his identification," Arkady said.

Max took hold of the situation like the director of a film. It looked like a stage set: wet marble steps, vying strobes, the fairy lights of tracers in the clouds. "My identification burned in the car. It doesn't matter because a dozen reporters here will vouch for me. Anyway, I think I recognize this character. His name is Renko, one of Prosecutor Rodionov's gang. Ask *him* for identification."

Dark eyes stared through the masks. Arkady had to admit that Max had defined the moment neatly; here his identification could condemn him.

"He's lying," Arkady said.

"Is his car a wreck? Is my friend dead?" In the clamor of the steps, Max's whisper was all the more effective. "Renko is a dangerous man. Ask him whether he killed someone or not. See, he can't deny it."

"Who was your friend?" the smaller guard asked through his mask. Though he had no face to go by, Arkady thought he had heard the voice before. The guard could have been militia like the traffic officer at the bottom of the steps or a private bodyguard.

"Borya Gubenko, a businessman," Max said.

"*The* Borya Gubenko?" The guard seemed to know the name. "He was a *close* friend?"

Max answered quickly, "Not close, but Borya sacrificed himself to get me here and the fact is that Renko brutally killed him and tried to do the same to me. Here we are surrounded by the cameras of the world. The world is watching these steps tonight and you can't afford to let a reactionary agent like Renko near anybody. The main thing is to get him out of sight. If you do trip and accidentally shoot him in the back it will be no loss to the world."

"I don't do anything accidentally," the guard assured him.

Max began to sidestep to continue his climb. "As I said, I have colleagues here."

"I know you do." He lifted off his mask. It was Beno, Makhmud's grandson. His face was almost as dark as his mask, but it was lit by a smile. "That's why we came, in case you tried to join them."

The larger guard pulled Max back by the tail of his jacket.

Beno said, "We were looking for Borya too, but if Renko took care of him, then we can concentrate on you. We'll start by asking about four cousins of mine who died at your apartment in Berlin."

"Renko, what is he talking about?" Max asked.

"Then we'll talk about Makhmud and Ali. We'll make a night of it," Beno said.

"Arkady," Max appealed.

"But since it is going to get dangerous here in about an hour," Beno said, "we'll do our talking someplace else."

Max wrested free of his jacket and ran diagonally down the steps. On the bottom one he slid on wax, crashed through the line of veterans, regained his feet and fought his way through the circle of worshipers around the priest. The larger Chechen raced after him. Beno waved calmly to a group in the crowd and pointed in Max's direction. In his white shirt he was easy to follow.

Beno regarded Arkady. "Are you staying? It's going to be bloody here."

"I have friends here."

"Get them out." Beno slipped his cap back on and adjusted the holes over his eyes. He took one step down. "If you don't . . . good luck." Then he plunged, a dark figure, into the crowd.

Arkady climbed the rest of the way to the jostling lights at the top of the steps, arriving just as a spokesman emerged from the door protected by guards carrying bulletproof shields. Ringed by cameras, the spokesman was outside just long enough to announce that snipers had been seen on the roofs of nearby buildings. He ducked back inside, but the journalists stayed in clear sight to check notes.

Irina had appeared with the spokesman and remained. "You came," she said.

"I said I would."

Her eyes were set deep with exhaustion and brilliant with exhilaration at the same time. "Stas is inside on the second floor. He's on the phone to Munich. They still haven't cut the wires. He's broadcasting right now."

Arkady said, "You should be with him."

"Do you want me to?"

"No, I want you with me."

As more tracers fanned across the sky, the bullhorn insisted futilely on an absolute blackout. Cigarettes reappeared, along with gas masks —a perfect Russian blackout, Arkady thought. As the sound of patrol boats approached on the river, the lights of a convoy appeared on the far bank. The women on the outer line had started to sing, and parts of the crowd picked up the song and swayed, so that in the dark they looked like the surface of a sea or a plain of grass in a wind.

"Let's wait with them," Irina said.

They walked down the steps, through the defense ring of the Afghan vets and past a row of candles freshly lit. Other vets in wheelchairs had arrived and had run chains through the spokes of their wheels. Women shielded them with umbrellas. Now, that must have made a parade on the way here, Arkady thought.

"Keep walking," Irina said. "I didn't get down here before. I want to see."

People were sitting, standing, slowly circulating as if at a fair. They would all have different memories later, Arkady was sure. One would say that the atmosphere around the White House was quiet, grim, purposeful; another would remember a circus air. If they lived.

All his life Arkady had avoided marches and demonstrations. This was the first one he had ever willingly come to. The same could be said, he suspected, of the other Muscovites around him. Of the construction workers who formed the unshaven and unarmed inner troops. Of the mousy apparatchiks who set down their briefcases to hold each other's hands and form a human ring, so many that there were fifty rings of them around the White House. Of the women doctors who somehow, out of empty hospital storerooms, had scavenged bandages.

He had an urge to see each of their faces. He wasn't the only one. A priest moved along a row giving absolution. He noticed artists who were making white pencil portraits on black paper, passing them as gifts.

The mystery is not the way we die, it's the way we live. The courage we have at birth becomes hoarded, shriveled, blown away. Year after year, we become more alone..Yet, holding Irina's hand, for this moment, for this night, Arkady felt that he could swing the world.

A piece of paper was pushed into his other hand. Look at this face, it was familiar, it was the one he was born with. Sound grew as a vortex in the rain. Overhead a helicopter shook the air and shot a flare that dropped, a matchhead in a well.

IT WAS ALL FALLING

*An excerpt from Don Swaim's 1992 interview
with Martin Cruz Smith . . .*

*. . . in which the author discusses his visit to Russia after
the fall of the Soviet Union, his picnic with a Russian mafioso,
and the perils of waiting in line for vodka.*

Don Swaim: So, Arkady Renko is back . . . and he's back in, uh, relatively good graces—

Martin Cruz Smith: Relatively, yeah.

DS: I say relatively because he runs into a new, uh, Commissioner of Police . . . no, a new Head Prosecutor.

MCS: Yes, a new City Prosecutor—

DS: A new City Prosecutor with whom he butts heads, of course, which is not unusual for Arkady. It's been his pattern all along. The last time we saw Arkady he was on a fishing trawler, or a, uh—

MCS: A factory ship.

DS: A factory ship—

MCS: Yeah.

DS: —that processes fish, and was, uh, pulled out of his enforced retirement to solve a murder onboard that ship. Now he is back in Moscow as a special investigator with his own staff. This is kind of unusual, so tell me about that.

MCS: Well, I spent some time with a prosecutor's investigator in Moscow for this book. And, uh, he described to me how in fact he gets his, uh, he has his own investigators and they take in detectives from the militia. It's sort of a split system there. The prosecutor's a little bit like our District Attorney, and they put a team together for, uh, to investigate different crimes. And they do it partly, the, the person in charge is the investigator and then he has these detectives and you can, um, you can pick or choose your detectives there—who you want to use and who you don't want to use and quite often you take who you can get because you don't think you're going to get anyone better. Arkady, uh, has a typical Russian kind of hand, in that he plays what he's dealt, to some degree, which is, uh—there's one detective he would not necessarily want to use, a man named Minin, a Communist of the old school. And then he has Jaak, who's an Estonian, and probably, uh, not, *not* a party man at all. And he has Polina, a very forthright pathologist.

DS: She's great.

MCS: Yeah, I like her. It's, uh, a funny thing—

DS: Well, she almost takes over the investigation—

MCS: Yes. It's extraordinary to me. I had a, uh, back in *Polar Star,* remember the character named Natasha. She started taking over that part of the book. These books are in danger of being hijacked by the women who appear in them. And so Polina does make a bid for power there in the beginning of the book. Anyway, he's investigating the death of a black market speculator and banker named Rudy Rosen, whose demise we see in the first few pages of the book. And once again he runs into the power lines of Moscow, but these are, these are new power lines.

DS: Well, things, uh, everything has changed, hasn't it, since the last time? The demise of the Communist government.

MCS: Well, the, you know, it's—I went there expecting to see a collapse, but it's different. It's very—you know, it's a little bit like going, I went up to the Oakland Hills after the fire there. And you think you're prepared for it, but you're not, because you walk around Oakland and you see nothing but chimneys, and where there were cars there are puddles of aluminum. Hardened aluminum. And now, to walk around Moscow, you are walking around the remains—the ruins—of Communist rule. Of Soviet rule. And of course it was a sham, of course it was a façade, but when it came down it really made a mess. And this mess, it wasn't quite a mess at the point right before the coup when I'm writing, but it was all falling. It was mid-descent, mid-collapse, at the time *Red Square* is set. So I went expecting that, and I went expecting a more prominent role, a more visible role for the gangs, but I really didn't anticipate, uh, the . . . not even *brazen*. It goes beyond brazen. The simple fact of the gangs on the street, of the taxicabs that won't pick up anyone without cigarettes, vodka, or foreign currency, of the women who knock on your door in the middle of the night. At the, at the— you go to a tourist bar and it's full of racketeers. Russian racketeers. You go to the casinos and find the mafia there. You go into the streets and you find the black markets. Some of them, of course, a lot of the black markets are simply providing goods that are unavailable. That should be available for stores and are not. But a lot of—a number of the black markets are clearly selling stolen goods. And you'll find—you go to the right street and the entire block lined with men selling stolen goods— *and* protected by the police.

DS: This is essentially the setting for Rudy's demise. The explosion, enormous. The huge black market area where you can find almost anything.

MCS: Yeah.

DS: Meanwhile, you have a wonderful description on page 71 of, uh, Red Square and the almost empty GUM department store—

MCS: Yes.

DS: These are *really* interesting touches because here, where you can get almost any kind of good in a black market, you go into a department store and you can't get anything.

MCS: Yeah. But, you know, all this stuff that the black market has has been diverted from where it was, and there are different ways to divert it. One way is, of course, to steal it. But a simpler way, and one that is more the norm, is simply to pay somebody—to pay somebody in the government who will ship it your way. So there's this new hand-in-hand relationship between brazen, organized crime and the caretakers of the old system. Because they're operating, they're operating like, as if they're officers of a bankrupt company. The company doesn't function anymore, it doesn't make anything, it doesn't produce anything anymore, but it has a great deal of physical assets. It owned much of the country. And what it didn't own directly, what the Party did not own directly, it controlled. It controlled everything. So now it was selling off those assets to the highest bidder. And some of the highest bidders are foreign companies. And many of those bidders are also mafias—mafias which have the hard currency.

DS: And it should be noted that we're not talking about the Sicilian mafia.

MCS: No.

DS: This is a mafia—

MCS: It's interesting that they call themselves the mafia.

DS: Yeah, they've appropriated the term, but they're distinctly Russian, and they're actually many ethnic Russians—

MCS: Yes.

DS: —making up various factions of the mafia, as you point out in the book.

MCS: I spent, uh, I spent a day with a Russian Mafioso. He took me for a picnic. And, uh, I'd already spent a day with him before, questioning him, interviewing him about how he did what he did. And he was enormously successful, so we went out in a fleet of Mercedes, out to the picnic. And he starts—one of his underlings starts cooking up the *shashlyk*. *Shashlyk* is a shish kabob. And it was really, it was like a scene out of one of the *Godfather* movies, where they're stirring the spaghetti. And every few moments he goes over there and he kicks his underling, to ask how the *shashlyk* is coming along, as if he's a great expert—we're now dealing with a great chef of *shashlyk*. And I questioned him for a couple hours, and we eat, and we have some vodka and wine, and then at the end he has a question for me. And he says he's meeting some guys from New York. And he wants to know, he says he's very concerned—he wants to know how to act around these contacts from New York—and his question is whether the book *The Godfather* is accurate. Whether he can use that as the style that he should assume. So there was this very strange, they see themselves as patterning themselves to some degree on our own mafia.

DS: Where I think *Red Square* is an interesting and valuable book, not just because it's a good mystery, but it, uh, one of the few books that really has told us what is happening in the Soviet Union right now. These little slices of life—for instance, Polina standing in line for two hours to get beets—

MCS: Mmm. Yes.

DS: —and looking down and seeing the red juices from the beets on her feet and on the ground and so forth. Another interesting story, apparently—and maybe you can amplify this—apparently to buy vodka, you have to return the empty.

MCS: That's right. That's absolutely right.

DS: You can't buy two bottles?

MCS: Well, you know, nope. You gotta bring one back for every one you buy. When Gorbachev tried to control the flow of vodka, cut down the production of vodka, he was to some degree successful. The only thing that restrains, that cuts down the production of vodka now is they don't have enough bottles. Because those bottlers can't get their sand— you know, it's a collapse of supply. God knows there's the demand.

DS: Well, the point in this book, of the Russian tripping as he approaches the beginning of the line, and dropping his bottle—

MCS: Oh yeah.

DS: *What do you do?*

MCS: (*Laughs.*) There it goes.

DS: Where do you start? You want to get your first bottle of vodka, how do you start? How do you get it?

MCS: Well, actually, you can buy one on the street, from a street vendor, you just have to pay four times more. See? I mean, anything, if you have the hard currency, you can get anything.

(To enjoy the rest of the interview, visit the Wired for Books website at wiredforbooks.org.)

ABOUT THE AUTHOR

MARTIN CRUZ SMITH is the author of *Gorky Park, Polar Star, Havana Bay, Stallion Gate,* and *Rose*, among other novels. He lives in California.

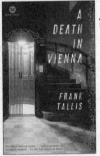